RISING
FIRE

RISING FIRE
THE JENSEN BRAND

WILLIAM W. JOHNSTONE
AND J. A. JOHNSTONE

PINNACLE BOOKS
Kensington Publishing Corp.
www.kensingtonbooks.com

PINNACLE BOOKS are published by

Kensington Publishing Corp.
119 West 40th Street
New York, NY 10018

PUBLISHER'S NOTE

Following the death of William W. Johnstone, the Johnstone family is working with a carefully selected writer to organize and complete Mr. Johnstone's outlines and many unfinished manuscripts to create additional novels in all of his series like The Last Gunfighter, Mountain Man, and Eagles, among others. This novel was inspired by Mr. Johnstone's superb storytelling.

All Kensington titles, imprints, and distributed lines are available at special quantity discounts for bulk purchases for sales promotions, premiums, fund-raising, educational, or institutional use. Special book excerpts or customized printings can also be created to fit specific needs. For details, write or phone the office of the Kensington sales manager: Kensington Publishing Corp., 119 West 40th Street, New York, NY 10018, attn: Sales Department; phone 1-800-221-2647.

PINNACLE BOOKS, the Pinnacle logo, and the WWJ steer head logo are Reg. U.S. Pat. & TM Off.

ISBN-13: 978-0-7860-4420-7
ISBN-10: 0-7860-4420-9

First printing: June 2020

10 9 8 7 6 5 4 3 2 1

Printed in the United States of America

Electronic edition:

ISBN-13: 978-0-7860-4421-4 (e-book)
ISBN-10: 0-7860-4421-7 (e-book)

THE JENSEN FAMILY
FIRST FAMILY OF THE AMERICAN FRONTIER

Smoke Jensen—*The Mountain Man*
The youngest of three children and orphaned as a young boy, Smoke Jensen is considered one of the fastest draws in the West. His quest to tame the lawless West has become the stuff of legend. Smoke owns the Sugarloaf Ranch in Colorado. Married to Sally Jensen, father to Denise ("Denny") and Louis.

Preacher—*The First Mountain Man*
Though not a blood relative, grizzled frontiersman Preacher became a father figure to the young Smoke Jensen, teaching him how to survive in the brutal, often deadly Rocky Mountains. Fought the battles that forged his destiny. Armed with a long gun, Preacher is as fierce as the land itself.

Matt Jensen—*The Last Mountain Man*
Orphaned but taken in by Smoke Jensen, Matt Jensen has become like a younger brother to Smoke and even took the Jensen name. And like Smoke, Matt has carved out his destiny on the American frontier. He lives by the gun and surrenders to no man.

Luke Jensen—*Bounty Hunter*
Mountain Man Smoke Jensen's long-lost brother Luke Jensen is scarred by war and a dead shot—the right

qualities to be a bounty hunter. And he's cunning, and fierce enough, to bring down the deadliest outlaws of his day.

Ace Jensen and Chance Jensen—*Those Jensen Boys!*
Smoke Jensen's long-lost nephews, Ace and Chance, are a pair of young-gun twins as reckless and wild as the frontier itself . . . Their father is Luke Jensen, thought killed in the Civil War. Their uncle Smoke Jensen is one of the fiercest gunfighters the West has ever known. It's no surprise that the inseparable Ace and Chance Jensen have a knack for taking risks— even if they have to blast their way out of them.

CHAPTER I

Big Rock, Colorado, 1902

Train whistles always had a little bit of a mournful sound to them. Or maybe she was just in a gloomy mood, Denise Nicole Jensen thought as she leaned a shoulder against one of the posts holding up the roof over the train station platform.

A train like the one that would be pulling into Big Rock in a few minutes had taken Denny's twin brother, Louis, back East, along with Louis's wife, Melanie, and stepson, Brad, so Louis could attend law school at Harvard. Denny had put on a smile and a brave face and hugged all of them when they left, but this was the longest she'd been separated from Louis since they were born, and she missed him.

On this day, Denny looked a little like an illustration on the flimsy yellow front cover of a dime novel. Her blond hair was tucked up under a flat-crowned brown hat with a rattlesnake band. She wore a brown leather vest over a butternut shirt with the sleeves rolled up a couple of turns, revealing deeply tanned forearms. The pair of jeans she wore weren't exactly baggy, but they didn't hug her hips and thighs tightly, so her shapely female form wasn't apparent at first glance. The jeans were tucked into high-topped brown boots.

A gun belt strapped around her waist, with a holstered .38 caliber Colt Lightning revolver attached to it, completed the picture of a young gunfighter. Almost, anyway. She didn't have a smoldering quirly dangling from her lips. Denny had never acquired the habit.

A voice from behind her said, "Howdy, sweetheart."

Denny winced. Without straightening from her casual pose, she looked slowly over her shoulder and asked, "How'd you know it was me, Sheriff?"

"Well, I recognized you, I guess, even though in that garb, you look like Young Wild West," Sheriff Monte Carson said. "I've seen you wearing that hat before, I think. It's not new, is it?"

"No, it's not," Denny said. "You have a keen eye."

"For an old codger, eh?" The sheriff chuckled.

"Don't let my pa hear you calling yourself an old codger. That would mean *he's* getting on in years, too."

"Well, Smoke's not a spring chicken anymore, even though he's not as old as me." Monte rubbed his chin. "Funny thing is, as far as I can tell, he hasn't lost a step. His draw is just as fast as it ever was. And your ma . . . well, I'd have to say that she's just as pretty as she was the day I first laid eyes on her, all those years ago. Prettier, even."

"I don't think anybody who knows her would argue with you about that."

Monte gestured toward the gleaming steel rails

that ran beside the station platform. "You here to meet the westbound? Expecting somebody, maybe?"

"Yes to the first, no to the second. I'm not expecting anybody. But I rode into town with Pearlie on the buckboard. He's down at the store picking up some supplies. I didn't see any point in standing around waiting while he does that."

"So you strolled down here." Monte leaned toward her and lowered his voice a little. "Can't say as I blame you. In the old days, we used to get excited whenever a stagecoach would roll in and break the monotony. Now everybody waits for the train to arrive. Kind of makes you wonder what folks will get excited about in the future, doesn't it?"

Denny just shrugged as the train whistle sounded again, louder this time. The *chuffing* of its steam engine could be heard now, too. That noise got louder, and brakes squealed and steam hissed as the locomotive reached the station and slowed so that the passenger cars came to a stop next to the platform. The baggage and freight cars were farther back.

As the train clattered to a halt, Denny straightened and took a step away from the post where she'd been leaning. She hooked her thumbs in the gun belt and watched with idle interest as porters put steps in place next to the cars so the passengers could disembark. A variety of men, women, and children got off, all of them strangers to Denny.

Then she drew in a breath so sharply that her nostrils flared slightly. She stood up straighter as her backbone stiffened. Her blue eyes fastened on two men who had just stepped down from one of the cars.

The first man was tall and slender, well dressed in

a brown tweed suit and dark brown bowler hat. He had light brown hair and a mild, pleasant-looking face. He held a small carpetbag in each hand.

The man who came down the steps next carried himself with an entirely different air about him. He had a self-assured spring in his gait, and as he paused, pushed his coat back, and rested his fists against his hips, he gave off so much confidence that it bordered on arrogance. He wore a dark gray suit and had a black slouch hat pushed back on thick, curly black hair. A smile broke out on his handsome, olive-skinned face as he looked around the platform.

"So this is Big Rock, eh?" he asked his companion. His voice had a slight accent to it.

"That's right, sir," the taller, diffident-looking man replied. "Big Rock, Colorado. I looked up the population and elevation and other interesting facts about the town, and if you'll give me a moment, I'm sure I can recall them."

The second man waved away the offer. "No, it doesn't matter. We're here at last, Arturo. You can go seek out accommodations for us."

"Of course, sir." Despite the Italian name, Arturo's voice had no accent at all, other than an educated, cultured one. "And where will you be?"

"When you've secured rooms and placed the bags in them, ask someone for directions to the best dining and drinking establishment in town."

Arturo inclined his head in a gesture that was almost a bow and said, "As you wish, sir."

Over by the pillar, Denny was still watching the two men when Sheriff Carson nudged her and said, "They're a pretty fancy pair, aren't they?"

"You could say that."

Monte looked more closely at Denny and asked, "Are you acquainted with those fellas? You're glaring at them sorta like you wouldn't mind whipping out that Lightning and blazing away at them."

"I don't know the taller one," Denny said, "but the other man . . . I'm acquainted with *him,* all right. You're not far off the mark, Sheriff. If anybody ever deserved to be shot, or at least horsewhipped, it's—"

She didn't get to finish what she was about to say, because at that moment, exactly the sort of thing Denny had just been talking about happened. Five rough-looking men in range clothes who had drifted onto the platform yanked pistols from their holsters and opened fire on the two well-dressed newcomers to Big Rock.

CHAPTER 2

The black-haired man's cocky grin and casual attitude vanished in a fraction of a second. In the time it took the gunmen to draw their weapons and start shooting, the man dived at Arturo and tackled him. The carpetbags went flying.

Both men sprawled on the platform as guns blasted and bullets sizzled through the space where they had been standing only a heartbeat earlier. Some of the slugs smacked into the side of the railroad car; others whined dangerously off the car's metal undercarriage.

The would-be killers had spread out as they approached, so they had their intended victims almost surrounded. Most of the people on the platform screamed or shouted in alarm and scattered when the shooting started. With so much open area around them and no place to take cover, the intended victims were doomed.

Or they would have been if Denny and Sheriff Carson hadn't been there. Denny's right hand dropped to the pistol on her hip and swooped back up, gripping the gun. The draw was almost too fast for the eye to follow. Flame spouted from the muzzle as Denny triggered the double-action revolver.

The .38 caliber slug from Denny's Lightning ripped into the back of a gunman's left shoulder and knocked him halfway around. He howled a curse and stumbled to the side but stayed on his feet. His head jerked from side to side as he tried to figure out who had shot him.

His eyes widened as his gaze lit on Denny. He still had his gun in his right hand. He lifted it to take aim at her.

Denny didn't let him get the shot off. She had waited a second to see if the man would collapse or drop his weapon, but it was obvious he wasn't going to do either of those things. She had already drawn a bead on him, so she shot him between the eyes before he could pull the trigger. His head snapped back as the bullet bored into his brain, leaving a red-rimmed hole that looked like a third eye peering out from between the other two.

Monte Carson, who had been a hired gun as a young man before setting out on a long career on the right side of the law, still possessed a fighter's instincts. As soon as gunplay erupted, he moved swiftly to his left, away from Denny. He pulled his gun smoothly from its holster, pointed it at the nearest of the would-be assassins, and shouted, "Drop it!"

The man had turned partially around, probably in response to the sound of Denny's gun, and caught sight of the sheriff. He threw a fast shot at Monte but missed. As the bullet whipped past his head, Monte fired. His shot ripped a gash along the gunman's forearm and caused the man to yelp and drop his revolver.

A few yards away, Denny wheeled behind the roof-support pillar as one of the other gunmen fired at her. The bullet struck the post and chewed splinters from it, only inches from Denny's head. This wasn't the first gunfight she'd been in, so she appeared cool and calm, no matter what might be going on inside her, as she dropped to a knee, leaned to her right, and triggered the Lightning again. She grimaced as the shot missed and struck one of the train's wheels instead.

With the gunmen having to defend themselves from Denny and Monte Carson, that gave the two newcomers a chance to get out of the line of fire. The black-haired man scrambled to his feet and lunged for the steps leading up to the platform at the back of the railroad car, where he had disembarked only moments earlier. He reached the platform in a couple of bounds and disappeared through the open door into the car.

Arturo wasn't as fast on his feet. Flustered and afraid, he managed to stand up but then froze, standing there whipping his head back and forth in wild-eyed panic. Behind him, one of the killers aimed at him.

Denny saw the man about to gun down Arturo, but Arturo was between her and the would-be assassin and she didn't have a clear shot at him. She was about to shout a warning, even though it probably wouldn't do any good, when another shot rang out and the man who was about to blast Arturo staggered under a bullet's impact instead.

He caught his balance and turned, his face twisting

in hate, and fired toward a man who had just emerged from the depot building. This man crouched and triggered his weapon again as the killer's bullet plowed into the platform only a few feet in front of him.

The second shot punched into the gunman's belly and tore through his guts. He dropped his gun, doubled over, and collapsed. Agony made him writhe on the platform and leave a crimson smear of blood on the planks.

Three of the hard cases were still on their feet, although one of them was wounded and had dropped his gun. Clutching his bleeding arm, he shouted, "Let's get out of here!" and followed his own advice, leaping off the platform and running alongside the train until he reached a spot where he could duck between cars and flee on the other side of the tracks.

The other two scattered as well, heading in different directions. Denny lined up a shot on one of them, intending to knock his legs out from under him, but before she could pull the trigger, he ducked behind a stack of bags that had been unloaded from the baggage car, and then he darted through the door into the station lobby. Denny lowered her gun and made a face because she hadn't had a good shot at him.

She looked around to see if the other man had gotten away. It appeared that he had. Monte Carson had a disgusted expression on his face as he thumbed fresh cartridges into his gun's cylinder.

"Three of the varmints lit a shuck out of here," he told Denny, then snapped the Colt's loading gate closed. "But at least they didn't kill anybody. That's a miracle, the way they had those two hombres dead to rights. Instead, it looks like a couple of them were the only ones to cross the divide."

One of the targets, the tall, slender man named Arturo, still stood on the platform near the railroad car, pale and shaken from his close brush with death. Beads of sweat stood out on his forehead. He swallowed hard, pulled a large handkerchief from his pocket, and wiped it over his face.

The man who had saved Arturo from being shot from behind approached the gut-shot assassin. He hooked a boot toe under the man's shoulder and rolled him onto his back. The way the gunman's arms flopped loosely was mute testimony that he was dead. So was the large pool of blood he had left on the platform.

For a moment, Deputy United States Marshal Brice Rogers stood gun in hand and looked down at the man he had shot. Then, evidently satisfied that the hard case was no longer a threat, he pouched his iron and turned toward Denny and Monte Carson.

"I'm not sure what was going on here, Sheriff," Brice said, "but I'm glad I came along when I did. When I saw that fella about to gun somebody down from behind, I figured I had better try to stop him."

"I don't have any idea what it's all about, either, Brice," Monte said, "but you did the right thing. Those hombres were trying to commit cold-blooded murder."

Denny was reloading, too. When she finished, she holstered the Lightning and studied the face of the man she had shot in the head. He had fallen on his back, and other than the neat bullet hole between his eyes, his features were unmarked and looked oddly puzzled, as if he couldn't quite figure out why he was dead. Denny didn't recognize his hard-planed, beard-stubbled face, but she had seen plenty like it belonging to other ruthless gunmen she had encountered.

She called over to Monte and Brice, "Do either of you know these men?"

"Never saw them before, as far as I recall," the sheriff answered.

Brice shook his head and said, "Nope."

"I'll go through the reward posters in my desk," Monte went on. "There's at least a chance they'll turn up on some of those. I've got a hunch this wasn't the first bushwhack they ever tried to pull off."

Brice Rogers, a medium-sized, athletic young man with brown hair and a quick, friendly grin—most of the time, when he wasn't dealing with lawbreakers—approached Arturo and asked, "Are you all right there, pardner? None of that lead flying around nicked you?"

Arturo swallowed hard and shook his head. "No, I . . . I'm not hurt."

"You came mighty close," Denny said as she walked up to them. Now that the shooting was over, the crowd was drifting back out of the building and onto the platform, morbidly curious now. Monte Carson motioned them away from the bodies and told one of the townies to fetch the undertaker.

Denny nodded toward the man Brice had downed and told Arturo, "That hombre was about to ventilate you from behind when Marshal Rogers winged him and then dropped him."

Arturo looked at Brice and said, "Thank you, sir, for saving my life." Then he frowned, turned toward Denny to stare at her, and exclaimed, "My word! You're a young woman!"

Brice chuckled and said, "I've had some suspicions along those lines myself."

Denny ignored his attempt at banter and asked Arturo, "What did you think I was?"

"A boy," Arturo said. "I mean, a young man, I suppose, based on your clothing. But clearly I was wrong. Still, you . . . you shot that man over there."

"He needed shooting," Denny said. "And a gun doesn't know if the finger pulling the trigger is male or female."

"Yes, I suppose—" Arturo stopped short, as if something had just occurred to him, and looked around frantically again. "The count! I must see if the count is all right!"

"I'm fine, Arturo," a voice said from the railroad car. The black-haired man came down the steps to the platform. His hat was cocked at a jaunty angle on his head now, and when he reached the platform, he brushed off any dirt that might have gotten on his suit when he dived to the planks with Arturo as the killers opened fire.

"Thank heavens for that," Arturo said, "and thank *you* for saving my life, too. I never would have reacted swiftly enough on my own when those villains opened fire."

"I think we both owe some thanks to this young fellow here for disrupting their attack—" the man began as he turned to Denny. He stopped short and let out a surprised oath in Italian, then said, "Can it be? Truly? It's really you, Denise?"

"It is," Denny said.

Then she hauled off and slapped him across the face as hard as she could.

CHAPTER 3

The blow took the man by surprise, striking him hard enough to make him stumble a couple of steps to his right. He caught his balance, smiled, and lifted a hand to his face. Taking hold of his chin, he worked his jaw back and forth, then announced, "Nothing broken, it seems. I suppose I had that coming."

"You most certainly did," Denny said coldly. "That, and worse."

His smile didn't waver as he spread his hands and said, "*Cara mia,* are you not glad to see me?"

Denny just let out a contemptuous snort, turned on her heel, stalked across the platform to the door into the train station lobby, and disappeared through it. The man she had just slapped watched her go with a wryly amused expression on his face.

"What in blazes did she do *that* for?" Brice asked.

"Denise and I have a . . . complicated history, I suppose you could say," the man replied. He held out his hand. "I believe she mentioned that you're a lawman of some sort?"

"Deputy United States Marshal," Brice said as he clasped the stranger's hand. "Name's Brice Rogers."

"I am Count Giovanni Malatesta," the man introduced himself with a more formal note in his voice. He inclined his head toward his companion. "My butler, valet, and all-around manservant, Arturo Vincenzo."

"Hello," Brice said. Arturo didn't offer to shake hands, but he did that little almost-bow again.

A commotion elsewhere on the platform made the three of them turn and look. The undertaker's wagon had drawn up next to the steps at the end of the platform, and the black-suited man and his helpers were coming to retrieve the bodies of the slain gunmen. The crowd that had gathered drew back to give them room.

With that grim chore being taken care of, Sheriff Monte Carson came over to join Brice and the two newcomers to Big Rock. Brice said, "Monte, this is Count . . . Giovanni Malatesta." He stumbled slightly over the name. "Count Malatesta, meet Sheriff Monte Carson."

Malatesta shook hands with Monte and said, "Please, gentlemen, you must call me Johnny. We are in America, and there is no place for titles of nobility. And Giovanni is Italian for 'John.' Since I wish for all of us to be friends, there is no need for formality between us."

"Do you plan on staying in Big Rock for a while?" Monte asked.

Malatesta laughed. "Perhaps, if it proves an amiable place in which to spend time."

"We like it here." Monte frowned a little. "Did I see

Denny slap you a minute ago? You didn't say something to offend her, I hope."

Brice said, "As far as I could tell, the count—I mean, Johnny—didn't do a thing other than ask if it was really her when he recognized her."

"Then you two know each other?" Monte asked.

Malatesta said, "We became well acquainted when Denise—Denny, as you so quaintly call her—was in Europe a few years ago with her brother. Is Louis here, too?"

"You missed him, but not by much," Monte said. "He headed back East to go to law school a few weeks ago."

Malatesta shook his head and said, "A shame. I would have liked to see him again. I had no idea he and Denise would be here. I recall her telling me that their father owns some sort of large farm out here on your frontier, but I never expected to run into them again when I set out on my tour of the American West."

"I wouldn't call Sugarloaf a farm," Monte said. "It's more of a ranch. A big ranch."

"Really?" Malatesta cocked an eyebrow. "I knew that Denise's family was well-to-do, otherwise she would not have been living in England and taking jaunts to the Continent, but you sound as if her father is quite successful."

"You could say that. Smoke Jensen is one of the most respected men in the state. In all of the West, in fact."

"Smoke?" Malatesta repeated. "His name is Smoke?"

"Well, his given name's actually Kirby, but everybody

calls him Smoke and has for a long, long time. Are you saying you never heard of Smoke Jensen?"

The count shook his head. "Perhaps I just never traveled in the right circles to do so. And Denise never spoke that much about her family."

With a noticeable intentness in his voice, Brice asked, "Were the two of you particularly close, over there in Italy?"

"Very close," Malatesta said as that arrogant grin reappeared on his face. Brice frowned and stiffened. The count chuckled and slapped him on the arm. "But do not worry, my dear marshal. Anything that was between Signorina Denise Nicole Jensen and myself has long since passed into the realm of friendship and friendship alone."

Brice nodded slowly. "All right."

The bodies had been toted off by now, the crowd on the platform had thinned, and the train was getting ready to pull out. The leather-lunged conductor leaned out from one of the cars and bellowed, *"Boooaaarrrddd! All aboooaarrrddd!"*

Malatesta rubbed his hands together and turned to Arturo. "Now that this grisly business is concluded, we can return to our original plans. I'm sure these gentlemen can tell you where to find the best hotel in Big Rock . . ."

Monte Carson said, "Hold on a minute, Count."

"Johnny, please," Malatesta said.

Monte's voice remained more formal, however, as he went on, "I'm asking as the sheriff now. Why did those hombres try to kill you?"

Malatesta spread his hands innocently. "I assure you,

I have no idea. I assumed they were mere brigands, bent on robbery."

"And they just happened to pick you and Mr. Vincenzo out of the crowd?"

"My garments are expensive, and Arturo dresses in a suitable fashion for a gentleman's gentleman. Those . . . *desperadoes* is the accepted western term, is it not? Those desperadoes probably looked at us and assumed that we were suitable targets for their larcenous intentions."

Monte rubbed his chin and said, "Yeah, maybe."

"I believe that if you find any of those wanted posters you mentioned with those men listed on them, you'll find that they have long histories of being thieves."

"More than likely," Monte agreed with a shrug.

"Now, if you can recommend a hostelry . . ."

"The Big Rock Hotel is the best place in town to stay."

"And an establishment that offers fine dining and drinking?"

"Longmont's," Monte said without hesitation. He provided directions to both businesses.

Malatesta made a shooing motion at Arturo and said, "Scurry on about your business, my friend." He tipped a finger against the brim of his slouch hat and told Carson and Brice, "Good day to you, gentlemen. It was a pleasure meeting you, even under these somewhat trying circumstances, and I hope to see a great deal of you in the future."

With that, the count strolled away, whistling under his breath.

The two lawmen watched him go, and as Monte

Carson's eyes narrowed, he asked, "You believe what he said about why those hombres tried to kill him?"

"Not for one minute," Brice replied.

Wes "Pearlie" Fontaine was standing on the high porch and loading dock in front of Goldstein's Mercantile, talking to Leo Goldstein, the store's proprietor. A couple of Goldstein's clerks had just finished loading the supplies into the back of the wagon Pearlie had driven into town that morning with Denny coming along to keep him company.

The lanky former hired gunman and longtime foreman of the Sugarloaf—now retired—had his hat tipped far back on his head, and his hands were tucked in the back pockets of his jeans. Like most of the other men on the streets of Big Rock in these early days of the twentieth century, he wasn't wearing a gun, although that still felt funny to him at times. It was said of some men in the West, "He packed iron for so long he walked slanchwise." Pearlie was such a man.

As he looked along the street and saw Denny walking toward the mercantile, he stopped the small talk he was making with Leo Goldstein. The young storekeeper noticed her, too, and commented, "Miss Jensen looks just about mad enough to chew nails."

"Yep, and then spit 'em out to fasten somebody's hide to the barn."

Denny took the steps at the end of the porch two at a time. As she came up to Pearlie, she asked sharply, "Are you ready to go?"

"I reckon. Leo's clerks just finished loadin' us up.

I sort of figured we'd get some lunch in town before headin' back out to the ranch, though."

Denny shook her head. "No, I want to go now."

Pearlie considered that and slowly nodded. "All right," he said. "That'll be fine. So long, Leo."

He shook hands with the young merchant and then started to reach out to help Denny onto the wagon seat. She ignored his hand and made the long step from the porch onto the driver's box without any assistance.

Pearlie climbed up beside her, unwound the reins from the brake lever, and flicked them against the horses' backs to get the team moving. He guided the wagon through a wide turn across Big Rock's main street and then headed west toward the Sugarloaf.

When they were on the road and the town was falling behind them, Pearlie said without looking over at Denny, "I heard all the shootin' a while ago. Sounded like it was comin' from the direction of the depot, and since I knew you'd gone down there, I started to go see what it was all about. But I ran into Phil Clinton along the way, and he told me what had happened. He said you were all right, but that you'd been mixed up in the ruckus."

Denny maintained her stony silence for a moment, then relaxed a little and said, "I didn't notice Mr. Clinton there, but I'm not surprised. I'm sure he'll put a story about the trouble in his newspaper." She paused. "That means he'll probably talk to . . ."

"Talk to who?" Pearlie asked when Denny didn't go on.

"Count Giovanni Malatesta." Denny said the name like it tasted bad in her mouth.

"Who?"

"Nobody," Denny snapped. "Nobody worth writing about in the newspaper. Nobody even worth knowing."

"You sound like *you* know him, right enough," Pearlie pointed out.

"I wish I didn't," Denny said. Her voice grew softer as she turned her head and stared off into the distance. "I wish I had never met or even heard of Giovanni Malatesta . . ."

CHAPTER 4

Venice, Italy, two years earlier

It was the fanciest, most exclusive ball of the season, with only the most illustrious members of Italian society there, along with many distinguished visitors from England and the rest of the Continent. The great, glittering hall in one of the palaces overlooking the Grand Canal was packed with aristocracy, wealth, power, and influence. Ladies in exquisite gowns, with jewelry shimmering on their fingers and wrists and around their milky white throats, swirled around the dance floor in the arms of dashing, expensively dressed gentlemen as a small orchestra played.

Nineteen-year-old Denise Nicole Jensen was perhaps the loveliest young woman in the vast room. Her blond hair was coiffed in an elaborate arrangement of curls that tumbled around shoulders left bare by her pale blue gown. The dress was cut fashionably low, cinched tight at her trim waist, and flared out around her hips. A smattering of lace decorated the neckline and sleeves.

The ball had not been under way for long, and at the moment, Denny was dancing with her twin brother, Louis, who shared the same fine features and slender build but had sandy brown hair instead of blond. They were making one of their periodic tours of the Continent, during a break from the school Louis attended in England.

When they were younger, they had always been accompanied on these journeys by their grandparents, their mother Sally's mother and father, who owned the estate in England where Denny and Louis had grown up. Louis's poor health as a child had prompted Smoke and Sally to seek the very best medical care available for him, and that had been in Europe. Rather than split up the twins, Denny had gone with her brother to live on the Reynolds estate. Smoke and Sally hated to be apart from their children, but they had to do what was best for Louis.

These days, now that the twins were almost fully grown, they traveled on their own, although their grandmother still wasn't too keen on the idea. So far on this trip, they had been to Paris, Rome, and now Venice.

"I have a feeling you're about to be swarmed," Louis said quietly as they danced. "All the young men at this ball are waiting to swoop down on you like a pack of vultures. Quite a few of the older men are, too."

"What a lovely image," Denny said caustically. "I always enjoy being compared to a piece of carrion."

"Oh, now, that's not what I meant, and you know it. I'm just saying that as the prettiest girl here, you're going to get the most attention. It's inevitable."

"I'm hardly the prettiest girl here," Denny scoffed. "Look at all those gorgeous Italian signorinas and

French mademoiselles and Spanish señoritas. Poor little old me can't hold a candle to them."

"You underestimate yourself," Louis assured her.

Denny laughed. "What do you know about it? You're my brother."

"That doesn't mean I'm blind."

"It doesn't mean you're right, either."

The song came to an end. The dancers paused and applauded lightly, and some shuffling of partners went on. Denny supposed she would dance with Louis again, but before the music resumed, a man's voice said from behind her, "Please, signorina, you must help me. My life is in danger!"

Denny turned quickly. An elegantly attired, dark-haired young man a few years older than her stood there with a smile on his handsome face. He was well built but not overly tall. His gray eyes and Denny's blue ones were almost on the same level.

Denny cocked her head a little to the side, frowned, and said, "It doesn't look to me like your life is in any danger. You look perfectly healthy to me."

"Ah, but that is because you cannot see my heart, signorina. There is no way for you to know that it will break completely in two if I do not have this dance, and all the other dances this evening, with you."

Denny glanced at Louis, who shrugged as if to say, *I told you so.* Then she turned back to the stranger.

"Does that approach actually *work*?" she asked him. "Don't women laugh in your face when you say such things?"

"My face, it is strong enough to withstand a beautiful woman's laughter, because when she laughs, she also smiles, and a smile from a beautiful woman is worth any risk. Especially a woman as lovely as you, signorina."

Denny studied him for a moment, then said, "Whatever I say, you're going to have an answer for it, aren't you?"

He shrugged. "I speak only the truth, as any noble-man must." He took her hand and bowed low over it. "Allow me to introduce myself. I am Count Giovanni Malatesta, from the beautiful island of Sicily."

Even though Denny hadn't grown up in the American West, the courtesy of the frontier ran in her veins, along with the blood of the Jensens. She said, "I'm Denise Jensen. This is my brother Louis."

Count Malatesta pressed his lips to the back of Denny's hand, then murmured, "It is a great pleasure to meet you, Signorina Jensen. Denise . . . a lovely name for a lovely girl."

He straightened, held on to Denny's hand for a second longer, then let go of it and forthrightly stuck out his own hand to Louis. "And an honor to meet you, my friend." He looked back and forth between them. "Such a distinct resemblance. You are perhaps twins?"

"We are," Louis acknowledged as he shook hands with the count.

"And Americans, of that there is no doubt."

"Why?" Denny asked. "Because you think we're bumpkins, as so many Europeans do?"

Malatesta pressed his right hand to his chest and shook his head. "Never! No Italian would ever be so ungracious as to think such a thing. Now, a German might hold such an opinion, perhaps . . .

a Frenchman, most definitely! But not me or any of my countrymen."

The first notes of the next song came from the musicians. Malatesta held out his hand.

"Please, signorina. Have mercy on my poor heart. Do not let it break in two."

Denny couldn't help but smile. She put her hand in Malatesta's and said, "Oh, all right. We're guests in your country, after all."

"And very welcome guests, I assure you."

"But this one dance is all I'll promise you."

"I will cast my fate to the winds of fortune and the mercy of a beautiful woman," Malatesta said.

He clasped her left hand with his right, put his other arm around her waist as she rested her right hand on his shoulder, and led her into a waltz. He was a very skilled dancer, moving perfectly in time to the music and making certain that she did, too. He didn't pull her too close, instead maintaining a proper distance, but even so there was an undeniable intimacy in what they shared.

After a few minutes, he asked quietly, "You are enjoying yourself?"

"I am," Denny admitted. "You dance very well."

"I do a great many things very well."

"Including boasting?" she asked.

"It is not boasting if one can accomplish the things he claims," Malatesta said.

"In other words, as they say where I come from, no brag, just fact."

"That is one way of putting it. And where, exactly, is it that you come from, Signorina Jensen? America is your homeland, I know, but it is a vast country."

"Quite vast," Denny agreed. "Actually, I was born in Boston and have spent a great deal of time in England. I've picked up some of the accent."

"Not much," Malatesta said. "You still sound like an American to me."

"But my parents live in the West, in a state called Colorado, and since that's my heritage and I've visited there enough, I consider myself a western girl."

"Colorado," Malatesta repeated. "I believe I have heard of it. A place full of murderous desperadoes and wild, bloodthirsty Indians, is it not?"

"Only in dime novels. Oh, there are still desperadoes, I suppose. There have always been men on the wrong side of the law and there always will be."

"Certainly quite probable."

"But the threat from the Indians is over, except in widely scattered places," she said as they continued turning and swooping gracefully in time to the music. "The country is civilized now, or so they say." She sighed.

Malatesta frowned slightly and said, "You sound almost disappointed that it is so."

"Well, my father and mother had such exciting adventures when they were young and just married, and quite a few since then, too. It just seems hard to believe that so little time has actually passed since then. Only a few decades."

"History moves slowly when one studies it in books, but speeds along swiftly indeed when one is busy living it."

She looked squarely at him and said, "That's a pretty profound thing to say."

"Forgive me," he replied hastily. "The last thing I feel like being this evening is profound. And most people of my acquaintance would laugh at the very idea of me saying anything that might make a person think."

"Maybe so, but I'm enjoying dancing with you . . . *and* talking with you."

"Then my evening is already a spectacular success and will only get better from here, I think!"

Denny didn't dance *every* dance with Count Giovanni Malatesta at that ball, despite his pleading, but she found herself in his arms quite often even though she tried to spread her attention around to some of the other single men in attendance.

He was insistent, though, and eventually she gave up the battle, telling Louis, "I think it'll be easier dancing with him than trying to avoid him."

"He does seem very determined," Louis said.

Denny looked over at her brother and asked, "What do you think of him?"

"The count? He's a charmer, no doubt about that. How genuine it is, I couldn't tell you." Louis paused. "He also seems to have a very high opinion of himself. Perhaps it's deserved. After all, he *is* young, rich, handsome, and a nobleman. I'm sure a lot of the ladies here would love to be dancing with him."

Denny made a dismissive sound. "He thinks he can just come along and sweep me off my feet. This isn't some Henry James novel. He's not some sophisticated European taking advantage of the crass, crude Americans."

But despite her wariness, Denny said yes the next time the count asked her to dance, and after that they spent most of the rest of the evening together.

When the hour grew late and the ball began to break up, Malatesta took hold of both of Denny's hands and asked, "Would you do me the honor of allowing me to escort you back to your hotel?"

"I came here tonight with my brother."

"And I've spent enough time talking with Louis to know that he's an intelligent, enterprising young man. I have no doubt he can find his own way back without your assistance."

Denny shook her head. "I'm sorry, but no, Count."

"Please, after all the time we've spent together this evening, you should call me Giovanni." A smile lit up his face. "Or perhaps even Johnny. That is how you Americans would say my name, is it not?"

"Let's just leave it at Count Malatesta, shall we?" Denny replied coolly.

"As you wish." He held up his hands in surrender. "I should not move so fast, I know. It's just that my resistance is always so weak in the presence of such a beautiful woman."

"Well, you'll just have to be strong. Louis and I are going back to the hotel in the same carriage that brought us here."

"Of course." He took hold of her hand and bent to kiss the back of it again. "But you and I, we will see each other again. It is written in the stars, *cara mia.*"

She and Louis were in the carriage, on their way back to the Hotel Metropole, before she said, "What does *cara mia* mean in Italian?" Louis had always had a better flare for languages than she did.

"I believe it translates to 'my beloved,' or something very close to that. Why?"

"I heard someone say it tonight."

Louis looked over at her in the shadows of the coach. "Count Malatesta?"

"Never mind." Denny rolled her eyes. "The whole thing is ridiculous."

But as she gazed out the carriage's window at the cobblestone street rolling past, she realized she had a smile on her lips.

CHAPTER 5

It wasn't exactly a whirlwind courtship, but once it got started, it moved along pretty fast.

Count Malatesta sent flowers to Denny at the hotel the next day, and the day after that, but he didn't come to call until the third day. Denny had considered suggesting to Louis that they go ahead and leave Venice, but she found herself strangely unwilling to do so.

Her reluctance to go couldn't have anything to do with the way Giovanni Malatesta was attempting to woo her so determinedly, she told herself. It was just that Venice was such a beautiful city, and she and Louis hadn't yet seen everything there was to see. That was why they couldn't leave yet.

She knew Louis would have scoffed at that reasoning—and in the back of her mind, she did, too.

When Malatesta showed up at the hotel and asked her to go with him to the Piazza San Marco and St. Mark's Basilica, Denny couldn't come up with a good reason to refuse the invitation, especially after Malatesta asked Louis to come along, too. That proved the Italian nobleman didn't have any improper intentions, or if he did, he was being sly about them.

"I don't need a chaperone," Denny said to her brother as they were getting ready to leave the hotel. Malatesta had gone back downstairs after telling them he would meet them in the lobby.

"Good, because I wouldn't amount to much as one, even if there was any trouble," Louis said.

Denny looked over at him. Louis wasn't frail, exactly, but he wasn't the picture of health, either. He had been born with a flaw in his heart that often left him pale, weak, and struggling for breath. In times of trouble, Denny was more likely to be the one taking the bull by its proverbial horns.

She hated that he thought less of himself because of his condition. It was no fault of his own, and as far as she was concerned, no girl had ever had a better brother.

She put her arms around him, hugged him, and said, "Don't you ever think anything like that. You don't know how much I depend on you, Louis."

"Well, I'm glad to hear it," he said with a rueful smile. "I just hope I don't ever let you down."

"You won't," she assured him.

They went downstairs, where Malatesta greeted them in his jovial, booming voice as if they were old friends he hadn't seen for years, instead of having left them at the door of their hotel room less than a quarter of an hour earlier. He ushered them toward the entrance doors of the vast, elaborately furnished lobby with its golden mosaics, jeweled tapestries, and gleaming marble floor.

The Hotel Metropole was a square, four-story building with its name emblazed on a large sign that ran across the front, above the entrance. Steps on the other side of the small plaza in front of it led down to the Grand Canal, where gondolas and other boats waited to carry passengers along the watery thoroughfares of this ancient city. To the left as Denny, Louis, and Giovanni Malatesta walked toward the Grand Canal was one of the many graceful arched bridges to be found in Venice, this one crossing a smaller canal that ran alongside the hotel.

Malatesta led the two Americans to a waiting gondola manned by a stocky, swarthy gondolier in the traditional outfit of tight white trousers, loose colorful shirt, and flat-crowned straw hat adorned by a small ribbon. The count took Denny's hand and helped her step into the boat, then started to assist Louis as well, only to have him say, "Thanks, but I can manage."

"Of course, my friend." Malatesta boarded with the grace of a large cat and took Denny's hand again as they sat on one of the sumptuously padded benches. Louis sat opposite them, facing backward.

The gondolier pushed off with the long pole that was the tool of his trade and sent the gondola gliding smoothly through the water. With expert skill, he guided the boat into the traffic on the Grand Canal.

"With all the bridges, it is possible to walk from the hotel to St. Mark's," Malatesta said as he leaned back against the cushioned seat, "but I did not know if the two of you had ridden in a gondola yet. It is an experience that every visitor to Venezia must have."

"It just so happens that we've been to Venice before," Denny said, "and this isn't our first ride in a gondola. But it's been a while, and it's always a nice thing to do."

Despite the waterways that made it distinctive, in many ways Venice was like most of the other cities in Europe: a striking blend of beauty and squalor, wealth and poverty, and an assault on the senses. Nearly everywhere a person looked were gracious old buildings that were works of art every bit as much as the treasures some of them housed. But underlying the stunning visions that met the eye was the perpetual stink of dead fish. It was impossible to eliminate in a city built on the water. The canals themselves were lovely from a distance, but up close, trash floated in them. No one ever mentioned that. It was as if everyone in Venice, citizens and visitors alike, had agreed to turn a blind eye to the unavoidably ugly parts of life that went on here as they did everywhere else.

The trip to the vast Piazza San Marco, with its busy shops and museums on three sides and the massive, magnificent edifice, St. Mark's Basilica, at the far end, didn't take long. Once they were there, Denny, Louis, and Malatesta joined the throngs of people strolling around the plaza, gazing at the wide variety of beautiful goods on display. They were in no hurry, and considering the crowds, it wouldn't have done them much good if they had been. It took them more than an hour to reach the huge church, and they spent another hour inside, staring raptly at the statues and icons and tapestries and paintings, masterworks of art from all over Europe, some of them dating back hundreds of years.

Later, back out in the plaza, Denny sat on one of the benches to rest. Malatesta sat beside her while Louis wandered off to look at the wares in one of the shops.

Not far away, water bubbled in a fountain adorned by a statue of a naked cherub. Denny didn't know if the statue was a work of art or just a decoration. She supposed it didn't matter.

"Are you enjoying yourself?" Malatesta asked.

"I am," she admitted. "It's getting a little warm, though." She was grateful for the hat she had worn, with its broad, floppy brim. The shade it provided for her face was welcome.

"We can go back to the hotel soon," Malatesta told her. "You will want to rest before I take you to supper tonight."

Denny laughed. "Who said I was going to have supper with you?"

"But you must eat at the Café Top Rosso Elegante." Malatesta kissed his fingertips and then blew that kiss off them. "The best food in all of Venice. You cannot pass up the chance to dine there."

"I don't believe I've heard of that place."

Malatesta waved away her comment. "The ones who actually live in a city always know the best places to eat there. The café is, how you say it, off the beaten path. But you will love it, I give you my word."

"Is Louis invited to dinner as well?"

Malatesta smiled slightly. "No offense to your wonderful brother, but it was my fondest hope that perhaps this evening, the two of us could spend some time alone together, *cara mia*."

"Isn't that rather bold of you, referring to me as your beloved?"

"Fortune favors the bold," the count replied. "Isn't that what they say? But as for me, I care not for fortune. All that matters to me is that Signorina Denise Nicole Jensen favors me. Say that you do, and my heart will leap so high, there is no way of knowing where it will come down."

Denny looked at him for a long moment, then finally said, "You're starting to grow on me a little, I suppose."

He exclaimed in Italian as a brilliant smile broke out across his face. "My heart, she soars out of sight," he added in English.

"Better hold on to your heart," Denny advised him drily. "You might need it."

He shook his head. "No, because the joy of being in your presence fills my chest instead and beats as warmly and strongly as my heart ever could."

"What you're full of is . . . fancy talk," Denny said, the smile on her face taking any sting out of the words.

"So you will have supper with me?" he persisted.

"I will," Denny said. His flowery, grandiose proclamations amused her—quite possibly, intentionally on his part—and there was no denying that he was handsome and charming. It wasn't going to hurt anything to spend more time with him.

But she wasn't going to lose her heart to him. She was absolutely certain of that.

Despite her best intentions, Denny spent most of every waking hour with Count Giovanni Malatesta during the next week, and even though she told herself that it was crazy, that she hadn't come to Venice to have some sort of whirlwind romance with a dashing Italian nobleman, she realized that she was falling in love with Giovanni.

They ate in the finest restaurants and coziest cafés. They explored the shops, from the most expensive and luxurious to the quaint, hole-in-the-wall establishments that always struck Denny as the slightest bit shady. They visited the great palazzos where the noble families opened their homes so visitors could admire all the beautiful treasures within. The very best of art, music, and fine food, Giovanni laid at Denny's feet. And in between, the gondolas carried them along the city's canals as glittering scenery slid smoothly past them.

She had vowed to herself that no Italian count was going to sweep her off her feet, no matter how handsome and dashing he might be—but that was exactly what Giovanni Malatesta did.

Poor Louis was left out most of the time, of course, and Denny felt bad about that, but he assured her that he was enjoying the visit and could take care of himself.

"I hope I can say the same of you," he commented to her, one day in the hotel as he gave her a meaningful look. "That you can take care of yourself."

"I know what you mean. Just because you're a few minutes older than me doesn't mean you have to start playing the protective big brother."

"I just don't want you to get hurt, Denny."

"I'm not going to," she said confidently. "Honestly, Giovanni has been a perfect gentleman so far."

"Let's hope that continues."

The thing of it was, Denny wasn't sure she *wanted* Giovanni's gentlemanly behavior to continue. She found herself growing more and more curious what it would feel like to have his strong arms around her, to taste the warmth of his mouth with hers . . .

That evening, they dined again at the Café Top Rosso Elegante, where they'd had dinner for the first time in Venice. The food was as good as ever, the candlelight dim and subdued, the atmosphere romantic. When they left, Giovanni suggested a stroll along the canal before he hailed a gondola and took her back to the Metropole.

"I think I'd like that," Denny said.

Arm in arm, they walked along the cobblestones with the canal at their right. Up ahead, a bridge arched up and over one of the smaller canals.

"The Bridge of the Roses," Giovanni told her. "Legend has it that lovers come here, after they have been . . . intimate . . . and each tosses a rose into the canal. If the current carries the roses away together, the couple will stay together forever. If the current separates the roses, so, too, will the lovers drift apart."

"So it's either romantic . . . or terrible."

"Such is life," Giovanni said with an eloquent gesture. "Shall we walk across the bridge?"

"We have no roses."

"Not yet," he said, smiling.

Denny hesitated, then said, "I don't suppose walking across it will hurt anything."

"Perhaps we will find someone selling flowers on the street, on the other side."

"Perhaps," Denny said.

The hour was late enough that the streets and the canals weren't as busy as they often were. The two of them were the only ones on the bridge, in fact. It was dimly lit by lamps at either end, but at the top of the arch in the middle, thick shadows gathered.

Giovanni stopped there, turned to her, and said in a husky voice, "Denise . . . Denny, *cara mia* . . ."

When he put his hands on her shoulders and bent his head to hers, she didn't stop him.

The kiss was long and lingering and started her heart pounding almost painfully in her chest. Her hands clutched at the front of his shirt. He moved his hands down to the swell of her hips and held her close to him.

Denny felt herself weakening. She already had her hands on his broad chest. She pushed against it, moved her head back to break the kiss, and whispered, "Giovanni, no . . ."

"My apartment is near, *cara mia*," he said. "And I have roses there."

She shook her head a little. "We can't . . . I can't . . ."

"No one will know. No one will be harmed. And there will be joy for you, joy unlike any you have ever known."

She pushed harder against his chest, shook her head more emphatically. "I've had a wonderful time with you, these last two weeks," she said, "and I want to go with you, I really do, but—"

She didn't know what he would do next. She was afraid he would try to force her to go with him, and if he did that, she would fight back. And if that happened, he would be surprised just how much of a wildcat he had on his hands.

But those decisions were taken out of her hands, because at that moment, rapid footsteps slapped against the bridge and Giovanni let go of her so he could whirl around and face the handful of shadowy figures charging toward them. Denny heard the men's rasping breath and harsh words she thought were Italian curses.

Then Giovanni exclaimed, "Thieves!"

They were under attack.

CHAPTER 6

Giovanni sprang to meet the would-be robbers. He lashed out with a fist at the man in the lead and slammed a blow to the man's jaw. The thief flew backward and got tangled up with one of the other men.

But there were three more of them, and one of them darted in and swung a short club of some sort at Giovanni's head. Denny thought it was going to smash his brains in, but at the last second, Giovanni ducked his head and twisted aside so that the club caught him on the back of his shoulder instead. It still packed enough power to make him grunt in pain and stagger to the side.

The other two closed in on him and started hammering him with their fists.

So far, none of the thieves had paid the least bit of attention to Denny. She would show them that was a mistake. She lunged at the one with the club and leaped onto his back.

It wasn't easy in the expensive gown she wore, but she managed to wrap her legs around the man's waist and hang on with one arm around his neck. An opponent's ears were often vulnerable, her father had taught her during one of her visits to the Sugarloaf.

Sally had chided Smoke for the rough-and-tumble lessons with their daughter, but the things she had learned had come in handy more than once.

She grabbed the man's right ear and twisted as hard as she could. He cried out in a mixture of surprise and pain, then lurched back and forth and dropped the club so he could use both hands to reach back at her. She bent her head down to avoid his grasp and kept twisting his ear until she felt something give and hot blood spurted over the back of her hand.

By now he was writhing around and flailing at her in a crazed fashion. They were near the waist-high stone wall along the side of the bridge, so Denny dropped her feet to the ground and shoved hard as she planted her shoulder in the small of the man's back. Taken once again by surprise, he stumbled forward and she rammed him against the wall. He said, *"Ooof!"* as the impact bent him forward over the stone barrier.

Denny acted almost quicker than the eye could follow, especially in the poor light. She reached down, grabbed the man's ankles, and heaved upward. Already bent over the wall, he couldn't stop himself as his weight shifted. He screamed as his head went down, his feet went up, and he flipped right over the wall and plunged the twenty feet or so to the canal. Denny heard the splash as he hit the water.

She didn't know how Giovanni was doing with the other attackers. As she whirled around toward the center of the bridge, her foot struck the club the man had dropped. It rolled away with a clatter. Denny pounced on it, snatched it up, and waded into the knot of struggling figures a few yards away.

In the shadows, it was hard to tell which of the men was Giovanni. She spotted one she definitely knew *wasn't* him, though, because he was too tall and thin. She laid into him from behind with the club, whaling away at his head and shoulders, as far up as she could reach, anyway.

The man yelled and swept out an arm as he turned quickly toward her. His arm struck her wrist and sent the club flying. Snarling and cursing, the man came at her with his arms outstretched.

Denny stood her ground and kicked him in the groin. Her foot landed hard and on target. The man howled in agony and collapsed as he tried to fold up around himself.

The sound of running footsteps made her look around. It appeared that the rest of the thieves were fleeing down the slope of the bridge. Giovanni stood at the top of the arch, his hair disarrayed, his expensive suit torn and disheveled, and shook his fist at them as he shouted defiantly in Italian after them.

He turned sharply as Denny came up to him and said, "Giovanni." He gripped her arms.

"*Cara mia,* you are all right?" he asked anxiously. "Those horrible men, they did not harm you?"

"I'm fine," she told him. "A little shaken, that's all." She pointed at the man who lay there moaning as he clutched himself. "One of them didn't get away. You can call the police—"

"No *polizia*. This man insulted your honor and dared lay hands on your person! I will deal with him personally!"

He reached under his coat, and Denny saw starlight glitter on the blade of the dagger he pulled out.

She grasped his wrist and said, "No! You don't have

to kill him. I'm all right, Giovanni, really. Let's just . . . let's just get out of here."

He hesitated but finally said with obvious reluctance, "All right." He slipped the knife back in its hidden sheath under his coat. "Come with me."

He took her hand and led her down from the bridge. Denny was surprised that the encounter hadn't attracted any attention, but the street seemed to be deserted. Giovanni took her to an elegant building that appeared to have been a palazzo belonging to one of Venice's old families at some time in the past. It had been turned into apartments, and Giovanni led her to one.

Denny recalled what he had been saying before the would-be thieves attacked them. Giovanni had gotten her into his apartment after all, but under the circumstances, he couldn't have anything amorous in mind. Both of them were too shaken by the attack.

And Giovanni was hurt, too, Denny saw as he lit an oil lamp sitting on an elaborately carved sideboard. Crimson trickled down the side of his face from a cut on his forehead.

"You're bleeding!" she exclaimed.

"It is nothing," he said with a dismissive wave. "A wound suffered in the defense of a woman is a badge of honor. Especially when the woman is as lovely as you, *cara mia*."

"This is no time for flattery," she snapped at him. "I need to clean that up. Where can I get some hot water and a cloth?"

"The kitchen is there," he said, pointing. "There should be some embers in the stove."

Denny nodded. She always felt better when she had a task to accomplish. She went into the kitchen, stirred up the fire in the stove, and added some wood to it from a bin in the corner. On the other side of the room was a basin with a pump. She put some water in a pot and set it on the stove to heat, then began opening cabinets in search of a cloth she could use to clean Giovanni's injury.

When she came back into the other room, carrying a tray with a porcelain bowl of hot water and a clean cloth on it, she saw that he had taken off his coat and vest and cravat and stood there in shirt-sleeves. And he was unbuttoning the shirt as well. It was already open enough to reveal a muscular chest thickly furred with dark hair.

"My apologies for the indecency," he said. "The lady who does my laundry, she would be very upset if she had to clean bloodstains from my garments."

"You don't need to get blood on such fine clothes, anyway," Denny said as she set the tray on the sideboard next to the lamp.

He peeled off the shirt and tossed it onto a claw-footed divan with the other things he had taken off. Denny got the cloth wet and stepped close to him. Since there wasn't a great difference in their height, she had no trouble reaching the cut on his forehead. He winced as she began dabbing at it.

"I'm sorry if I hurt you," she said.

"It is a pain I suffer willingly, even gladly," he assured her. "All in a good cause."

"Defending me?"

"That is what gentlemen are born to do, defend noble and beautiful ladies." He cocked his head a little to the side. "Although, from what I saw while engaged in my own combat, you gave a good account of yourself. I never would have dreamed you would leap into the fray like that."

"I've always been a fighter. You can ask my brother."

Giovanni gave her a dubious smile. "Eh, I am not sure I will mention this affair to Louis. It is over, no harm was done, and there is no reason to worry him."

Denny just about had the blood cleaned off his face. She pressed the cloth to the cut to stop any further bleeding and said, "No harm done?"

"Not to you, and this . . . this is nothing. It will be a scar well earned."

"You never even hesitated when those men jumped us. You went right after them, even though the odds were five to one."

"They gave me no choice," he said quietly. "And I never paused to think about my own safety."

"No," Denny said, "I don't believe you did."

"All I thought about, *cara mia* . . . was you."

She took the cloth away from the cut and said softly, "I think it's stopped bleeding now. And I don't believe . . ." She was getting a little breathless and found it difficult to talk. "I don't believe you'll need any stitches . . ."

He took her wrist in his left hand, gently plucked the cloth from her fingers with his right, and tossed it onto the tray.

"Let us have no more talk of blood and stitches, of robbers and danger. Fate had brought us here, Denny, and there . . . there are the roses I promised you."

He nodded toward a vase containing a dozen beautiful roses. It was on a table next to an open door, and through that door Denny could see part of an elegant old four-poster bed. The light from the lamp didn't reach very far into the room, and most of the bed was in shadow—but she knew it was there.

"Giovanni," she whispered, "I . . . I never . . ."

"Shhh," he told her. "All is well. Follow your heart, and you will know happiness unlike any you have ever known." His fingers moved over the bare skin of her forearm, strayed up to her shoulder and then behind her neck as he leaned in and kissed her. She felt the heat from his body, bare from the waist up, and couldn't resist the temptation to reach out and touch it. A tingle like the shock of electricity went through her as she rested her fingers on his chest. She opened her lips to his.

He had risked his life to save her. If she'd ever had any doubt about the genuineness of his feelings for her, it had vanished now. And her own feelings were calling out to her stronger than she had ever experienced. All of that together, combined with the nearness of that bed, was more temptation than Denny could stand.

So she stopped fighting it and whispered, "Yes."

To Giovanni, and to herself . . .

CHAPTER 7

Without opening her eyes, Denny stretched and yawned, luxuriating in the sensation of bare skin against smooth silken sheets. A warm breeze blew through the room, moving a curling strand of blond hair against her cheek. That touch tickled. She lifted a hand to push the hair away. The movement made the sheet fall away from her, and that finally alerted her consciousness to her state of undress.

Her eyes popped open and widened in alarm as she realized she was lying in Count Giovanni Malatesta's bed.

She grabbed the sheet and pulled it over her again as she sat up and hurriedly looked around. The lamp still burned in the other room. Enough light spilled into the bedroom for her to see that she was alone. She swung her legs off the soft mattress and stood up, taking the sheet with her. She wrapped it around her as she stepped to the door between rooms and called softly, "Giovanni?"

When there was no response, she called his name twice more before deciding she was alone in the apartment. She leaned against the doorjamb, closed her eyes, and tried to gather her scattered thoughts.

The knowledge that her life had changed and would never be the same again clamored in the back of her mind. She wasn't upset about that fact, necessarily; she had known that sooner or later she would meet the right man and take the step she had taken tonight.

She had never expected that man to be an Italian count, however. She had figured that she would be married, or at the very least, her first experience would be with a man she intended to marry.

Try as she might, she just couldn't imagine Giovanni living on a ranch in Colorado, and she had decided several years earlier that she intended to return to the Sugarloaf and make her permanent home there, probably in the fairly near future.

The medical advances to be had in Europe may well have saved Louis's life, but during the past year, more than one doctor had told him that they had done all they could for him. Their best advice, in fact, had been for Louis to spend more time in the open air and try to make himself more robust that way. There was no better place to do that than the Colorado valley where the vast Jensen ranch was located.

When Louis went home to stay, Denny intended to, as well. She and her brother had both spent too much time away from their parents. It was time for the Jensen family to be together again.

If she came home with a husband, Smoke and Sally would welcome him and do their best to make him feel right at home at Sugarloaf. Denny had no doubt of that. But would Giovanni ever consider such a thing? Venice had become home to him, after he'd come here from Sicily.

"Oh, Denny, you're such an impulsive fool," she

whispered to herself. Passion had welled up so strongly and unexpectedly inside her that she hadn't been able to withstand it. She had allowed Giovanni to ruin her.

"Stop that," she told herself, louder and more firmly this time. She wasn't ruined. This was the twentieth century, after all. Morality wasn't as strict and stringent as it had been in the past. Anyway, she knew good and well that a lot of the so-called rules regarding proper behavior were more honored in theory than they were in practice. Plenty of western brides had walked down the aisle already in the family way.

Her eyes widened again at that thought. What if she was . . . That wasn't possible, was it? A girl didn't get like that on the very first time, did she? That wouldn't be fair at all!

A practical streak a mile wide ran through Denny, always had. What was done was done. Her jaw firmed and her chin lifted. Whatever results the future held, she would face them head-on, without flinching.

Right now, she had to think about getting back to the Hotel Metropole. She could tell by a glance out the window at the darkness that the hour was late. Louis was bound to be worried about her, and probably he would be upset when she got back. But at least she could ease his mind about her safety.

The sound of an angry voice made her frown and look around. She was convinced that she was alone in the apartment and had no idea where Giovanni had gone. After a moment, she realized that the voice came through the open window in the bedroom. Curious, she moved over to it and looked out.

The apartment was on the second floor of the old palazzo, on the side overlooking a narrow street instead of the canal. Streetlamps were few and far between, but enough glow filtered along the cobblestones from one about fifty yards away for Denny to make out the shapes of three men standing and talking in front of the house.

Denny frowned. One of the men was the right size and shape to be Giovanni, but she couldn't be sure it was him. The other two were in the shadows and were even more obscure. She made out a blob of white where one man's head ought to be. A mask of some sort?

She caught only a few of the heated words being spoken. They were in Italian and rattled along too fast for her to comprehend them. Then the man she thought *might* be Giovanni turned on his heel and stalked toward the palazzo's entrance. Watching the way he moved, Denny was convinced that he was indeed Giovanni.

And no doubt he was on his way back up here. Hurriedly, she tossed the sheet onto the bed and started looking around for her clothes.

She was fully dressed by the time Giovanni opened the door and strode into the apartment. At the sight of her standing there, he exclaimed, "*Cara mia,* you are awake!"

"Did you plan to let me sleep all night?" she asked coolly. She wasn't angry with him, but for some reason, at this moment she felt the need to keep a little distance between them. Under the circumstances, it would be too easy to open herself completely to him unless she stayed on her guard.

"Of course not," he answered as he shook his head. "That would worry and upset your brother. Actually, the hour is not all *that* late. You can tell Louis that we were strolling along the canal and lost track of the time."

"Lie to him, in other words."

Giovanni spread his hands. "It's not a lie, not exactly. We *did* stroll along the canal, and after that, *I* was not thinking about the time, and I fervently hope that you were not, either."

"You don't have to worry. I have no intention of telling Louis what happened tonight. The attack by the thieves . . . or anything else."

He came to her and rested his hands on her shoulders. "Denise, you have nothing of which to be ashamed."

"I didn't say I was ashamed. I just don't think it's any of his business."

Giovanni nodded and said, "I will get you back to your hotel. Unless . . . you would rather stay . . ."

"I can't," Denny said. She started to look away, but then forced herself to meet his eyes. If she claimed she wasn't ashamed, she didn't need to act like she was. "I have to think about what's happened, Giovanni. I'm not upset, but I still have to think about it."

"I understand," he said, but she had a feeling he was just trying to be agreeable.

"I'm curious about one thing, though. Who were those men you were talking to just now, out on the street?"

His hands still rested on her shoulders. They tightened slightly as he frowned, shook his head, and said, "I was not talking to anyone."

"Yes, you were," Denny insisted. "I saw you from the window in the bedroom. You were talking to two men."

Grinning, he lifted both hands from her shoulders

and waved them expressively. "Oh, *those* two! Minor annoyances, I assure you. They sent word that they wanted to see me, and since I have known them practically forever, I should have known what they were after. They wanted to borrow some money, only I know that were I to give them any, I would never see those lire again! Still, they are old friends, so I could not refuse to speak with them."

"No, I suppose not," Denny said. Giovanni's words had the ring of truth to them. She went on, "I need to get back to the hotel now."

"Yes, of course. There are still some gondolas available, even at this hour. But before we go . . ." He gripped her hands. "*Cara mia,* I want you to know just how happy you have made me and how deeply I care for you."

He leaned in and kissed her again, not urgent and passionate this time, more of a gentle caress with his lips. Denny responded without thinking, putting her arms around his neck and returning the kiss.

Yes, everything had changed, she thought, but she believed . . . and hoped . . . that this might be the start of something even better.

Louis was upset when she came into their suite at the Hotel Metropole, even a little angry, just as Denny expected. She thought he also suspected that something had happened between her and Giovanni, but he was too much of a gentleman—or too embarrassed—to press his sister for details about such a thing.

However, over breakfast in their sitting room the next morning, he did say, "I think we should leave

Venice. We've already been here a lot longer than we intended."

"I'm not ready to go yet," Denny said.

"If we stay much longer, we won't be able to stop at all the other places on our itinerary. We'll have to start back to England."

"I don't care. We've already been everywhere anyway. What does it matter whether we make the entire grand tour this time?"

Louis didn't prolong the argument, but Denny knew he wasn't happy with her. She didn't want to annoy him—but she wasn't ready to leave Giovanni, either.

They continued spending most of their time together, but no matter where they went, they nearly always wound up back in Giovanni's apartment in the old palazzo, making love in the big four-poster bed while soft evening breezes blew in through the window, carrying the faint strains of romantic songs being sung by the gondoliers poling their boats through the canals. Denny didn't understand most of the words, but the language of love was unmistakable.

She was so distracted by the unexpected affair with Giovanni that perhaps she wasn't as alert as usual, but even so, eventually she came to realize that someone was following them.

More than once, she caught a glimpse of a man lurking in the shadows as they strolled along the narrow streets. It wasn't always the same man, either. Sometimes the watcher was tall and thin, other times short and stocky.

Denny's mind went back to the night they had been attacked on the Bridge of Roses, a fateful night in more ways than one. Maybe the men who had jumped them hadn't been random thieves after all. Maybe they had had a more sinister purpose to their assault, although she had no idea what that might have been. She might have gotten around to asking Giovanni about it . . .

But then some of the answers presented themselves, in an unexpected and unpleasant way.

CHAPTER 8

Denny and Giovanni were having dinner in one of the city's finest restaurants when a man came over to their table. Denny saw the way Giovanni stiffened when he spotted the man approaching and knew something was wrong.

She took a closer look and realized that despite the stranger's expensive suit, he looked out of place in these elegant surroundings. The cruel, hard-planed look of his face reminded her of some of the men she had seen in Big Rock during the visits she and Louis had made to the Sugarloaf.

Hard cases had definite similarities, whether they were in Colorado or Venice.

"Count Malatesta," the man said with an insincere smile as he stopped beside the table. "I bid you good evening on behalf of Signor Tomasi."

Giovanni jerked his head in a curt nod and said, "Tell Signor Tomasi good evening in return, if you will."

"Of course. The signore would be pleased if you and the signorina would join him in his private salon."

Giovanni shook his head. "My apologies to the

signore, but that will be impossible. Signorina Jensen and I were just about to take our leave."

They hadn't finished their meal, so that took Denny by surprise. But she supposed Giovanni had a good reason for not wanting to accept the invitation from this Signor Tomasi, whoever he was.

"Are you certain, Count?" the rough-looking stranger asked. "The signore will be very disappointed."

"This is the way it must be," Giovanni answered.

The man's broad shoulders rose and fell. "I will convey your regrets to the signore."

"*Grazie.*"

The man looked at Denny for a second, and she saw the coldness in his gaze. He definitely made her feel uneasy, and that feeling remained even after he had walked off.

"My apologies for that unpleasantness, *cara mia,*" Giovanni said as he reached across the table and clasped one of her hands in both of his. "I did not expect such an intrusion to take place tonight."

"Who was that man?" she asked. "Who's Signor Tomasi?"

As usual, Giovanni waved away a question he didn't want to answer. "No one important. A business associate."

That was puzzling. Giovanni had never mentioned business, and he hadn't shown any signs of working. Since he was a member of the nobility, Denny had assumed he was wealthy and didn't need a job. From the way he talked, his family owned a great deal of property and was important in Sicily.

"If you need to talk to him, I don't mind . . ."

A sharp shake of his head caused her voice to

trail off. "Please, put the matter out of your mind. I already have."

"Of course," Denny said. She smiled.

But she was still puzzled, and she suddenly wondered if this Tomasi might have something to do with the men who had attacked them on the Bridge of Roses. It could be his men who had been following them . . .

Keeping those suspicions to herself for the time being, she took her napkin from her lap and placed it on the table. "You told that man we were about to leave," she reminded Giovanni. "That's fine with me."

"I just said that to get rid of him. We don't have to cut our meal short—"

"No, really, I don't mind."

Giovanni squeezed her hand. "I, too, am anxious to return to my apartment," he said. "But we should at least finish the wine in our glasses."

There wasn't much wine left in the glasses. A couple of swallows took care of it. Then Giovanni held her chair for her and draped her shawl around her shoulders as he helped her up. They left the restaurant and turned toward the nearest canal where they could find a cruising gondola, walking arm in arm with Denny on Giovanni's left.

They reached some steps leading down to a landing where a couple of torches burned in holders. They walked down the steps, then Giovanni raised his right arm to signal to a passing gondola with a lantern hanging from its high-arching stern. The gondolier moved his pole to the other side of the boat and angled it in their direction.

The gondola hadn't reached the landing when the gondolier abruptly reversed course. As the boat's prow swung away, Giovanni called to the man in Italian and sounded angry. The gondolier shook his head and poled the boat farther away.

Denny had gotten a good enough look at the man's face to know that he had been scared off by something he had seen. That was enough of a warning to make her turn her head and look back over her shoulder.

"Giovanni," she said quietly as she saw four men standing at the top of the steps.

He cursed under his breath and seemed a little frantic as he glanced around. With the men blocking the steps, there was nowhere for them to go unless they wanted to jump into the canal and swim for it.

"I am sorry, *cara mia*," he told her. "I had no wish for you to become involved in my troubles."

"If they're your troubles, they're mine as well," Denny told him without hesitation. She was a little afraid—under the circumstances, it would have been foolish not to be—but she was more than a little angry as well. She was certain these men intended to harm Giovanni and maybe her as well, but they would learn that Jensens always fought back, no matter what the odds. Some of them might be well aware of that already, if they had been part of the bunch that had jumped them on the Bridge of Roses.

"Count Malatesta," one of them called as he swaggered down a couple of steps. "Signor Tomasi would like to know if you have reconsidered. It's not too late to do so."

Denny recognized the voice of the man who had come to their table in the restaurant. As he came slowly down the steps toward the landing, she saw his face in the torchlight. He had lost his mask of politeness and looked more like an outlaw than ever. The other three men trailed him down the steps. They were more roughly dressed and had the same brutal look about them.

In a tight, angry voice, Giovanni said, "Tell Tomasi that I will deal with him later. Tonight, if he wishes. But first I must escort the young lady back to her hotel."

"No, the signorina stays. Signor Tomasi has run out of patience. You must settle your accounts with him now." The man put his hands in his trouser pockets and smirked as he came to a stop on the bottom step, just above the landing. "Perhaps the signore would consider the signorina as part of your arrangement with him."

Fear welled up even stronger inside Denny at the vile implication of those words, but more anger rapidly replaced it. How dare the man even suggest such a thing? If her father had been here, Smoke Jensen wouldn't take kindly to his daughter being threatened.

Smoke might not be here, but another Jensen was. Denny's right hand slipped into the small, stylish bag she had brought with her tonight.

"What will it be, Count?" the man said. "The decision is up to you."

"Denny, get behind me," Giovanni said from the corner of his mouth. "I will not allow them to harm you."

The leader of the Italian hard cases slowly shook his head. "You have no say in this any longer, Malatesta. The signore's orders are clear. But we will be merciful. We will take the signorina with us, to hold as . . . security, shall we say . . . until you pay what you owe." The man shrugged. "Of course, you will be in no shape to worry about that for a while. But not to worry. We will keep the signorina occupied."

He jerked his head, and the other three men stepped around him, obviously ready to rush Giovanni and give him a beating before they carried Denny off to whatever sordid fate they had in mind for her.

Denny pulled the short-barreled, .32 caliber Smith & Wesson revolver from her bag and leveled it at the leader.

"If those men take one more step," she said, "I'll put a bullet in your brain."

She had never shot a man before, had never even pointed a gun at anything except a target or some predator she had helped her father hunt down on the ranch. But no one would ever guess that from the calm, cool, flint-edged voice in which she spoke. This fellow had a lot in common with a wolf or a mountain lion, Denny told herself, and she believed she could pull the trigger if she had to. She was downright certain of it, in fact.

The man gestured sharply to his companions to stop their rush before it started.

"Denise, what are you doing?" Giovanni exclaimed.

"This is a mistake, Malatesta," the leader rasped angrily. He sneered. "And I'm surprised to see you hiding behind a woman this way. I thought you were a nobleman."

Giovanni's face flushed darkly in the torchlight at that insult. He said, "Denise, put that gun away. Or better yet, give it to me."

"The signorina is not the only one who is armed." The leader made another sharp motion to the other three. Knives came out from somewhere. The red glare from the torches glittered on the blades.

"None of that will do *you* any good," Denny said. "You'll be dead before they can reach us." She paused. "Anyway, if you kill Giovanni, who's going to pay the man you work for? That's what this is about, right? A debt that needs to be collected? Maybe something can be done about that."

The leader cocked his head slightly to the side. "What do you propose, signorina?"

"No!" Giovanni cried. "This is not right! This is none of your affair, *cara mia*—"

"If I'm really your beloved, then I think it *is* my affair, too," Denny said. To the leader of the toughs, she went on, "Go back to your boss and tell him that things will be worked out if he'll just be a little more patient. I give him my word, and Jensens don't lie. You think he'll go along with that?"

"I would not presume to speak for the signore without talking to him first."

"Then go talk to him," Denny snapped. "Or keep crowding us and we'll see what happens."

From the corner of her eye, she saw Giovanni glaring furiously at her, but she kept most of her attention focused on the man she was looking at over the revolver's sights. He seemed pretty observant. He must have noticed that even while holding a gun on him, her hand was rock steady.

After a long moment, the man shrugged. "I will speak to Signor Tomasi, but I make no promises. The day of reckoning may be postponed, but the debt must still be settled. You know this, Malatesta. And the next time . . . there will be no woman for you to hide behind."

Giovanni growled and started to move forward, but

he stopped himself and with a visible effort controlled his rage. "Go," he told the men. "Run away like the craven dogs you are."

For a second, Denny thought the insult was going to be more than the men could stand. She was ready to pull the trigger if she needed to. She didn't figure she could gun down all four of the men before any of them reached her, especially with the small-caliber weapon. If her father had been here with a Colt .45 . . . with Smoke Jensen's deadly speed and accuracy . . .

But Smoke wasn't here, she reminded herself again. She was the lone Jensen, so it was up to her to uphold the family name. The Jensen brand was on her, just like it was on all those cattle roaming the lushly grassed meadows of the Sugarloaf.

Without saying anything else, the leader turned and motioned for the men with him to go back up the steps. He trailed them, pausing at the top to cast one last hostile look over his shoulder at the man and woman on the landing. Then he was gone like the others, vanishing into the shadows.

"Denise, I am so sorry. This . . . this is terrible—" Giovanni began.

Denny lowered the gun slightly but didn't put it away. "Maybe you should see if you can attract the attention of another gondolier. I don't think I want to go back up there, and we need to get somewhere we can talk."

CHAPTER 9

"I never meant for my difficulty to involve you, *cara mia*," Giovanni said as he poured wine from a bottle into glasses on the sideboard in his apartment. "A signorina as beautiful as yourself should never have to trouble herself over something as ugly and sordid as gambling debts."

"That's what you owe to this man Tomasi?" Denny asked. "Gambling debts?"

"Salvatore Tomasi makes a business of buying debts from gambling houses and individuals alike. I had a run of terrible luck." Giovanni shrugged. "I would have recouped my losses sooner or later, but Tomasi is not a patient man. He demands payment now."

"And you don't have the money," Denny guessed. It wasn't really a question.

"I have experienced . . . financial reverses. Much as it pains me to admit it, I lack the funds to satisfy Tomasi's demands."

"Can't you get your family in Sicily to advance some money to you?"

Giovanni laughed, but there was no humor in the sound.

"I am, what do you call it, the black sheep of the Malatesta family. My family cannot strip me of my title, but neither are they inclined to share their riches with me. I have my own money, of course, but much of it is tied up in investments and is not actually available to me at present."

"You could borrow on it," Denny suggested.

"A well I have gone to before, on occasion, to live in the lifestyle to which I am accustomed," Giovanni said with a slight grimace. "Not a viable alternative at the moment, unfortunately."

She finally took the glass of wine he held out to her and downed a healthy swallow. "There's only one thing we can do," she said. "How much do you need to get Tomasi to leave you alone?"

"No! Take money from a woman, from my beloved? No, I say, a thousand times no!"

With anybody else, she might have thought he was being too dramatic. But such flamboyance was just who Giovanni Malatesta was, Denny told herself.

"There's nothing wrong with letting someone who cares about you help you out of a problem," she argued. "My grandparents are wealthy, and my father's ranch is one of the biggest and most lucrative in Colorado. All I need to do is send a few telegrams, and I can have the money wired to a bank here in Venice. Just give me the details of where it should go and how much you need, and we can take care of this first thing in the morning."

Stubbornly, Giovanni shook his head and said, "I cannot do this. Bad enough that I had to hide behind your skirts . . . *and* your gun . . . when Tomasi's men cornered us."

"They were threatening me, too, you know," she

reminded him. "And I'm sure they'll continue to do so, now that they know I'm someone important to you. Men like that are no different than the outlaws my father has dealt with back home. They'll use any leverage they have to get what they want."

"This is true," Giovanni admitted. "Salvatore Tomasi and the men who work for him are ruthless."

"So it's in my interest to help you with this, too," Denny said. "Please, Giovanni, let me help. Tell me how much you need."

For a long moment, he stood there, glaring, then he abruptly lifted his glass and drank down all the wine in it.

"All right. I don't like it. This still seems wrong. But I will pay you back, every bit." He named an amount that sounded enormous to Denny and must have seen the look of surprise on her face, because he added hastily, "That is in lire. In American money, a bit more than ten thousand of your dollars."

That was still an awful lot of money, Denny thought, especially to have lost it gambling. But she said, "I can get that much. My grandparents may not be happy about it, but when I tell them it's important, they'll do it."

"They are in London?"

"They have an estate not far from there where they spend time every year, but their home is in America, like mine." She had explained to him about Louis's medical condition and why they had spent so much time in Europe, as well as mentioning that she considered herself an American and that her true home was in Colorado, where her parents lived. "Right now they're in Boston, but I'll wire their bank in London as well as sending them a telegram directly. It may take a few days to arrange everything, but you'll get the money to settle your debt with Tomasi. Will he wait that long?"

"*Sì*, I believe so, once he knows the funds will be forthcoming." Giovanni put his hands on her shoulders. "You must promise me that once the debt between the two of us is settled, we will never speak of this matter again. It is too humiliating to contemplate."

Denny smiled. "There's no need for you to feel like that, Giovanni. I'm glad to help . . . when it's someone I care deeply about."

A moment later, they were wrapped up in each other's arms again, and Denny didn't think anymore about gambling debts.

For a while, anyway.

Louis was opposed to the idea when she told him about it, but Denny expected that. And she didn't really blame him, either. He didn't know Giovanni as well as she did. She didn't believe he would ever allow himself to get tangled up in such a situation again.

She spent all the next day burning up the telegraph wires between Venice, London, and Boston, and by the time she was finished, she had overcome her grandparents' reluctance to wire the money to the bank in Venice. She met Giovanni in the Hotel Metropole's lounge that evening to give him the good news.

"The money will be in your account sometime tomorrow," she told him over glasses of wine. "I'd like to know one thing, Giovanni."

"Ask me anything, my dear," he said. "My life, like my heart, is completely open to you."

"Those men who attacked us that night on the Bridge of Roses . . . were they working for Tomasi?"

He shook his head. "No, they were thieves, plain and simple, just as we thought at the time."

"You're sure?"

"Of course. I'm not acquainted with *all* of Tomasi's men, but I know none of them would have attacked us like that unless they were working under Gian-Carlo's orders. He would have been with them."

"Gian-Carlo is that hard-faced man who approached us in the restaurant?"

"That's right. He is Tomasi's second-in-command and takes a personal interest in all such matters. I believe he . . . enjoys . . . hurting people. Since he was not there on the bridge that night, we can be sure that Tomasi had nothing to do with that attempt on our lives."

Denny nodded and said, "All right." She wasn't completely convinced, but she supposed Giovanni knew a lot more about what was going on than she did. "Where are we going to eat dinner this evening?"

Giovanni made a face. "To my everlasting regret, *cara mia,* we cannot dine together tonight."

Denny was surprised. They had been together almost every night for the past two weeks. "Why not?"

"I received an unexpected message a short time before I came here to see you. My grandfather has sent an emissary to Venice, and I must meet with him."

"Your grandfather," Denny repeated.

"*Sì.* As I told you, I have been . . . estranged . . . from my family for some time. But now, it seems that my grandfather wishes to explore the idea of restoring friendly relations. So he asked one of his associates who was going to be coming to Venezia anyway to look me up and broach the subject. The old man wishes to have dinner with me tonight." Giovanni shrugged. "While I wish there was some other way to do it, if I am restored to my grandfather's good graces, it will ensure that unpleasant situations such as the one with Salvatore Tomasi never again trouble us."

"You can avoid that yourself," Denny told him. "Just don't pile up any more big gambling debts."

"Of course, of course. That is my intention, I assure you. But life is uncertain. Problems arise. They are much easier to deal with when one has ample resources at one's command. Besides . . ." He smiled. "It will be good to be welcomed back into the bosom of my family, if such a thing is possible."

When he said that, Denny felt a little ashamed of herself for doubting him. He just wanted his family to forgive him for his black sheep ways and take him back. She could understand that. Her family had never shunned her, but at the same time, she knew she hadn't turned out exactly like they had expected. She had her own wild streak and often gave in to her impulsive nature.

She took Giovanni's hand and smiled across the table at him. "I understand," she said. "You go ahead and do whatever you need to do this evening."

He returned the smile. "I will be thinking of you the entire time! That will help me endure what I am sure will be a tiresome evening with the old gentleman. Then, tomorrow morning I will go to the bank and take care of the final obstacle standing between us and happiness!"

"Would you like for me to come with you?"

Giovanni shook his head emphatically. "No, I don't want you anywhere near Tomasi, Gian-Carlo, or any of those other louts! You must stay here at the Metropole with your brother, where you will be safe, and then, when all is concluded, I will call for you tomorrow evening. We will have a special celebration! And soon, if all goes well with my grandfather's emissary, I will be able to pay you back for your oh-so-generous assistance."

"Don't worry about that," she told him. "There's no hurry."

"Actually . . ." He picked up his glass of wine. "The hurry is now. I must prepare for this evening's meeting. Wish me luck."

Denny clinked her glass against his. "Good luck, Giovanni . . . always."

They drank, then stood up. Giovanni hugged her, planted a brief kiss on her forehead, and left the lounge. As Denny watched him go, an idea stirred to life in her head.

He might not have wanted her to come with him to this meeting with his grandfather's emissary . . . but he might enjoy it if she were to surprise him at his apartment afterward. In fact, Denny mused, she was confident she could see to it that they both enjoyed that little surprise.

CHAPTER 10

Denny didn't tell Louis where she was going that evening. She had dinner with him and then, knowing that he had a habit of turning in early, waited until he had gone into his bedroom in the hotel suite and closed the door. She had said she was going to bed, too, but instead she dressed in simple clothes so she wouldn't stand out on the street, then lingered a little longer just to make sure before she left the hotel.

She knew the way to Giovanni's apartment, of course, and she didn't have to take a gondola to get there. The two of them had walked all over Venice, and Denny had a keen, instinctive sense of direction. She followed the dark, narrow, winding streets, keeping her hand in her bag. Her fingers were wrapped around the butt of the Smith & Wesson. She didn't expect to run into trouble, but if she did, she would be prepared.

The canals were still busy at this hour, the streets and bridges less so. Denny was wary when passing groups of rough-looking men, but other than calling out to her in Italian, they didn't bother her. She didn't know all the words they said, but it wasn't difficult to get the general idea of their comments. They probably thought she was a prostitute.

She didn't let them bother her. She had been hearing the same sort of thing from men for a number of years now, especially whenever she and Louis visited France. The Italian men weren't quite as aggressive verbally—although they were more likely to pinch a girl's rear end if she got within reach of them.

When she reached the street that ran in front of the palazzo where Giovanni's apartment was, she paused to look up at the building. Most of the windows were already dark, but light still glowed in some of them.

Including, Denny realized as a frown creased her forehead, Giovanni's bedroom window.

Maybe he had left a lamp burning, although that wasn't very likely. She hadn't expected him to be back from the meeting with his grandfather's friend yet, but she supposed that was possible. The meeting might not have gone as well as Giovanni had hoped it would.

Denny hoped that wasn't the case. She wanted Giovanni to be on good terms with his family again, and not just because of the financial advantages that would give him. Family was important. No one needed to be cut off from the ones who were supposed to love them the most.

The best way for her to find out what had happened was to go on up there, she told herself. Giovanni would be surprised to see her, but she hoped he would be pleased, too.

She went in and walked up the stairs to the second floor. Cooking odors from that night's supper lingered in the air in the stairwell, a heady mixture of garlic and other spices. When she reached the second-floor hallway, she walked along it to the door of Giovanni's apartment. Her hand lifted, poised to rap on the panel.

The shrill, strident laughter of a woman came from inside the apartment before Denny's knuckles could fall.

She caught her breath and stepped back sharply as if she had just been slapped across the face. A deeper laugh with the rumble of a man's voice in it came to her ears. She knew that sound, knew it all too well. She had heard it often during the past few weeks. And the laugh held a tone of intimacy that Denny recognized, too.

Her heart slugged painfully hard in her chest. Giovanni was in there with a woman . . . laughing . . . and Denny's mind whirled desperately, searching for something that would explain what she had just heard.

Maybe . . . maybe the emissary sent by Giovanni's grandfather had brought along some members of Giovanni's family. That might be his sister laughing in there, or his mother or aunt. That was possible, wasn't it?

No, Denny told herself as the woman giggled. No, it wasn't. That wasn't the sort of sound a woman made when she was visiting with a long-absent relative. There was passion in it, and excitement, and . . . and . . .

With her pulse hammering in her head, Denny leaned closer to the door and carefully pressed her ear against the panel.

". . . villa on the Mediterranean." That was Giovanni's voice. "The most beautiful place you have ever seen, and it will be just the two of us, *cara mia.*"

Denny caught her breath again, the air hissing between tightly clenched teeth. This time she felt like she'd been punched in the gut, and it was all she could do not to let out a groan.

She held it in, because she didn't want the two people in the apartment to hear it and realize someone was out here.

The woman spoke then, low enough that Denny couldn't make out the words at first, but she caught the final part of the question the woman asked.

". . . afford that?"

She had an English accent. Giovanni seemed to like women who had spent time in England, Denny thought wildly.

He chuckled and said, "Don't worry about that. With the money the American girl is having wired to my bank, we can live in luxury for months. And she will have no idea where to look for us, so you need not concern yourself with that, *cara mia.*"

Denny wished he would stop calling her that. She squeezed her eyes shut to hold back the tears that wanted to well out.

She could still hear, though, even if she couldn't see at the moment. The Englishwoman said, more clearly now, "It took you long enough to get that money out of her. And I'll wager you enjoyed every second of it, you scoundrel!"

"She was quite a pleasing companion," Giovanni agreed. "But not half so beautiful and exciting as you."

"What about that Tomasi fellow? From what you told me, he sounds rather dangerous."

"He has given me until tomorrow evening to meet him and settle accounts, and we will be long departed from Venice by then. Tomasi will not be able to find us, either," Giovanni said.

So at least he had been telling the truth about the money he owed to Salvatore Tomasi. That hadn't been yet another lie, part of the big act he had put on to convince Denny to part with ten thousand dollars—and more.

"I tell you, Vanessa, I have thought of everything. Soon we will be living the life that we deserve."

No, Denny thought, what he *deserved* was for her to kick this door open and go in there shooting with the Smith & Wesson in her bag. She realized that she was still gripping it, so tightly that her hand was starting to go numb.

But that would be cold-blooded murder, she told herself, and Jensens didn't do such things. Giving Giovanni a thorough beating, up one way and down the other, would be all right, but she lacked the physical ability to do that and so did Louis.

Anyway, she would never tell her brother about this. It was too humiliating. Louis didn't need to know how badly she had been fooled by that . . . that *snake*!

There was something else she could do, she realized. As the idea took shape in her mind, her face settled into cold, hard lines. That mask threatened to crack when she heard new noises coming from inside the apartment, noises that left no doubt what Giovanni and his Englishwoman were doing, without even having the decency to go into the bedroom.

Denny's resolve hardened even more. She straightened, taking her ear away from the door. She didn't need to hear what was going on in there. She had heard plenty already.

She left the palazzo and walked back to the hotel. If any of the Italian men she passed made crude comments, she didn't notice them this time. She was focused completely on what she had to do next.

When she reached the Hotel Metropole, she went up to the suite for a few minutes and then returned to the lobby. She crossed the ornately furnished room to the desk and told the clerk, "I need to send some telegrams."

"The telegraph office will be closed at this hour, signorina," the man said with a helpless shrug.

Denny reached into her bag, but instead of taking out the gun, she brought out a wad of money and slapped it on the desk in front of the clerk.

"This is important. Offices can be opened if the price is high enough. Give me some telegraph forms and wake up one of your bellboys. We've all got work to do."

The clerk probably wasn't used to such a tone of command coming from a woman, but if he had any misgivings, the look in her eyes—and the money—must have caused him to set them aside. He swallowed hard, bobbed his head up and down, and said, "Sì, signorina."

Louis woke up to a whirlwind of activity the next morning. Denny was packing, had in fact finished with some of the bags already.

"What's going on here?"

"We're leaving," she told him. "I've had more than enough of Venice."

He stared at her. "Just like that?"

"Yes," Denny said as she fastened the clasp on a bag. "Just like that." She gestured toward several bags resting on a table in the sitting room. "I packed some of your things, but you can finish up. We're catching a train to Naples, and from there there's a boat going to England."

"I know that," Louis said in exasperation, "but why now?"

She looked at him and said, "It's time."

Louis cocked his head to the side, squinted at her, and said, "This is about Giovanni, isn't it? The two of you have had some sort of falling-out!"

"Can't I just want to go back home?" she asked. She couldn't quite keep the note of misery out of her voice.

Louis heard that and went to her, still in his dressing gown, and took her in his arms, patting her lightly on the back. "Of course you can," he told her. "To tell you the truth, I've seen plenty of Venice myself. I don't care if we never come back here."

"Neither do I," Denny said, her voice tightly controlled now. "You'd better hurry."

"Won't there at least be time for breakfast?"

"On the train."

The bags had been loaded on a small boat, and a gondola was waiting at the landing in front of the hotel to take them to the train station. Denny stood there, waiting, dressed in a blue traveling outfit with a matching hat on her blond curls. Louis was next to her in a brown tweed suit and brown felt hat.

"I thought you were in a huge hurry," he said.

"We are," she said, "but we need to wait just a minute longer."

She caught sight of Giovanni then, hurrying along the street, hatless, his hair slightly askew as if he had just raked his fingers through it when the insistent knock on his apartment door pulled him out of bed with the Englishwoman Vanessa. His clothes were a little disheveled, too. But when he spotted Denny and Louis, he bounded down the steps to the landing and pasted the usual big smile on his face.

"*Cara mia,*" he said, "what is so important that you must see me so early in the morning?"

"I wanted to catch you before you went to the bank," Denny said, "so you won't waste your time."

Giovanni managed to keep smiling but frowned in confusion at the same time. "I don't understand," he said. "I thought everything was arranged—"

"It was," Denny said, "but I've *un*arranged it."

He shook his head. "What?"

"You can go to the bank if you want, but there won't be any money waiting there for you. I sent more wires last night canceling everything."

Now he looked shocked, angry, and a little scared. "Cancel . . . Why in the world would you do that?"

She wasn't going to give him the satisfaction of telling him that she had eavesdropped on him and his mistress, although more than likely he would figure that out if he stopped and thought about it. Instead she said coldly, "I have my reasons."

"But you cannot do this!" he burst out. "I need that money. Tomasi is expecting—"

"I don't care," Denny said. "You'll have to handle that problem yourself, some other way. But it won't be with my family's money." She paused. "Maybe you can talk to your grandfather's *emissary* again."

His eyes widened. She had said too much, she realized. She turned away quickly, motioned Louis toward the gondola.

"Let's go."

"Wait!" Giovanni grabbed her arm. "*Cara mia,* please! Whatever you think, you are wrong, mistaken—"

"What I think is that you'd better get your hand off me, mister," Denny ground out.

With only inches separating their faces, Giovanni looked into her eyes for a couple of seconds and then released her arm. He stepped back, his face stricken.

"You do not know what you're doing to me," he said.

"I've got a pretty good idea," Denny said, "and I still don't care."

With that, she held out a gloved hand to Louis, who took it and helped her into the waiting gondola. He stepped in after her and they both sat down on the padded seat. Louis nodded to the gondolier, who pushed the boat away from the landing and poled it farther out into the canal.

Giovanni Malatesta stood there on the landing, staring after them.

Quietly, Louis said, "I suppose I should be glad you didn't haul out that hogleg of yours and shoot the varmint, as folks in Colorado would say."

"How did you know I was considering it?" Denny asked without looking over at her brother.

"Because *I* felt like doing the same thing," Louis replied. "If I'd had a gun, I just might have."

For the first time in a while, Denny smiled. It wasn't much of one, but it was still a smile.

"I seriously doubt you would have done that."

"Don't be so sure," Louis said. "And just for the record, I have no doubt at all *you* would have, if he hadn't let go of you when he did."

"Well," Denny said, "you're right about that."

CHAPTER 11

The Sugarloaf, 1902

Denny never told Louis all the details of what had happened, and he didn't press her for them. She knew how smart he was, so she didn't speculate on how much he might have figured out. She wanted to put the whole thing behind her, to never think about Count Giovanni Malatesta or that trip to Venice again, and for the most part she had succeeded.

But deep down, she knew the experience had hardened her, made her less likely to trust anyone again—especially handsome, glib-tongued strangers. Maybe that was why she kept Brice Rogers at arm's length some of the time, even though both of them knew they were attracted to each other. Brice wasn't glib or arrogant—far from it, in fact, more like humble and down-to-earth—but even so, Denny was leery of opening her heart again. She figured she would get over that someday . . .

But she had never expected to see Giovanni Malatesta step off the train in Big Rock, as handsome as ever and evidently doing quite well for himself, with his fancy clothes and his manservant and his tour

across the American West. He must have found some
other way to settle up with Salvatore Tomasi.

"You been about a million miles away the whole
trip out from Big Rock," Pearlie commented from
the wagon seat beside her. They were almost back
to the ranch headquarters.

"I'm sorry. I guess the way it turned out, I wasn't
very good company after all."

"This have somethin' to do with that ruckus at the
train station?" Pearlie squinted over at her. "I know
you've been in a heap of gun trouble for a gal, especially a gal your age . . . No, a heap for *any* gal. You've
been as cool-headed as any child of Smoke Jensen
ought to be, but still, it's got to bother you a mite
when you have to kill a man, like you did back there."

"You think when we get home, I'm going to take to
my fainting couch?" Denny asked, forcing a note of
dry humor into her voice.

"No, not hardly. I'm just sayin' that if anything's
ever botherin' you, you ought to talk to your pa.
Smoke's done a heap of shootin' over the years, but
I know for a fact he never killed nobody who didn't
have it comin'. I don't reckon he's ever lost a minute
of sleep over it."

"Neither have I," Denny said, "and I don't intend
to start now."

Pearlie nodded slowly and said, "Well, all right. I
won't pester you about it no more. But you can always
talk to me, too. I know how close you and your
brother are, and with Louis gone, if you ever need a
sympathetic ear . . ."

She patted him on the knee and said, "Thank you,
Pearlie. I'll keep that in mind."

The big main house, the bunkhouse, the barns

and corrals, and the other buildings of the ranch headquarters were visible up ahead now. As Pearlie kept the wagon rolling toward the main house, Denny told herself to put all thoughts of Giovanni Malatesta out of her head.

As far as she knew, her parents had no idea anything unusual had happened in Venice two years earlier. Louis had promised not to say anything to Smoke and Sally, and Denny believed him. She had persuaded her grandparents not to mention the money she had arranged to have wired to Venice, then backed out of the deal before the transfer could be made. Denny didn't know if they had kept that promise or not, but her mother had never brought up the subject, so she believed there was a strong possibility they had honored their word.

So there was a good chance the subject was dead and buried. She wanted it to stay that way.

Unfortunately, Monte Carson had seen her slap Malatesta, there on the train station platform. The sheriff might say something to Smoke, and Smoke would know there had to be a good reason for what she had done. His daughter didn't go around just slapping random strangers.

Brice had witnessed the unexpected encounter, too, she reminded herself, but Brice wasn't one of her father's best friends and wouldn't have any reason to mention it to Smoke. Monte Carson was the weak spot in the wall Denny had built to keep all those bad memories at bay. All she could do was hope that it wouldn't crack.

"There you go, wanderin' off in the hinterlands again," Pearlie said as he brought the wagon to a halt in front of the house. "You must have a whole heap of things on your mind today."

More than the ex-foreman knew, Denny thought as she jumped gracefully down from the driver's box. "I'm going for a ride," she announced. She started toward the barn, taking long strides. That would puzzle Pearlie even more, and she figured he would probably say something to Smoke and Sally about it. But it couldn't be helped. Denny wanted to be alone right now. She had a lot of thinking to do.

And she wished she knew if there was some hidden reason Giovanni Malatesta had shown up in Big Rock like that.

The sharp, precise rap of knuckles sounded three times on the bedroom door, followed by Arturo calling, "Count?"

Knowing that Arturo would repeat that twice more in his usual annoying pattern if he received no response, Malatesta stopped pacing and stepped to the door to jerk it open.

"What is it?" he demanded as he looked past Arturo into the sitting room of the suite in the Big Rock Hotel. It was the hotel's finest accommodation, and paying for it would take just about all the money Malatesta had left. *If* he paid for it, of course. Such things were always open to question and a matter of the circumstances in which he found himself.

"The sheriff is at the door and wishes to speak with you," Arturo reported.

Normally, that was the sort of news Malatesta never wanted to hear. A visit from the law always brought unpleasantness with it. But since he had just arrived in Big Rock a couple of hours earlier, he couldn't think of any reason he needed to skip town yet.

Malatesta had taken off his coat and loosened his collar. He quickly remedied those two things to make himself presentable and told Arturo, "By all means, let the sheriff in."

Arturo nodded and went to the corridor door. By the time he opened it, Malatesta was standing nonchalantly by the window, lighting a thin black cigar.

"Ah, Sheriff . . . Carson, was it? So good to see you again." Malatesta shook out the match he'd been using, dropped it in a glass ashtray on a small table near the window.

"That's right, Monte Carson's the name," the lawman said. "I hope you've gotten settled in good here at the hotel."

"Of course. These are very comfortable accommodations."

"Probably not what you're used to, being a European nobleman and all."

Malatesta smiled and said, "I have stayed many places, Sheriff, and have always found that the pleasantness of the people is more important than the luxuriousness of the furnishings. So far, I have to say that Big Rock is a pleasant place."

"Mighty generous of you," Carson said drily, "considering that as soon as you stepped off the train, folks started shooting at you."

"Ah, but those scoundrels were not citizens of your fine community, were they?"

"That's what I came to tell you. I had a look through the wanted posters in my office, like I said I would, and I turned up those two fellas who are down at the undertaker's now."

Carson pulled a couple of sheets of folded paper from his pocket and held them out to Malatesta. The count took them, unfolded them, and studied the words and likenesses printed on them.

"'Casey Murtagh and Wilbur Morrell,'" Malatesta read. "'Wanted for murder, assault, train robbery, arson . . .'" He looked up from the reward dodgers. "Outlaws, just as I thought."

Arturo had been standing in the background, listening. He said, "They sound like villains from some American dime novel."

"Yeah." Carson took the wanted posters back and put them in his pocket again. "I have to say, the posters make those two seem a mite more impressive than they actually were. They're known to have run with a man named Ned Yeager. You may have noticed his name on the posters as being the leader of the gang. Yeager's the genuine article, a really bad man. If you want somebody dead, he's the man you hire." The sheriff looked intently at Malatesta. "What I'm curious about, Count, is who wants you dead bad enough to hire somebody like Yeager?"

Malatesta took the cigar out of his mouth and blew a perfect smoke ring that hung in the air for a couple of seconds before starting to dissipate.

"Unfortunately, Sheriff, I have no idea," he said in reply to Carson's question. "I wish I did, because if someone has such a grudge against me, it would be a good thing for me to know."

"Yeah, I imagine so."

"But on the other hand," Malatesta said, "isn't it still possible that those men just intended to gun me down and then steal whatever they could find on my body? They're thieves. Those wanted posters said so."

Carson shook his head slowly and said, "That fracas didn't strike me as a simple robbery. They were waiting to ambush *you*."

"I can't help you, Sheriff," Malatesta said flatly. "I have no enemies that I know of in America."

"How about in Italy, or somewhere else over there?"

"Do you really believe trouble would follow me all the way across the ocean?"

"You tell me."

Malatesta put the cigar back in his mouth. His teeth clamped on it harder than before.

"I can't tell you, Sheriff, because I don't know," he said. His smile had disappeared, and there was an edge to his voice. "But I'm confident that with you on the job, I'll be safe as long as I'm in Big Rock."

"You can rest easy on that score," Carson said with a little edge in his own voice now. "And I'll assume that if you think of anything I ought to know, you'll tell me."

Malatesta made a gesture of agreement with the cigar.

"Don't reckon there's anything else to say." Carson started to turn toward the door.

"One moment, Sheriff, if you would."

"Sure. What is it?"

"Those two men, Murtagh and Morrell . . . The only reason you have those posters with their pictures on them is because there are rewards posted for them. Correct?"

"That's right," Carson said.

"Dead or alive?"

"That's usually the way it works."

"Then since Miss Jensen killed one of them and Marshal Rogers took care of the other, I suppose they are entitled to those rewards?"

"Well, as a federal lawman, Brice Rogers can't claim a reward like that," Carson explained. "And the bounty on Murtagh . . . he's the one Denny ventilated . . . is only three hundred dollars, so I doubt if she'd bother to collect it."

"Because she is rich, or at least her father is," Malatesta said.

"Because Denny's not really the sort of person to be interested in blood money."

"Yes, I would say you are correct about that. She looked very different today than she did the last time I saw her, two years ago in Italy. I'm sure she is still the same sort of person she was then."

"She's a fine gal," Carson said. "One of the finest I've ever known."

"Then we are in total agreement on that, Sheriff," Malatesta said with a smile. "I have never met another woman quite like Denise Nicole Jensen."

CHAPTER 12

Harkerville, Wyoming

Eight people on horseback sat their saddles and looked down at the settlement in the valley below them. Evergreens grew thickly atop the ridge where the riders had paused, and on this cloudy afternoon, the shadows were thick enough that anybody in Harkerville, half a mile away, who glanced up here wouldn't be likely to spot them.

"Place don't hardly look big enough to have a bank," one of the men said with a sneer of contempt. He added to the impression by leaning over in his saddle and spitting on the ground. "That's a one-horse town if I ever seen one."

"The place is small and that's the way the folks who live here like it," a thickset man dressed all in black replied. "But all the ranchers who own big spreads on up the valley have to have someplace to put their money, and Harkerville's the closest town. Yeah, they've got a bank, Curly." He chuckled. "You can bank on that."

Curly Bannister, whose tangled mass of brown hair

that fell to his shoulders had given him his nickname, said, "I'm not doubtin' your word, Alden, just sayin' that looks can be deceivin', I reckon. If you say there's a bank down there and it's worth takin', I believe you, one hunnerd percent."

Alden Simms nodded. Curly was his second-in-command, and a good one, so he was in the habit of cutting Curly some slack whenever he got mouthy, which was too often, to tell the truth. One of these days, Curly would catch Alden in a bad mood when he made one of his snide comments, and Alden would put a bullet through the snaggletoothed varmint's brain. He'd be sorry to kill Curly, he supposed, but he'd get over it.

Another rider edged forward to join Alden and Curly, who were slightly ahead of the rest of the gang. "How much do you believe is in there?"

The rider's husky but undoubtedly female voice, along with the long, straight dark hair that hung down her back from under the flat-crowned black hat, marked her as a woman. So did the lack of beard stubble on her lean face, which otherwise was as hard-featured as those of the male outlaws.

"Could be ten, twelve thousand, I'd say," Alden replied.

"That's only a little more than a thousand apiece."

"How else you gonna earn that much money, Juliana?" Curly asked. "You sure never did when you was workin' in the Duchess's place in Rapid City."

Juliana Montero fastened a cold gaze on Curly and said, "That's because the Duchess's customers were cheap owlhoots who never had any money because they were stupid. That description remind you of anybody, Curly?"

Curly's cocky grin disappeared and he tightened his grip on his reins, as if he was about to turn his mount toward Juliana's. Alden said sharply, "Hush up that squabbling, you two. I swear, the way you pick at each other, I'm surprised neither of you has shot the other one yet."

"Could happen any day now," Juliana said.

"No, it won't. We've got a job to do, and we're all going to get along." Alden turned to look at the rest of the men. "Isn't that right, boys?"

A couple of the outlaws muttered their agreement, and the others nodded.

Alden looked hard at Curly and Juliana and said, "Well, what about you two? A truce? No more arguing until we finish this job?"

The two of them looked at each other. Curly sniffed. Juliana said, "All right. Truce. For now." She pointed a slender finger at Curly. "But you keep your dirty cracks to yourself."

"Just remindin' you of where you came from, darlin'," Curly drawled.

"It doesn't matter where somebody came from," Alden snapped. "The only thing that's important is where they wind up. And for me, I plan on that being San Francisco, once I've got enough money saved up." He nodded toward the settlement. "This is just one more step along the way."

It was true that Harkerville didn't look very impressive. A single street lined with maybe a dozen and a half businesses. A scattering of dwellings ranging from substantial houses to log cabins to ramshackle hovels with tar paper and tin roofs. Not a single building in town was constructed of brick or stone. The largest and most impressive structure was a false-fronted saloon. But almost as large was a building made of thick beams. Alden pointed to it and said, "That's the bank. Billy Ray said he saw several gents who looked like successful cattlemen going in there."

A small young man with a ratlike face nudged his horse ahead as if responding to hearing his name spoken. "That's right," he said eagerly. "I done a good job of scoutin' the place, didn't I, Alden?"

"You sure did. Nobody ever noticed you hanging around, did they?"

"No, sir! Nobody ever notices me."

That was the truth. Whenever folks looked at Billy Ray, they immediately dismissed him from their thoughts. That made him a valuable asset for the Simms gang. They never rode into a town to pull a job without Billy Ray going in first to have a look around. Twenty-four hours in a town and he knew it intimately.

Juliana crossed her hands on the saddle horn and leaned forward. She dressed like a man, in a long, dark brown duster over jeans and a gray shirt. She carried an old Colt Navy in a cross-draw rig on her left hip.

"So when do we hit this bank?" she asked.

Alden pulled a turnip watch from the pocket of his black trousers and flipped it open. "No time like the present," he said after checking the time. "The bank'll be closing in half an hour. We'll split up and ease into town between now and then, so folks won't be as likely to notice this many strangers showing up.

You and Curly and me will go in and get the loot. Billy Ray, you'll be in charge of the horses, as usual."

Billy Ray bobbed his head and grinned.

"Childers, Hamilton, Britt, Dumont," Alden addressed the other four members of the gang, "you'll wait outside the bank and try not to look too suspicious. But if there's any trouble, it'll be up to you to keep those townspeople from getting in there until we're ready to light a shuck . . . *especially* the local law."

Alden knew from Billy Ray's scouting that Harkerville had a town marshal, a fairly young man with a wife and two little kids, but he was the settlement's only star packer.

The plan was identical to the one they had followed in holding up banks in half a dozen other towns in Wyoming. They had been working their way south and now weren't far from the Colorado border. Only one of the robberies had played out differently because Juliana hadn't been feeling well that day and Childers had had to take her place inside the bank. But everything had gone all right and the substitution hadn't caused any problems.

Since everyone knew what they were supposed to do, there wasn't any point in waiting. A few of the men wished each other good luck, and then they scattered to ride into Harkerville from different directions. None of them would arrive together except for Alden, Curly, and Juliana, who would be siding each other as they entered the bank.

They angled down the slope and struck the road that led into the settlement from the east. They didn't get in a hurry as they approached the edge of town. They wanted to walk into the bank no more than five minutes before it was supposed to close for the day.

As they rode, Curly said quietly, "Hey, Juliana, I'm sorry about what I said earlier. You know I didn't mean nothin'. I just like to pick at you a little. Shoot, I don't care what you used to do for a livin'."

"I wouldn't think so, since *you* were one of the regular customers at the Duchess's place."

Curly grinned. "We had some good ol' times there, didn't we?"

"Good for you, maybe. You just got what you came for and left." Juliana shrugged, then reached over and patted him on the leg. "But you were always nicer than some, I'll give you that. You talked too much, but there are worse things."

"You was always my favorite, you know."

"I know."

The three of them were ambling along the street now, with the bank up ahead to their right. They angled toward an empty hitchrack that wasn't directly in front of the bank but was nearby. They left their horses there, and as they stepped up on the boardwalk, Alden glanced both directions along the street and spotted the rest of his men, Britt and Hamilton on this side of the street, Dumont, Childers, and Billy Ray on the other. None of them paid any attention to the others. Once Alden, Curly, and Juliana were inside the bank, Billy Ray would start gathering up the horses and bring them, one by one, to the hitchrack where the three ringleaders of the gang had left their mounts. He was very good at being unobtrusive about what he was doing, but when the time came for them to make their getaway, all the horses would be waiting together.

The bank had double doors with glass in the upper halves. One of them opened when the three outlaws were less than twenty feet away. They didn't slow down as a man stepped out of the bank and started to turn in the other direction. That fella had had a close call and didn't even know it.

But he didn't keep going. Instead, he stopped, looked back over his shoulder, and then turned around to face the three of them. He was young, medium-sized, wearing a gray suit and vest and a black hat. He looked at Juliana and exclaimed, "Caroline?"

All three of the outlaws stiffened. Caroline was the name Juliana had used when she was working for the Duchess in the house in Rapid City. What were the odds that they would run into one of her former customers in this one-horse town, as Curly had called it, hundreds of miles away?

Gruffly, Juliana said, "I don't know what you're talking about, mister. That ain't my name, and I don't know any Caroline."

"Well, you look mighty different dressed like that," the man said, "but I would've sworn—"

"Sorry, friend," Alden said. "The lady told you you've made a mistake. Now, if you'll excuse us, we have some business we need to take care of."

"Sure, sure." The man held up both hands, palms out. "No offense meant. It's just that there's a remarkable resemblance between this lady and a, uh, woman I used to know . . ."

The motion he had made had caused his coat to swing out a little, revealing a five-pointed star pinned to his vest. Alden's mouth tightened, and Curly's eyes got wide with surprise. The man must have noticed that reaction, because his voice trailed off.

Then he said, "Hold on a minute. Three of you, going into the bank . . . just before it's supposed to close . . . Seems like I've read something like that, in notices from other peace officers . . ."

"Well, you've put it all together," Juliana said. "Drat the luck."

Her Colt Navy came out of its holster fast and smooth and flame spurted from its muzzle as she fired, almost touching the marshal's vest with the star pinned to it. The .36 caliber round slammed into his chest at close range, driving him off the boardwalk with his arms flung out to the side. He landed in the street on his back so hard that his legs flew up in the air for a second.

"I guess you shouldn't have been frequenting houses of ill repute," Juliana said.

CHAPTER 13

Big Rock

According to Arturo, who had asked the desk clerk in the hotel about it, the best place to eat in Big Rock was Longmont's, a combination dining, drinking, and gambling establishment that had food to rival any of the fancy restaurants back East. The owner, Louis Longmont, who had once been a deadly gunman with a reputation that almost rivaled Smoke Jensen's, brought in the best chefs he could find and paid them more than they could have made in New York, Chicago, or San Francisco.

As a result, when Count Giovanni Malatesta dined there that evening, he enjoyed a delicious, perfectly cooked steak with all the trimmings, along with an excellent bottle of red wine. It was a French vintage, not Italian, but Malatesta was willing to forgive that.

Unlike in most frontier saloons, a number of women came to Longmont's with their husbands. That was because they felt safe in these refined, comfortable surroundings. Yes, there was gambling on one side of the room, but the games didn't get loud and raucous like they sometimes did in other saloons because nobody wanted to get on Louis Longmont's bad side. He was middle-aged and distinguished, with considerable gray in his dark hair, but most folks in Big Rock knew how dangerous he had been in his earlier days. He had sided Smoke Jensen in more than one epic battle against a variety of badmen. Nobody wanted to test whether he might have lost any of his edge.

That was what Arturo had gathered from asking around, anyway, and then passed on to Malatesta. Arturo was very good at coming up with information, and he was patient about waiting for his salary. If things didn't work out the way Malatesta planned and he had to leave Big Rock in a hurry, he would owe Arturo a considerable amount that would never be paid. He almost felt a little bad about that. Almost.

One of Longmont's hostesses paused beside the table and asked, "Would you like more wine, Count Malatesta?"

The women who worked here dressed in a more subdued fashion than run-of-the-mill saloon girls and soiled doves. No short, low-cut, spangled dresses that showed off their sometimes dubious charms.

But they were undeniably lovely. Longmont clearly had a good eye for feminine beauty. Malatesta smiled up at this young woman, a brown-eyed blonde, and said, "I believe I've had enough, especially since you're so intoxicating, my dear. If you'd like to sit down with me, I could easily spend another hour just drinking in the exquisiteness of your eyes."

She smiled and said, "You *are* a flatterer, aren't you? Mr. Longmont said he wanted to speak with you when you finished your meal. I'll send him on over."

"I'll be happy to meet him," Malatesta said, "but he will be a poor substitute for you."

She laughed, shook her head, and went toward the bar.

A few minutes later, a tall, well-dressed man sauntered up to the table and said in a voice that retained just the faintest of French accents to mark his Cajun heritage, "Count Malatesta, I'm Louis Longmont. I own this place."

Malatesta stood up and extended his hand. "A pleasure and an honor to meet you, signore." After shaking hands, he waved toward the empty chair on the other side of the table. "Please, join me."

"Thank you. Don't mind if I do." The two men took their seats, then Longmont went on, "I hear there was some excitement when your train arrived this morning."

"Indeed. One of your notorious western gunfights. I was fortunate to escape with my life, thanks to the intervention of Sheriff Carson, Marshal Rogers, and Miss Jensen."

Longmont cocked an eyebrow. "Who then slapped you, from what I hear. Miss Jensen, I mean."

"Indeed she did," Malatesta said with a chuckle. "I make the assumption, Signor Longmont, that you, too, have been slapped by a beautiful woman in your lifetime?"

"Once or twice," Louis agreed drily. He took a couple of cheroots from his vest pocket. "Cigar?"

"*Grazie.*" Malatesta took one of the cigars, smelled it, and nodded in approval.

"I have to say, I'm curious why Denny would do that. She's not usually the type to fly off the handle."

"You know her well, I imagine, since you and her father are good friends?"

"You seem to know quite a bit about the folks who live in Big Rock and hereabouts," Longmont said without actually answering the question about the friendship between him and Smoke.

"My valet makes a habit of learning what he can about the places we plan to visit. As for the lovely Denise . . . she and I became acquainted when she and her brother visited Venice a few years ago, on a tour of the Continent while they lived in England."

"And you became friends with them?"

"Friendly," Malatesta said with a shrug.

"It must not have ended that way, though, for her to have slapped you like that as soon as she laid eyes on you."

Malatesta laughed and said, "You know how women are, signore. Volatile. They lose their temper easily, especially with men they care about."

"And Denny cared about you?"

"Modesty prevents me from saying more," Malatesta replied, trying not to smirk.

"Uh-huh." Longmont put the cigar in his mouth and clamped his teeth on it without lighting it. "I'm going to speak plainly, Count Malatesta."

"Please do."

"What brings you to Big Rock? Are you here because of Denny?"

"Seeing Denise was as much of a surprise to me as it was to her," Malatesta said. "I'm simply making an educational excursion across your vast and fascinating country, as Denise and her brother were touring the Continent when we first met."

Longmont nodded slowly. "All right," he said,

apparently accepting Malatesta's story. "My apologies if it seemed like I was prying into something that's none of my business. Out here in the West, we try not to ask too many questions about a man's past. I don't mind admitting, though, that I feel somewhat protective of Denny, considering that she's the daughter of my oldest and best friend."

"No need to apologize," Malatesta said, waving casually with the hand that held the cigar. "Your concern is perfectly understandable."

"But probably unnecessary," Longmont went on. "I suppose you noticed during that incident at the train station . . . Denny's pretty good at taking care of herself."

Malatesta threw back his head and laughed, drawing some curious glances from diners at nearby tables. "That, my friend, is very much an understatement. I don't believe I've ever encountered a woman *more* capable of taking care of herself than Denise Jensen."

"You're right about that." Longmont got to his feet. "Can I interest you in another bottle of wine? It's on the house."

"Now that you mention it, I believe I will accept your kind offer. Providing, of course, that you can arrange to have the lovely blonde in the green dress deliver it."

"Sophie?" Longmont nodded. "I think I can do that. She *is* lovely." He held out his hand. "Good evening, Count. Enjoy your stay in Big Rock."

"Oh, I intend to," Malatesta said as they shook hands again. He sank back in his chair and watched as Longmont went to the bar and spoke to the blonde called Sophie. A few minutes later she came over to the table with a bottle of wine in her hand, along with two glasses.

"Mr. Longmont sent this over," she said. "It's one of the best vintages we have."

"And delivered by the most beautiful woman in the room. No man could ask for more."

"I can sit down and visit with you for a spell, too, if you'd like."

"Ah, I am corrected!" Malatesta said. "A man *can* ask for more. Please." He held her chair for her and then sat back down across from her. "But you must share the wine with me."

"I can do that. It's why I brought two fresh glasses."

"Allow me to pour . . ."

A few minutes later, they clinked glasses and Malatesta sat back to enjoy both the wine and the company. This was where he belonged, he thought. If everything worked out as he intended, he might not ever have to leave, although he was always prepared for that contingency.

Louis Longmont had asked him why he was in Big Rock, but the answer Malatesta had given him was not exactly the truth. Far from it, in fact.

He was in Big Rock because he intended to escape his past, forever and at long last.

CHAPTER 14

Sicily, seventeen years earlier

Twelve-year-old Giovanni Malatesta ran so hard up the hill that it felt as if his heart were about to burst in his chest. He heard the sheep bleating on the other side of the crest and knew he had to catch up to them before it was too late.

He hadn't meant to go to sleep. He'd been sitting under a tree, keeping an eye on the flock, but the heat of the sun splashing down over the rugged Sicilian hills had lulled him into a stupor. He had been distracted to start with by all the thoughts of Serafina Alcani that filled his brain night and day.

Serafina was the same age as Giovanni and seemingly overnight had transformed from a spindly-legged annoyance into a gorgeous creature the likes of which he had never seen before. He had tried to persuade her to go with him into the shed behind his grandfather's farmhouse, but so far his efforts had been unsuccessful.

She was just being coy, Giovanni told himself. Sooner or later, he would convince her. He wasn't exactly sure what would happen if he ever succeeded in his quest, but he was certain it would be glorious.

Between the heat and dreaming of Serafina with her long dark hair and lissome body, he had forgotten all about his grandfather's sheep and gone to sleep, only to jolt awake an unknowable time later and discover that the woolly idiots were gone. They had wandered off somewhere, and Giovanni sprang to his feet knowing that he had to find them.

He had run this way and that and then stopped short as he heard them bleating. He had followed the sound, his legs pumping hard, his sandaled feet slapping the ground, sweat soaking his homespun shirt. The bleating grew louder. Just over the next hill, he told himself. He paused for a moment to drag in a couple of deep breaths, then resumed the chase.

Now he could even hear the bell on the collar around the thick neck of the old ram. A few more lunging steps and he reached the top of the hill.

He stopped short and looked down the slope. The sheep were headed along a winding road that was almost white in the brilliant sunshine. Their cloven hooves kicked up enough dust to form a cloud around them, but not so much that Giovanni couldn't see the three figures around the flock.

The sheep hadn't simply wandered off. They were being *driven* away.

They had been stolen.

And it was those no-good Capizzi brothers, Alessandro and Lorenzo, who had done it, along with their dim-witted friend Luca. Alessandro and Lorenzo were a year older than Giovanni, while Luca was three years older and enormous. Together, they made a formidable trio who did whatever they wanted, terrorizing the other youngsters in the area.

Alessandro and Lorenzo's father was rumored to be an important man in the Cosa Nostra, so all the adults were afraid of him and advised their children to steer clear of the Capizzi brothers and their oafish minion if at all possible. Giovanni always tried not to draw attention to himself whenever they were around.

At this moment, seeing the sheep that his grandfather relied on for a living being driven away, Giovanni didn't think about any of that. Rage boiled up inside him, and with an incoherent yell, he charged down the hill after them.

Alessandro was closest, heard the shout, and turned to see Giovanni sprinting toward him. He called to his brother and Luca, asking them for help. The younger boy was too close, though, and moving too fast. He left his feet in a diving tackle that carried him into Alessandro. Both of them crashed to the ground among the suddenly startled sheep. Bleating crazily, the animals stampeded. Hooves hammered against Giovanni.

He thrashed around and fought his way clear of them. The stench of the sheep combined with the swirling dust choked him. He coughed and pawed at his eyes. He couldn't see anything.

A fist shot out of the dust and slammed into his jaw, knocking him onto his back again. A weight landed on top of him. Desperation made him buck it off. He rolled onto his belly and even though his vision was blurry, he made out Alessandro lying a few feet away. Alessandro had to be the one who had punched him.

Giovanni scrambled toward his enemy. Alessandro and Lorenzo were a year older than him but roughly the same size. He was willing to fight them, even two against one, as long as he could stay out of Luca's grip. The fifteen-year-old was slow and lumbering. Giovanni thought he could outmaneuver Luca. He could certainly outwit him.

Alessandro hadn't made it to his feet when Giovanni rammed a shoulder into his chest and knocked him flat on his back. Giovanni straddled the other boy and hammered punches into his face as rapid footsteps sounded nearby. A glance to his left told Giovanni that Lorenzo was almost on top of him. He ducked and threw himself to the side.

Unable to halt his charge, Lorenzo sailed through the space where Giovanni had been a heartbeat earlier. He landed on his belly with a loud *"Ooof!"* His legs were on top of his brother, keeping Alessandro pinned to the ground momentarily.

Giovanni took advantage of that opportunity to kick Alessandro in the head, driving the heel of his sandal against the other boy's temple.

Over the frenzied bleating of the sheep, Giovanni heard a bellow of rage from Luca. He rolled, sprang to his feet, and darted to the side as Luca charged at him with arms outstretched. If Luca ever managed to get those arms around him, the larger boy would squeeze mercilessly until Giovanni's ribs cracked and splintered. He couldn't allow that to happen.

Once Luca got some momentum going, he had a hard time stopping. Giovanni thrust his leg out and Luca tripped over it, pitching forward so that his face plowed into the dusty road. Giovanni knew that wouldn't stop the giant for long, but he seized the few moments' respite it gave him and whirled toward Lorenzo, who had pushed himself up on hands and knees and was trying to make it to his feet.

Giovanni clubbed his hands together and brought them down as hard as he could on the back of Lorenzo's neck. Lorenzo collapsed and groaned. Alessandro was still senseless from the kick to the head.

Giovanni swung around. Luca was trying to get up. Giovanni searched rapidly for a weapon of some sort. He spotted a good-sized rock half buried in the hillside not far away and ran to it. He got hold of it and tried to pull it loose. As he worked at that, grunting from the strain, he glanced over his shoulder and saw that Luca had made it to his knees. Giovanni's lips pulled back from his teeth in a grimace as he redoubled his efforts.

The rock came loose just as he heard Luca pounding toward him. He turned with the rock in both hands, swung it up over his head, and pitched it at his attacker. Luca was too dumb to get out of the way. The stone smashed into his forehead. He went down like Goliath.

For a second, Giovanni believed he had killed the fifteen-year-old. Then he saw Luca's broad chest rising and falling in a ragged rhythm. The older boy was alive but out cold. Blood welled from the gash that the rock had opened on his forehead.

Alessandro and Lorenzo were still down, too, and too stunned to pay any attention to Giovanni. He looked at the rock, which was lying on the ground where it had fallen next to Luca. If he acted quickly, Giovanni could use that stone to batter the brains out of all three of his enemies. They were too senseless to stop him from killing them.

For a moment, he considered it. But if Giuseppe Capizzi really was a member of the Cosa Nostra, killing his sons would be inviting too much trouble. Giovanni left the stone where it was and ran around the sheep, herding the flock together and starting it back toward his grandfather's farm. As he prodded the creatures along, he looked back over his shoulder. The other three boys were still down. If they didn't regain their senses for a while, he might actually have a chance to get away.

But this wasn't over, he told himself bleakly. Probably Alessandro and Lorenzo had decided to steal the sheep just for fun, but it wasn't fun anymore. They would be furious that Giovanni had not only dared to stand up to them, he had actually defeated them and taken the sheep back. They would regard that as a humiliation, and they couldn't allow that because it might loosen the grip of terror they had on all the other youngsters in the area. If Giovanni got away with what he had done, others might be emboldened to defy the Capizzi brothers.

So he knew he was still in danger, but at least he could get his grandfather's sheep back home. Later, he would figure out what to do about Alessandro, Lorenzo, and Luca.

But with a sigh, he realized he was already starting to regret that he hadn't bashed their brains out when he had the chance.

CHAPTER 15

Giovanni's grandfather didn't realize that the sheep had ever been missing, which was a relief. The old man had been kind enough to take Giovanni in when the boy's mother and father had both succumbed to a fever that swept through Sicily a couple of years earlier, but he also had a temper and had been known to take his walking stick after his grandson when Giovanni did something to displease him. He would have been very upset to know that he had almost lost the entire flock.

But the old man might be even more upset if he knew that Giovanni had earned the enmity of the Capizzi brothers. All the way back to the field where the sheep grazed, Giovanni had debated what to tell his grandfather. In the end, he decided to say nothing about the incident.

For a few days, it appeared that was the right decision. Giovanni halfway expected Giuseppe Capizzi to show up at the farm to kill him and the old man, but Giuseppe didn't appear and neither did Alessandro and Lorenzo. When Giovanni went into the village with his grandfather, he paid particular attention to the gossip in the marketplace, figuring that what had happened to the Capizzi brothers and their friend Luca would be big news.

No one mentioned it, as far as Giovanni could tell. Maybe when Alessandro and Lorenzo regained their senses, they had decided to keep quiet about the whole thing. Luca would do whatever they told him, of course. They might see ignoring it as the best way for them to hang on to their power—as long as Giovanni didn't go around boasting about what he had done.

He didn't say a word. If fate had presented him with a way to avoid further trouble, he was going to take it. He was no fool.

Then, at Mass on Sunday, he laid eyes on his enemies for the first time since the encounter. They might not be talking about it, but it was obvious that *something* had happened.

Alessandro had a bruise on his head where Giovanni had kicked him. He kept his cap pulled down except while he was in the church, but it didn't conceal the mark completely. Also, he sort of shuffled along when he walked, and Lorenzo kept a hand on his brother's arm to steady him. Alessandro's eyes had a dull look to them, as well. Giovanni remembered seeing a man in the village who had been kicked in the head by a mule. That was what Alessandro looked like. It frightened Giovanni that he had done that, but at the same time, it made him a little proud.

Luca wore a bandage wrapped around his head, covering the gash the rock had given him. Other than that, he seemed normal, though. Giovanni supposed it was difficult to damage something that didn't work all that well to start with, such as Luca's brain.

Giuseppe Capizzi had a dark scowl on his face during Mass, but that was nothing unusual. He always looked like that, as if he was angry at the entire world. The fact that his sons had gotten into a fight wasn't necessarily the cause of his ire. Giovanni wondered just how much Alessandro and Lorenzo had told him. With Alessandro in the state he was in, they wouldn't have been able to pretend nothing had happened.

But despite that, Giovanni clung to the hope that maybe things wouldn't go any further—until after the service, when the brothers came up to him outside the church.

Lorenzo did the talking, low-voiced and intense. "Don't think you've gotten away with it," he told Giovanni. "You'll get what you've got coming to you." He added a few colorful curses, making sure he spoke quietly enough that the priest, standing over in the doorway of the church, wouldn't overhear.

Alessandro didn't say anything, just stood there looking at Giovanni. Now that Giovanni was closer, he could tell that Alessandro's eyes weren't dull after all. A fierce hate burned in them as he cast a hooded, baleful glare at Giovanni.

"He hasn't said anything since the other day, and sometimes he can't move right," Lorenzo said when he saw Giovanni staring at Alessandro. "*You* did that."

Giovanni was scared, but he was also defiant. "You

shouldn't have stolen my sheep. What did you expect me to do?"

"We weren't stealing them. We would have left them somewhere you could find them. It was a joke, you idiot."

Giovanni didn't believe that for a second. They would have kept the sheep, all right, and sold them. Or perhaps driven them off a cliff out of sheer meanness. He wouldn't put anything past the Capizzi brothers.

"You shouldn't have fallen asleep while you were supposed to be watching them," Lorenzo went on. "If you'd been doing your job when we came along, we wouldn't have bothered them. But when we saw you sleeping, we figured it would be funny to think about the look on your face when you woke up and realized the sheep were gone. So it's all your fault, everything that happened. And you'll pay for it."

"You don't scare me," Giovanni said, even though actually he was so frightened he thought his knees might start knocking together. The fear got even worse when Alessandro leaned closer to him, still not saying anything, but Giovanni could hear the rasp of his breathing now.

"Just remember," Lorenzo said. "You'll pay."

He took his brother's arm, and they walked off. Giovanni stood there and after a minute dragged the back of his hand across his forehead to wipe away the beads of sweat that had sprung out there.

Despite the threats, nothing happened. Days dragged past. A week, then two. When Giovanni saw the Capizzi brothers at church, he thought Alessandro looked better. Steadier on his feet. Still silent, though, and when he looked at Giovanni, chills went down the younger boy's back. His enemies—were still his enemies. But all he could do was remain watchful.

After Mass the third Sunday following the fight over the sheep, Giovanni was outside the church with his grandfather when he heard his name being called. He looked around and saw Serafina Alcani standing with some other girls. She waved at him, and when he returned the wave, all the girls giggled and started whispering to one another. He wondered if they had dared Serafina to call to him.

She kept talking to her friends, but while doing that, she glanced around at him again, and the smile that passed briefly over her face when their eyes met made his heart start thumping harder in his chest. He felt his face getting warm.

His grandfather cuffed him on the back of the head, hard enough to get Giovanni's attention. "Come on, boy," the old man growled. "We've attended to the spiritual, now we must attend to the physical. There's work to do, even on the Sabbath."

"Yes, Grandfather." Giovanni followed the old man, but he cast a last look over his shoulder at Serafina, standing there slender and beautiful in a pale blue dress, the sunlight gleaming on her hair, dark as a raven's wing, her head thrown back slightly, her lips parted as she laughed at something one of her friends had just said.

He had never seen a more beautiful sight in all his life.

* * *

Late that afternoon, his grandfather sent him out to check on the sheep, who were grazing today in a fenced meadow about a quarter of a mile from the house.

Giovanni had a stout tree branch he took everywhere on the farm with him these days. He had cut it and trimmed it and kept it close at hand. His grandfather laughingly called it his walking stick, but actually it was a beating stick, or it would be if he had to fight off another attack by the Capizzi brothers and their dim-witted friend. He wished he had a knife, but until he could get his hands on one somehow, the branch was a better weapon than nothing.

The sheep were in the meadow, just like they were supposed to be. Giovanni leaned the branch against the fence, then rested his arms on the top rail and looked at the woolly creatures without really seeing them. He conjured up that image of Serafina standing outside the church again. She had been on his mind all afternoon.

He knew better than to let himself get *too* distracted, though. A part of his brain remained alert. Because of that, he was aware of the Capizzi brothers approaching him before they got too close. As he turned, he snatched up the branch and held it with both hands at a slant across his chest, ready to strike if he needed to.

Lorenzo held up his hands, palms out, and laughed. "Take it easy, Malatesta," he said. "We're not looking for trouble."

Alessandro stood beside him, smiling but not saying anything.

"Then why are you here?" Giovanni asked, making

an effort not to allow his voice to tremble. His hands clutched the branch so hard it felt like he was going to snap it, even though it was thick enough that that wasn't possible.

"We're tired of the bad blood between you and us. We want to call a truce. And just to show you that we mean it, we brought you a present."

Giovanni frowned. Neither of them held anything—not that he believed for one second the Capizzi brothers would be sincere about giving him a present.

"You don't need to do that," he told them. "You leave me alone and I'll leave you alone. I haven't said anything about what happened, and I won't. That's enough."

"No, no, we've already got your present. You have to accept it, or there won't be a truce." Lorenzo reached under his shirt and pulled out what looked like a wadded-up piece of cloth. He tossed it at Giovanni's feet, and as the light blue cloth unfurled, he recognized it for what it was—a large piece of the same material as the dress Serafina had worn to church that morning.

No, Giovanni thought as an icy cold began to flow through him, it wasn't just the same material. It was a large piece of the dress itself, ripped and dirty as if it had been dragged across the ground.

"We saw you looking at the Alcani girl after Mass this morning," Lorenzo went on. "She's really pretty, isn't she, Malatesta? Alessandro and I were talking about her, and we decided she's pretty enough and old enough that she ought to be broken in properly. Did you know she likes to go walking by that brook on the other side of the village on Sunday afternoon? That's where we found her, and nobody else was around, so it seemed like the right time and place . . ."

Giovanni's chest heaved as Lorenzo went on talking, describing what they had done to Serafina. His heart pounded so hard he thought it was going to explode, and his brain, too. He took a step forward, clutching the branch.

Lorenzo put a hand in his pocket and brought out a small pistol that he pointed at Giovanni. "You better stay right where you are," he warned. "My papa taught me how to shoot. I'm good at it. Why don't you drop that stick?"

Giovanni couldn't find any words. He knew, though, that Lorenzo just wanted an excuse to pull the trigger. The branch slipped through his fingers and thudded to the ground at his feet.

"Anyway, once we were through with her, we thought you might like a souvenir of what happened," Lorenzo continued. He nodded toward the torn remnant of Serafina's dress. "You know what else we did when we were finished?"

Giovanni couldn't make his voice work. Anyway, Lorenzo didn't really want an answer. He was just tormenting Giovanni by talking to him this way.

Even though he knew that, he wasn't prepared for what Lorenzo said next.

"We gave her to Luca."

Giovanni doubled over and dropped to his knees. His hands scrabbled in the dirt, clutched the torn dress. He picked it up and his hands moved back and forth as if he was trying to rip it more, but there was no real awareness of what he was doing in his stunned face.

He vaguely heard Lorenzo and Alessandro laughing as they walked away. That was the first sound he'd heard Alessandro make since the fight, but Giovanni didn't really think about that. The stunned look in his eyes faded. He pressed the dress against his shirt-front as he began to sob.

He stayed there on his knees like that for a long time after his enemies were gone.

CHAPTER 16

Serafina's parents sent her to stay with her aunt and uncle in Palermo. Nothing was said openly in the village about the reason why, but Giovanni knew the old women speculated eagerly about it. Usually when something like that happened, it was because the girl was in the family way and had no husband. Serafina was a little young for that, but it wasn't outside the realm of possibility, as the old crones discussed with hateful glee.

Giovanni hated the gossip and rumors that went around about Serafina, because he blamed himself for what had happened to her. It was no fault of her own at all. If he had just killed his enemies when he had the chance . . .

He had been relieved when he found out the girl was still alive. A brute like Luca could have killed her, either deliberately or accidentally. The one time he had caught sight of her in the village, she didn't appear to be injured, but she was so hollow-eyed that it made her face look gaunt. And when she moved, there was a tentativeness to it that made it seem painful.

Then she had turned her head, as if sensing him

looking at her, and what he saw in her eyes made him gulp and tremble. She looked like she had stared into hell, close enough to feel the flames—and she blamed him for it.

He knew then that Alessandro and Lorenzo had told her *why* they were doing what they did to her. Without a doubt, they blamed it all on Giovanni.

He wanted to rush across the village square to her, explain everything that had happened, apologize to her and throw himself at her feet to beg for her mercy . . . but he did none of those things. Instead he stood there as if his feet were rooted to the ground like an olive tree and listened to the whispers and snickers that came from the villagers when Serafina walked past with her mother and father. The shame of it seemed to make her eyes sink even deeper into her head.

It was the next day when Giovanni heard that Serafina was going to Palermo. He was glad that her parents were getting her away from the evil-minded villagers but sad that he might never see her again, might never have the chance to make things right for her.

Then he realized that in this world, there was no way to make things right. Once something was broken—a chair, a human being, whatever—it might be mended but it would never be the same. Nothing could put it back like was, not even revenge.

But when revenge was all a person had . . .

Over the next few weeks, Giovanni seldom saw the Capizzi brothers except at Mass. He wouldn't have been surprised if they tried to attack him again, but they seemed to be steering clear of him. Some people might think they were ashamed of what they had done and didn't want to face him, but Giovanni knew better than that.

Monsters had no shame. That was why they were monsters. And that was a very valuable lesson to learn, Giovanni told himself.

No, it was more likely that to their perverse way of thinking, what they had done to Serafina was enough to punish him, at least for now. Probably, they would decide to come after him again, sooner or later.

Alessandro's condition continued to improve. He talked again, although sometimes his speech had a strange halting gait to it. Every now and then his eyes glazed over for a few moments, too. Just like Serafina, he would never fully recover from the damage that had been done to him. The difference was, he'd had it coming.

Finally, Giovanni caught Luca by himself in the village one day, while Giovanni's grandfather was at the butcher shop. Luca stood in the shade under some trees, watching several small children rolling a hoop around, laughing and playing. He looked like he wished he could get right in there and join them, even though he was three times their size, maybe more.

"Luca," Giovanni said. "I need to talk to you."

Luca's head jerked around. A scowl creased his forehead, where the scar from being hit with the rock showed as a pale, jagged line.

"What do you want?" he asked. "I'll pound you if you try to hurt me."

Giovanni put a smile on his face and spread his hands. "Luca," he said in his most amiable voice, "why would I want to hurt you, even if I could? And I don't think I could. I mean, look at you. You're the size of Mount Etna!"

Luca nodded and looked pleased by the comparison. "Yeah, I'm pretty big." He shrugged those massive shoulders. "I just thought you might be mad at me. You know, because of that girl."

"Serafina, you mean?"

"Yeah. She was really pretty. Or she would have been, if she'd ever stopped crying. I tried not to hurt her, I really did."

He sounded like he actually meant it, and for a second, Giovanni thought maybe the big oaf was just too dumb to be blamed for what had happened.

Then, Luca went on, "But Lorenzo and Alessandro said I had to, because of what you did, so what else could I do?"

Giovanni's resolve came flooding back, stronger than ever. Luca, like the Capizzi brothers, would pay for what he had done.

But right now, still sounding friendly, Giovanni said, "I was wondering if you could do me a favor, Luca."

"Why would I do that?"

"Because Alessandro and Lorenzo will be happy if you do. I just want you to give them a message for me."

Luca scowled again. He had an animal's natural wariness. "What kind of message?"

"Tell them I'll be in old man Cannizarro's barn at dusk this evening. I want to settle things with them."

"What do you mean, 'settle things'?"

"You know, talk it all out. Put the trouble behind us. Get on good terms with them again."

Luca shook his head. "They don't care if you like them. They just care if you're afraid of them."

"I *am* afraid of them. That's why I want to talk to them." Giovanni paused, but only for a second. "I want to find out what it will take to make them leave me alone from now on."

There it was, the bait that he hoped the Capizzi brothers would be unable to resist taking. If half of the rumors about their father were true, then extortion was in their blood. If they believed they could make him pay, they would show up at the old stone barn that was full of straw at this time of year.

"I dunno . . ." Luca said.

"If you tell them what I just said, exactly the way I said it, they'll be pleased with you, Luca. I promise. Can you do that?"

Luca scoffed. "Of course I can. I'm not as dumb as people think I am. Do you think I'm dumb, Giovanni?"

"No, but you can show everybody you're not. Just deliver the message for me, all right?"

Slowly, Luca nodded. "Yeah, I can do that. Old Cannizzaro's barn at dusk."

"I'll be there," Giovanni promised.

Luca nodded and went back to watching the kids playing with the hoop. Giovanni hoped he wouldn't forget to talk to Alessandro and Lorenzo.

But if that happened, he would just try something else. He would be as patient as he needed to be, because some things were worth waiting for.

Despite having that attitude, Giovanni was both pleased and relieved when he saw Alessandro,

Lorenzo, and Luca stroll into the old barn that evening. He was watching from a grove of chestnut trees about two hundred yards from the stone structure with its thatched roof. With the shadows of twilight gathering around the thick-trunked trees, he was confident they wouldn't spot him.

Luigi Cannizarro had one of the largest farms in the area. His barn was surrounded by fields, so there was nothing too close to it. When Giovanni had started looking around the area and planning, he had thought of this place and realized he could make good use of it.

He had to move quickly now. The Capizzi brothers would be wary as wolves and wouldn't hang around long if he didn't show up. As soon as they disappeared into the barn, along with Luca, Giovanni left the grove of chestnut trees and walked quickly toward the barn.

Only one side of the double doors was open, and that only partially. Giovanni had arranged it that way. As he approached the opening, he heard Alessandro and Lorenzo talking inside, their voices echoing slightly in the high-ceilinged chamber.

"—might be a trap." That was Lorenzo.

"Not Malatesta," Alessandro replied. "He's too much of a cowardly l-little r-rat." He struggled a little to get the words out. "We'll take his m-money, however much it is. And then we'll k-kill him."

"He said he wanted to be friends." That rumble came from Luca.

"I don't care what he said," Alessandro snapped. "He lied. And even if he didn't, I don't want to be friends with him. I want him dead!"

There it was. Exactly what Giovanni expected. He had no choice now.

But deep down, he knew he hadn't *wanted* a choice. What he was about to do was exactly what he *did* want.

He paused beside the open door, where a small keg sat. He pulled the top off the keg, reached into it, and took out a wine bottle he had prepared earlier.

Then he stepped into the opening and called to them, "Here I am."

The gloom was thick enough inside the barn that the three boys were just shadowy shapes as they turned toward him. It was easy to tell which one was Luca because of his size, and Alessandro was stooped a little, almost like an old man instead of a thirteen-year-old boy.

Or maybe he had turned fourteen by now. Giovanni didn't know when his birthday was. Not that it mattered.

Alessandro stepped forward and demanded, "What do you want?"

"For the trouble between us to end," Giovanni said. "That's why this time I brought *you* a present."

He held out the wine bottle.

"A bottle of wine?" Alessandro said. He sneered. "A lousy, stinking bottle of wine?"

"That's all?" Lorenzo said.

Luca said, "Why does it have a rag stuck in it?"

Of the three of them, it was Luca, surprisingly, who had taken note of the most important detail. But the question the giant asked was enough to warn the Capizzi brothers. Lorenzo let out a frightened,

inarticulate yell and charged forward. Alessandro
tried to follow him but stumbled and fell to a knee.

Using his thumbnail, just as he had practiced for
hours, Giovanni snapped to life the match he had
taken from his pocket and held the flame to the coal
oil–soaked rag stuffed in the neck of the wine bottle.
It caught fire instantly. Giovanni threw the bottle as
hard as he could. It sailed over the heads of Alessandro, Lorenzo, and Luca, and just as he expected, they
all turned their heads to follow its fiery flight toward
one of the huge piles of straw that filled the barn.

The burst of flame when the coal oil inside the
bottle exploded was bright enough to hurt the eyes.
The last thing Giovanni saw before he slammed the
barn door and dropped the bar over its brackets was
the sight of the three boys wincing and throwing their
arms up over their faces to shield them from the heat.

That wasn't going to do them any good. Not one bit.

Giovanni ran to pick up the other pieces of stout
board he had laid against the barn wall where they
wouldn't be noticed. He wedged one under each of
the brackets on the doors to reinforce them. Luca
was big and strong enough he might have been able
to batter his way out despite the bar, but not with
those extra boards wedged in place. Giovanni had already prepared the rear door the same way. Also, he
had nailed the small door up in the loft shut, so they
wouldn't be able to budge it. There was no way out
for his enemies.

The stone walls wouldn't burn, but all the straw
stored in there would, and so would the wooden
rafters. The thatched roof would catch fire and collapse, too, but probably by that time Alessandro,

Lorenzo, and Luca would be dead already. The smoke would kill them and the flames would consume their bodies.

Right now, however, they were still alive, and Giovanni smiled as he heard their panicked yells, so loud he could make them out through the thick walls. He heard the crackling, too, as the fire grew stronger and stronger. The trapped boys started to scream. Maybe he imagined it, but the smoke escaping the barn seemed to take on the smell of cooking meat . . .

Giovanni was still smiling as he turned and walked away. After a minute, he broke into a trot, then a run. He didn't want to be discovered anywhere near here. In fact, it might be time for him to leave his grandfather's farm altogether. Maybe even go somewhere besides Sicily. There was a big world out there waiting for him, and even though he was just a child, he realized he wasn't afraid to face it on his own.

To survive, you just had to be prepared to do whatever it took. And always, always, strike back at your enemies harder than they hit you.

He didn't just smile as he disappeared into the night. He laughed.

CHAPTER 17

Stinking Gulch, Wyoming, 1902

There wasn't much to the place, just a combination saloon, whorehouse, and general store on the south side of the railroad tracks, with an adjoining corral and feed shed. To the north of the tracks lay a large array of cattle pens and a couple of loading ramps. The broad, shallow, dry wash that gave the tiny settlement its name ran from north to south, just west of town, and a long trestle carried the railroad tracks across it.

The settlement, about halfway between Laramie to the east and Rawlins to the west, served as a shipping point for the ranches in the area. It was a flag stop on the railroad, but most of the time the trains just barreled on through because there was no reason to raise the signal. On this night, one of the rare rainy nights in the area, the westbound was due to come through at 8:20.

The two men standing under the western end of the trestle didn't know if the train was on schedule or not. They hoped it was, because they didn't want to have to stay out in this mucky weather any longer than they had to.

"I don't know why in blazes it had to pick tonight to rain," Curly Bannister said. "It ain't rained around here in a month of Sundays, so why tonight?"

"Don't ask me," the outlaw called Childers replied. "I ain't in charge of the weather."

He finished tying a bundle of dynamite to one of the support posts but didn't attach a fuse to it yet. The rain was falling fairly hard, and quite a bit of water dripped through the gaps between the planks that formed the trestle's floor.

Curly glanced nervously to the north along the gulch, which was barely visible on this dark night. "I wonder if it's gonna rain so much there'll be a flash flood."

"I think it'll have to rain a lot more than it has so far," Childers said. He didn't sound worried. He had a stolid, unexcitable nature, which made him a good man to work with explosives. "It only started about half an hour ago."

"I know, I know," Curly said. "But I wish it'd stop. How are we gonna set off this blast if it's rainin'?"

"Fuse is special made so it'll burn even in the rain," Childers said. "So that won't be a problem." He held his hand under one of the drips coming from the trestle. "Anyway, I think it's lettin' up."

"I sure hope so. I hate gettin' wet!"

"That's what I would've figured from the way you hate takin' a bath."

Curly glared at his companion even though he couldn't see Childers hardly at all in the thick shadows under the trestle, and Childers couldn't see him.

"Did you just make a joke?" he demanded. "I don't

recollect you ever makin' a joke before, Childers. And as far as I'm concerned, you don't have to make a doggoned habit of it." Curly paced back and forth. "Ain't it time for that blasted train to be gettin' here?"

"Should be along soon," Childers said, as imperturbable as ever. "Too bad we didn't have time to pay a visit to Foley's place. I've heard that the girls he's got working there are pretty good."

Oscar Foley ran the lone business in Stinking Gulch, or rather, ran the saloon and whorehouse side of it while his wife ran the store. Foley had four soiled doves working for him—a Chinese gal who claimed she was a princess back in her homeland, a sullen half-breed, and two sisters who'd decided they would rather do anything than grueling labor on their pa's farm back in Kansas and seemingly had set out to prove it.

The girls had a pretty easy time of it except when a ranch crew showed up with a herd to be shipped back East. Then they were mighty busy for a night or two. Because of that relative ease, they had survived in a profession that tended to chew up girls and spit them out on a pretty regular basis.

"Yeah, that would've been nice," Curly agreed with the other outlaw's comment. "I came through these parts a few years ago and stopped for a night at Foley's. Not bad at all, and I hear the same gals are still there. But I reckon stoppin' that train and takin' whatever's in the express car safe is more important than a little slap and tickle with some dove."

Childers snorted. "That's easy for you to say."

"What do you mean by that?"

"I mean you got Juliana, while the rest of us are pretty much high and dry."

"Juliana's Alden's girl!"

"Yeah, but he don't mind if you have a go at her now and then, and neither does she. None of the rest of us are allowed that privilege, even though she used to tumble into bed with whoever had the price in his pocket."

"Don't you go talkin' like that about her," Curly warned. "She don't take kindly to it."

"You jape at her about it."

"That's different. Her and me are old friends."

"I reckon you could call it that," Childers drawled.

Curly said, "You know the real reason you ought to watch your mouth? Because if you get Juliana's dander up, you know what she's liable to do. She shot that marshal up in Harkerville when he wasn't doin' nothin' but standin' there gawpin' at her!"

"Yeah, that's true," Childers admitted. "Anyway, there's plenty of other whorehouses in the world besides Foley's."

"You're right about that." Curly lifted his head and looked around. "Hey! Has it stopped rainin'?"

"You know, I believe it has."

And as if that were the cue for which it had been waiting, the wail of a train whistle drifted through the night to the ears of the two men.

The flags that signaled the train to stop were mounted on posts located beside the tracks two miles out on either side of the settlement. That distance gave the locomotive room to stop once the engineer spotted the signal.

Alden Simms and Juliana Montero sat on horseback fifty yards from the tracks. A few minutes earlier, when they had spotted the train's headlight in the distance, Juliana had ridden up to the signal and raised the flag, then returned to Alden's side. They watched now as the locomotive rolled past. The engineer blew the whistle to announce the train's arrival, and they heard the squeal of the brakes as they engaged, too.

Both of them still wore slickers even though the rain had stopped a couple of minutes earlier. A few drops still dripped from their hat brims. They were far enough back from the rails that they knew nobody on the train would have spotted them.

"The engineer's going to be pretty puzzled why the flag's up at night like this," Juliana said. "They wouldn't be loading cattle on a westbound, anyway."

"No, but from time to time some important person might want to get on here," Alden pointed out. "There are some big spreads in this area, and those cattle barons don't like to be kept waiting. Anyway, the regulations say they stop when the signal flag is up. That's what they're going to do."

"We can hope so, anyway." Juliana lifted her reins and turned her horse. "We'd better get moving if we're going to get there by the time the train stops."

"I know." Alden nudged his mount into motion as well. They ran their horses at a fast lope toward Stinking Gulch.

This was the first job the gang had pulled since the bank robbery at Harkerville a week earlier, which had netted them just more than ten thousand dollars and had gone off without any more hitches after Juliana gunned down the marshal who'd been one of her old customers. After that killing, everybody in Harkerville had scrambled into their holes like frightened rabbits.

Normally they would wait longer before striking again, but Alden was getting impatient. That was why they were changing things up and hitting a train this time instead of a bank. Sometimes trains carried a lot of money in their express cars. He had heard tell of holdups that paid off to the tune of thirty or forty thousand dollars. If they could get their hands on that much loot, he could put the owlhoot trail behind him and head for San Francisco to live out his days. He hoped Juliana would come with him, but that was up to her.

If things didn't work out that well with this job, the gang would push on into Colorado and hunt up some banks there. Alden was eager to be a respectable citizen instead of a robber and murderer, but he was also willing to be patient if he had to be. For a while, anyway.

The lights of the train were visible off to the left as it slowed down. Alden and Juliana were moving faster than the locomotive now, so they drew even with it by the time it reached the settlement. The train was barely moving as the big Baldwin locomotive rolled past the cattle pens.

Hamilton, Britt, Dumont, and Billy Ray had been waiting in the saloon all evening, but if they had followed the plan, they would have left the place and mounted up as soon as they heard the train whistle. Alden had confidence in them, but to tell the truth, their part in the plan was the least important. That was why he and Juliana had handled the signal flag themselves and why Curly and Childers were in charge of dynamiting the trestle. Alden trusted those two more than he trusted any of the others except Juliana.

Alden spotted four moving figures on horseback in the light that spilled from Foley's. They rode toward the locomotive, whooping and shooting. The train lurched forward as the engineer realized it was a holdup and leaned on the throttle, but the train was going so slow now that it would take quite a while to work up any speed.

Alden didn't intend to give his quarry that much time.

He and Juliana veered their horses toward the first passenger car, right behind the tender. As they drew alongside the platform at the rear of the car, Alden reached over and grabbed the railing, then kicked loose from the stirrups and swung from saddle to steps. He pulled himself up, turned, and held out a hand to Juliana, but as usual, her independent streak made her ignore the offer of help and swing up onto the platform on her own.

"All right?" he called to her over the clatter of the rails.

She jerked her head in a nod.

They both drew their guns and plunged into the car, heading up the aisle toward the front. Lanterns burned at front and back, but the light was dim. The passengers realized something was going on, though. A few women cried out, a man shouted a question while another man cursed, and a young cowboy stood up and jumped into the aisle, facing Alden and Juliana and blocking their path.

"Hey!" the cowboy yelled. "What're you—"

Alden didn't let him get any further than that. The gun in his fist roared and bucked, and the cowboy slapped his left hand to his chest as he cried out in pain. Blood welled between his splayed fingers. With his right hand, he fumbled at the holstered pistol on his hip. Alden shot him again, this time in the forehead. The man's head snapped back, and he collapsed as his knees buckled. Alden kicked him out of the way as he fell.

The shots were deafening in the close confines of the railroad car. Terrified screams from some of the female passengers added to the din. Another passenger, probably a salesman from the looks of his clothes, managed to draw a small pistol from under his coat, but Juliana shot him between the eyes before he could even lift the weapon. His derby hat flew off his head, and blood and brains painted the window behind the man as he fell back onto the bench where he'd been sitting.

Juliana turned, swept her gun from left to right, and triggered three more shots as quickly as she could, not caring if she hit anything. She just wanted the rest of the passengers cowering on the floor and wetting themselves in terror, so that they wouldn't cause any trouble behind her and Alden.

Then the two of them were out of the car and Alden began using the grab irons to climb onto the tender while Juliana guarded his back. Once he was up there, he watched over her while she joined him.

The train was still moving slowly enough that a man walking fairly fast could have kept up with it. The four outlaws on horseback had peeled off. Up in the cab, the engineer and the fireman probably thought they had avoided the trap and were going to get away. The sound of the wheels changed as the locomotive crawled out onto the trestle over the gulch.

Moving carefully over the coal piled in the tender, Alden and Juliana saw the sudden blossom of flame in the darkness up ahead. Even over the locomotive's rumble, they had heard the heavy thump of the explosion. The engineer had to know the far end of the trestle had just been blown to kingdom come.

There was nothing he could do except haul back on the Johnson bar and pray the locomotive could stop in time.

Alden threw his arms out to the side to help him keep his balance while the train jerked underneath his feet. Once it steadied and continued skidding forward while the brakes screamed, he hurried ahead with Juliana right behind him. They took the engineer and fireman completely by surprise as they leaped down into the cab.

The engineer flung his hands up as he whirled toward them. The fireman tried to fight back, though, swinging his shovel at Alden's head. Juliana drilled him before the blow could fall. The fireman dropped the shovel and doubled over as the bullet tore into his guts. He toppled backward out of the cab with a strangled cry.

"Mister, we're gonna go over!" the engineer yelled as his eyes bulged with fear.

"No, we're not," Alden said as he covered the man. "I calculated the speed and distance. We'll stop with twenty feet to spare."

He was wrong about that. When somebody measured later, it was exactly eighteen feet and seven inches from the tip of the cowcatcher to the edge of the hole Curly and Childers had blown in the trestle.

But it didn't matter, because by that time the gang had taken over the train completely, robbed all the passengers, gunned down two more men who unwisely put up a fight, forced the express messenger to open the safe by putting a bullet in his knee—Juliana had done that—looted it of a disappointing eight thousand dollars, approximately, and were dozens of miles away. Juliana had been upset enough over the meager loot that she'd shot the messenger twice more, the bullets making his head look like a shattered pumpkin.

But if she hadn't killed him, Alden would have. He was disappointed, too. A man had to approach things on a practical basis, though.

There were still banks down in Colorado just waiting to be robbed.

CHAPTER 18

The Sugarloaf

"Smoke, I just saw Denise go out to the barn," Sally said. "Maybe this would be a good time for you to go talk to her."

Smoke tried not to grimace. He didn't want his wife to see the reaction her comment provoked. He would rather face fifty armed gunmen—something he had, in fact, actually done in his adventurous life—than upset Sally.

But she was already upset, he reminded himself, so he swiveled his chair away from the desk in his office, where he had been going over the ranch's accounts, and stood up.

"I'll talk to her," he said, "but I don't guarantee that it'll do any good."

"Even if you just find out what she's in such a snit about these days, it would be helpful."

Smoke nodded, stepped out of the office past Sally, and paused just long enough to kiss her gently on the forehead.

"Snit" was an understatement, he thought as he left the house and headed toward the barn. Denny had been as surly as an old possum for the past week, ever since she had gotten mixed up in that shoot-out on the train station platform.

He was confident the gunplay wasn't what was bothering Denny. She had faced down plenty of trouble before, and she had inherited his cool head, fast draw, and pragmatic outlook on life. On more than one occasion, circumstances had forced her to kill, and as far as Smoke could tell, she had been able to put those incidents behind her, knowing that sometimes violence had to be met with violence if evil was going to be defeated.

The shoot-out wasn't the only thing that had happened that day, however. Smoke knew from talking to his old friend Sheriff Monte Carson that a couple of strangers had gotten off the train just before the ruckus broke out, and after all the powder burning was over, Denny had slapped one of the newcomers. Clearly, he was no stranger to her, but she had steadfastly refused to talk about it.

The man's name was Giovanni Malatesta, Monte had told Smoke. He was some sort of European nobleman, Italian from the sound of his name, and insisted that he had no idea why those hard cases had bushwhacked him.

Denny had been to Italy several times while she was living in England on the estate that belonged to Sally's parents, the most recent trip having been a couple of years earlier. It seemed pretty obvious that Denny must have met Malatesta on one of those jaunts. And as for why she just as obviously held a grudge against him . . .

Smoke felt his jaw tightening as he approached the barn. He had speculated on why Denny might be angry with Malatesta and had come up with a reason, but it wasn't one he wanted to think about. Even less so would he be comfortable discussing it with his daughter. But Sally had asked him to have a talk with her, so here he was, about to step into the barn—and wishing he was facing those fifty gunmen instead.

The shrill sound of a horse's angry whinny met his ears as soon as he entered the barn. He frowned as he walked quickly along the broad center aisle and made a turn into the shorter aisle that formed a T shape at the rear of the barn.

"Denny, what are you doing?" he asked as he saw his daughter about to open the gate on one of the stalls back there. Inside was a magnificent black stallion, tossing his head up and down and moving around skittishly.

Denny jerked her head toward Smoke. "I'm tired of this horse thinking he's got me buffaloed. I'm fixing to show him there's no horse that can't be ridden."

"Rocket's a killer, you know that," Smoke said.

"He's never killed anybody."

"Not for lack of trying. If he had thrown you when he ran away during that race, the day of your brother's wedding, there's no telling what might have happened. It wouldn't have surprised me if he'd gone after you with his hooves."

Denny's expression hardened at the reminder of that incident. It had started a chain of events that had ended badly. Smoke knew the whole business had hurt her, although as always, she tried not to show it.

Denny turned back to the gate and reached for the latch. "I still intend to ride him. I've done it before, and this time I won't let him run away with me. He'll see who's boss."

"Maybe you're trying to show somebody else who's boss," Smoke said.

Again, Denny turned her head sharply to look at him. "What do you mean by *that?*"

Smoke drew in a deep breath and said, "I mean, riding Rocket isn't going to prove anything to that Count Malatesta fella. He's probably long gone from these parts by now and won't even know a thing about it."

"He's not long gone," Denny said with a curt shake of her head. "He's still in Big Rock."

"How do you know that?"

Denny hesitated.

"Cal rode into town yesterday, didn't he?" Smoke went on, making a shrewd guess. "Did you ask him to check and see if Malatesta is still there?"

Calvin Woods, who was now the foreman of the Sugarloaf after spending years on the spread as a top hand, would do just about anything for Denny, as would the other members of the ranch crew. It wouldn't surprise Smoke at all if Cal had agreed to do a little spying on Denny's behalf, even though he probably felt a mite guilty about it.

"You don't know anything about Malatesta—" Denny began.

"That's right," Smoke interrupted her. "Because you won't tell us anything about him. Whatever's going on, you've got it all locked up inside you, Denny. We can't help you as long as you're doing that."

"That's just it, Pa," she said in a low voice as she looked down at the ground. "I don't need any help."

"You don't."

"No." She raised her eyes and met his gaze boldly

and defiantly. "I can shoot that no-good skunk myself just fine if he ever dares to set foot on the Sugarloaf!"

Big Rock

Brice Rogers was walking along the hotel's front porch when he had to stop short to avoid running into a man who had just stepped out through the double doors.

"Ah, Marshal Rogers!" Count Giovanni Malatesta said with a smile. "Very nimble of you, I must say. I thought we were about to collide."

"Sorry, I didn't see you until it was almost too late," Brice said. He was being polite, more so than actually apologetic. He figured Malatesta should have been watching where he was going. But the man was a foreigner, so Brice supposed it was best to be tolerant. Malatesta didn't know western ways.

"It's quite all right," Malatesta said with a dismissive wave of his hand.

He looked quite dapper today, as usual, in a charcoal gray suit and black Stetson. Brice figured the count must have purchased the hat at Goldstein's Mercantile, since it wasn't the sort of thing a European nobleman would have brought with him.

"I hope things have been going well for you since the last time we met," Malatesta continued.

"Well enough," Brice said. "I had to ride up to Red Cliff—that's the county seat—to testify in a trial, so I was gone for a few days. Nobody's tried to ventilate you in the meantime, have they?"

"Ventilate?" Malatesta frowned and cocked his head to the side, clearly puzzled, then grinned as he realized what Brice meant. "Ah, you mean shoot! No, there have been no further attempts on my life, for which I'm very grateful."

"You haven't happened to think of why somebody would want to ambush you like that?"

"As I said before, it must have been a holdup, Marshal. Those men intended to rob me."

Brice nodded slowly. "Yeah, maybe. And I'm just a deputy marshal. The chief marshal for this region has an office in Denver and is named Long."

"I see. So I should call you Deputy?"

Brice hadn't forgotten about Denny slapping this hombre for some mysterious reason, so there was a limit to how cordial he wanted to be as long as that mystery remained.

But his own natural courtesy caused him to say, "Why not just call me Brice? If you're going to be staying around these parts for a while, there's no reason we shouldn't get along."

"No reason at all!" Malatesta said. "And you must call me Johnny. I may not be an American, but you know the old saying."

Brice shook his head. "I don't reckon I know what old saying you mean."

"When in Rome, do as the Romans do! Only in this case, it's when in America, do as the Americans do. To be precise, when in Colorado, do as the . . . Coloradans? . . . do. I've never encountered a friendlier group of people."

"I think you'll find that most folks in the West are friendly, as long as a fella's not looking for trouble."

Malatesta held up a hand, palm out. "Trouble is the farthest thing from my mind, I assure you, Brice. Now, as for my suggestion . . ."

Brice looked puzzled again.

"Call me Johnny!" Malatesta reminded him.

"Oh. Yeah, sure. Johnny, it is."

Malatesta clapped a hand on Brice's shoulder. "Very good, my friend. Now, I'm sure you can tell me the way to the Sugarloaf Ranch."

"The Sugarloaf? Smoke Jensen's spread?"

"That is correct. I sent my man Arturo to make arrangements to rent a buggy and horse for the journey out there, and I believe that is him coming now."

Malatesta looked along the street. Brice followed his gaze and spotted the buggy rolling toward the hotel, pulled by a big, good-looking gray gelding. Brice recognized the buggy as one that could be rented from Patterson's Livery Stable and Wagonyard. Malatesta's servant and companion, Arturo Vincenzo, was handling the reins and doing a fairly good job of it, from what Brice could see. He maneuvered through the traffic on the street and brought the vehicle to a stop in front of the hotel.

"Will this be satisfactory, Count?" Arturo asked.

"Very satisfactory," Malatesta replied. He turned to Brice. "Now, if you would be so kind as to tell Arturo and me how to find the Sugarloaf? I was going to ask Sheriff Carson, but since you're already here . . ."

"Wait a minute," Brice said. "You're going out to the Jensen ranch? I thought since there was bad blood between you and Denny—"

"Bad blood? Ha! As I explained before, her behavior during that encounter was simply a matter of her being surprised. The sight of me clearly stirred up some old emotions for her."

"Yeah, I'd say so," Brice responded drily. "She slapped you, after all."

"What can I say, she is a hot-blooded young woman."

The smile on Malatesta's face as he said that irritated Brice, but he kept a tight rein on his temper.

"And I am certain that by now, those emotions of hers have cooled off," Malatesta went on. "While her presence here in Big Rock was a surprise to me, as well, I really would like to see her again. The two of us shared too much while she was in Italy for me to ignore this opportunity to renew our special friendship, unexpected though it may be."

The way Malatesta was hinting around about what had gone on between him and Denny in Italy got under Brice's skin, but he controlled himself and said, "I'm not convinced she's going to be glad to see you."

"Perhaps not, but I would still like the chance to explain myself to her."

Brice supposed most hombres deserved a chance like that, whether they were annoying foreigners or not. He nodded and said, "All right, but I won't tell you how to get to the Sugarloaf."

Malatesta continued smiling, but anger flashed in his eyes. "I'm sure I can find someone else in Big Rock willing to do so."

"I reckon you could, but what I meant was, I'll ride out there with you and show you the way."

Brice knew he was acting impulsively, but some instinct told him not to let Malatesta go out there and confront Denny alone. She had slapped the count once already. What if the next time she saw him, she took a gun to him? As a lawman, it was Brice's duty to keep the peace.

Malatesta looked like he didn't care for Brice's offer, but he couldn't think of any way to gracefully decline it. So he nodded and said, "As you wish, my friend. Arturo and I appreciate your assistance and will enjoy your company."

"I believe I could have found the place without any help," Arturo said, but neither of the two men on the hotel porch paid any attention to him.

"My horse is tied at that hitch rail right down the street," Brice said. "Let me get him and we'll be on our way, if you're ready to go now."

"By all means," Malatesta said, doing one of those elegant hand waves that seemed to be a habit of his. "Lead on, my friend . . . and I mean that literally."

The part about leading the way, he might have meant literally, Brice thought, but the other . . .

For some reason, he didn't believe that he and Giovanni Malatesta would ever actually be friends.

CHAPTER 19

The main road leading west out of Big Rock twisted among the foothills of the Rockies that rose majestically in the distance. It ran between thick stands of trees, rugged outcroppings of rock, and rolling grasslands. This was beautiful country, and nearly everyone who saw it deemed it so.

But trouble could lurk hidden in beauty, and that was the case today.

Six men on horseback sat in the trees on a slight rise overlooking the road, about three miles west of town. It wasn't likely anyone would spot them up here as they kept an eye on the trail, obviously waiting for something—or some*one*.

"You better be right about this, Seth," one of the men said in an impatient voice.

"I saw 'em leavin' Big Rock, Ned," another man replied. "That Eye-talian count and the fella who works for him. That young federal lawdog was with 'em. The marshal's on horseback, and the other two are in a buggy. You just wait and see."

"We've *been* waiting," Ned Yeager growled. "They should have been here by now."

Yeager was a stony-visaged man in his forties with cold, blue-gray eyes that looked like chips of ice set deep in the flat planes of his face. His hat was thumbed back on thinning fair hair. Like the other men, he was dressed in range clothes that had seen better days. Their horses and saddles were well cared for, though, and their guns especially were, because those weapons were the tools of their trade.

Yeager glanced around at the others. Fred Kent and Gene Rice had ridden with him the longest. They had been with him at the train station in Big Rock during that disastrous ambush a week earlier, and he trusted them.

The other three—Seth Billings, Edgar Norris, and Ben Steeger—were acquaintances. Yeager had never worked with them before. But they had decent reputations as gunmen, and anyway, he hadn't had a lot of choice in the matter. After losing two men, he'd needed to recruit more quickly, and those three were the ones he'd come up with.

If they got themselves killed, it wouldn't matter much to Yeager—as long as the Italian count wound up dead, too. The chance to kill that meddling lawman was just a bonus.

If it hadn't been for the marshal and that gunswift kid who had taken a hand, Malatesta would be dead and Yeager would have collected the promised payoff by now. He and his men would be a long way from Big Rock, taking it easy until the money ran out and it was time to look for another job.

Instead, he had been forced to flee with the target still alive. Yeager didn't cotton to failure. Never had. It left a bitter, sour taste under his tongue.

So he had set out to rectify the situation. He had found Billings, Norris, and Steeger at a road ranch that was a known haven for men of their stripe, owlhoots and hired killers. Then he had sent Billings into Big Rock to keep an eye on Malatesta, since Billings had never been there before and wouldn't be recognized. The rest of them had camped in a little canyon about a mile from the settlement. Billings was supposed to hurry out there and let them know if Malatesta did anything that would expose him to another attempt on his life. Since arriving in Big Rock, Malatesta had stuck close to the hotel and to Longmont's, and neither place was a good spot for an ambush.

Today, though, Billings had galloped into camp with the news that Malatesta was on his way out of town in a buggy driven by his servant. For some reason, the federal marshal was tagging along, too.

Ned Yeager didn't care where Malatesta was going or why Brice Rogers was with him. All that mattered to Yeager was the chance to finish the job. He and the other men had saddled and mounted quickly, then galloped parallel to the road until they found a good spot to bushwhack Malatesta and his companions.

But where in blazes were they?

Ben Steeger suddenly pointed and said, "Look yonder."

Yeager looked and saw something moving along the road. A screen of trees that grew beside the trail partially obscured the view. But then, after a moment, the buggy and the man on horseback came out into the open, and Yeager knew their quarry had arrived at last.

He reached down and loosened the gun in the holster on his hip.

"Get ready, boys," he said. "We'll let 'em get a little closer, then when I give the word, sweep down there and blast 'em to pieces. We'd better get rid of that lawman first, since he's the one most likely to put up a fight. But whatever you do, remember . . . Malatesta dies today."

They were only about a mile from Big Rock when the horse pulling the buggy started to give trouble, balking and holding up his right forehoof.

"What in the world is wrong with this beast?" Arturo said. He slapped at the horse's rump with the reins. "Go on! Go on there, I say!"

Brice had been riding alongside the vehicle and had reined in when the horse stopped. "Wait a minute," he said to Arturo. "Something's wrong with his hoof. He probably picked up a rock in his shoe."

"Oh. I'm sorry. I shouldn't have been trying to force him to continue, then, should I?"

"There's probably no real harm done. Let me take a look."

Brice swung down from the saddle and let his horse's reins dangle, knowing the well-trained mount wouldn't go anywhere. He approached the buggy horse carefully, talking softly in a soothing tone, then stroking the animal's nose to calm it down even more. The horse allowed him to pick up the troublesome hoof and examine it.

"Yep, got a little rock stuck in there just like I thought," Brice announced as he held the horse's leg up. "Give me a minute and I'll dig it so I can see how bad the bruise is. It might not be anything to worry about."

"I hope not," Malatesta said from the seat behind where Arturo was perched. "For the poor brute's sake, of course, and because it would be a shame to have to turn around and go back to Big Rock."

Brice thought maybe it was fate trying to keep Malatesta away from Denny, but he didn't say that. Still, he wouldn't be upset if the count's plans didn't go as intended.

He pulled out his folding knife, opened it with his teeth, and went to work on the hoof. It took him only a few moments to pry out the small rock that had lodged under the horseshoe. The damage it had done appeared minimal, and when Brice set the leg down and the horse put weight on that hoof again, the animal didn't flinch.

"I think he'll be all right now," Brice said. He would have liked to see Malatesta turn around and go back to Big Rock, rather than bothering Denny, but he wasn't going to lie about the horse's condition.

"Excellent," Malatesta said. "Drive on, Arturo."

Arturo got the buggy moving while Brice mounted up. He fell in alongside the vehicle again.

"Just how large is this ranch that belongs to Denise's father?" Malatesta asked. "I assume that you've been there, since you seem to be a friend of the family?"

"I hope the Jensens consider me a friend," Brice replied. "I don't know the exact acreage of the Sugarloaf, but it's big. It takes up most of the valley where it's located. It's one of the most successful ranches in Colorado."

"And yet this fellow Smoke Jensen is best known as a gunman instead of a rancher."

"There are dime novels about him," Arturo put in. "I've read some of them. Quite thrilling tales."

"Most of those are based on things that happened in Smoke's life when he was younger, before he married his wife and settled down to be a cattleman," Brice explained. "And if you ask Smoke about them, he'll tell you that most of those books are just wild stories made up by fellas who are too drunk or eccentric to care about the truth." He shrugged. "Still, Smoke's led a pretty exciting life, and there's no denying that."

"So he actually is skilled with a gun?" Malatesta asked.

"Maybe the best the West has ever seen," Brice answered simply.

Arturo said, "For a time, I was in the employ of a young man named Conrad Browning, whose father is Frank Morgan, another famous gunman."

Brice was a little surprised by that, but he nodded. "I've heard of Morgan. He's supposed to be mighty fast with a gun, too. I'm not sure how he'd stack up against Smoke, but if those two ever faced off, it would be a sight to see, let me tell you. More than likely it won't ever happen, though, because I've heard that they're actually friends. And to be honest, they're both getting on in years, too. Morgan's older than Smoke, I believe. He's probably hung up his guns for good by now."

"Perhaps," Arturo said.

Malatesta was starting to look impatient with this conversation. He leaned forward in the buggy's rear seat and asked, "How much farther is it to the Sugarloaf?"

"Between four and five miles, I'd say," Brice replied. "It won't take us long to get there."

They rode on in silence for a few minutes. Arturo might have felt chastised by his employer's sharp question about the distance. He didn't bring up the dime novels and Smoke Jensen's reputation again.

Brice had enjoyed their conversation, though, and was especially interested in Arturo's comment about working for Frank Morgan's son. As a lawman, Brice had heard quite a bit about Morgan, who was also sometimes known as the Drifter, and he had heard Smoke speak about him as well, but he had never met the man.

Brice was still thinking about that as they traveled past a line of trees close beside the road and entered a stretch with open ground on both sides, although to the right, about a hundred yards away, was a wooded rise. He wasn't looking in that direction, but from the corner of his eye he caught a sudden flash among the trees. The ingrained instincts of a man in a dangerous profession made him look sharply toward the rise.

Because of even that tiny warning and Brice's swift reaction, it didn't take him completely by surprise when half a dozen men on horseback burst out from the cover of the trees and charged toward the road, the guns in their hands spouting flame and lead as they opened fire on Brice, Malatesta, and Arturo.

CHAPTER 20

Smoke had talked Denny out of riding Rocket again, at least for the time being. Sooner or later, though, she was going to teach that big stallion who was boss.

The problem with Rocket was that he was unpredictable. Sometimes he was calm and didn't seem the least bit inclined to cause any trouble—and then he'd explode and take off running, and nothing a rider did would bring him back under control.

Some people were like that, Denny mused, too volatile to be around without worrying about what was going to happen next. If she was being really honest with herself, she might have to admit she could be like that at times, too.

Being too antsy to just sit at home today, she saddled a different horse, one of her regular saddle mounts, and set off toward Big Rock. She hadn't been to town since the shoot-out at the train station, and she didn't have any legitimate reason for going there today, but she didn't want anybody thinking she was staying away just because of Giovanni Malatesta.

She wouldn't even allow that possibility to float around inside her own head.

She was dressed in riding clothes—boots, jeans, man's shirt, and vest—but she hadn't bothered tucking her blond hair up under her hat, nor was she wearing her gun belt and holstered Colt Lightning today. She didn't expect to need a gun, but the stock of a Winchester carbine stuck up from a sheath strapped to her saddle, just in case. Few westerners rode the range unarmed, because there was always a chance you'd run across a snake—or some other low-down varmint—that needed shooting.

Denny jogged along the road at a leisurely pace on the big chestnut gelding she had picked out for today's ride. It was a pretty day, and she successfully let her mind wander as she enjoyed the beautiful weather and surroundings. Worry and resentment and old hates still lurked in the back of her head, but she managed to ignore them.

In fact, the ride had calmed her down to the point that when she heard shots up ahead, it took her a couple of seconds to realize what they were.

Then the booming reports of handguns finally penetrated her brain, causing her eyes to widen and her jaw to tighten. It sounded like somebody was fighting a small-scale war up there, and even though she was no longer on Sugarloaf range and technically the ruckus was none of her business, she couldn't just ignore it.

Not and call herself Smoke Jensen's daughter.

She leaned forward, grabbed the carbine, pulled it out of its scabbard, and levered a round into the Winchester's chamber.

Then she held the carbine in her right hand, the

reins in her left, and heeled the horse into a gallop, straight toward the sounds of battle.

"Go! Go!" Brice shouted to Arturo as he reined in and fell behind the buggy. "Fast as you can! Stay on the road!"

There might be some cover up ahead, but Arturo would have to leave the trail to reach it, and Brice didn't know if he could handle the buggy well enough for that.

Arturo responded instantly, slashing the horse's rump with the reins and calling out to the animal. The horse leaped ahead so abruptly that Malatesta was thrown back hard against the rear seat. Brice heard his alarmed shout.

Then the buggy was racing along the road, and the group of attackers changed course slightly, angling to their right in an attempt to cut it off as they continued firing.

Brice drew his gun and rode hard, staying at the buggy's right-rear corner as he opened fire on the bushwhackers. The range was too great for any real accuracy with a handgun, but the attackers were sweeping closer with each passing second. Brice figured if he hit any of them or their horses, it would be sheer luck. He just wanted to come close enough to spook them and blunt their charge.

That didn't appear to be happening. The riders thundered closer with powder smoke and flames spewing from their gun muzzles.

Brice became aware that shots were coming from the buggy as well. He knew Arturo couldn't be firing them; the servant would be too busy handling the buggy and the lunging horse hitched to it. That meant Malatesta was armed and putting up a fight, too, something he hadn't done that day back at the train station when he had gone diving for cover.

Maybe he hadn't had a gun then. Maybe the attempt on his life was what had prompted him to buy one.

It didn't really matter. What was important was that they were under attack *now*.

The hammer of Brice's Colt fell on an empty chamber. He slowed his horse slightly, fell behind the buggy again, and then swung around to the other side so he wouldn't be in Malatesta's line of fire as he drew alongside the careening vehicle. He guided the horse with his knees and began reloading, dumping the empty brass from the cylinder and thumbing in fresh cartridges from the loops in his shell belt.

Those actions were automatic, so his attention was elsewhere. He spotted a clump of large boulders up ahead, close beside the road, and knew Arturo could get behind them if the buggy could reach the rocks before the attackers intercepted it.

That was their best chance, so they had to give it a try. He urged his horse ahead a little more, yelled over the pounding hoofbeats, "Arturo!"

When the man glanced over at him, Brice waved his free hand toward the boulders.

"Head for those rocks!"

Arturo jerked his head in a nod of understanding.

Brice dropped back again and angled to the right as the buggy hugged the left side of the trail. Malatesta leaned forward on the rear seat, thrust a pistol out of the buggy, and continued firing toward the ambushers. His shots didn't appear to be having any more of an effect than Brice's. But at least they were putting up a fight. That had to count for something.

Although it wouldn't, Brice supposed as he triggered the Colt again, if all three of them wound up dead . . .

Just then, one of the attackers' horses fell, its front legs folding up abruptly underneath it. As the unfortunate animal plowed into the ground, its rider sailed out of the saddle. The man had kicked his feet free of the stirrups in time to avoid having the horse roll on him, but he wasn't out of danger. His arms and legs flailed wildly. He wasn't able to control his fall. He crashed to the ground and rolled over and over. Luckily, none of the other horses trampled him.

He didn't get up when his momentum came to a stop, though. Instead he just lay there, sprawled awkwardly. Whether he was unconscious, badly injured, or even dead, he seemed to be out of the fight.

That cut down the odds a little, but not enough to do any real good.

The buggy came even with the rocks, but Arturo didn't head behind them, instead whipping the horse on. For a second, Brice didn't understand, but then he saw how deeply rutted the ground was on this side of the rocks. If Arturo had left the road and tried to drive over that, he would have busted an axle or overturned the buggy.

Instead, he swung around the far side of the boulders, even as bullets began kicking up dust in the trail near the buggy's wheels. Brice followed, trying not to think about how close the shots were coming now. He felt as much as heard the wind-rip of a slug as it passed through the air near his head.

Then he and his horse were behind the rocks and

had some cover at last. Nearby, the buggy still swayed slightly from the abruptness of its halt. Frothy sweat covered the flanks of the horse hitched to it. A cloud of dust swirled around rocks, horses, and men.

Brice had already holstered his Colt. He threw himself from the saddle and dragged his Winchester out of its scabbard. He wedged into a narrow opening between the boulders as he worked the rifle's lever.

The attackers were still coming, despite the loss of the man who'd been unhorsed. Brice settled his sights on one of them and squeezed the trigger.

The man jerked but remained mounted and even continued firing the gun he clutched in his fist. Brice felt like he had hit the hombre, but probably only a nick. That wasn't going to stop the attack. He levered the Winchester and fired again, grimacing as his shot missed. It was difficult to hit fast-moving targets like that, and the bushwhackers had started to split up and weave slightly to make themselves even harder to hit.

More shots blasted not far away. Brice glanced right and left and saw that both Malatesta and Arturo were getting in on the fight. The small-caliber pistols they were using didn't pack much punch, though, and weren't noted for their accuracy beyond a few feet. Brice's rifle was the only real threat to the bushwhackers.

They had scattered out enough that he knew what their next move would be. They would circle the rocks and try to surround their quarry, maybe even catch them in a cross fire. The plan stood a good chance of working, too, if Brice couldn't pick off a couple of them and persuade them that this ambush was going to come with a higher price than they were prepared to pay.

With all the dust and powder smoke floating in the air, he hadn't gotten a good look at the men yet, but he felt like there was a good chance that some of them were the same men who had tried to kill Malatesta at the train station. If that was true, it ruined the count's theory that the attack had been an attempted robbery—not that Brice had ever put much stock in that idea. He knew a would-be killing when he saw one, and those men had wanted Giovanni Malatesta dead.

It appeared that they still did—and if he and Arturo bit the dust, too, that would be just fine with the attackers.

"I'll watch the flanks!" he shouted to Malatesta and Arturo as he levered the Winchester again and turned. "Protect the front!"

He spotted a rider through the haze and triggered the rifle. The man fired at the same time. That shot hit the boulder beside Brice, coming too close for comfort and whining off wickedly. Brice jacked the Winchester's lever to try for another shot.

The sharp cracks of another rifle suddenly intruded on his awareness. He jerked his head to the right, peered along the road to the Sugarloaf, and saw another rider coming from that direction.

Coming fast and blazing away with a carbine . . .

The newcomer's hat hung by its chin strap, and blond hair streamed in the wind. That could mean only one thing.

Denny Jensen was joining the fight.

CHAPTER 21

As Denny galloped east along the road, she spotted a cloud of dust rising ahead of her. That probably came from a vehicle moving fast, or else a large group of riders. Stagecoaches no longer used this road and hadn't since the railroad had arrived in Big Rock many years earlier, but wagons, buckboards, and buggies traveled it on a regular basis.

The number of gunshots made her wonder if outlaws had ambushed someone on the road. That explanation made more sense to her than anything else.

Many people believed that the day of the outlaw had come to a close with the turn of the century, and it was true that lawlessness wasn't as widespread as it had been when her parents were young.

But Denny knew from experience that there were still plenty of desperadoes around, and if a gang of them had gone after some unfortunate pilgrim, they were about to get a surprise.

She rounded a bend in the trail where it dropped down to a level stretch through which the road ran straight as a string. A buggy rolled along at breakneck speed with a lone man on horseback accompanying it. More riders swept in from Denny's left, obviously trying to cut off the fleeing buggy. They were all shooting. Denny could see the smoke and muzzle flames.

Return fire came from the buggy and the rider with it. They were outnumbered, and the closest place to take cover was a cluster of boulders next to the road ahead of them. The buggy might make it in time, but it would be a close race.

Denny thought maybe she could give them a little more breathing room. She brought the carbine to her shoulder and tried a long shot, aiming instinctively as she squeezed the trigger.

One of the attackers' horses went down hard, throwing the rider. Denny made a face as she lowered the carbine and worked the lever. She hated that she had hit the horse instead of the man, but when he didn't get up, she thought she might have done some good anyway. One less attacker that way.

She sent the chestnut charging along the road while she worked the carbine's lever. Ahead of her, the attackers began to spread out while the buggy reached the rocks and wheeled crazily behind them. The rider followed, and Denny's breath caught in her throat as she realized the man looked familiar. She couldn't be sure because of all the dust in the air, but she thought he might be Brice Rogers.

Her heart had started pounding harder because of the excitement of the fight, she told herself. The thought that Brice might be in danger had nothing to do with it.

The attackers were trying to circle around the rocks and get behind the defenders. One of them veered in Denny's direction, and as he did, he must have spotted her. He swung his gun toward her. Even in the bright sunshine, Denny saw flame gush from the gun's muzzle. The bullet kicked up dirt in the trail a good twenty yards in front of her.

That handgun might not have the necessary range, but her carbine did. She whipped it back to her shoulder and cranked off three rounds as fast as she could work the lever. The chestnut gelding was used to the sound of gunfire and the smell of powder smoke and continued running straight and steady as Denny fired.

The man went backward out of the saddle like a giant hand had slapped him off the horse. That was the second of the varmints Denny had accounted for. The odds were getting closer to even now.

The attackers weren't giving up, though. They continued firing at the men in the rocks even though Denny was galloping closer and spraying lead in their direction. Evidently they were determined to wipe out whoever it was they were after.

Denny realized her carbine was going to run dry if she kept up this barrage. She needed to make her shots count, because she might not have a chance to reload. She hauled back on the reins, brought her mount to a halt, and settled the carbine against her shoulder to take aim. She drew a bead on one of the circling riders, just like Smoke had taught her to, and squeezed the trigger.

Just as she did, however, her target threw his arms in the air and pitched off his horse to land in a limp heap on the ground. Denny knew one of the defenders in the rocks had drilled the man. Her shot had missed because the man had fallen off his horse a split second before the bullet got there.

Well, there were still three more of the varmints, she told herself as she worked the carbine's lever.

Except losing three out of the six of them appeared to be enough for the surviving attackers. They jerked their horses around and took off for the tall and uncut, galloping away in three different directions. Denny lifted the carbine and took aim at one of them, and she was pretty sure she could hit the broad back that presented itself to her as a target.

Then she muttered a curse that would have made her mother turn pale and lowered the Winchester. Carefully, she let the hammer down off cock. Shooting a man in the back to protect the life of someone else was one thing, but gunning him down from behind when he was fleeing was too much like murder as far as Denny was concerned. And more important, she figured Smoke wouldn't have done it. When he absolutely had to kill, it was always from the front.

Denny stayed where she was, watching alertly until all three of the gunmen disappeared in the distance. Then she nudged her horse into motion and walked the animal toward the rocks. A man stepped out from behind one of the boulders and waved his hat in the air above his head in a signal that it was all right for her to come on in.

She was certain now that man was Brice Rogers. He went back into the cluster of rocks.

Denny rode up a few minutes later but didn't dismount. She could see the buggy now and thought it looked like one from Patterson's Livery Stable in Big Rock. The vehicle partially obscured her view of a man sitting on a rock slab on the other side of it. He had his coat off, and Brice was wrapping a makeshift bandage around the bloodstained right sleeve of his shirt.

Denny recognized Arturo Vincenzo, and that was enough to tell her who else was here. She supposed that in the back of her mind, that suspicion had been there all along. She knew Malatesta was still in the area, and he was plenty stubborn enough to believe that he could ride out to the Sugarloaf and plead his case to her, whatever it was.

The next moment, her hunch was confirmed as Malatesta himself stepped around the rear of the buggy and said, "*Cara mia!* I should have known it was you riding to our rescue!"

Denny didn't think about what she was doing. She just lifted the carbine to her shoulder and eared back the hammer in one smooth motion. At the same time, the cocky grin disappeared from Malatesta's face and his hand came up with a pistol in it. In the blink of an eye, the two of them were staring at each other over the barrels of their guns.

Brice had turned his head to look over his shoulder as Denny rode up. Arturo had lost some blood and was pale from the pain he was in, but he wasn't badly wounded, just a bullet graze on the arm. Brice was trying to stop the bleeding. Arturo would be fine once they got back to Big Rock and he could get some actual medical attention.

Brice figured that Denny wouldn't be happy to see Giovanni Malatesta. He had thought that ever since he'd left the settlement with Malatesta and Arturo. But he hadn't expected them to point guns at each other. He exclaimed, "Hold it, you two! Put those guns down before somebody gets hurt."

"Please listen to the marshal, *cara mia*," Malatesta said. "I would hate more than anything else in the world to have to shoot you. I would hate it more than you can possibly know."

"Stop calling me that," Denny snapped. "And I don't believe you. You enjoy hurting people."

"You are wrong—" Malatesta stopped short, causing Brice to figure that he was about to use the endearment again, out of habit. The count went on, "I am going to lower my gun now. I apologize for pointing it at you to start with. It was merely a reflex action, that's all." Slowly, he lowered his arm. "Now, if you still wish to shoot me, I can do nothing to prevent you from doing so. And if that will soothe your troubled heart, I understand."

"You . . . you dad-blasted . . . I ought to . . . Oh!" Denny shook her head in what seemed like self-disgust and pointed her carbine at the ground next to her horse. "You're a heck of a lot luckier than you deserve, mister."

"To know you, I am fortunate indeed," Malatesta said. His grin was trying to come back.

Denny glared at him a couple of seconds longer, then turned her head to look at Brice. "How bad is Signor Vincenzo hurt?"

Arturo replied for himself, saying, "Not terribly badly, Signorina Jensen. A bullet cut my arm. It could have been much worse."

"I reckon so," Denny said.

She still held the Winchester, and Malatesta still had the pistol in his hand, so Brice said, "Why don't both of you put those guns away, so I can get back to patching up Arturo? I'm not sure I trust either of you enough to turn my back on you while you've got irons in your hands."

Denny glared at him, but she shoved the carbine back in its saddle sheath. Malatesta reached under his coat and replaced his pistol in the shoulder rig where he had gotten it.

"I was on my way to your father's ranch to see you," he said to Denny. "Dare I hope that you were on your way to town to see me?"

Denny snorted and said, "Not hardly. I was just out for a ride, that's all."

"Then we were quite fortunate you came along when you did."

"That's the truth," Brice added as he knotted one of the strips of cloth he had wrapped around Arturo's arm. "We had pretty good cover in these rocks, but I'm not sure we could have held off two-to-one odds for very long."

"Who were those hombres shooting at you, anyway?" Denny asked. An odd look came over her face as she added, "Maybe I should have found that out before *I* started shooting at *them*. I didn't know who I was blowing out of the saddle. I still don't."

Brice stepped back from Arturo, nodded in satisfaction at the bandaging job he had done, and said, "Why don't we go and see if we can find out?"

CHAPTER 22

They left Arturo sitting there on the rock and walked out to where the nearest of the fallen bushwhackers lay. This was the last man who had gone down. Denny figured one of Brice's shots had drilled him, because she had seen the man fall from his horse just a fraction of a second before she fired at him. It was unlikely Malatesta or Arturo had made a shot like that.

The dead man lay on his side with one arm flung above his head. The fingers of his other hand had dug furrows in the dirt as he clawed at the ground in his death throes. His hawkish, beard-stubbled face was twisted in lines of agony, and his wide-open eyes stared sightlessly.

"Ever see him before?" Brice asked, glancing to either side of him at Denny and Malatesta. He had been careful to stay between them during the walk out here, just in case they got any more ideas about throwing down on each other.

"Never in my life," Malatesta declared. "But he looks like a thoroughly disreputable character."

Brice grunted. "A hard case if I've ever seen one, I reckon," he agreed. "How about you, Denny? Recognize him?"

Denny opened her mouth to say something, then closed it abruptly and shook her head.

"No."

Actually, there *was* something familiar about the man, but Denny decided to keep that to herself for now. She was still suspicious of Malatesta's reasons for being in Colorado, and nothing that had happened so far had done anything to lessen those suspicions. More was going on here than was apparent on the surface.

She didn't have to lie when they walked over to the second fallen bushwhacker and Brice rolled the man onto his back with a boot toe hooked under the corpse's shoulder. He had rusty hair and a broad, florid face. The front of his shirt was sodden with blood from his wounds. Bullets from Denny's carbine had hit him at least twice.

"Never laid eyes on him before," she said honestly.

Malatesta added, "I'm not acquainted with the gentleman, either."

"I reckon it's safe to say he was no gentleman," Brice pointed out. "He wouldn't go around bushwhacking folks if he was."

They had to circle the rocks to reach the third man, who lay near the horse Denny had shot out from under him. Denny held the Winchester carbine ready and Brice slipped his Colt from its holster as they approached the man, since he apparently hadn't been wounded and they didn't know if he had survived being thrown from his horse. He might be alive but still unconscious.

Or he could be shamming, pretending to be out cold until they got close enough that he could start shooting again.

Before they ever reached him, though, the unnatural angle of his head and neck made it obvious that he wasn't alive. The hard fall had broken his neck. He lay on his back, so they got a good look at his coarse-featured face, which still wore a surprised expression.

"A stranger to me, as well," Malatesta said without waiting to be asked.

"And me," Denny said, hating to agree with that insufferable man about anything. Again, though, she was telling the truth. Only the first man whose body they had checked out had been familiar to her, and she was pretty sure where she had seen *him* before.

"So it's a mystery," Brice said as he pouched his iron. "Just like at the train station that day, you don't have any idea why these men would want to kill you."

Malatesta pursed his lips and said, "None at all. Perhaps we should interrogate Arturo and find out if he has any old enemies who might wish him harm."

"Arturo doesn't strike me as the type of hombre who'd bring bushwhackers out of the woodwork," Brice commented drily.

"And I do?" Malatesta asked as he cocked an eyebrow.

Brice shrugged and said, "You tell me, Count."

"I believe I have told you everything that I know," Malatesta replied. His voice held a hint of coolness now. "And speaking of Arturo, I should get back to him and make sure he is all right."

He walked toward the rocks and the buggy. Brice

watched him go and said quietly, "I didn't figure the count was the sort who'd worry all that much about the health of somebody who worked for him."

"He isn't," Denny said. "All he cares about is himself."

Brice looked at her but didn't press her for details about why she felt that way. She was glad he didn't. She didn't want to dredge up all those old memories again. She had been brooding about them too much recently. And she sure didn't want to share them with Brice. What had happened in Venice between her and Malatesta was none of his business.

Instead, Brice changed the subject by saying, "That was a pretty good shot I made, all the way from those rocks with a handgun."

"Wait a minute. You believe *you* shot this fella's horse out from under him?"

"That's right. I was aiming at him when I fired, and the horse went down."

Denny shook her head. "I'm the one who shot that poor horse, from that little rise in the trail just west of here. I was aiming at the son of a gun riding him."

"Although you didn't know who he was," Brice reminded her. "For all you knew when you opened fire, those six hombres could have been a posse of lawmen."

"They weren't acting like lawmen," Denny snapped. "Chasing you and shooting that way."

"We could have been owlhoots they were after. Thieves and killers."

"Well, that's not the way it worked out, is it?"

"I'm just saying, Denny, it might be a good idea not to jump in with both feet before you know what's going on."

She glared resentfully at him, but it was hard to

argue with what he was saying. He was right and she knew it. Just because she had guessed correctly this time didn't mean she always would.

"Fine," she said through clenched teeth. "I'll try to remember that."

She stalked back toward the boulders where Malatesta and Arturo waited with the buggy. Brice waited a few seconds before shaking his head ruefully and following her.

"I know we were on our way out to the Sugarloaf when those fellas jumped us," Brice said when they had rejoined the two Italians, "but I really think we ought to take Arturo back to Big Rock so Dr. Steward can take a look at his arm."

"It's really not that bad," Arturo said. "I don't want to inconvenience anyone—"

"Nonsense," Malatesta interrupted him. He put a hand on the shoulder of Arturo's uninjured arm. "Your health is of paramount importance. I would suggest that Marshal Rogers here can drive the buggy back to Big Rock."

"I suppose I can do that," Brice said. "I can tie my horse on behind—"

Once again Malatesta broke in to what somebody else was saying. "I had more in mind that you would be so kind as to loan me your horse, Marshal, so that I might continue on to the Sugarloaf with Signorina Jensen."

Denny stiffened.

"Nobody invited you," she said.

"But what about your world-famous western hospitality, eh?"

"That doesn't extend to low-down sons of—"

Brice said, "I'm afraid that animal of mine is a

one-man horse, Count. He seems well behaved, but if anybody besides me tries to ride him, he turns into a bucking fool. My conscience won't let me loan him to you and take a chance on you getting hurt."

Malatesta's lips thinned. He didn't like having his suggestion vetoed like that, Denny knew.

"I would hold you blameless in the event of any such unfortunate occurrence, signore."

"Maybe, but I'd still blame myself." Brice shook his head. "Nope. Just can't do it. But I *will* be happy to take both of you back to town and see to it that Arturo gets to the doctor's office."

"Very well." Malatesta didn't sound happy about it. He climbed into the buggy's rear seat without offering to share it with Arturo or helping the servant climb into the vehicle.

"Arturo might be more comfortable back there," Brice said. Denny got the feeling that he was deliberately trying to put a burr under Malatesta's saddle now.

"No, that's all right, I'd rather sit up front," Arturo said before his employer could respond.

"Whatever you want," Brice replied with a shrug. "Let me go get my horse and tie him on the back."

His horse had wandered off about fifty yards and was cropping contentedly at some grass. Denny knew the animal was well trained enough that it would have come back if Brice whistled for it, but he walked toward the mount to retrieve it.

She also knew that it wasn't a one-man horse at all. Brice had shaded the truth there.

She walked with him, leading the chestnut, and when they were out of easy earshot of the buggy, she said quietly, "I appreciate what you did back there."

"You mean not letting the count borrow my horse?"

"That's right. I don't want that man on my parents' ranch. I especially don't want him in their house. It would be fine with me if he'd just go back where he came from."

"He seems determined not to do that just yet." Brice paused. "I know there's bad blood between the two of you, even if I don't know why. That's none of my business."

"You're blasted right it's not."

"But for what it's worth, he seems like he really wants to make amends. I get the feeling that he's planning on staying in these parts until you've forgiven him for whatever it is, Denny."

She felt her expression hardening as she said, "That's never going to happen. Anyway, you're wrong about that being what he wants."

"Then why *is* he so determined to stay around here and win you over?"

She looked back over her shoulder at the buggy and thought about the man she had recognized earlier as one of the gun-wolves who tried to kill Malatesta at the train station. Whatever had brought Malatesta to Colorado, trouble had trailed him here, she was certain of that.

"I don't know what he's after," Denny said, "but you can be sure that whatever Giovanni Malatesta is trying to do, he's up to no good."

CHAPTER 23

Dr. Enoch Steward stepped back from the examining table where Arturo sat and said, "There, that ought to do it."

Arturo looked down at the neat bandage encircling his arm and said, "Thank you, Doctor. Your stitches were very precise . . . and painful."

The sandy-haired physician chuckled. "I offered to give you something for the pain, you'll recall. You claimed that you preferred to remain clearheaded."

"That is the case." Arturo picked up the blood-stained shirt he had taken off earlier and started to slip it on. "A servant never knows when he will be called upon to perform his duties for his employer."

"That's an admirable attitude, I suppose."

"One that I endeavor to live by," Arturo said as he buttoned up the bloody shirt.

"I'll come by the hotel this evening and check that dressing," Steward went on briskly. "You'll need to make sure the wound stays clean. As long as it doesn't become infected, I believe you'll heal up just fine. And since this is hardly the first bullet wound I've patched up, I think you can put some stock in my opinion."

"Indeed I do. But I'm curious . . . In this modern day and age, you still have to treat numerous gunshot wounds?"

"Smoke Jensen lives less than a dozen miles from here," Steward said with a smile. "Also, he has brothers and nephews who come to visit him from time to time, and they seem to be just as much of a magnet for trouble as he is. Just because it's a new century doesn't mean that things have changed that much. As long as there are Jensens around . . ."

The doctor left that comment unfinished except for an eloquent shrug.

"Very well." Arturo tucked in his shirt, and then Steward draped a black silk sling around his neck and over his shoulder. Arturo arranged his wounded arm in the sling and carried his coat and tie over his other arm as he left the doctor's examination room.

Brice Rogers and Giovanni Malatesta waited in the office, where they had been joined by Sheriff Monte Carson, who had been summoned by one of the townspeople Brice spoke to as he drove the buggy into town. The sheriff was talking to them about the ambush on the road to the Sugarloaf.

"I'll let the undertaker know what happened, and he can go out there with his wagon to collect the bodies," Monte said. He frowned at Malatesta. "You're sure you don't have any idea why they jumped you?"

Malatesta blew out an exasperated breath. "Must everyone constantly ask me that question?"

"We're just looking for answers," Monte said.

"You've got to admit, circumstances sure make it look like somebody's out to get you."

"I cannot help how it looks. And I cannot give you answers that I don't have, Sheriff."

Monte nodded and said, "Fair enough." He didn't sound convinced, though, and Brice looked skeptical, too.

Malatesta ignored them, stood up, and said to Steward, "You took good care of my friend, eh, Doctor?"

"That's right," Steward said. "The wound bled quite a bit but looked worse than it really was. I cleaned it, took a few stitches to close it up, and bandaged it. Mr. Vincenzo will need to take it easy for a few days and keep his arm in that sling most of the time."

"But rest assured, Count Malatesta, I'll still be able to take care of my duties," Arturo said.

"Nonsense!" Malatesta gave him a hearty slap on the back. "For the time being, our roles are reversed, eh? *I* will take care of *you*."

Arturo looked quite uncomfortable at that idea, but he didn't say anything about it. Instead he turned to Steward and said, "I suppose we should settle our account, Doctor."

Malatesta said, "You were injured while in the course of performing your duties for me, so I will be held accountable for your medical expenses."

"Seems fair to me," Brice put in.

Steward said, "It doesn't really matter to me, as long as I get my three dollars."

Malatesta took three silver dollars from his pocket and gave them to the doctor.

"If you require additional payment later, sir, please let me know."

"If there aren't any complications—and I don't expect any—everything should be fine."

"We should get back to the hotel, then," Malatesta said, "so Arturo can rest." He looked at Brice and Monte. "Unless you gentlemen have any more questions . . . ?"

Monte shook his head. "No, I don't reckon I do. I'll go notify the undertaker."

"I'll come with you," Brice said.

The two lawmen left the doctor's office. Steward promised again to check on Arturo later, and then Malatesta ushered him out of the office and they walked along the street toward the Big Rock Hotel.

"I really do hate to be a burden," Arturo said.

"You are no burden, my friend," Malatesta assured him.

"I just don't understand why people keep trying to shoot us!" Some of the frustration he felt came out in Arturo's voice.

Beside him, with a hand on Arturo's arm, Malatesta sighed and shook his head. Solemnly, he said, "It is a great mystery, indeed."

New York City, four months earlier

The area known as Little Italy lay between Houston Street on the north, Worth Street on the south, Lafayette Street on the west, and the Bowery on the east. The neighborhood in lower Manhattan had been known originally as Mulberry Bend because Mulberry Street ran through the center of it. At first it had been a mixture of nationalities and cultures, but during the past decade and a half, more and more Italians had moved in, until now at least 90 percent of the population had either immigrated from Italy or been born to Italian immigrants. To anyone walking along Mulberry Street, the sights and sounds and smells might have led them to believe they had been transported around the world to an Italian village.

Johnny Malatesta tugged his cap down tighter, lowered his head, and hunched his shoulders against the chilly wind blowing through the canyons formed by the brownstone buildings. The frigid fingers clawed right through the thin, threadbare jacket he wore, almost as if the garment wasn't there. Johnny clenched his jaw to keep his teeth from chattering. It might be spring according to the calendar, but the weather here was still miserable.

He opened a gate in a wrought iron railing and went down some steps to a small area below street level with a plain door opening into the basement of one of the buildings. When he pushed the door back, welcome warm air gushed out around him, wrapping him in the smells of garlic, fresh-baked bread, and the acidic tang of wine. Johnny closed the door behind him.

He had taken only a single step through the restaurant's foyer before a mountainous figure emerged from a curtained doorway and blocked his path.

"Stop right there," the man rumbled. "Where do you think you're goin'?"

Even though years had passed since all the trouble back in Sicily, for a second Johnny's mind flashed back to the massive, brutal youngster called Luca. Dead and gone for a long time, Luca was, along with the Capizzi brothers, but every now and then Johnny still had nightmares about them and about what had happened to Serafina. And about the fiery end he had put to his enemies, as well.

Those weren't nightmares, however. What he had done to the Capizzi brothers and Luca still gave him intense satisfaction.

But this man standing in front of him now was not Luca. He was much older and even bigger. Everybody in the neighborhood called him Pete and walked carefully around him, not wanting to get on his bad side because he was the strong-arm and right-hand man for Nick Scaramello.

And Scaramello, despite being half Pete's size, was even more feared.

Pete was mostly bald, with tufts of brown hair sticking out above his ears and trailing on around to the back of his head, which was somehow reminiscent of a stone block. The finger he poked painfully against Johnny's chest was as thick and square and blunt on the end as a board.

"You hear me?" he said. "What you want here?"

"I need to talk to Nick," Johnny replied.

"Talk to Nick?" Pete said. "A guy like you don't just waltz in here and talk to Nick. You gotta arrange it with Ant'ony, you know that."

Anthony Migliazzi was Nick Scaramello's bookkeeper and general factotum. He and Pete handled day-to-day matters for their boss while Scaramello sat here in this restaurant, eating and drinking and pulling strings that ran from one end of Little Italy to the other.

Sometimes, though, things required Nick's personal attention, and the problem Johnny faced now was one of them—at least, in Johnny's opinion, it was.

"This is about the Lavery business," he said.

"The Lavery business?" Pete's voice boomed and his bushy eyebrows crawled up his forehead. "Well, why didn't you say so? You can go right in!"

He moved aside and waved toward the curtain behind him.

Johnny started to step past him, but then Pete's hand came down on his shoulder and clamped shut. Before Johnny fully understood what was happening, Pete flung him backward. He backstepped across the foyer, unable to stop himself, and slammed into the now-closed door. The back of his head thudded against the panel hard enough to make him see stars for a second.

"What's wrong with you?" Pete yelled as he planted a hamlike hand against Johnny's chest and pinned him to the door. "You got a problem, you talk to Ant'ony or me, you don't come in here bold as brass and say you've gotta see the boss! You're lucky I don't take you out back in the alley and pound you until you got gravy runnin' out your ears—"

"Pete. What are you bellowing like a bull about?"

The voice was quiet and carried not a hint of menace. But it made Pete drop his hand from Johnny's chest and step back quickly.

"Uh, sorry, boss, if the racket was disturbin' you. This little pissant thought he could just walk right in and bother you—"

Nick Scaramello pushed the curtain aside, stepped into the foyer, and faced Johnny with a curious look on his blandly handsome face.

CHAPTER 24

"Hello, Johnny," Scaramello said. "I thought I gave you a job to do. You having a problem with it?"

Even a simple question like that was enough to chill the blood of most people in Little Italy. Nobody wanted to incur the wrath of Nick Scaramello.

"Not really a problem, Nick," Johnny said.

Scaramello insisted that everybody call him by his given name. That was his way of furthering the self-created illusion of being one of the common people, instead of the boss of the dreaded Black Hand.

"I just need some advice, that's all," Johnny went on. Scaramello liked it when people acted like he was the favorite uncle of everyone in the neighborhood.

"It was a simple job," Scaramello said, spreading his hands as if he couldn't understand how Johnny would have any trouble carrying out his instructions. "Talk to Patrick Lavery and make sure he understands how things are going to be around here from now on."

"Yes, sir, I know. I did talk to him."

"And?"

"He won't listen to reason," Johnny replied with a

rueful shake of his head. "He says he's always had an arrangement and he expects it to be honored."

"He *had* an arrangement." Scaramello's voice hardened. "Things have changed. I say what goes on around here now."

Patrick Lavery was a hardheaded Irishman who operated a pawn shop a few blocks up Mulberry Street, one of the handful of businesses in the neighborhood owned by someone who wasn't an Italian. He had been there for more than twenty years, running the place in a scrupulously honest fashion, making small payoffs to previous bosses so he could remain open without interference. That had started in the days of the Irish mobs and continued after the Italians moved in.

So far, since taking over fourteen months earlier, Nick Scaramello had maintained the arrangement with Lavery, but recently he had decided that the percentage the Irishman paid had to go up. Double, in fact. And the old mick hadn't liked it.

Anybody could have predicted that. Johnny knew good and well that when he approached Lavery about the new terms, the man was going to balk. He had, in fact, grabbed a shillelagh and threatened to break Johnny's head if he didn't get out, all the while blustering about the "Eye-talians."

Trying not to stammer out of nervousness, Johnny explained this to Scaramello, right there in the foyer of the restaurant that the boss used as his headquarters. Scaramello hooked his thumbs in his vest pockets and nodded as he listened. When Johnny was finished with his explanation, Scaramello asked, "So, what do you think is the next step?"

Johnny swallowed and said, "I thought maybe you

could send some men with me when I go back there. You know, enough to show him that we mean business."

"I see." Scaramello turned his head to look at Pete and nodded again.

Pete took a quick step toward Johnny and hooked a heavy fist into his midsection. The punch hit like a thunderbolt. Johnny felt like it went all the way to his spine and blasted it in two. He doubled over, stunned by both the pain and the unexpected savagery of the attack, and would have fallen if Pete hadn't clamped a hand around his throat, straightened him up, and slammed him back against the wall again.

The blow had driven all the air out of Johnny's lungs, and with Pete's fingers like iron bands closing off his windpipe, Johnny couldn't inhale. His chest began to feel like it was on fire. His pulse hammered like drums inside his skull. A red haze closed in on his vision from both sides.

"That's enough," he heard Scaramello say. The man's voice sounded like it came from a million miles away.

The terrible pressure on Johnny's throat eased. It didn't go away completely, but he was able to breathe again. He dragged air into his body. The frantic breaths rasped and wheezed in his throat, which Pete still squeezed, just not as tightly. He kept Johnny pinned against the wall and lifted him enough that Johnny was forced to stand on his toes.

Scaramello moved closer and said, "Listen to me, Johnny." He still sounded friendly and avuncular. "If I give a man a job, it's because I believe he's capable enough to handle it. When you come back to me asking for help like this, it makes me doubt my own judgment, like you're not as good a man as I thought you were. I don't like doubting myself, Johnny. What do you think we can do to fix this problem?"

Pete eased off the pressure even more, so that Johnny could stand flat on his feet again even though he was still trapped against the wall. He croaked past the hand on his throat, "I . . . I can handle it . . . Nick. You're . . . not wrong . . . about me. I'll go back . . . to Lavery's place . . . and talk to him again."

Scaramello reached up and patted Johnny lightly on the cheek.

"Now, that's what I like to hear. I know you won't let me down."

He nodded to Pete again, and this time the big man let go of Johnny. Johnny sagged forward and might have collapsed, but Pete's hand on his shoulder steadied him. He stood there breathing deeply for several moments, then straightened and nodded to Pete.

Scaramello pushed the curtain aside and started to go back into the restaurant's dining room. He paused to say, "Next time you come see me, Johnny, you bring me something I want to hear. You do that, I'll have more jobs for you."

"Yes, sir," Johnny said. His throat hurt, but he got the words out. "I'll do that, Nick."

Scaramello nodded and let the curtain fall closed behind him. Johnny started to turn toward the street door, but Pete stopped him by saying, "What Nick meant, kid, was that if you don't have anything good to report . . . don't come back. In fact, if he's gonna be disappointed in you again, you'd be better off runnin' as far and as fast as you can." Pete leaned closer, his ugly face creasing in a mean grin as he added, "But that won't be far enough to keep Nick from findin' you. And when he does . . ."

Pete left the threat unfinished, but Johnny got the idea, loud and clear.

When he went back to see Old Man Lavery, his life would be on the line.

The saloons, the restaurants, and the gambling joints in Little Italy stayed open late, so there were people out and about on the streets until well after dark. Because of that, the possibility existed that somebody might need a little extra cash, so Lavery kept his pawn shop open late, too. The yellow light that spilled through its front window illuminated the shop's sign and the three balls that were the hallmark of the pawn business.

Johnny stood a block away and stared at that blob of light. Part of him wanted to go ahead and get in there and get the job done, while another part wanted to turn and run away. Not just from the pawn shop, but from Little Italy in particular and New York City in general. Maybe it was time to try his luck elsewhere.

He had been scrambling for survival ever since he'd arrived here nearly a year and a half earlier. He had gotten out of Venice just a few steps ahead of Salvatore Tomasi's goons, using what little money he had cached to get to Naples, where he'd signed on as a crew member on a tramp steamer bound for America.

That miserable voyage was quite a comedown for "Count" Giovanni Malatesta. He had done well for himself, these last few years, using his natural charms and his pose as a phony Sicilian aristocrat to fleece money primarily from American and English women. He lived in the style to which noblemen were accustomed, partially because it was good for business, partially because he enjoyed it. He had come a long, long way from herding his grandfather's sheep around the Sicilian hills, and he was determined never to go back to a peasant's life.

Then he had encountered Signorina Denise Nicole Jensen. Most of the women he targeted weren't as attractive as she was. In fact, he would venture to say that she was the most beautiful woman he had ever been with.

Unfortunately, she was also the cleverest, and somehow she had discovered the truth at the worst of all possible times: right when Giovanni's love of gambling and reckless impulses were catching up to him, in the form of Tomasi's enforcers.

So his days as an aristocrat were over, although he remembered them fondly as he shoveled coal, deep in the steamer's bowels, as a member of the vessel's black gang. When he got to America, he would have to start over, but he told himself that he was capable of doing that. Just give him time, and he would be riding as high as ever.

He had jumped ship in New York, sought out familiar surroundings, and disappeared into the teeming warren of Little Italy. Since then he had survived hand to mouth, working at odd jobs and stealing when he had to. Then, after long months of such a precarious existence, he had been fortunate enough to start running numbers for a low-level employee of Nick Scaramello's. He had worked his way up until he caught the attention of Scaramello himself, who had given him the task of dealing with Patrick Lavery.

Johnny understood now that the job had actually been a test—a test that he had failed miserably. But Scaramello had given him a second chance, and he didn't intend to waste it.

He drew in a breath and walked quickly toward the pawn shop. As he came up to the window, he saw through the glass that a customer was just leaving. The man pushed out through the door, stuffing money into his pocket, the loan for whatever he had just hocked.

Lavery was alone in the shop now, as far as Johnny could tell.

He went in, closed the door behind him, thought about locking it but didn't. Maybe Lavery would be reasonable this time, and everything would go quickly and smoothly. No fuss. That was the way Johnny liked it.

That didn't appear to be what was going to happen, though. As soon as Lavery saw Johnny, he reached under the counter and brought out the shillelagh again, clutching the gnarled club in both hands. He lifted it slightly, as if daring Johnny to come within reach of a swing, and said harshly, "What're ye doin' back here, ya filthy Eye-talian? Go back to yer greasy boss and tell him I won't pay him a nickel more! I'm done wi' the likes o' ye!"

CHAPTER 25

Johnny held up both hands, palms out, as he said, "Take it easy, Mr. Lavery. I'm not looking for trouble."

"Then what *are* ye lookin' for?" Lavery sneered. "A deal on some merchandise, maybe? Somethin' ye can't get yer thievin' wop fingers on to steal?"

Johnny eased closer, still with his hands held out, as he said, "No, I just hoped we could talk some more—"

Lavery snarled and slashed the air in front of him with the shillelagh.

"There's nothin' to talk about," he declared. "I always honored my deal with the old *paisans*. I'll even honor it with that rat Scaramello. But not a nickel more! Not a penny!"

"Things change—"

"Not a man's word!" Lavery slammed the club down on the counter to punctuate his exclamation.

Considering how red the old man's face was, if he kept this up he might just die of apoplexy, Johnny thought. The man was thickly built, with a prominent gut, and even when he wasn't upset, his face bore a resemblance to a slab of raw beef topped by curly gray hair that retained a hint of its original rust color.

Now he was breathing hard and his eyes bulged, and Johnny found himself hoping that the stubborn mick would just drop dead. That would certainly simplify things. Johnny didn't know if Lavery had any heirs, but even if he did, Scaramello would be able to run them off without much trouble and the pawn shop would pass into Italian hands, which was only right and fitting.

"What'd you say yer name was?" Lavery demanded.

"Johnny Malatesta."

"Look, *Giovanni,* you're wastin' yer time here. Run along afore I come out from behind this counter and teach ye the folly of annoyin' a good Irishman."

"My name's Johnny," he snapped. "I don't go by Giovanni anymore. I'm an American now."

For some reason, Lavery calling him by his given name bothered him more than the old man's stubborn refusal to go along with Nick Scaramello's demands. He was trying hard to fit in here.

"An American?" Lavery repeated. "Don't make me laugh! You're a greasy little wop, and you'll never be anything except a greasy little wop. They barely tolerate the Irish in this country. What makes you think they'll ever put up with the likes o' you?"

"When I'm rich, they will," Johnny shot back. "A rich man is always welcome anywhere."

"Aye, ye might have somethin' there. But how'll ye ever get rich beggin' for scraps at the heels o' scum like Nick Scaramello?"

"I won't always be doing that."

"You're not fit for anythin' else, ye no-account Eyetalian mongrel—"

While they were talking, Johnny had edged closer and closer to the counter. Now he was right across from Lavery, so close that he was afraid some of the enraged spittle flying from the man's mouth might strike him in the face.

Close enough that he was able to lunge across the counter and get both hands on the shillelagh.

Clearly, Lavery wasn't expecting that, but he clung to the club and tried to pull back away from Johnny. Johnny hung on tightly, and they swayed back and forth above the counter as they struggled. Lavery's lips drew back from his teeth in a grimace. Neither man said anything now. The only sounds in the pawn shop were grunts of effort and breath hissing through clenched teeth and shoes scraping on the floor.

Lavery had the better position, but Johnny was a lot younger. The Irishman's grip weakened first. Johnny jerked the shillelagh loose. He turned it and rammed one end into Lavery's stomach. The club sunk deep in the roll of fat around the man's mid-section. The force of the blow made Lavery gasp and bend forward over the counter.

Johnny stepped back to give himself some room and swung.

The club smacked sharply into the side of Lavery's head above his left ear and knocked him sprawling behind the counter. Johnny glanced toward the pawn shop's front window, worried that some passerby might have seen the fight and witnessed the possibly fatal blow he had just struck. He hadn't meant to kill the Irishman, but Lavery's venomous insults had gotten under his skin and he'd lost his temper.

Nobody was looking in, though, and a groan from behind the counter told Johnny that the old man wasn't dead after all. He put his hands on the counter, vaulted up onto it, and swung his legs over. He dropped into the area behind the counter where Lavery was stretched out, pawing weakly at his head. Blood welled from a gash in his gray curls and turned them red again.

Johnny dropped both knees on Lavery's chest and pinned the man to the floor. Lavery gasped in pain. Johnny put the shillelagh across Lavery's throat and bore down on it. They were below the level of the counter, so if anybody looked in through the window now, they wouldn't see anything out of the ordinary.

"It wouldn't take much for me to crush your windpipe," Johnny said in a low, angry voice. "Then you'd suffocate, and I could just sit here and watch you die while I laughed about it. But that wouldn't put any money in Signor Scaramello's pockets, would it?"

Lavery moved his hands like he was going to try to strike at Johnny, who responded by pressing down harder on the club. Lavery's face started to turn purple.

Johnny leaned closer and said, "You think I won't do it, old man? I'll kill you right here and now, and there's not a blasted thing you can do about it. Maybe I'll just beat your brains out with this club of yours. How about that?"

Lavery gurgled and with fierce hate burning in his eyes stared up at Johnny. Lavery was weakening, though, from lack of air. It really wouldn't take much effort to kill him now, Johnny realized, and the knowledge that this old man's life was in his hands was a heady feeling, indeed.

"You think maybe you'd better go along with what

Nick wants? He's not asking for a lot, you know. Just a little higher percentage."

That wasn't strictly true, since Scaramello intended to double the percentage, but that wasn't much when you were talking about living or dying, was it?

"Come on, you stupid mick," Johnny urged. "Tell me you'll go along, and there won't be any more trouble. What do you say, old man?"

Johnny eased off on the pressure so Lavery could talk—just like Pete had let off on his grip on Johnny's throat earlier this evening. That similarity wasn't lost on Johnny. He didn't hold it against Pete, though. A man with power had to use it. Otherwise, what good was it?

Lavery's tongue came out. He made some gurgling sounds as he tried to form words.

The voice Johnny heard, though, came from behind him.

"What are you doing to my grandfather? Get off him!"

Johnny's head jerked around. A woman in a green shirt and long brown skirt rushed toward him through the area behind the counter. She must have been somewhere else in the shop, a back room, more than likely, and heard the commotion.

"Get off him!" she cried again as she reached for him.

Without getting up, Johnny twisted toward her and jabbed the shillelagh in her belly, just as he had done to Lavery. That stopped her in her tracks. He leaped to his feet as she staggered back a couple of steps, bent over and moaning.

Instead of hitting her a second time, as he had done with the old man, he grabbed her arm and forced her back along the counter. They came out at the far end. He pushed her behind a set of shelves with various tools displayed on them. That would help keep them from being seen through the front window.

A scrabbling noise behind him made Johnny look over his shoulder. Lavery was struggling to get to his feet. Johnny pointed the shillelagh at him and yelled, "Don't you move, old man! You stay right there if you don't want this girl to get hurt!"

"Leave her alone!" Lavery wailed pitifully. "Don't you have any decency in yer soul, ya young scut?"

Johnny ignored that question and turned back to the girl. He had taken her for a woman at first because she was fairly tall, but he saw now she was no more than fifteen or sixteen, rawboned and scrawny, all freckles and frizzy red hair and not at all pretty.

But definitely female. He pressed her against the wall and ran his free hand over her body while he held the shillelagh poised to strike.

"Don't fight me or I'll brain you," he warned her.

She shuddered under his touch. Her eyes were wide with terror.

"Wh-what are you going to do to me?" she asked.

"What do you think I ought to do?" He leered as he leaned in closer. "That stubborn old grandfather of yours is causing trouble for my boss. Maybe I ought to teach him a lesson by teaching *you* a few lessons. What do you think?"

Her lips trembled as she stared out at him. She forced out words. "P-Please . . . no. Please don't."

And just like that, he could hear Serafina saying the same thing. He hadn't been there on that awful day by the stream, didn't know exactly what words had come from her mouth, but he was certain it would have been something like the plea this Irish girl had just husked out. His face twisted as he drew back. Was he just as bad as the Capizzi brothers, as Luca?

Then he remembered what Pete had said about not coming back if he failed again, about running away—but still being unable to escape Scaramello's vengeance. He thought about money and power and all the doors they would open. A man had to start somewhere. He had already started over more than once in his life, which was why he was Johnny Malatesta now instead of Giovanni. He didn't want to have to flee for his life again. This time, he might not make it.

So he just had to accept things as they were. Maybe when he was younger, he hadn't been as bad as the Capizzis and Luca—but that was then and this was now.

He rammed his body against the terrified girl and kissed her. She tried to twist her head and get her mouth away from his, but he gripped her chin so tightly it had to be hurting her.

"Mother of mercy, no!" Lavery choked out. "I'll do whatever you say! I'll pay Scaramello whatever he wants! Just leave her alone. Please, I'm begging you."

Johnny pulled his head back. His chest heaved as he struggled with the thoughts and emotions whirling through him. Maybe he didn't have to hurt this girl after all. But the old mick had to pay somehow for defying Nick Scaramello.

"Stand up," he told Lavery.

Shaking, the old man struggled to his feet. He had to lean both hands on the counter in order to keep from falling.

"Stay there, just like that," Johnny said. He looked at the girl. "Don't you move."

"Please don't hurt us," she whispered.

Johnny didn't respond to that. He stepped out in front of the counter and walked along it until he was across from Lavery again.

"I'm going to leave now," he said. "When Nick's man comes around to collect, you give him what you're supposed to and not a penny less, you got that?"

Lavery jerked his head in a nod. All the fight had gone out of him in the face of Johnny's savagery.

"You don't mouth off, you don't argue, you just pay up."

Another nod.

"And in case maybe you forget, this'll remind you," Johnny said.

He slammed the shillelagh down on Lavery's left hand as hard as he could, breaking most of the bones in there, if not all of them. Lavery screamed as he staggered back and held the shattered hand in his other one, pressing it against his chest in horror and agony.

"Hey, what are you yelling about? I left you one, didn't I?"

He grinned at the girl, who started to rush behind the counter toward her grandfather but stopped short when Johnny looked at her. He motioned with his head for her to go on with what she was doing.

Then, whistling and carrying the shillelagh canted over his shoulder, he left the pawn shop and strolled along Mulberry Street. A cold wind still blew, but Johnny didn't feel it anymore. For a moment there, he had almost forgotten that a guy did what he had to in order to survive. But he remembered now, and he was going to do more than just survive. He might be close to the bottom of the ladder right now, but he knew how to climb.

He brought the shillelagh down from his shoulder, held it in one hand, and smacked it solidly in the palm of the other hand. Those micks might be dumb as dirt, but they knew how to make a pretty good club.

He was going to put it to good use, too.

CHAPTER 26

Johnny's rise in Scaramello's gang was dizzying. Within two months, he had risen to a position of authority second only to that of Pete and Anthony Migliazzi. He did this by being utterly ruthless in carrying out every job Scaramello gave him, culminating in the night he had followed one of the boss's ambitious, would-be rivals and jumped him right on the stoop of the man's own home. The guy managed one yell of alarm, but by the time his wife stepped out to see what was wrong, she found her husband sprawled on the steps, his brains leaking out of a skull shattered by the shillelagh Johnny had taken from Old Man Lavery's pawn shop.

Scaramello had laughed and laughed when Johnny told him about that, then invited Johnny to sit with him at his private table in the restaurant.

He might not be an important man yet, Johnny thought, but he was on his way.

As soon as he started making better money—and Nick Scaramello was a generous employer—he began dressing better as well. In Italy, Johnny had developed a flair for dapper suits and good-quality hats. He carried the shillelagh with him when he was working but otherwise left it in the room he rented. A gentleman didn't carry around a club, and a gentleman was what Johnny had aspired to be ever since he left Sicily.

When he could afford to dress the part, he frequented the nicer restaurants and saloons. They were still in Little Italy, but the best the neighborhood had to offer. The sort of places that catered to well-to-do businessmen and also customers from other areas of New York, the wealthy types who liked to venture down to lower Manhattan on a lark. To them, a jaunt like that was an adventure, something to spice up their lives.

One evening when he didn't have anything to do for Scaramello, he was loafing at the bar in Frederico's, an upscale eating place that featured dining and drinking on the first floor and gambling on the second, when he noticed a group that had just come in.

There were two men and two women, and from the way they were laughing, they had been drinking already. Both women were blond, as was one of the men. The other man had red hair. It was possible that some of them were Italian, but that didn't seem likely. They were expensively dressed, so Johnny pegged them for uptown swells who were slumming in Little Italy.

He turned back to the bar and grimaced as he looked down into his drink. Then, as he sat there, his attitude slowly changed. Instead of the resentment he felt toward the interlopers, he began to see this as an opportunity. He turned his head and watched as the maître d' seated the foursome at a table. A few minutes later, a waiter brought glasses and a bottle of wine to the table. The group didn't appear to have ordered any food and just intended to continue drinking.

Judging by their laughter and loud talk, they were having themselves a good time. Without appearing to, Johnny studied them closely, especially the two women. One was rather vapid-looking and clearly not too bright. The expensive clothes and jewelry and stylish hair failed to conceal her cowlike nature. Obviously she had plenty of money and that interested Johnny, but the other woman looked just as well-to-do and was considerably more attractive.

She had the sort of brittle beauty many women displayed when they were within shouting distance of middle age. Her sleek good looks had not yet started to leave her—but they were thinking about it. She was with the red-haired man, and as Johnny watched the way he doted on her, it became clear who had the money—and the power—in their relationship.

Without thinking too much about what he was doing, Johnny let his old instincts take over. He had the bartender refill his drink, then left the bar and sauntered toward the stairs that led up to the gaming room on the second floor. To get there, he had to pass the table he had been watching, and as he did, he pretended to stumble slightly.

The liquor in his glass went all over the crisp white shirtfront of the redheaded man.

The man leaped to his feet and cursed loudly. He turned toward Johnny. His fists clenched.

But Johnny already had his handkerchief out and started patting at the spilled liquor as he said, "A thousand apologies, signore! How terribly clumsy of me. I never meant for this to happen. Please, allow me to clean this up."

His Italian accent was perhaps a bit thicker than it usually was. He had learned to speak English quite well as a young man in Italy and could carry on a conversation with either a British or an American accent if circumstances demanded. At the moment, however, he didn't want to conceal his Italian ancestry.

"You should watch where you're going," the redhead blustered as Johnny dabbed at his shirt with the handkerchief. "And you're just making it worse!"

"The maître d' will be able to clean this. I'll get him."

"You don't have to—"

Johnny had already lifted a finger in a signal, though, and the maître d' was there at the table instantly, almost as if by magic. Everyone who worked at Frederico's knew who Johnny Malatesta was—and none of them wanted him to leave there unhappy.

"My friend here has had a small mishap," Johnny said. "Perhaps you could take him out to the kitchen and help him."

"Of course, Signor Malatesta," the maître d' murmured.

"I don't want to go to the kitchen—" the redhead began.

Johnny put a hand on his shoulder, and the strength of his grip caused the man to stop talking and take a sharp breath.

"Please, let me do this for you," Johnny said. "And I assure you, I'll see to having that shirt cleaned or buy you a new one."

"That . . . that's not necessary," the redhead managed to say.

The maître d' took the man's other arm and said, "Please, signore, come with me. Everything will be attended to."

"I . . . I . . . all right."

As the maître d' led the redhead away, Johnny turned to the others at the table and said, "My apologies to you, as well, for ruining your evening."

"My evening's not ruined," the attractive blonde said as she ran her eyes over Johnny from head to foot. The drinks she'd had this evening were making her bold—or maybe that was just her nature. "In fact, I think perhaps it's just starting to get interesting."

"I might say the same thing." Johnny bowed slightly. "Allow me to introduce myself . . ."

He almost said the name he was using now. He had believed he was putting that other life behind him, never to be resurrected. But then, on a whim, he realized that maybe it didn't have to be that way.

"Count Giovanni Malatesta," he said. He took the blonde's hand where it lay on the white linen tablecloth and lifted it, pressed his lips to the back of it. "At your service."

The other blonde, the bovine one, tittered and said, "He talks fancy."

"Yes, he does." The first blonde took her hand back and went on, "I'm Mrs. Felicia Brighton."

Johnny's eyes went to her hand again, specifically the ring finger, which was bare.

"I'm a widow," Felicia Brighton added.

"I'm sorry for your loss," Johnny said.

"Don't be," she told him with a shake of her head. "It was a long time ago, and besides, he was a terrible man. Rich, mind you, but still terrible. I suppose money makes a man's flaws more bearable, don't you?"

"Just as beauty has the same effect on a woman's flaws."

Her eyes flashed deep blue fire, and for a moment he thought she was going to be angry with him. But then the fire went away, and her laugh was genuine amusement, not brittle insincerity.

"No one who's honest with themselves could deny that."

The other man evidently decided that he'd been left out of this long enough. He stood up, stuck out his hand toward Johnny, and said, "I'm Clarence Hamilton the Third."

"Count Giovanni Malatesta," Johnny introduced himself again. He shook hands with Milhorn.

"And this is Miss Beatrice Sterling," Milhorn said, gesturing toward his companion.

Despite the fact that she was nowhere near as beautiful as Felicia Brighton, Johnny didn't want Beatrice Sterling to feel left out. He bent over the hand she offered him and kissed the back of it, too, making her giggle and blush.

"You don't ever do anything nice and Continental like that," she said as she looked up at Milhorn.

"I'm not a European." He looked at Johnny. "You're Italian?"

"Sicilian, to be precise."

"A beautiful, charming island," Felicia said. "My late husband and I spent a summer there, many years ago." She cocked her head a little to the side. "We visited with many of the best families. I don't seem to recall any Malatestas . . ."

"Our estate is rather isolated," Johnny said. "My grandfather was the sort who never enjoyed much company. He was content with what he called his flock. He cared for them, and they depended on him."

"It sounds positively feudal," Milhorn commented.

Johnny shrugged. "In some ways, my homeland has changed very little in the past five hundred years." He turned back to Felicia. "But enough about me. Since your companion for the evening is temporarily unavailable, I hope you'll consider me a suitable replacement. For the time being, of course."

"Of course," she said. "What did you have in mind?"

Before Johnny could reply, Milhorn said, "I'm sure Ted won't be gone long—"

"I made such a terrible mess that it may take some time to set things right," Johnny said. Even though he hadn't been able to talk to the maître d' and make sure the man understood what he wanted, he had a hunch the redhead would be stuck in the kitchen for quite a while. "Please, I'd really like to make up for any inconvenience my clumsiness has caused you."

"What did you have in mind?"

Johnny inclined his head toward the stairs and said, "There's a gaming room upstairs, if you'd care to visit. It's rather . . . exclusive . . . but I'm sure there wouldn't be a problem if you wanted to go up there."

"As long as I'm with you?"

Johnny spread his hands. "They know me here."

"Hang on," Milhorn said. "We didn't come out tonight to do any gambling, Felicia."

"I think it sounds exciting," Beatrice put in.

"And when Ted comes back, if he finds us gone—"

"There's quite an easy solution to that, Clarence," Felicia interrupted him. "You and Bea can stay here and tell poor Ted where I've gotten off to."

"You mean we can't come?" Beatrice asked, pouting.

"Perhaps later, dear," Felicia said. She patted Beatrice's hand and then stood up and extended her hand to Johnny. "Lead on, Count Malatesta."

"It will be my pleasure," Johnny said as he took her smooth, cool fingers, and he meant every word of it.

CHAPTER 27

Johnny's affair with Felicia Brighton proceeded faster—and burned even brighter—than his rise in the Black Hand organization. Within days of their meeting at Frederico's, they were lovers. Within a few weeks, he was spending most of his time at her big house on Riverside Drive, although he kept his rented room to remind him of his adopted roots in Little Italy.

Of course, he still had to devote some of his attention to his job. Nick Scaramello had proven to be a surprisingly tolerant boss, but there were limits to his understanding and Johnny knew that. Whenever Nick needed something done, Johnny was there to take care of it. But the rest of the time, Johnny and Felicia spent dining and drinking, gambling and taking in shows, making love in the giant, four-poster bed in her bedroom in the big house. It might not be the so-called Gilded Age anymore, but they lived as if it were.

And Felicia paid for everything. All of Johnny's old tricks from his days in Venice as Count Malatesta came back to him, and although he successfully maintained the illusion of wealth, it was Felicia who forked over for all the expenses, without seeming to mind or even notice.

One night as Johnny entered the foyer of the nameless, all-but-unknown restaurant where Scaramello held court, Pete leered at him and said, "The old bat let you off the leash tonight, eh, kid?"

Anger immediately bubbled up inside Johnny.

"Shut up, Pete," he snapped, confident that he was well positioned enough in the organization to say such a thing. "Felicia's not an old bat, and I don't wear a stinkin' leash."

Pete cuffed him on the arm, playfully but with enough force to knock Johnny a step to the side.

"Watch your mouth, bambino. You're doin' pretty good for yourself these days, but I been around a lot longer than you. I've seen how things don't always last."

Johnny straightened his coat and sniffed.

"I'm not worried about that," he said.

"Maybe you better be."

"What do you mean by that?" Johnny asked with a curious frown. "I've been doing everything Nick asks me to do, and a pretty good job of it, too."

"I'm just sayin'," Pete rumbled, "that guys who start ridin' too high are usually ridin' for a fall."

Johnny just shook his head disgustedly, pushed past the big man, and walked into the restaurant's main room. He headed for the big table in the back where, at the moment, Scaramello sat talking to Anthony Migliazzi.

The bookkeeper was a scrawny, dark-haired man who always looked like he'd just bitten into a lemon. He wore spectacles and his dark suits were always a little dusty and threadbare, even though as one of Nick's top subordinates, he could afford to dress much better. He was saying something to Scaramello, but his trap snapped shut when he saw Johnny approaching the table.

Scaramello had both hands resting flat on the table. He lifted the index finger of the right one in a signal to Migliazzi and said, "We'll talk more later, Anthony."

Migliazzi nodded, stood up, and left.

Scaramello waved expansively as Johnny came up to the table.

"Sit down," he invited, then added as if they had just happened to encounter each other, "It's good to see you again, Johnny."

"I saw you just a couple of days ago, Nick," Johnny said as he sat down. "It hasn't been that long."

"And you have somebody else a lot prettier to spend your time with now, eh?" Scaramello grinned as he spoke, but his eyes glittered with possible anger.

"You know Felicia's not nearly as important to me as you, boss." Johnny wanted to head off any problems before they got blown out of proportion. "I still do my job, and I always will. If you've got something you want me to handle, just say the word and it'll be handled."

"Nah, that's not it. I admire you, kid. Mrs. Brighton's still a good-looking woman . . . and she doesn't mind paying for things, am I right?"

Johnny shrugged and said, "She likes buying things for me."

"Like that ring."

Johnny glanced down at his hand. The ring, with a large opal in an elaborate gold setting, was on the gaudy side, but Johnny liked it. When he'd admired it in a jewelry store window, Felicia had insisted on buying it for him.

"It's a nice ring," he said to Scaramello.

"Sure, sure. Hey, we've gotten off the track here. You know Georgie Anselmo?"

"The guy who owns Frederico's?" Johnny asked with a frown. "Sure. What about him? He giving you trouble? You want me to pay him a visit?"

Scaramello waved that away.

"No, no, not at all. Georgie and I talk from time to time, and he was telling me about what happened that first night you met Mrs. Brighton. He said there was a little trouble upstairs . . ."

"Nothing important," Johnny said, shrugging it off. "That guy she came in with, Ted Bassingham, came upstairs looking for her and got his nose out of joint because she was with me by then and didn't want to leave with him. He took a poke at me and I put him on the floor, but I didn't really hurt him. Then a couple of Anselmo's men hustled him out of there, and that was the end of it."

"Bassingham's old man is important. Owns a bank and part of a steamship line and a railroad. He's making noises about trying to have you arrested, but I can make sure that doesn't ever happen. Still, it draws attention to me in other parts of town, and I don't like that."

"I'm sorry, Nick," Johnny said, and meant it. "I never intended for that to happen. I just—"

"You just saw a chance to get next to a rich, good-looking woman and took it." Scaramello shook his head. "I could never blame you for that, kid. I'm just saying, keep your wits about you from now on. You're young, sometimes you do things without thinking, especially if there's a woman involved."

"I'll be careful," Johnny promised.

"Like that ten grand, for example."

Johnny frowned and said, "Ten grand? What ten grand?"

"The money you dropped at the roulette wheel in Frederico's that first night, showing off for the lady and betting with money that Georgie advanced to you."

"Oh," Johnny said. "So that's what this is about. Anselmo wants his money." He shook his head. "I'm good for it, Nick, you know that. He'll get it. I'm making good money working for you. I just need to save up a little more."

There was a little bit of truth to that. Johnny *was* making decent money—but he wasn't saving any of it. Even with Felicia picking up the tab for a lot of things, that wasn't enough for him to live the way he wanted to, so just about everything that came in went right back out again.

"Mrs. Brighton has plenty of loot," Scaramello said.

Without thinking about what he was doing, Johnny shook his head, defying his boss.

"I don't mind letting her pay for things, but I haven't asked her for any money outright yet," he said. "I'd just as soon not do that, Nick. But I'm sure if you talk to Anselmo again, he'll understand. Just tell him I'll pay him back when I can. I mean, who's gonna argue with you?"

Scaramello sighed, leaned back in his chair, and nodded.

"That's true," he admitted. "Georgie will go along with whatever I say."

Glad to have that little problem behind him, Johnny leaned forward eagerly and said, "So, you have something you need done this evening?"

"No, no." Scaramello made a small gesture as if sweeping something off the table. "I just wanted to discuss these matters with you. You know I take an interest in the lives of everybody who works for me. I like to look out for all the people in the neighborhood."

"Sure, Nick. That's why everybody loves you."

"Why don't you just go on home . . . or to Mrs. Brighton's place, I should say . . . and enjoy the rest of your evening?"

"You're sure?"

"I'm certain. I'm always certain when I say something."

"All right," Johnny said as he got to his feet. "But if you need anything, anything at all, you just let me know. I owe you a lot, Nick."

"Yeah. Yeah, you do. Good night, kid."

Still feeling vaguely troubled, Johnny left the restaurant. He caught a horse-drawn cab and had the driver take him to Riverside Drive. Earlier in the day, he had told Felicia not to expect him tonight since he knew he was supposed to go see Scaramello at the restaurant and figured the boss would have something for him to do. She had pouted when he told her, but maybe she would be happy to see him. Even if she wanted to stay mad, he was sure he could cajole her out of her bad mood.

"This is good," he told the driver when the cab was still a couple of blocks away from Felicia's house. Johnny stepped out and paid the man, adding a generous tip. He didn't have much ready cash right at the moment, but he could always act as if he did. Maintaining an illusion was a big part of making it a reality.

He strolled along the sidewalk. He enjoyed looking at the big, fancy houses with their well-manicured lawns and flower beds enclosed by ornate wrought iron fences. That was why he'd gotten out of the cab early. Spending time at Felicia's place was fine, but someday he was going to own a house like one of those for himself. He would be the big boss, the man whose word made everybody jump.

He was still half a block from his destination when a figure stepped out of some shadows up ahead and said, "Malatesta."

The voice was dry as dirt and made Johnny think of a grave. Fear jumped up inside him for a second, but then he calmed himself. He didn't have the shillelagh, but he had a knife in his pocket and didn't mind using it. Besides, there was something familiar about the voice, even though he didn't recognize it right away.

Then he did as the man went on, "Nick wanted me to talk to you."

"Anthony!" Johnny exclaimed. He hardly ever heard the bookkeeper speak. That was why he hadn't recognized Migliazzi's voice right away. "You scared me there for a second." Johnny frowned. "What're you doing here? You say Nick sent you to find me? He's got a job for me after all?"

"I said he sent me to talk to you," Migliazzi corrected. "He said that after your conversation, it was apparent you didn't fully understand the situation and required a better explanation."

"A better . . . What're you talking about, Anthony? What situation?"

"The money you lost at Frederico's."

"That again?" Johnny didn't bother trying to keep the irritation out of his voice. "Is Anselmo already crying again? I told Nick, I'll get the guy his money, it's just a matter of time—"

"That's what you don't understand," Migliazzi interrupted. "George Anselmo runs Frederico's, but he doesn't *own* it. Nick does." The bookkeeper moved closer. "You don't owe that ten thousand dollars to Anselmo. You owe it to Nick."

That news surprised Johnny but didn't throw him completely for a loop. Now that he thought about it, he supposed it made sense. Nick didn't like to draw attention to himself. He probably owned a lot of businesses in Little Italy that people didn't know about.

"All right, I get it. I owe the money to Nick. But the same thing still goes. I'll pay him back. I mean, he ought to know better than anybody else that I'm good for it. I work for him, for Pete's sake!"

"He also knows that a debt left outstanding too long starts to stink, like a fish. You can get the money, Malatesta." The bookkeeper leaned his head toward Felicia's house. "All you have to do is ask for it."

"I can't do that! It would make me look like a—"

"Sleazy, low-class gigolo?"

For the second time tonight, anger surged up inside Johnny. He stepped toward Migliazzi and grabbed the man's shirtfront, bunching his fists in the material.

"You little weasel!" Johnny said as he jerked Migliazzi toward him. "Did Nick send you to put the strong-arm on me? *You*? Why, I can bust you in half—"

"No," a voice like distant thunder rumbled behind

Johnny. "Nick just sent Ant'ony to try to talk some sense into you. He sent *me* to strong-arm you."

Johnny let go of Migliazzi and tried to turn around, but he was too late. Pete's massive fist slammed into the side of his head and drove him to the sidewalk.

"'For Pete's sake,' you said. That's funny. You didn't know ol' Pete was standin' right behind you."

Johnny rolled onto his back and held up his hands toward the giant figure looming over him, saying desperately, "Listen, you don't have to do this—"

"Sooner or later, everybody gets too big for his britches and has to be taught a lesson. You got there faster than most, kid. I guess that's because you got too much ambition in you. You think you're too smart to listen to advice. But we can take care o' that."

"Wait!" Johnny cried.

But of course, Pete didn't wait. His foot slammed into Johnny's side. Johnny gasped in agony and tried to curl up around the pain. Pete didn't let him do that. Another kick straightened him out, and then Pete bent over him, got hold of Johnny's shirt in his left hand, and lifted him a little off the sidewalk. The big man's right fist sledged down, again and again, until Johnny didn't feel it smashing into his face anymore. He wasn't even aware of the final two kicks that Pete gave him and didn't know it when he was dumped in the back of a wagon that rolled away from Riverside Drive and the big houses looking down upon it.

CHAPTER 28

Later, Johnny became aware of the swaying, jolting motion of the wagon, but he didn't fully regain consciousness until he was lying in the dirt of an alley behind the rooming house in Little Italy where he lived. He was sprawled on his belly and had grit and a horrible taste in his mouth. He tried to lift his head so he could spit, but when he did that, his head seemed to explode, flying apart in a million pieces. He groaned as he let it slump to the ground again.

The pain inside his skull gradually receded. As it did, he realized how much he hurt all over. At first his brain was too stunned to remember what had happened, but slowly it came back to him. Pete and Migliazzi . . . the money he owed, not to George Anselmo as he had thought but to Nick Scaramello instead . . . the brutal beating Pete had given him just down the block from Felicia's house . . .

Felicia! The thought of her made Johnny lift his head again, and this time he pushed aside the resulting pain. Would Scaramello go after her, try to muscle the ten grand out of her? Johnny didn't think so, but who could be certain what that animal was capable of?

He struggled to his hands and knees. He had to get to her, warn her. But if he showed up looking like this, covered with blood and bruises from a beating, she would be horrified. She would realize he was just a cheap crook and wouldn't have anything else to do with him. He had to get cleaned up first, before he went to see her. He'd probably still look pretty bad, but not as bad as he must now.

When he got to his feet, he couldn't stop the low cry of pain that came from his lips. With every step as he stumbled out of the alley and around to the front of the building, he seemed to feel Pete's fists hammering into him again. A twinge in his side every time he took a breath made him think he probably had a cracked rib.

As long as it was just cracked and not fractured and stabbing into his lung, he could live with it, he told himself.

Scaramello wasn't likely to hurt Felicia. She was his best bet when it came to getting that money. Johnny could get it out of her. Of course he could. He had done the same thing with other women, plenty of times, although usually not for such a large sum.

In fact, the last time he had tried to get ten grand out of a woman had been in Venice, with Denise Jensen. That hadn't worked out. It had almost been his downfall, permanently.

But not this time, he vowed as he started struggling up the steps to the front door of the brownstone. Felicia would give him what he needed.

"Well, what in the world has happened to you? Not that you don't deserve it, whatever it was."

For a second, Johnny thought he'd imagined the gloating voice. Then he turned his head, setting off more little explosions in his head, and saw Ted Bassingham standing there on the sidewalk with another man. In the faint light that came from nearby windows, Johnny could tell that the redheaded man was smirking.

The man with Bassingham was a burly gent in a derby and overcoat, even though the night was fairly warm. He said, "This is the guy, isn't it, Mr. Bassingham? I told you I could find him. Looks like somebody else has already worked him over."

"Yes, Harcourt, this is the man," Bassingham answered. "And I don't really care what else has happened to him tonight. By the time I'm finished with him, he won't be in any shape to ever go near Mrs. Brighton again. Even if he does, his face won't be pretty enough anymore to interest her."

Johnny leaned against the railing alongside the steps and stared in amazement at Bassingham. The twists that fate could take in a man's life!

After a few seconds, he laughed hollowly.

"You're going to teach me a lesson, are you, Ted? You tried that at Frederico's. It didn't work out very well for you, did it?"

Bassingham's face darkened as he scowled. He clenched his fists and stepped forward.

"Tonight's going to be different."

"Yeah, because I'm already hurt. I can't put up much of a fight. And you've got that gorilla there to help you. What's he going to do, hold my arms while you pound me?"

"It'll still be *my* fists landing on that smug face of

yours," Bassingham said. His upper lip curled as he came closer and poised himself to attack.

Johnny never knew where he found the strength, but as Bassingham lunged at him, he clung to the railing, lifted his right leg, and drove the heel of that shoe into the wealthy young man's chest. The kick threw Bassingham backward. He windmilled his arms and would have fallen, but the man called Harcourt was there to catch him.

By then, Johnny had turned to try to run up the steps and get inside the building. If he could lock the front door behind him, he might be safe.

But he couldn't force his legs to move fast enough. Kicking Bassingham had taken too much out of him. Just as he reached the top step, somebody tackled him from behind. He went down hard, banging his knees against the step and causing more pain to shoot through him.

He writhed over onto his back, wincing as the sharp edges of the steps cut into him. Harcourt was the one who had tackled him. The man was big and strong and clearly an experienced brawler. Johnny had no chance against him, especially in his current condition. He had to try to fight, though. He threw a couple of ineffectual punches.

Harcourt didn't even grunt when the blows landed. He batted Johnny's arms aside and clipped him with a short punch to the jaw. Many more of those and he'd be out cold again. He was already starting to feel pretty hazy . . .

His fingers brushed against a lump in his trouser pocket. It was the knife he carried, he realized. Acting mostly on instinct, he slid his hand in there and closed his fingers around the weapon. It opened easily with a flick of his wrist as he pulled it out. He thumbed the button that locked the blade into place. Above him, Harcourt lifted his right fist to strike again.

Johnny drove the knife into his throat.

Johnny couldn't see Harcourt's face that well, but he imagined the man's eyes suddenly got as big around as saucers from the pain and shock. As he made a gurgling sound, wet heat flooded down over Johnny's hand. That was blood, Johnny knew. Instinct—or maybe just fate—had guided his thrust perfectly.

"Don't knock him out," Bassingham called from the sidewalk, blithely unaware of what was really going on. "I want him awake to know what I'm doing to him and suffer through every minute of it."

Harcourt sagged forward. Johnny pulled the knife free, ripping it to the side as he did so to open an even more hideous wound. With a groan of effort, he got his hands on Harcourt's shoulders and rolled the dying man to the side. Having that weight off him was a huge relief to Johnny.

"Harcourt?" Bassingham said, not sounding nearly as confident and arrogant all of a sudden.

Johnny caught hold of the railing with his left hand and hauled himself up. He didn't hurt anymore. It was as if the blood pouring down over him had revitalized him, like bathing in a life-giving elixir. In the back of his mind, he knew that he was just caught up in the heat of battle, operating on the emotions running riot inside him, but he didn't care.

There would be time for aches and pains later—after he had dealt with his enemies.

He lunged down the steps toward Ted Bassingham, who shrieked in terror as he turned to run.

It would be difficult to say who would have won a race between the two young men under normal circumstances. These circumstances were far from normal. Johnny caught up with Bassingham before they had gone a block. He grabbed Bassingham from behind and rode him to the ground. The impact with the sidewalk almost jolted them apart, but Johnny managed to hang on. He tangled his fingers in Bassingham's red hair and jerked the man's head up.

"No!" Bassingham screamed. "Please, no—"

Johnny slashed his throat, pressing down hard on the blade so it cut deep. He thought he felt the steel scrape on Bassingham's spine, but he wasn't sure about that.

Bassingham bucked and heaved underneath him. So much blood came out of the man's neck that it sounded like a bubbling brook back in Sicily. His struggles lasted only a few seconds before he went limp in death.

Johnny put a hand on the corpse's back to brace himself as he pushed to his feet. Only then, when he was standing again, swaying slightly, did he think to look around. A dozen people could have been standing on the street, watching him murder Ted Bassingham.

Instead, the sidewalks were empty, and no wagons or carriages moved along the cobblestones. Johnny lifted his head to peer at the buildings surrounding him. The windows were about equally divided between being darkened and showing light from the rooms behind them. He didn't *see* anybody watching him from any of those windows, but that didn't mean it was impossible. Someone could have been peering out, taking in all the details of the grisly killings, and then pulled back out of sight mere seconds before he checked. He had no way of knowing.

The same was true of witnesses on the street. Somebody could have seen what was going on and ducked into a doorway or an alley.

This was Little Italy. Most people were smart enough not to get mixed up in things that were none of their business.

He couldn't count on all of them to be that discreet. If somebody saw what had happened, they might go to the police. The law was mostly corrupt, just like any other business, but Ted Bassingham was rich and came from a wealthy, powerful family. The police would feel like they had to at least try to solve his murder. And once an investigation started, who knew where it would lead?

Nick Scaramello would protect him. Nick looked after everybody in the neighborhood, didn't he? And Johnny worked for him. He didn't have anything to worry about.

Despite trying to convince himself of that, he couldn't do it. Just tonight, Scaramello had sicced Pete on him, had him beaten up over a piddling ten-grand gambling debt. If the police came after Johnny for murder, Scaramello would protect himself and toss him aside like a piece of discarded trash.

Knowing that, he forced his aching muscles to work again and bent to grasp Bassingham's ankles. He dragged the body off the sidewalk and down some steps into a basement entryway, getting a little satisfaction out of the way Bassingham's head thudded against the steps on the way down, even though the guy couldn't feel it anymore. Moving the corpse might slow things down a little, even though a huge pool of darkening blood remained on the sidewalk as gruesome testimony that something horrible had happened there.

Johnny knew Harcourt weighed too much for him to move, the shape he was in right now. So he circled the buildings and came up to the one where he lived from the back alley. The rear door was locked for the night, but he opened it easily with the knife. He took off his shirt, used it to wipe blood off the blade, then threw it in the incinerator along with his sodden coat. In trousers and undershirt, he climbed the rear stairs to the third floor and let himself in to his room.

He had to move fast now. The flyspecked mirror told him that his face was bruised and swollen and covered with dried blood. He couldn't do anything about the bruises and swelling, but he washed the blood off and by the time he was finished, he thought he looked passable. Like somebody who had been in a tussle, sure, but you couldn't tell by looking at him that already tonight he had been beaten up by a Black Hand enforcer and knifed two guys to death.

Every second that passed gnawed at his guts, but he took care in getting dressed, pulling on some of his best clothes. He had to look like Count Giovanni Malatesta for a while longer tonight. He couldn't stay in New York, not with those murders looming over his head, but if he just panicked and ran, he would do so with almost no money. He would be broke in no time, and then what would he do?

Once he was satisfied that he looked as good as he

could under the circumstances, he left the building through the back door, the way he had come in. Somewhere, several blocks away, a police whistle sounded. Had somebody finally reported Harcourt's body and the big puddle of blood on the sidewalk?

Johnny didn't know, but he wasn't going to hang around to find out.

"Oh, merciful heavens!" Felicia exclaimed when she saw Johnny's face. She tightened the belt of the fine silk robe around her waist. "What happened to you, Giovanni?"

The butler hadn't wanted to show him into the parlor and awaken Felicia, who evidently had turned in early, but Johnny had persuaded him to do so by claiming it was an emergency. That wasn't a lie, and his battered state must have helped the butler believe him.

"Were you in an accident?" Felicia went on.

"You could say that. I trusted a fellow I shouldn't have. Is that an accident or just a stupid mistake?"

On the way here, Johnny had spent quite a bit of time figuring out exactly what he was going to say. In his experience, a mixture of truth and fiction usually worked best, especially with a little humble chagrin thrown in for good measure.

For that reason, it sounded genuine—and was—when he went on, "I made a foolish wager a while back, *cara mia*, and lost a considerable amount of money to a man I believed was a friend. Now he's pressing me for the money."

"Can't you just pay him?"

"Of course I can . . . once some funds I'm expecting arrive from Sicily. Unfortunately, they won't be here for at least another week."

"Surely the man can wait that long."

Johnny shrugged and said, "I certainly thought so. But when I suggested that, he took exception and . . . well . . ."

He gestured helplessly toward the bruises on his face.

"That's terrible! You should go to the police."

"Over an illegal gambling debt?" Johnny smiled ruefully and shook his head. "I do not believe that would be wise, *cara mia.*"

She stepped closer to him, put a hand on his arm. Her hair was a little tousled, and without cosmetics the lines on her face were more visible than usual, but she was still lovely.

"I can loan you the money, Giovanni, dearest."

Without hesitating, he responded with an emphatic shake of his head.

"I could never do such a thing," he said. "It would bring dishonor on me, and upon my whole family."

"I don't see how in the world it would! There's nothing dishonorable about a friend helping out another friend. And actually . . . I believe we're more than friends."

He smiled, even though it hurt his face, and reached up to stroke his fingertips over her cheek.

"Oh yes, *cara mia,* much more than friends."

She rested her hands on his shoulders and said, "Besides, the rest of your family would never even know about it. You'll just pay me back as soon as your money comes in."

"At what rate of interest?" he asked, still smiling.

Felicia laughed. "I don't need any interest," she assured him. "Especially since it'll be for such a short time. However, if you wanted to pay me back a little bit extra . . . I'm sure we could figure out a way for you to do that . . ."

Her voice trailed off, but it didn't matter because the next instant Johnny kissed her and would have silenced her anyway.

After a long, passionate moment, Felicia broke the kiss and asked, "How much do you need, anyway?"

Johnny started to ask for the whole ten, but then he realized he didn't actually need that much. If what he intended to do didn't work out, it wouldn't matter how much money he had. A corpse floating in the East River couldn't spend anything.

"Five thousand," he said. "A mere bagatelle."

"Well . . . maybe not quite that mere," Felicia said with a slight frown. "But I can certainly manage to let you have that much. I can write you a bank draft—"

She stopped as Johnny shook his head.

"It would be better in cash, so I can settle things with my former friend tonight," he said. "I don't want to have to deal with that scoundrel for one minute longer than absolutely necessary!"

"After what he did to you, I can understand why. Still, I'm not sure I have that much cash in the house. I'll have to look . . ."

Again, Johnny shook his head, more vehemently this time.

"No, this is a sign," he said. "I should never have asked you. It was wrong of me."

"Don't be ridiculous. Anyway, I asked you, you

didn't ask me. You didn't even want to tell me what happened to you, remember?" She leaned forward, pecked his lips again. "Wait right here. I'll go see what I can rustle up. All right?"

"If you insist, my *bella signorina*."

She left him there in the parlor for ten minutes that seemed much longer. When she returned, she handed him a bundle wrapped in brown paper and tied with a string.

"There's just over four thousand dollars there," she told him. "I also put in a little bag with some jewelry that's worth at least another thousand. Do you think your friend . . . former friend . . . will be willing to take them instead of the rest of the cash?"

"I think so," Johnny said. "But I hate to take your precious jewelry . . ."

"That's all right. It's true, the pieces do have some . . . sentimental value. But my late husband gave them to me, and we both know what an ass he was."

"So you have said, *cara mia.*"

"It's the truth," Felicia said. "I'd rather them go to help you than just sit in a jewelry box gathering dust." She pressed her hands against his as he held the bundle. "Take them and go deal with this terrible man and then come back to me. Unless you have something else you need to do tonight . . . ?"

"Nothing that could be as important as making you happy." He tucked the bundle of money and jewels under his arm and slid his other hand behind her neck, cupping her head as he leaned closer to her. "You have saved my life, *cara mia.* I feel for you something I have never felt before for any woman in my life."

"And you've saved me, too," she whispered. "Saved me from a life of turning to simpering fools like Ted Bassingham just to relieve my boredom."

"You need never think of Signor Bassingham again," he told her honestly, then kissed her again with enough passion to leave her breathless as he smiled and slipped out of the parlor, taking the bundle with him.

Forty-five nerve-wracking minutes later, with his muscles aching and his chest tight from constantly looking over his shoulder for the police or Nick Scaramello, Johnny Malatesta left New York City on a train bound for Chicago.

By the time Count Giovanni Malatesta left Chicago a couple of months after arriving there, he had acquired not only a more extensive wardrobe but also a servant to go along with it. For a change, Lady Luck had been kind to him at the gambling tables, and he had run his stake up to a considerable amount, enough to live comfortably in a hotel in his pose as an expatriate Sicilian nobleman. He had enough money that he could have sent what he owed back to Nick Scaramello, but why would he do that? Scaramello would never find him.

Then one day, while sitting in an expensive restaurant and enjoying a brandy and a cigar after a fine dinner, he had chanced to be glancing through a newspaper when a familiar name leaped out of a story at him.

The story was about the famous rancher and gunfighter Smoke Jensen, detailing some contretemps or other that had involved a great deal of violence and bloodletting, and evidently Jensen's own daughter had been mixed up in it.

"Denise," Malatesta breathed as he looked at the newspaper. Evidently, she had returned home to her family's ranch, this time to stay. A smile spread slowly across his face. *"Cara mia."*

The one who had gotten away from him. But not again, Malatesta vowed. Not this time.

CHAPTER 29

New York City

The butler opened the door of the late Cyrus Brighton's study and announced, "Mr. Crabtree is here, madam."

"Show him in, Dawes," Felicia Brighton said from behind the desk that had once been her husband's. The smooth, polished top was empty except for a folder containing bank drafts and a pen and inkwell.

She was dressed soberly and conservatively in a dark blue dress. Her hair was pulled back tightly behind her head. The severe appearance was a far cry from how she had looked during the days and nights she had spent gadding about the finest restaurants, clubs, and theaters in New York, always with a handsome young man on her arm.

There had been no handsome young men since Johnny Malatesta. And the way she looked now accurately reflected the bitterness and hate that threatened to consume her.

Dawes opened the door again and ushered a man in a brown tweed suit into the study. The newcomer was tall and broad-shouldered, a little thick through the chest and midsection, but from the way he carried himself, it was obvious his bulk was muscle, not fat. His face was long and rather horsey. He held a brown derby in his left hand, revealing that he had graying sandy hair. He nodded to Felicia and said, "Ma'am."

"Mr. Crabtree," she said as she rose to her feet behind the desk. "I take it you have news? I hope you do."

"Yes, ma'am. I've received a wire from one of my associates in Chicago. Count Giovanni Malatesta was there less than two weeks ago."

"He's still using the same name?" Felicia couldn't quite keep the surprise out of her voice.

"Apparently. My man found several hotel employees who said he stayed in the place where they work, and the description they gave fits your man to a T."

"He's hardly *my* man, Mr. Crabtree." She almost added *Not anymore,* but she controlled the impulse. One only revealed so much of oneself in the presence of the hired help.

"Well, the man you're looking for, anyway," Angus Crabtree said clumsily.

"Indeed he is." Felicia shook her head and laughed quietly. "And to tell the truth, I'm not really surprised that he's still using the same name. He was always the sort who believed he could get by on his charm and good looks. He never actually had to *think* all that much."

"No, ma'am," Crabtree responded, with the air of a man who didn't know what else to say.

Felicia thought about what he had told her and then went on, "You said Giovanni was there two weeks ago. He's no longer in Chicago?"

"Not at the same hotel. He checked out. He might be staying at some other hotel under a different name. Or he may have left Chicago entirely. I have my operative working on it."

"That's not good enough, Mr. Crabtree."

He gestured with the derby he held and said, "I don't know what else I can—"

"I want you to go to Chicago yourself. Now that you've picked up Giovanni's trail, I don't want you to lose it. You *are* regarded as one of the best private detectives in the country, aren't you?"

"Yes, ma'am," he said. "Twenty years' experience with the Pinkertons before I started my own agency, and I always got the job done."

"Yes, but the *way* you got the job done is why you eventually had to leave the Pinkerton agency and go out on your own, isn't it?"

Crabtree frowned. "I don't know what you're talking about, Mrs. Brighton."

With a determined air, she leaned forward and rested her hands on the desk.

"I'm talking about how your methods were too extreme even for the Pinkertons, an organization notorious for the brutality of some of its operatives." Felicia straightened and smiled. "Honestly, Mr. Crabtree, what does it take to be too much for goons who make their living breaking strikes . . . and heads . . . to stomach?"

Crabtree's jaw tightened. His face flushed with anger. He said, "I don't care for being talked to that way."

"And I don't care what you care for," Felicia said. "Not as long as I'm paying your fee."

"Maybe we'll just say the job's over." Crabtree clapped the derby back on his head. "Good day, missus, and good luck finding that scoundrel you're after—"

"One more moment, sir." Felicia opened the folder of bank drafts and took out one she had already written. She pushed it across the desk toward him and said, "Take a look at this, please."

She could tell that Crabtree, despite his anger, was too curious—and too mercenary—not to look. He scowled as he stepped closer to the desk and peered down at the piece of paper. The scowl went away, replaced by a look of surprise.

"That's a lot of money," he said.

"Five thousand dollars," Felicia agreed. "A small fortune for some people . . . including, I suspect, private detectives."

"It's worth that to you for me to find that fellow Malatesta?"

"No, Mr. Crabtree. It's worth that much to me for you to find Count Giovanni Malatesta . . . and kill him."

Big Rock

Brice Rogers stepped into the sheriff's office and said, "You wanted to see me, Monte?"

Even though Monte Carson was much older than Brice, an informality existed between the two of them because they were fellow lawmen, although Brice was always careful to be respectful to the older man when other folks were around.

Right now Monte was alone in the office, sitting

behind the big, scarred desk he had been using for two decades. He pushed several pieces of paper across the desk toward Brice and said, "I finally got around to checking through all the reward dodgers for those bushwhackers from the other day. Those are the three whose carcasses got brought in."

Brice spread out the three wanted posters and studied them.

"Gene Rice, Seth Billings, and Edgar Norris," he read the names. "All three of them with pretty bad reputations. Murder, attempted murder, robbery, rape . . ."

"Yeah, but here's something interesting." Monte tapped the notice with Gene Rice's name and picture on it and went on, "Rice is known to be part of a bunch that's headed up by a man named Ned Yeager. Remember that shoot-out at the train station?"

"It'd be hard to forget it," Brice said.

"Well, the two men you and Denny killed that day were also part of Yeager's gang."

Brice's eyebrows rose.

"So Yeager was responsible for both ambushes?"

Monte nodded and said, "It sure looks like it."

Brice frowned in thought and scraped a fingernail along his jawline. After a moment, he said, "That sort of explains something else I've been thinking about. When we checked out the bodies after the shooting was over, Denny claimed never to have seen any of these three before, but with one of them I got the feeling that maybe she wasn't being a hundred percent truthful." He rested a finger on Gene Rice's wanted poster. "This one."

Monte leaned back in his chair and nodded.

"She recognized the varmint from that day at the train station," he said.

"That's my guess, too," Brice agreed. "Which is just one more indication that this Ned Yeager is the one who's trying to kill the count. Maybe you'd better ask Signor Malatesta about that."

Monte sighed. "I already did, when I realized Yeager might've been involved with that first attack. He claimed he has no idea who Yeager is or why some western owlhoot would want him dead."

"He's lying," Brice snapped.

"The count? Maybe. Ambushes like that don't come out of nowhere, especially when the fellas doing the ambushing are determined enough to try a second time."

"And maybe a third?"

"Can happen," Monte allowed. "It's probably going to get on the count's nerves, but I think I need to have another talk with him."

"What about those other two?" Brice asked. "Billings and Norris. I don't see anything on these posters to indicate that they rode with Yeager."

"Maybe they didn't, until now. After Murtagh and Morrell got killed at the train station, Yeager could have gone off to recruit some more gunmen before he made another try for Malatesta. You said there were six bushwhackers on the road to the Sugarloaf. Yeager might've found three men to throw in with him to replace the two who were killed earlier."

Brice nodded and said, "Makes sense. Are you going to see Malatesta now?"

Monte scraped his chair back and stood up.

"I thought I would. You want to come along?"

"It's not a case that falls under federal jurisdiction, but if you don't have any objection . . ."

Monte grinned. "I don't. I wouldn't have invited you if I did."

"Then I'd be curious to hear what the count has to say."

Denny and Smoke swung down from their saddles in front of Longmont's. As they wrapped their reins around the hitch rail, Smoke said, "I'll walk down to the telegraph office and send that wire while you go to Goldstein's, then I'll meet you back here. We'll get a bite to eat and say hello to Louis."

"Sure," Denny nodded. Normally, she would have taken more of an interest in the telegram her father was sending to a cattle buyer in Kansas City. She knew that in all likelihood, she would be running the Sugarloaf someday, so she usually tried to learn as much as she could about every little detail of operating a large, lucrative cattle business.

These days, however, she was having trouble concentrating on such things. She didn't like feeling that way, but she supposed it would just have to work itself out.

Besides, her mother had asked her to stop in at Goldstein's and pick up a bolt of cloth she had ordered, and Denny had agreed to do so.

Smoke strode off toward the telegraph office. Denny glanced toward the entrance of Longmont's. As far back as she could remember, she had known that her brother was named after her father's old friend Louis Longmont. But when Smoke said "Louis," sometimes she had to stop and think about which one he meant. She hadn't grown up here, so to her, "Louis" was always first and foremost her brother.

She was pondering that, knowing that it was really irrelevant, and it cost her a few seconds. When the door of Longmont's swung open and Count Giovanni Malatesta stepped out onto the boardwalk, followed by Arturo Vincenzo, Denny inwardly cursed the delay that had brought her face-to-face with the man.

Malatesta's face lit up with a smile.

"Denise!" he said. "How wonderful to see you again." Then he pretended to duck and look around nervously. "Should I be searching for gunmen who seek to ambush us?" He straightened and let out a booming laugh.

Denny reined in the surge of anger she felt and said, "Having somebody shooting at you is no laughing matter."

Malatesta sobered and nodded.

"Indeed it is not," he agreed. "Especially when such incidents place you in danger as well. Never would I wish that a single hair on your head should be harmed, *cara mia.*"

Denny was about to tell him again to stop using that endearment when someone called Malatesta's name from the street.

"Count Malatesta! Could we talk to you for a minute?"

Denny turned her head to look over her shoulder. Sheriff Monte Carson was the one who had spoken, but he wasn't alone. Brice Rogers was with him, the two lawmen walking side by side across the street toward the boardwalk in front of Longmont's.

Denny saw the frown that creased Brice's forehead.

He was unhappy about something. Was it the sight of her standing there talking to Malatesta?

Brice wasn't stupid. Surely he had figured out by now that she detested the man. How she felt about Brice . . . how she would feel about him in the future . . . she couldn't decide those things right now, but he couldn't possibly be jealous of Malatesta. Could he?

A glance back toward the boardwalk caught the angry glare that flashed quickly across Malatesta's face. He wasn't any happier to see Brice than Brice was to see him. Was that because he regarded Brice as a rival? Could he seriously hope to rekindle a romance with the woman he had betrayed so callously in Venice?

Brice and Monte Carson came to a stop, and that left Denny standing directly between Brice and Malatesta. It was an uncomfortable position, and she wasn't the only one who noticed that.

"My word," Arturo said, "this is a bit awkward, isn't it?"

CHAPTER 30

"Arturo, return to the hotel," Malatesta snapped.

"Of course, sir," the servant murmured. He looked suitably chastened as he bowed slightly and scurried off, Denny thought. At heart, Malatesta was a feudal lord, or at least that was what he aspired to be.

"Sorry to interrupt your conversation, Count," Brice said. He didn't sound sorry at all. "The sheriff and I have a few questions we'd like to ask you."

"If this is about those men who attacked us the other day—" Malatesta began.

"It is," Monte interrupted him. "I've identified them."

"Highwaymen, no doubt, who would have attacked any travelers they happened upon, with the intent of robbing and probably killing them."

"Not exactly," Monte said. "I think some of them were the same bunch who came after you at the train station, and the others were new guns who had thrown in with them. I suspect the man behind both attempts was an outlaw named Ned Yeager."

"Yes, you spoke to me before of this man called

Yeager. I never heard of him until you mentioned him to me. I have no idea why he would want to harm me. Really, I don't know what else I can tell you, Sheriff, and frankly, I'm getting a little impatient with this persistent but futile questioning."

Monte said, "I'm just trying to get to the bottom of this. I don't like it when folks start getting shot at in my bailiwick."

"I'm sure the ones being shot at like it even less."

Monte looked like he was about to lose his temper, but he controlled it and said, "I'm going to send some telegrams to other lawmen about Yeager, see if I can find out anything about what else he's been up to recently. Maybe the answer is in that."

"Perhaps. I hope so." Malatesta tilted his hand to the side in an eloquent gesture. "My apologies, Sheriff. This is as trying and frustrating to me as it is to you."

"Well, that's probably true. I'll let you know if I find out anything." Monte paused. "And if you think of anything you haven't told me so far, you'll let *me* know, I hope."

"Of course."

"I'll let you get back to your conversation with Miss Jensen. Sorry for the interruption."

"No apology necessary, Sheriff," Denny said. She looked narrow-eyed at Malatesta. "The count and I were finished talking. In fact, I think we said everything we have to say to each other a long time ago."

Malatesta frowned and pursed his lips but didn't make any other response.

"I'm headed over to the mercantile," Denny added as she turned in that direction.

"I'll walk with you," Brice said.

She started to tell him that she didn't need any company, but then she reconsidered. With her brother gone back East, Brice was the best friend she had in Big Rock. And as she remembered a few moments they had shared in the past, usually right before all hell broke loose, she had to admit they were more than just friends. They had the potential to be more than that, anyway.

So she made no objection as she started toward Goldstein's, and Brice fell in alongside her.

After a moment, he ventured, "I get the feeling you wouldn't mind if Count Malatesta were to just rattle his hocks out of Big Rock."

"Don't you feel the same way?"

Brice shrugged and admitted, "It would be all right with me if he was gone. I don't have anything against the man, personally, I suppose, but for whatever reason, I just don't like him."

Denny drew in a deep breath, blew it out, and said, "I *do* have something against the man. The preachers say that we shouldn't hate anybody, but sometimes, with some people, hate's mighty hard to let go of."

"You don't owe me any explanations, Denny."

"No. I don't reckon I do." She stopped and leaned both hands on an empty hitch rail they had been passing. She looked intently at Brice, who also stopped, and went on, "But you know what? You and I have been through enough trouble together that I know I can trust you. It might feel good to get some of this weight off my shoulders."

"I'm happy to listen," Brice said. He rested a hand

on the hitch rail, too, not touching either of her hands but not far from one of them.

"You know I was acquainted with the count while my brother and I were in Europe. We met him while we were in Venice. And you're smart enough to figure out that he, well, pursued me. Romantically speaking."

Brice suddenly looked like maybe he wished he hadn't been so willing to listen after all. Almost like he wished he was somewhere else.

"Don't worry, I'm not going to start spouting a lot of things that are none of your business. You may be a deputy marshal, but this isn't a confession. Let's just say that Count Malatesta and I were friends for a while, over there. And then he did something that hurt me."

"It must have been pretty bad, the way you've been treating him ever since he showed up here in Big Rock."

"Bad enough," Denny said. "But after Louis and I left Venice, I didn't figure I'd ever see him again. I just put the whole thing behind me." She paused, then added with some venom, "I sure as blazes haven't been pining away over the son of a—"

"No, I understand that," Brice broke in.

"Anyway, that's why I wish he would just clear out. Given what I know about him, I can't help but think that he's up to no good."

"But what could he want here in Big Rock?"

Denny just tilted her head a little to the side and gave him a look.

"I mean, besides trying to start things up with you again," Brice went on hastily.

"That's probably enough. He's a swindler, Brice. He probably figures he can make up with me, get me to fall in love with him again, and wind up marrying me. He may believe that would land him the Sugarloaf."

"Fall in love with him *again*?" Brice repeated.

Denny felt her face growing warm. "I told you, I'm not confessing anything. But for a man like Malatesta, who preys on women, the Sugarloaf would be a mighty tempting target." She frowned. "And if he needs money, that usually means he's in trouble. In Venice, there was a man trying to kill him over some gambling debts."

"That would explain the attempts on his life here," Brice said with a note of excitement in his voice. "Somebody's after him, and they've hired Ned Yeager to kill him. Malatesta's hoping that if he can land you . . . and the Sugarloaf . . . that will be enough to get him out from under."

"That all makes sense," Denny said, nodding.

"You think it's the same hombre he had trouble with in Venice?"

"Maybe. But to tell the truth, Giovanni's the sort of conniving scoundrel who's going to make enemies everywhere he goes. So there's really no telling who's got a grudge against him right now."

Brice gave her a funny look for a long moment, until Denny finally lost her patience and said, "What?"

"There's no chance he's going to win you over, is there?"

"Not a chance in the world."

Denny glanced along the street and saw that Malatesta had lingered on the boardwalk in front of

Longmont's. He was still standing there smoking a cigar, and although he wasn't trying to be obvious about it, she could tell that he was watching them. She reached over with her right hand, lightly touched Brice's forearm with an air of familiarity and intimacy, and smiled.

Brice smiled, too, but he said quietly, "You're just doing that for his benefit, aren't you, because he's still keeping an eye on us?"

"Am I?" Denny asked with a slight toss of her head. "You tell me."

Denny would have—but honestly, at this moment, she didn't know the true answer to Brice's question.

Malatesta puffed hard enough on the cigar that a cloud of smoke wreathed his head. Anger roiled his guts as he watched Denny talking to Brice Rogers. He didn't stare directly at them, but he saw them plainly enough from the corner of his eye.

His teeth clamped down on the cigar as Denny rested her hand on Rogers's forearm. Malatesta knew from experience the warmth of that touch, knew how it could start a man's heart beating faster. He thought for a second that she might actually lean over and kiss the marshal. The minx was perfectly capable of doing that just to get under his skin.

Instead, she turned and started on toward the mercantile that she had announced as her destination. Rogers walked with her. A moment later, they both disappeared into the store.

Malatesta dropped the cigar butt onto the boardwalk, ground it out with the heel of his shoe, and kicked the shredded remains into the street. He needed a drink, but he didn't turn and go back into Longmont's even though it was the best such establishment in Big Rock. He was in the mood for something a little . . . less civilized.

And as his eyes narrowed in thought, an idea began to stir in the back of his head.

CHAPTER 31

The Brown Dirt Cowboy Saloon had been a fixture in Big Rock for more than two decades. Plenty of other saloons had come and gone in that time, but the Brown Dirt Cowboy was still there, catering to customers who wouldn't be comfortable drinking in a fancy place like Longmont's.

Besides, the girls who worked at Longmont's, lovely though they might be, didn't go upstairs with the customers or even make arrangements to meet a fella somewhere else after work, while the gals at the Brown Dirt Cowboy did a steady business in the saloon's second-floor rooms. From time to time, the respectable ladies of Big Rock got their noses out of joint and tried to convince the sheriff to shut down that part of the operation, but as long as the town council didn't make it illegal, Monte Carson wasn't going to step in on somebody else's say-so.

Claude Brown, who'd been running the place all these years, always told his girls to be discreet. No drugging and robbing the customers, and if any of the cowboys got too rough, the girls were supposed to let Claude know and he would have his burly bartenders and bouncers take care of them. Just because he sold booze and soiled doves, Claude liked to say, that didn't mean the place had to be a hellhole.

But despite Claude's best intentions, trouble *did* break out from time to time, and one such incident appeared to be taking place now as Malatesta rested his hands on top of the batwings at the entrance and peered over them into the saloon.

The brawl had already overturned several tables and broken a couple of chairs. The action at the moment appeared to be concentrated at the rear of the barroom, where a knot of men surrounded and pummeled the objects of their wrath.

The two men being ganged up on fought valiantly against what appeared to be overwhelming odds. Those odds improved when one of the battlers managed to grab a chair and swing it like a club. He lambasted a couple of the attackers and knocked them to the floor, where they promptly got tangled up with the legs of other brawlers. While those men were off-balance, the second would-be victim went on the offensive and plowed into them with his arms spread wide, swooping in on his opponents like a vulture. He drove them off their feet, and that created an opening for his companion to wade through, still swinging the chair right and left around him.

As far as Malatesta could tell, so far the battle had been fought with fists instead of weapons, other than the chair currently being wielded. No guns or knives were in evidence. But that changed suddenly as one of the men who had been knocked down struggled back to his feet and clawed a revolver from the holster on his hip. He was behind the two battlers at the center of the action and undoubtedly intended to gun them down without warning.

Malatesta moved fast then, letting his instincts guide him as he often did. He slapped the batwings aside, moved into the saloon, and plucked his own pistol from the shoulder rig under his coat. He lined the gun on the man who had just pulled iron, eared back the hammer, and said in a loud, clear voice that cut through the hubbub, "Don't."

The sharp command caught the attention of the man trying to raise his gun so he could open fire on the two battlers. He froze before his Colt came level. As he stared into the muzzle of Malatesta's pistol, he gulped and said, "Don't shoot, mister!"

The confrontation, with its threat of imminent gunplay, made the other men stop what they were doing, too. The man with the chair held it poised above his head, ready to bash in somebody else's skull. His friend, who had gotten to his feet after tackling several of their opponents, stood with his right fist cocked beside his ear while his left hand held the shirt of the man he was about to punch.

"That's enough from all of you," a new voice said. Paunchy, balding Claude Brown braced a sawed-off shotgun on the bar and let his finger caress the triggers. Staring into the twin muzzles of a scattergun like that was enough to restore reason to most men's brains.

"Break it up now," Brown went on. "Lukens, pouch that iron."

The man who had been about to start the ball when Malatesta threw down on him swallowed and said, "But . . . but, Claude, that fancy pants is still pointin' his gun at me!"

"He's trying to stop trouble, not start it," Brown replied. "Now holster it!"

Grudgingly, the man lowered his gun and slid it back into leather.

"Good," Brown went on. "Now get out."

"It was Bridwell and Nelson who started the fight!"

"And I'm ending it. You know the rules. I don't kick up too much fuss about fighting as long as you boys pay for the damages, but when somebody brings a gun out, that's all she wrote. If you start blowing holes in each other, Monte Carson'll use that as an excuse to close me down. I don't want that."

Muttering to himself about how unfair life was, Lukens shuffled out of the saloon, circling wide around Malatesta and casting angry but nervous glances at him as he did so.

From behind the bar, Claude Brown said, "You can put your own gun up now, mister. Or rather, Count, isn't it? I've seen you around and heard talk about you."

Malatesta smiled as he holstered his pistol and said, "Yes, my good man, Count Giovanni Malatesta, at your service."

Brown replaced the shotgun on a shelf under the bar and came around the end of it.

"It's an honor to have you in my place, Count. We don't get many Italian noblemen in here."

One of the cowboys laughed and said, "I reckon this here fella's the first one, Claude."

"Yeah, you're probably right about that." Brown looked around and went on, "Fight's over. Go back to what you were doing."

The swamper and a bartender, both wearing

aprons, started setting up overturned tables and chairs, putting things back to rights. The hostile atmosphere in the room evaporated surprisingly quickly.

That was typical of these westerners, Malatesta had learned. They were swift to anger and equally swift to forget about it. They didn't hang on to grudges as stubbornly as people in the old country did.

At least that was true of the men. The women— and Denise Jensen was a prime example—weren't like that. Clearly, Denise had nursed her hatred of him all this time. Women were unforgiving no matter where they came from, Malatesta supposed.

"Let me buy you a drink, sir," Brown went on, smoothing down the few strands of hair on his head as he did so.

One of the men who had been at the center of the brawl sauntered up and said, "You're gonna have to wait your turn, Claude. Me and Dave owe this fella a drink first. If it wasn't for him, Lukens mighta ventilated one of us."

Brown's bushy eyebrows lowered, but he said, "All right, Bridwell, but don't think I've forgotten that it was you and Nelson who actually caused that trouble."

"Naw, it weren't," the man called Bridwell responded. "When that hombre started gettin' too rough with Rosemarie, we had to step in. She's our favorite, you know."

"Yeah, I know," Brown said drily. "But I expect the two of you to kick in half the damages if you want to keep drinking here. I'll split up the rest of it amongst the other fellas in the ruckus."

"That ain't hardly fair—"

"This is my place," Brown cut in. "I decide what's fair."

"Well, we'll hash it out later, I reckon," Bridwell said with a shrug. "Come on over here and sit down with us, mister. Claude, send over a bottle."

Brown rolled his eyes but nodded in agreement.

Malatesta went with Bridwell and Nelson to one of the tables and sat down with them. Bridwell stuck his hand across the table and introduced himself.

"Benjy Bridwell. This here's my pard Dave Nelson."

Bridwell was a tall, rangy, lantern-jawed and carrot-topped man. His friend was shorter, with a round face and a drooping, dark mustache. Each had a suitably hard-nosed look, however, and Malatesta had seen with his own eyes that they were capable fighters.

"I'm Count Giovanni Malatesta," he said as he shook hands with them.

"We've heard about you," Bridwell said. Evidently he was the more talkative member of the duo. "I reckon ever'body in Big Rock has. It ain't every day some fancy nobleman from Europe shows up in these parts."

"Please, I'm just a man like any other," Malatesta said, knowing that employing a common touch would be effective with men such as these. "I enjoy a drink . . . and a good fight every now and then."

Bridwell chuckled and waggled his eyebrows. "And a pretty gal?"

"Well, of course," Malatesta answered with a smile.

"Well, then, here you go! The prettiest gal around here, and she's brung a bottle o' whiskey with her!"

Malatesta looked up to see that one of the saloon girls had approached the table. She was young, probably nineteen or twenty, and lacked the hard lines in her face that women in her profession inevitably acquired fairly quickly. Chestnut curls flowed over her shoulders, except for two strands that spiraled down in front of her ears. When she smiled, she looked almost innocent.

There was nothing innocent about the short, low-cut dress she wore, though, which revealed a goodly amount of her modestly curved figure. She carried a tray with a bottle and three glasses on it, and when she leaned over to place it on the table, the men got an even better look at her charms.

"Here you go, fellas," she said. "There's just, uh, one thing. Claude says you have to go ahead and pay for the bottle . . ."

"Why, sure," Bridwell said. He dug a couple of silver dollars out of his pocket and handed them to the girl. "There you go." He caught hold of her wrist as she started to pull her hand back. "How about you join us, Rosemarie?"

"As soon as I give Claude that money," she promised.

Bridwell nodded and let go of her wrist. As she walked away, he leaned back in his chair and sighed.

"Pretty little thing, ain't she? I would say she's as pretty as a speckled pup, but I ain't never seen no dog that looks as good as her!"

"The conflict was over the young lady, I believe you said?"

"Yep. Rosemarie's our favorite. We always pay her a visit when we drift through these parts."

"You don't work on one of the ranches in the area?" Malatesta asked.

"Naw, we tried cowboyin', but we wasn't really cut out for it."

"Then, what *do* you do?"

Nelson spoke for the first time, saying in a flat, hard voice, "This and that." His tone warned that it wouldn't be wise to pry further into their affairs.

Malatesta nodded. He kept his face impassive, but inside he was quite satisfied with what fate had delivered into his lap.

Bridwell poured drinks and slid glasses over to Malatesta and Nelson. Picking up his own glass, he said, "Here's to you, Count. You done us a big favor, and if there's ever anything we can do for you, all you gotta do is ask."

Malatesta could have put his plan into motion right then and there, but he decided to wait a little longer, until he was absolutely sure he was proceeding correctly. He smiled, nodded, and said, "And to you two fine gentlemen of the range, as well."

They downed the whiskey, then Bridwell chuckled and said, "Like I told you, we don't exactly ride the range, do we, Dave? More like the trails where most folks don't go."

Nelson frowned, as if he wished Bridwell would stop talking, but he didn't say anything.

Rosemarie returned to the table from the bar, where she had been talking to Claude Brown for the past couple of minutes. Malatesta got to his feet and held the empty chair for her, an act which appeared to surprise her quite a bit. He figured common courtesy wasn't all that common in a place like the Brown Dirt Cowboy.

"Would you care for a drink?" he asked her as he resumed his seat.

"Oh my, no. I don't drink whiskey." She lowered her voice confidentially. "What you see the girls drinking with customers is just tea."

"Oh," Malatesta said, who had known perfectly well what girls who worked in places like this drank with their customers.

Keeping her voice low, Rosemarie went on, "Claude's over there toting up the damages. He'll expect you to pay up before you leave, boys."

Bridwell downed another shot and then toyed with his empty glass as he said, "Well, now, you see, that's gonna be a problem. Happens that those two silver dollars I gave you, darlin', were the last coins in my pockets."

"What about folding money?"

That question brought another laugh from Bridwell.

"I sorta remember what greenbacks look like," he said, "but it's been a long spell since I seen any of 'em!"

"So you're broke?" Rosemarie said in a tone of dismay.

"As can be," Bridwell confirmed.

Her features hardened a little. "How were you going to pay me, then, if you took me upstairs?"

"Well, we sorta figured—"

"Never mind," she cut him off. "I know what you figured. You were counting on me taking pity on you. You two have pulled that stunt too often—"

"A moment," Malatesta said. The other three at the table looked at him in surprise.

"I'm sorry, Count," Bridwell said. "You shouldn't ought to be burdened with listenin' to our problems."

"Not at all. Actually, I believe I may be in a position to help you with your problems." Malatesta looked around at all of them, including Rosemarie in his speculative gaze. "Including you, my dear."

"Me?" she said as her eyebrows rose.

"Indeed." The vague plan he'd had when he came in here had not only come together unexpectedly well, it had even expanded. "I'd like to discuss this further with you, but perhaps in some place more private. I'm sure you have a room upstairs."

"You want to go upstairs?" Rosemarie looked confused. "You mean . . . all four of us?"

Malatesta thought about it and shrugged. "Why not?"

"Well . . . if folks see us all going up together . . . they're liable to think . . . things."

Malatesta reached over, took her hand, and said, "My dear, I've long since learned to stop worrying about what people think. I only worry about what I want. And I'm reasonably sure that the three of you can help me get it." He squeezed her hand and smiled. "As for anything else . . . there's no reason we can't all enjoy the extra benefits of my plan."

CHAPTER 32

Brice walked with Denny all the way to Goldstein's Mercantile and went inside with her while she picked up the bolt of cloth her mother had ordered. They didn't talk anymore about Count Malatesta as they strolled back toward Longmont's, and he was grateful for that. He would always listen to anything Denny wanted to tell him, but he figured there were some things it was just better for him not to know.

They found Smoke waiting inside, sitting at a table with Louis Longmont. The gambler and former gunman greeted Denny with a hug and shook hands with Brice.

"I have my cook preparing steaks for the three of us," Longmont said with a gesture that took in himself, Smoke, and Denny. "Would you like to join us, Brice? I can always have him throw another steak on the fire, as they say."

"Actually," Smoke said before the lawman could reply, "I've got a message for you, Brice. Eddie over at the telegraph office is looking for you. Seems he's got an important wire for you. He was going to send one of his boys to look for you."

"Nobody's said anything about that to me until now," Brice said. "You reckon I ought to go on over to the office and see what it's about?"

"That's up to you," Smoke told him with a shrug. "I just told Eddie that if I saw you, I'd pass the word along. I didn't know you and Denny were together."

"We ran into each other earlier and walked down to Goldstein's," Denny explained. She didn't offer any more details than that.

"You get that cloth for your mother?"

"Tied to my saddle outside."

Brice said, "I'd better go see what that telegram's about. So long, Denny." He nodded to the other two men. "Mr. Jensen. Mr. Longmont."

"Good day to you, Marshal," Longmont said.

"See you around, Brice," Smoke added.

Brice didn't doubt that. Maybe it was time he spoke up more with Denny and let her know how he felt about her, if she wasn't aware of it already. He had a feeling she was. Considering the fact that he had kissed her several times in the past, she had to have a pretty good idea that he liked her. And he was fairly confident that she was fond of him.

It seemed like there was always some sort of ruckus looming, though, that prevented them from ever taking things further. It was hard to talk about romance or even think about it when bad hombres were shooting at you. His badge was a magnet for trouble, and evidently, so was the name Jensen.

Those thoughts rolled around in his head as he walked down the street to the telegraph office. When he came in, the manager and chief telegrapher looked up from behind the window in the counter and said, "There you are, Marshal. I have youngsters out scouring the town for you."

"They're not doing a very good job of it," Brice said. "I just walked down the street in plain sight."

"Be that as it may, I have a telegram for you." The man stood up and slid a yellow telegraph flimsy across the counter. "It came in about forty-five minutes ago."

Brice picked up the message and turned away to read it. As he scanned the blocky, pencil-printed letters, he wasn't surprised to see that the wire was from Chief Marshal Long in Denver. It was a warning that a gang of bank robbers seemed to be headed in Brice's direction. The outlaws had held up banks in Flat Rock, Colby, Moss City, Harkerville, and several other settlements in Wyoming. They had wantonly gunned down more than a dozen people, including the town marshal of Harkerville, and seemed to have no compunctions at all about killing.

Their most recent job had been a change of pace, of sorts: they had boarded and stopped a westbound train just outside a hamlet known as Stinking Gulch, just across the Wyoming border. They had killed two of the train crew and murdered two passengers, as well. Given the history of their crimes, it very much appeared that they were working their way south toward Colorado and might have crossed the state line already. It was even possible the gang had struck again, and word of it hadn't yet reached the chief marshal's office.

The exact number of outlaws was uncertain. Estimates ranged from six to twelve. Some witnesses seemed to believe that one member of the gang was a woman, but that hadn't been confirmed, either.

The looting of the mailbag in the train they had stopped brought them under federal jurisdiction, so Brice was advised to be on the lookout for them and to pursue any leads he might get to their where-abouts.

That was a lot of information to pack into a telegram, but Marshal Long was good at being suc-cinct, and Brice had learned how to read between the lines. His boss wanted him to track down these varmints. He didn't like the idea of leaving Big Rock while Count Giovanni Malatesta was still around, the source of potential trouble in more ways than one, but his job might require it.

"Any reply, Marshal?" the telegrapher asked.

Brice hastily printed out a message letting Long know he had gotten the wire and understood, then composed wires for all the county sheriffs and town marshals he could think of between Big Rock and the Wyoming border, asking them if they knew anything about the gang of robbers and killers. He paid for sending the messages, making a note of the cost for his expense account, and left the telegraph office.

He cast a glance in the direction of Longmont's, thought about walking down there and telling Denny what was going on, then discarded the idea. There would be time enough to talk to her about it once he got some replies to the telegrams he had sent out and had a better idea what he was going to do.

The town was called Burnley, Colorado. It was big enough to have *two* banks, not just one, Billy Ray re-ported after scouting the place. After listening to him as the gang sat around their campfire in an isolated canyon, Curly spoke up, saying, "I got an idea."

Juliana rolled her eyes and said, "That's not necessarily a good thing."

"Now, now, let's just hear him out," Alden said. "What's your idea, Curly?"

"There's eight of us. That's enough."

"Enough to what?"

"To rob both banks at once!"

Alden winced and shook his head.

"I was afraid you were going to say that. Did you ever hear of a place called Coffeyville?"

"No," Curly said, frowning. "I don't reckon I . . . Wait a minute. There's a town by that name over in Kansas, ain't there?"

"That's right. How about Northfield?"

That brought an emphatic shake of the head from Curly. He said, "Nope. Never heard tell of it."

"Well, I have," Juliana said. "It's way up north in Minnesota or Wisconsin or some such frozen place. They're both settlements where outlaw gangs got too full of themselves and tried to do too much at once. And both times the fools got shot to pieces by the townspeople."

"Maybe, but that ain't gonna happen to us."

"How do you know that?"

"I . . . uh . . . Well, it just ain't, that's all!"

Alden turned to their scout and asked, "Billy Ray, could you tell which of the banks is bigger?"

"From what I heard around town, the Cattleman's is," the young man said. "There should be a decent amount of money in it, Alden."

"Then that's the one we'll hit," Alden said with a decisive nod.

Curly said, "What if Billy Ray's wrong and there's more money in the other bank?"

"Even if that's true, we'll never know because we'll be long gone. It's foolish to speculate on what you might have had. It's better to concentrate on what you can actually get."

Juliana, who was sitting on the ground, lay back and propped herself on an elbow. As she smirked at Curly, she said to him, "Sort of like women, where you're concerned."

He sneered back at her and said, "You best shut your mouth. I managed to get you plenty of times. But that don't mean I never thought about how I could've done better."

She stopped smiling as her hand moved toward the gun on her hip. Curly uncoiled from the rock where he was sitting and came up in a crouch with his hand poised near his own revolver.

"Quit it, you two," Alden said. "I swear, you're like two little kids picking at each other. You're as bad as a brother and sister."

Curly snickered. "Not like any brother and sister I ever knowed. Ain't that right, Juliana?"

"Shut up," she told him. "Go on with what you were trying to say, Alden."

He looked around the campfire at the entire group and said, "Here's how it'll be. We'll hit the bank in Burnley, and then we'll head southwest."

"What's southwest of there?" Childers asked.

"A little offshoot of the Rockies called the Prophet Mountains. Mostly empty these days, because it's rugged country and not much good for anything. Every rancher who tried to make a go of it in there went bust. There was some mining for a while, but all the veins played out. The only settlement was called Painted Post, and it's abandoned now, although from what I hear, most of the buildings are still standing. That'll make a good place for us to hole up for a while."

"How do you know all this, boss?" the outlaw called Hamilton asked.

"A fella told me about it at one of the robbers' roosts we stopped at, up in Montana. Said he'd gone to ground there once when a posse was after him and they never found him. He said if I ever found myself down in these parts and needed a place to hide out, Painted Post was a good one."

"I don't know about ghost towns," Juliana said. "Sometimes they give me the shivers. But I guess we don't have to worry about it just yet."

"That's right," Alden said. "First we've got to empty that bank in Burnley."

CHAPTER 33

The Sugarloaf

Denny reined in atop the ridge. She looked behind her to the northwest, at the black clouds gathering ominously over the mountains. They billowed so high that they blocked off the sun, and even though it had been bright midafternoon only a short time earlier, now a dusklike gloom hung over the landscape.

Skeletal fingers of lightning clawed through the clouds. Denny heard the rataplan of thunder, like the sound of distant drums. That made her horse skittish. So did the crackling feeling in the air. She tightened her grip on the reins.

Old-timers claimed they could predict the weather according to how their bones felt, but Denny didn't have that skill. When she had set out from Sugarloaf headquarters earlier today, she'd had no idea it was going to storm before the afternoon was over. She had delivered some supplies to a high-country line camp where a couple members of the Sugarloaf crew were staying.

She had volunteered for that errand just to have

something to do. The encounter with Malatesta in
Big Rock a couple of days earlier, followed by the
surprisingly intimate conversation with Brice Rogers,
still had her mind in a whirl.

She was all discombobulated, as Pearlie put it,
and she couldn't argue with that assessment. If
Malatesta would just move on, she believed she could
forget about him again, as well as what had happened
in Venice. She had been able to put it behind her
before—until she had the reminder of his smug face
in front of her again.

There was also the matter of whoever wanted Malatesta dead badly enough to pay some owlhoots to
take care of it. Denny didn't want that trouble touching her family through her connection with the son
of a—

That thought was going through her head when
thunder boomed again, louder and closer this time.
She was on her way home from the line camp, but it
looked like she might get wet before she got there.

Luckily, she had a slicker rolled up and tied to her
saddle. That was part of everyday equipment out on
the range. Since she had already brought the horse
to a stop, she swung down and started to untie the
lashings so she could shake out the slicker and put
it on.

She hadn't gotten it loose yet when some instinct
made her turn her head and look around. The back
of her neck had prickled under the blond curls that
were hanging loose today, and it wasn't from the electricity in the air.

She felt eyes on her.

That instinct was telling her the truth. Two men

rode out of the trees about twenty yards away. She didn't recognize the men or their horses.

There were plenty of good reasons why strangers might be riding across Sugarloaf range. Smoke didn't mind travelers taking a shortcut through his ranch as long as they didn't cause any trouble.

These two had trouble written all over them, though, Denny thought as they came closer. One was taller, a rawboned hombre who rode slouched in the saddle, while the other, who was smaller and sported a dark mustache, had a stiffer posture. Both wore rough range clothes and had the look of drifting hard cases about them.

Men such as that might be harmless, or they might decide that running across a young, attractive female by herself was a sign that they ought to have themselves a little sport.

But if they believed she was defenseless because she was alone, they were going to find out mighty quick-like that they were wrong.

Instead of untying the slicker, she reached for the carbine and slid it out of the saddle boot. The clack of the repeater's lever as she worked it coincided with another rumble of thunder, but the men saw what she was doing and both reined in sharply.

"Hold on there, ma'am," the bigger of the pair said. He held up his right hand, palm out. "You don't need that Winchester. We ain't lookin' for trouble."

In Denny's experience, nearly everybody who claimed not to be looking for trouble actually was. So she didn't let down her guard as she said, "Who are you? What are you doing here? This is Sugarloaf range."

"It is?" the man said. His bright red eyebrows

lifted. "We sure didn't know that. I reckon Sugarloaf's a ranch?"

"My father's ranch," Denny said curtly.

"I see. Well, my partner and me, we was just on our way to Red Cliff—"

"You're going the wrong direction, then," Denny interrupted him. "You need to turn around and go back the way you came from."

"Yes'm. We appreciate the help." The man turned to his companion and went on, "I done *told* you we got turned around, didn't I? Now that this pretty lady has set us straight, maybe we can get where we're goin'." He looked at Denny again. "We're plumb obliged to you—"

"No need for thanks. Just turn around and ride."

"Sure, sure. Just bein' polite. No call to get touchy."

The men lifted their reins and started to turn their horses. But as they did, Denny noticed that they wheeled their mounts in different directions. That had the effect of splitting them up, so she couldn't really cover both of them at the same time . . .

That thought set off warning bells in her mind, but not in time. The men kicked their horses and made the animals lunge toward her. She raised the carbine to her shoulder, twisted to her left, and fired at the bigger of the two men as he charged in on her.

She saw him jerk and thought she had hit him, but he didn't fall off his horse. Even worse, targeting him gave the smaller man time to get closer to her—close enough to leave his saddle in a diving tackle that rammed his shoulder into her and drove her off her feet.

Denny hit the ground hard with the man's weight on top of her. The impact forced all the air out of her lungs. Hooves pounded the dirt around her as her own mount danced around skittishly and the attacker's horse raced on by. Both Denny and the man she struggled with managed to avoid being trampled, though.

Somehow she had hung on to the carbine. Pinned to the ground as she was, she couldn't work the lever, but she swung the stock toward the man's head and tried to ram the butt against his jaw. He threw his shoulder up in time to block the thrust but grunted in pain anyway. He worked a knee between her thighs as if trying to force her legs apart, but she didn't think that rape was his intention, at least not right away. He was just trying to subdue her.

Instead, he had a wildcat on his hands. Even the short-barreled carbine was too awkward at close quarters like this, so she threw it aside and clawed at his face with her left hand while using her right to grab his left ear and twist it. He howled and bucked up away from her enough to give him room to hook a punch into her belly. Denny was already gasping for air, and that situation worsened as his fist sunk into her midsection.

He whipped his head to the side, away from her fingernails that had already left bleeding streaks on his cheeks. She lost her grip on his ear, but he'd left himself open for a side-hand blow to his throat. She landed that swift stroke and he rolled away, gagging and coughing.

Denny rolled the other way, putting some distance between them. She spotted the carbine lying on the ground where she had tossed it and pushed up onto her hands and knees to make a diving grab for it. She hadn't forgotten that the other man might still be a threat. She didn't know how badly he was hit or even if her shot had actually struck him.

She was in midair, reaching for the Winchester, when a kick thudded into her ribs, flipped her over, and knocked her away from the carbine. The first man stomped after her, spewing curses. As Denny rolled, she caught a glimpse of the bloodstain on his left sleeve and knew she had just nicked him. He was still able to use that arm as he reached down and caught hold of her shirtfront.

He hauled her to her feet, one hand bunched in the fabric of her shirt while he used the other to slap her, backhand and forehand. The blows knocked her head to one side and then the other and stunned her. Even though she tried to force her muscles to work so she could fight back, her knees buckled and she sagged in his grip.

The man drew back his fist to hit her again, but before the blow could fall, his smaller companion grabbed his arm and croaked, "Don't! You're liable to hurt her bad or even kill her, blast it!"

"The witch shot me!"

"Well, she dang near crushed my windpipe, too, but we don't want her dead."

The hoarse words finally penetrated the bigger man's brain. Snarling in anger, he lowered his fist and used the hand holding Denny up to give her a hard shove away from him. She stumbled backward, fell painfully on her rear end, and then sprawled on her back, breathing hard but otherwise unable to move.

"You better see how bad she wounded me," the bigger man said.

"After I get her tied up so she can't run off," the

man with the mustache said. He rubbed his sore throat. "I never figured a girl'd put up that much of a fight."

"Must be she ain't a normal girl."

Denny's brain had started functioning well enough again for her to hear those words and understand them. She was too stunned and battered to resist as the smaller man rolled her onto her stomach, yanked her arms behind her, and lashed her wrists together. Next he tied her ankles together and then left her there while he tended to his partner's injury.

"Shoot, this isn't much more than a bullet burn," he said when he'd examined the wound on the bigger man's arm. "I'll tie a rag around it and you'll be fine."

"It don't *feel* fine. It hurts like blazes."

"Take it easy. We got what we came for."

Her, Denny thought. She sensed now that this wasn't some random encounter. They must have followed her up here and waited for a good chance to grab her. She had no idea why, unless they planned to hold her for ransom because she was Smoke Jensen's daughter.

It didn't matter. What was important was that the bigger one was right. She *wasn't* a normal girl.

And as soon as she got the chance, they would find out just how much of a fight she really could put up.

CHAPTER 34

Her two captors, and seemingly life itself, weren't finished heaping indignities on Denny. As soon as Mustache, as she mentally dubbed him, had tied a makeshift bandage around Big Boy's wounded arm, he wadded up a bandanna, forced Denny's mouth open, and shoved the cloth in, then tied it in place with a short length of rope. The gag was very effective—and uncomfortable.

Then the rain started.

It was as if the heavens opened up and dumped giant buckets of water on the Sugarloaf. The sky had turned black as night as the clouds swept in, but that darkness was shattered by the near-constant flash of lightning. Thunder assaulted Denny's ears. The downpour was so strong that if she'd been lying on her back with the gag in her mouth, she might well have drowned.

"Grab that horse!" Mustache yelled at Big Boy as Denny's spooked mount started to take off running.

Big Boy lunged and just managed to snag the horse's reins. He set his feet and fought to bring the animal under control. That struggle must have pained his injured arm, because he bellowed curses at the horse.

Denny hoped lightning would strike both of the men who'd attacked her. It would serve them right to fry.

Unfortunately, that didn't happen. When Big Boy had the horse settled down somewhat, Mustache called to him over the continual rumble of thunder, "Hang on to that horse! I'll lift the girl onto the saddle!"

Denny didn't see how she was going to be able to ride with her legs tied together like that. A moment later she realized to her dismay that that wasn't what they had in mind. Mustache, who seemed to be extremely strong despite his smaller stature, picked her up in his arms and then slung her facedown over her horse's saddle. She landed on her belly with enough force that she would have said, *"Ooofff!"* if she hadn't been gagged. As it was, she couldn't make any sound as a wave of sickness washed through her.

With her arms hanging on one side and her legs on the other, Mustache tied them together under the horse's belly. The horse didn't like the rope rubbing against its underside and jumped around some more before finally settling down. By then, Denny was well and truly miserable.

And she figured it was only going to get worse before they got to wherever they were going.

With her helpless, the two men took turns hanging on to her horse's reins while they mounted up. Then they rode off through the stinging rain with Mustache leading Denny's horse.

She had never gotten that slicker out, so she had been soaked to the skin within a minute of the storm starting. She wouldn't have thought it was possible to get even wetter, but somehow she did during that long ride through day-turned-night.

She tried to twist her wrists back and forth to see if there was any play in the rope around them, but Mustache had done a good job of tying her. She might be able to work her way loose—in two or three days.

She didn't think she had that much time to spare.

Although she couldn't tell which direction they were going or how far they had traveled, she knew when their path sloped upward. She could feel that in the horse underneath her. The ground was muddy and the footing was tricky. Her captors had to slow down.

The rain wasn't falling as hard now, Denny realized. The thunder and lightning were still present but not constant. The storm was weakening. It might even break up completely or move on.

The trail leveled off again. The rain abruptly stopped hitting her, even though Denny could still hear it falling.

That was because they had entered a cavelike area underneath a huge outcropping of rock, she realized as she lifted her head again and looked around. The space was forty feet long and twenty feet deep, with the roof sloping down almost to the floor in the back. The gloom was thick in here, although Denny could tell that the sky was lighter outside now as the storm lessened in intensity.

The two men dismounted. Big Boy held Denny's horse while Mustache cut the rope between her wrists and ankles. She started to slide off headfirst, but Mustache caught her belt and stopped her from falling.

"Can't have you busting your head open," he said. He pulled her the other way and helped her down from the horse. Then he lowered her to the ground, which seemed to have a thin layer of dirt over solid rock.

Denny was all too aware of how her soaked clothes were plastered to her body, revealing every feminine curve. So far, though, they hadn't shown any real interest in molesting her, despite an occasional admiring glance that seemed almost involuntary.

How long that would continue to be true, she didn't know.

Big Boy put his hands on his hips and grinned down at her as he loomed over her.

"Sorry we can't make you more comfortable," he said. "Got to make sure you don't try to pull no tricks on us."

Muffled grunts came from Denny, a string of curses that were decidedly unladylike, although with the gag they were also indecipherable.

"Don't you worry, we're gonna take good care of you," Big Boy went on. "And as long as you behave, we ain't a-gonna hurt you. You're a mighty important gal, Miss Jensen. Worth a heap of money to us."

That was it, Denny thought. Confirmation that they had kidnapped her in order to demand ransom from her parents. That was why they didn't want to hurt her right now.

But she had seen their faces. No matter what her captors said, they couldn't afford to leave her alive to identify them. Once they got the payoff they were after, the only value she would have for them would be—as a corpse.

Unless somebody realized she was missing and found her first.

Big Rock

For two days, replies had been filtering in from Brice's telegrams to the other lawmen between Big Rock and the Wyoming border. None of them reported having seen the gang of bank robbers Marshal Long had wired about, but Brice hadn't heard from all of them yet, either.

A storm was lurking to the northwest, with dark clouds, rumbles of thunder, and occasional flashes of distant lightning. The air in Big Rock, though, remained still and oppressive at this point. Brice stood on the boardwalk in front of Hukill's Barbershop with Monte Carson, whom he had run into a few minutes earlier.

The sheriff took off his hat and rubbed his sleeve across his forehead. Then as he replaced the hat, he said, "When the air gets so heavy like this, I wish it'd just go ahead and rain to break things up."

"Yeah, it's pretty uncomfortable," Brice agreed. His hat was thumbed to the back of his head. "You know what they say, though."

"What's that?"

"Everybody talks about the weather, but nobody does anything about it."

Monte chuckled. "That's sure enough true. Sometimes I wish—"

Whatever it was that Monte wished, it went unspoken, because at the moment, a woman's voice said rather tentatively, "Marshal? Could I talk to you for a minute?"

Brice and Monte looked over to the end of this section of boardwalk, where two steps led down to an alley before the walk resumed again on the other side in front of Tompkins's Apothecary and Yates's Variety Store. Brice thought at first that he hadn't ever seen the woman who stood there, but then he changed his mind and decided that she was vaguely familiar for some reason.

"You want to talk to Marshal Rogers, not me?" Monte asked with a frown.

"Yes, sir, Sheriff, that's right," she said. "If . . . if that's not a problem."

Monte shrugged and said, "Sure, if you want to. It's a free country, and you've got a right to talk to whoever you like."

"Thank you, Sheriff."

Brice tugged his hat down, figuring this had to be official business, and asked, "What can I do for you, ma'am?"

The woman hesitated, and Monte said, "See you later, Brice." He walked off as another peal of thunder rolled over the mountains in the distance.

Brice moved closer to the woman and smiled reassuringly. She was pretty, although a mite on the mousy side in a grayish-brown dress and a matching hat pushed down on her chestnut curls. As she gave him a weak smile in return, he remembered where he had seen her before.

"You work at the Brown Dirt Cowboy Saloon," he said, then immediately regretted the surprised exclamation as she winced.

"That . . . that's right," she said. "Does it make a difference?"

"Not a bit," he hastened to say. "What can I do for you?"

"There's a man . . . He's been bothering me . . . I mean, I know it's my job . . . to associate with men, but this one . . . he scares me—"

Brice held a hand up to stop her.

"This really sounds like something you ought to talk to Sheriff Carson about. I'm a federal deputy marshal. There are only certain crimes that fall under my jurisdiction."

"I know that. But this man, he talked about how the federal law wanted him. He bragged about it. He . . . he even said he shot a deputy U.S. marshal over in Kansas."

Brice's heart rate kicked up a notch. "He killed a marshal?"

"Well . . . he didn't actually say he killed him, just that he shot him. But that's pretty bad, too, isn't it, even if it wasn't fatal?"

"Plenty bad enough," Brice replied grimly. "Where is he now?"

"I don't know. He was talking about leaving town."

"What's his name?"

"I don't know that, either. I'm sorry."

"What did he look like?"

"He was big . . . well, broad-shouldered, anyway . . . maybe forty years old. Brown hair getting thin."

That description could fit a lot of men, Brice thought.

"And he had a scar, here," the girl went on, tracing a path from her right cheek down over her jawline. "And another one above his left eye."

Brice nodded. That was more to go on. He could take that description and ask around town. He could also look through the wanted posters in Monte's office and even wire the chief marshal's office in Denver. If this varmint had gunned down a federal star packer, Brice wanted to get on his trail.

"All right," he told the girl. "I'll take care of it. Thank you for looking me up and telling me about it, Miss . . . ?"

"Sutton," she said. "Rosemarie Sutton."

"I'm obliged to you, Miss Sutton. If I find the man, or find out anything else about him, would you like for me to come to the Brown Dirt Cowboy and let you know, so you don't have to worry?"

"That would be wonderful, Marshal. Thank you." She reached out, rested the fingertips of a gloved hand on his forearm, just as Denny had done a few days earlier, and added, "You can come see me any-time you like."

CHAPTER 35

The cave

The rain stopped and the clouds broke up enough for sunlight to slant through here and there, but that occurred so late in the afternoon that it wasn't long before night fell and darkness closed in again. The shadows were thick as mud in the cavelike area under the rock.

It was crowded under there, too, with three people and three horses. Big Boy tied all three animals together with a lead rope and then anchored that rope with a large rock he hauled in from outside.

Mustache went to the back of the space and built a fire small enough that it would be difficult to spot from outside unless someone just happened to be in exactly the right spot to do so. He broke out a coffeepot, a frying pan, and a bag of supplies, then started rustling up a meal.

Denny couldn't do anything except lie on her side, watching with a limited field of view as her two captors went about their chores. The only bit of relief came when Big Boy walked over to her once he was finished with the horses and knelt beside her to remove the gag.

"Don't go to yellin'," he warned her. "I'll just put it back in there if you do."

Denny opened and closed her mouth and worked her jaw back and forth to get the stiffness out of it. The gag had left a foul taste in her mouth, but she couldn't do anything about that.

"I won't yell," she said when she trusted herself to speak again. "Out here in the middle of nowhere like this, what good would it do?"

"That's right," Big Boy agreed, unwittingly confirming that they were a long way from anywhere— but Denny had already had a pretty good idea that was true.

She knew that by now, her parents would have noticed she hadn't returned from the line camp. Smoke, Cal, Pearlie, and the other members of the ranch crew would soon be out searching for her, if they weren't already.

Since she hadn't been able to tell exactly where they were going, she wasn't sure they were still on Sugarloaf range. She didn't recall ever being in this particular spot before, but she didn't know every inch of the ranch. She was familiar with most of it, to be sure, but it was possible this location was still on her parents' land and she wouldn't know it.

Not that it mattered. Smoke would go anywhere, all the way to the ends of the earth if he had to, in order to find her.

The problem was, that downpour would have wiped out any trail the horses left. Smoke and the others would be searching blind.

Mustache had even picked up her carbine and hat before they rode off, not leaving behind any clue to indicate the spot where she had been taken captive.

Denny's stomach clenched as the smells of coffee, bacon, and biscuits began to fill the air, along with the smoke from the fire. Despite the various aches and pains she had accumulated during the fight with the two men, she was hungry and there was no denying it. Her resentment grew stronger as she lay there and watched them hunkering on their heels beside the fire, filling their bellies and slurping coffee from tin cups.

After a while, her irritation got the best of her. She said, "Hey! If either of you had even a shred of human decency, you'd feed your poor prisoner."

"Dadgum it, she's right, Dave," Big Boy said. "We been chowin' down and didn't even think about the lady."

Mustache—or Dave—winced as his partner said his name. But it was too late to call it back. He swallowed the last of the coffee in his cup, then picked up the empty tin plate he had just set aside. After placing a biscuit and a couple of strips of bacon on it, he poured more coffee into the cup.

"We don't have any fancy china or crystal, but I reckon you can make do," he said as he stood up and came toward Denny. The faint firelight made his shadow huge and grotesque as it fell over her. He told Big Boy, "Go stand on the other side of her."

Big Boy moved around so Denny couldn't see him anymore. Dave knelt in front of her, set the plate and cup on the ground, and took hold of her shoulders so he could lift her into a sitting position. She could have lashed out with her bound legs and kicked him, but she didn't see what good it would do at this point.

"Untie her hands."

Denny felt Big Boy's fingers working clumsily at the knots. The man swore under his breath, then said, "Beggin' your pardon, ma'am. I'm tryin' back here, but my friend tied you up mighty good."

"Cut the rope if you have to," Dave said. "We've got plenty more."

"No need to waste perfectly good rope. I'll get it . . . There, I think it's startin' to come loose."

The job of untying her required another couple of minutes, but finally the rope fell away from Denny's wrists. As it did, she felt the back of one of Big Boy's hands brush across the small of her back. It might have been an accident, or he might have enjoyed feeling her body, even through her damp shirt. He didn't pursue it beyond that, however, so she didn't waste any time or energy taking offense.

She already had plenty to be offended about, where these two were concerned.

She didn't realize how numb her hands had gotten while her wrists were tied until blood started flowing back into them and a million pins and needles jabbed into her flesh. She pulled her arms around in front of her and flexed her fingers to get the feeling back sooner.

Dave left the plate and cup within her reach as he stood up and backed off a couple of steps.

"Don't try anything," he warned her. "Benjy's standing behind you, and if you go to throw hot coffee in my face or anything like that, he'll clout you one. We don't aim to hurt you, but we're not going to let *you* hurt *us,* either."

"Hey, you said my name!" Big Boy—Benjy— exclaimed.

"Well, you said mine earlier."

"It ain't easy not to, is it? I mean, when we're used to callin' each other by name all the time."

Denny ignored their yammering and picked up the cup of coffee. The wet clothes and the high-country wind had settled a chill into her bones. The warmth that came through the tin cup as she wrapped her hands around it was mighty welcome. She sipped the strong black brew to get some of that warmth inside her.

She picked up a strip of bacon. It took some self-control not to shove the whole thing into her mouth. She nibbled on it instead, tore off a piece of biscuit and ate it, washing it down with more coffee. She felt strength seeping back into her from the food and drink.

After a few minutes, she looked up at Dave, gestured with the half-full tin cup, and said, "You know what would make this even better? A shot of whiskey."

"Whoo-hoo!" Benjy chortled. "I didn't expect her to come out with that, did you, Dave?" Obviously, they weren't going to worry about names anymore. "We figured you'd be some dainty little rich gal, ma'am."

"You can be rich without being dainty," Denny said. "Nobody ever accused me of being dainty. Now, how about that whiskey?"

Dave gave her a suspicious frown, pointed a finger at her, and said, "You stay right there. If she moves, you know what to do."

"Yep," Benjy said.

Dave went over to his horse, reached into a saddle-bag, and took out a silver flask. He came back to Denny, unscrewed the cap, and splashed a little whiskey into the cup she held out. She swirled around the mixture, sipped it, and sighed.

"Just like I said, that's a lot better." She took another drink. "You ought to try it. Just what is it you boys want with me, anyway?"

"Now, that's none of your business," Dave said.

"Well, then, whose business is it?" Denny demanded. "I'm the one who's the prisoner here. If you want money, I can arrange for you to get plenty of it. You obviously know who my father is."

"Yeah," Dave said, frowning worriedly. "Smoke Jensen."

"That's right. You know what sort of reputation he has, too."

Benjy said, "He's supposed to be a ring-tailed devil with a gun. But he's got to be gettin' kinda old by now. He must've slowed down some."

Denny laughed and then said, "Yeah. You just go on believing that."

"We don't want to tangle with Smoke Jensen," Dave said. "That's not what this is about."

"Then here's what you should do. Leave me here . . . Shoot, leave my ankles tied if you want, just toss a knife down outside where I can crawl to it. Take my horse with you, leave it a mile from here, and ride away. Just ride away. You'll have a good start, and chances are, you'll get away."

"Not interested," Dave said as he shook his head. "Your pa could still try to track us down."

"Then how about this? Do what I told you, with the knife and the horse, and then I'll stay the rest of the night right here. I won't ride back home until tomorrow, and when I do, I'll tell my folks I got lost and had to seek shelter from the storm. My father will never even know what you've done."

"Why would you do that for us?" Benjy asked.

Denny shrugged and said, "Well, other than knocking me around some, you haven't treated me as badly as you could have."

"That's right," Dave said. "You need to be sure and tell your pa that."

"I'd rather not tell him anything, and that's what'll happen if you boys take the deal I'm offering you. I mean, no matter how much ransom you ask for, is it going to be worth it if you have to spend the rest of your life looking over your shoulder for Smoke Jensen? And if that's not enough, I have a couple of uncles and some cousins who aren't going to be happy to hear about this, either."

Benjy still stood behind her, but she heard him swallow hard. He said, "I'm startin' to think maybe we bit off a mite more than we oughta be chewin', Dave. Maybe we should—"

"No!" Dave said. "She's just trying to mix us up and get us to do something stupid."

"Too late for that," Denny said. "That horse is a long way out of the barn."

Dave just glared at her, so she twisted her head and shoulders and looked up at Benjy.

"I'll sweeten the deal even more, if that's what you want. If you agree to ride off and leave me here, we can have a little fun before you go. Of course . . . you'd have to untie my legs first."

Benjy's eyes got bigger in the firelight. "Are you sayin' what I think you're sayin'?"

Before Denny could reply, Dave pointed his finger again and said, "You just stop that! That's serious business, and you don't need to be making sport of us about it. You're a respectable young woman—"

"Whoever told you that?" Denny asked. She laughed and shook her head.

"Dave, listen," Benjy said with a note of urgency in his voice. "I think she's tellin' the truth. She ain't a-gonna hold it against us. And she's derned near the prettiest gal I ever saw in my whole life!"

"No!" Dave was starting to sound really frustrated. "Blast it, we had a plan, Benjy. It was all worked out—"

"Plans can be changed. Sometimes, a *better* plan comes along, and you got to grab the chance while you got it."

Dave shook his head stubbornly. "We'll stick to what we said we were going to do."

Benjy stepped around Denny. He was the one pointing a finger now, and waving it in his partner's face.

"We've rode together for a long time and I don't want any trouble betwixt us, but we never shoulda gone into this like we done. The more I think about her bein' Smoke Jensen's daughter, the less I like it. What if he really *is* as fast as he ever was? There ain't no tellin' how many hombres he's gunned down over the years. I don't want him on my back trail. And what she's offerin' us . . . man, Dave, you know fellas like us ain't never gonna have another chance at somethin' like that!"

With his face now mottled with anger, Dave got right in his friend's face and said, "Now, you listen to me, you big bumpkin. We can't—"

"Bumpkin!" Benjy raised a fist and shook it in the air. "Boy, howdy, Dave, if you wasn't my pard, I'd—"

Denny didn't wait to hear what either of them was going to say next. Caught up in their argument, they weren't paying any attention to her, so she took them completely by surprise when she jackknifed up from the ground, lifting herself high enough that she was able to reach out and pluck Benjy's gun from the holster on his hip before she fell back.

CHAPTER 36

Benjy yelled, jerked around, and slapped at his now-empty holster. Dave jumped back and clawed at his own gun. He hadn't cleared leather yet when Denny leveled the Colt at him and said, "Don't!"

Dave froze with his gun halfway out of the holster.

"Pull it out slow and easy and throw it away," Denny told him.

Instead of following the order, Dave glared at his partner and grated, "You blasted fool!"

"Me?" Benjy said. "You was the one who was arguin'—"

"No, it was you—"

"Shut up, both of you!" Denny said. "Now, take that gun out carefully and toss it away from you. I'm not going to tell you again."

She was very tempted to just shoot both of them while she had the chance. In Dave's case, that would have been justified since he was trying to draw on her, but Benjy wasn't threatening her, and drilling him would have been murder to Denny's way of thinking. She'd almost done it anyway, and she would still pull the trigger if she had to.

But then Dave sighed, slowly and gingerly lifted his revolver from its holster, and tossed it toward the rear of the area underneath the bulging rock.

"Get your hands up, both of you," Denny said. "Back up, closer to the fire."

As they backed away, Benjy said bitterly, "We tried to be nice to you—"

"By hitting me and kicking me and tying me up?" Denny snorted. "I'd hate to see what you'd do to somebody you were trying to be mean to."

"You could have seen it, all right," Dave said, scowling. "I think we treated you pretty good, considering."

That was true, in its own bizarre way, Denny supposed. But she also didn't care. She said, "Benjy, take your knife out and toss it over here where I can reach it. If I even think you're about to throw it *at* me, I'll just kill you and let Dave do it."

"I ain't gonna try nothin'," Benjy grumbled. He slid the bone-handled knife from the sheath on his left hip and gave it a gentle, underhand toss that landed it in front of Denny and to her left. She'd have to struggle and stretch a little to reach it, but she didn't figure that would be a problem.

Sounding aggrieved, Benjy went on, "You wasn't ever plannin' to really let us have some sport with you, was you?"

"Of course she wasn't, you lunkhead," Dave told him. "She was just playing us against each other so we'd stop paying attention to her long enough for her to try some trick." He glanced at Denny. "And it worked."

Benjy heaved a big sigh and shook his head.

"Well, you can't blame a fella for dreamin'—"

Denny leaned forward to try to reach the knife. As

she did so, she took her eyes off the two men, and Dave suddenly darted toward the fire. He dragged his foot across the ground and kicked dirt over the flames.

The fire wasn't big to start with, and the dirt put it out almost instantly. Darkness enveloped Denny as if someone had dropped a thick black curtain over her head. But since she had been reaching for the knife anyway, she continued her lunge toward it and slapped her free hand on the ground, searching for the weapon.

Her fingers brushed the bone handle and closed around it. Hearing the fast shuffle of feet near her, she threw herself to the side and rolled. One of the men, probably Benjy since he'd been closer, brushed against her as he tried to tackle her in the dark. Denny lashed out with the blade, felt it hit something. Benjy howled in pain.

She came to a stop against the rock where it angled down low to the ground. As she heard one of the men coming toward her again, she jerked the gun up and pulled the trigger.

The muzzle flash revealed Dave looming over her. That lasted only a split second before darkness closed in again. Dave yelped and scrambled away. He was moving fast enough that Denny didn't think she had hit him, not seriously, anyway.

As Denny sat there with her back braced against the rock and her heart slugging furiously in her chest, she realized she could make out the opening of the cavelike area because of the starlight outside. As long as she stayed where she was, they couldn't come at her without her being able to see their silhouettes against that faint glow.

From somewhere near the entrance, Dave called, "Listen to me, lady. You don't want to do this. It's just going to make things worse."

"She cut me, Dave!" Benjy said. "The little witch cut me!"

Dave ignored him and went on, "You hear me, Miss Jensen? You're making this a lot harder on yourself than you have to."

Denny didn't respond to him. She was too busy leaning forward and using the knife to saw at the rope tied around her ankles. She felt the strands parting under the keen-edged blade.

"Miss Jensen?" Dave said tentatively. "Are you all right?"

Denny still didn't answer. Let the varmints wonder about her. As soon as the rope fell away from her ankles, she scooted slowly and carefully along the rock wall, feeling around as she went for the gun she'd made Dave toss away.

If she could get both guns, she'd stand a lot better chance, she reasoned.

"Missy, I'm plumb sorry I called you names just now," Benjy said. "My leg hurts like fire where you cut me. But I reckon I understand why you did it. You're scared of us, and you don't trust us. I don't blame you for feelin' that way. But I swear, we ain't out to hurt you."

Benjy's voice came from far to her right. Dave had been to her left. That was worrisome. They were flanking her, she realized, and soon would be moving in from both sides.

Maybe it was time to forget about that other gun and make her move now.

She gathered her legs underneath her and came up fast, springing to her feet and dashing toward the entrance. She wished she could have gotten one of the horses, but that seemed impossible under the circumstances.

They must have heard enough to figure out what she was doing. Dave yelled, "Stop her!"

"I'll get her!" Benjy cried.

Denny was almost to the entrance when he rammed into her from the right and knocked her off her feet. She rolled and felt his hands clutching at her, trying to get a secure hold on her. She thrust the gun toward where she thought he was and pulled the trigger again. Benjy screamed and his hands fell away from her.

Denny rolled again, and the ground fell out from under her. She was outside now, toppling out of control down a steep, rock-studded slope.

She grunted at the impacts that jolted her as she continued her downward plunge. It was pure luck she didn't dash her brains out against one of the rocks. Vaguely, she was aware of Dave and Benjy both shouting somewhere above her, so she supposed she hadn't killed Benjy with that second shot.

She fetched up hard against a tree trunk, hitting it with enough force to make her gasp. She slipped around it and staggered to her feet. After a few stumbling steps, the ground started to move under her feet.

No, not ground, she realized. Smaller rocks. She had wandered onto a talus slope, and as her feet shot out from under her, dust, racket, and flying pebbles surrounded her. She slid downward, feetfirst, picking up speed until it seemed like she was flying down the mountainside.

That slide probably lasted only a few seconds, but it seemed a lot longer to Denny. What waited at the end of it was worse. Suddenly she was in midair, plummeting toward an unknown fate. She might fall for hundreds of feet before she slammed to her death on the rocks below.

Instead, in two terrifying heartbeats, she hit water, cleaving deep into its icy grip.

Since she hadn't been able to see it coming, she hadn't caught her breath before she went under. Her lungs cried out for air and her pulse thundered inside her head. Somehow, she kept her wits about her, and when she stopped sinking and her natural buoyancy tried to lift her in the water, she stroked with both arms to help her rise.

That was the first time she realized she still held both the gun and the knife she had taken from her former captors. Somehow she hadn't dropped them during her mad plunge. She thought about letting go of them to lessen the weight pulling her down, but she didn't want to give them up. She might need them. The gun ought to work even after being submerged in water, and it probably still had either three or four rounds in it, depending on whether Benjy liked to carry the hammer on an empty chamber.

After another seemingly interminable interval, her head broke the surface. She gasped and then began dragging in as much air as she could, treading water as she did so. She had fallen into a good-sized creek. Its current carried her along at a steady pace.

She tilted her head back to look up at the slope looming on her right. She had rolled and slid and fallen from somewhere fairly high up there, and since Benjy and Dave wouldn't be able to take such a direct route down on horseback, she knew she had some time before they could mount much of a pursuit. For that reason, she was content to let the stream carry her farther away while she caught her breath.

It didn't take long, though, for the cold to penetrate her body until every bone ached and it felt as if her insides were about to turn to solid ice. Now that the storm had passed, the temperature itself wasn't that frigid, although the nights were cool in the high country. The streams, though, were fed by snowmelt most of the year and were always cold.

Despite the need to put more distance between her and her former captors, Denny knew she had to get out of the water sooner rather than later. Eventually the chill might paralyze her muscles and cause her to sink.

She stood it as long as she could, but between the cold and the weight of her clothes and boots dragging her down, she weakened quickly. She kicked her legs and angled toward the far side of the creek. A pang of relief went through her when her feet scraped on the rocky bottom.

Within moments, she had pulled herself out of the water and collapsed on the bank. Almost immediately, she began shivering. The night breeze wasn't very strong, but as soaked as she was, any movement of the air had a frigid bite to it. Although she was so weary that all she wanted to do was lay her head down on the grass and close her eyes, she forced herself up to hands and knees and then pushed all the way to her feet.

She swayed and put out her arms to balance herself as the world spun crazily for several seconds. When it settled down and stopped tilting every which way, she shoved the gun and knife behind her belt and then looked around to take stock of her situation.

That really wasn't a mountain on the other side of the creek, she saw now as starlight shone down on the landscape. More like a good-sized hill. Still it would take Benjy and Dave time to make their way down from their hideout—assuming Benjy could even travel. She was pretty sure she'd hit him with that second shot. He had screamed like he was shot, no doubt about that.

Even so, they would be hurrying, so it wouldn't be too long before they were down here searching for her. She turned to look in the other direction. This side of the creek appeared to be rolling, wooded terrain. At least it wouldn't be too much of a challenge to travel through.

And since she didn't know where she was, one direction was as good as another, she supposed. Her main goal was to find a place to hole up where she could get out of the wet clothes, maybe even make a fire to help her warm up and dry off.

She reached down to the pocket of her jeans, felt the familiar lump that was the small, waterproof tin container of matches Smoke insisted that she always carry with her when she was out on the range. She didn't know exactly *how* waterproof it was, but the storm and now the dunking in the creek would be good tests for it. First she had to find a good place.

She turned and walked into the trees, stumbling only a little from exhaustion, exposure to the elements, and the battering she had received at the hands and feet of her captors.

Luck had been with her tonight, she knew, but her own stubbornness had played a large part in her escape, too. It wasn't enough just to escape, though. She had a grudge against those two, and she intended to settle it.

First things first.

The woods swallowed her up.

CHAPTER 37

Denny hunkered over the tiny fire, trying to soak up every bit of the warmth the flames gave off. Earlier, she had taken off her wet clothes in the hope that she would be warmer out of them, but that hadn't proven to be the case since she didn't have a nice dry blanket to wrap up in. Her jeans and socks still hung on a low branch above the fire, but she had pulled her under-clothes and flannel shirt back on. They were still quite damp but an improvement over nothing.

Mostly, though, she would just have to remain cold and miserable while she waited for morning. She had kept the fire small because she didn't want Benjy and Dave to spot it. She could have built a big, roaring blaze to dry off and warm up much more quickly, but that would have led them right to her.

Her camp was tucked into a little nook at the base of a bluff, with little ridges sticking out on both sides of her and a thick stand of trees straight ahead. Several trees grew around her, as well. Not a perfect hiding place, by any means, but the best one she had come across before she was too stiff to continue searching.

With trembling fingers, she had found some broken

branches and arranged them in a pile, stuffed dried pine needles underneath them, and then opened the container of matches. As far as she could tell, they had remained dry during her dunking. Carefully, she tried to strike one of them.

She was shaking so bad, it had taken her several tries, but finally she got the fire going. Then she had taken off her clothes, given up on that idea, pulled the shirt back on, and knelt beside the flames.

The coffee and bacon and biscuits her captors had given her had been good. She could have done with something like that right now. Not at the cost of being a prisoner, though.

The pistol and the knife lay on the ground beside her. At every little sound in the night, her hand strayed toward the weapons and she listened intently for several minutes before relaxing again when it turned out to be nothing.

One of these times, it might *not* be nothing. She had to remain vigilant, alert for any potential threat.

She warned herself about that as sternly as possible— but despite her determination, she wasn't even aware of it when exhaustion overwhelmed her and she slumped down on the ground beside the fire to let sleep claim her.

"Now that is just about the prettiest sight I ever laid eyes on in all my borned days."

The jeering voice jolted Denny awake. She sat bolt upright and realized that it was morning. Sunlight flooded down around her. Under other circumstances, she would have enjoyed its warmth, but right now her blood ran cold in her veins because of the sight that met her startled eyes.

Benjy and Dave stood a few yards away, looking at her. A leer twisted Benjy's face, but it wasn't just Denny's partially unclad body that brought about that expression. He had a small wound on his cheek, covered with dried blood and surrounded by little red marks that looked like burns.

That was what they were, Denny thought—powder burns from when she had discharged the pistol right in his face. If she'd been holding it at a slightly different angle, she would have blown his brains out, and she would have been facing only one enemy right now.

That would have been all right with her.

The left leg of Benjy's trousers was dark with dried blood, too. She remembered him yelling about how she'd cut him when he tried to tackle her as she made her escape. That made three wounds she had given him, overall. She was whittling him down.

Dave appeared to be uninjured, though, as he pointed a gun at Denny.

"Get on your feet, lady," he told her. "We've been chasing you the whole blasted night. We're tired, and we're in no mood for any more trouble."

Benjy said, "With you just wearin' that shirt, I can tell you what we're in the mood for."

"Stop that," Dave snapped. "There's not going to be any of that, and you know why."

A surly scowl replaced the leer on Benjy's face.

"Yeah, yeah," he said grudgingly. "I know. But a gal like her puts ideas in a fella's head, especially when she looks like she does right now."

Dave ignored that, waggled the gun at Denny, and

said, "Come on. Get up and get dressed. We're going back. I won't tell you again."

Denny was still half-stunned from sleep. She was stiff and sore from the ordeal she had endured. But her brain was beginning to work. Quickly but thoroughly, she studied the two men and her surroundings, searching for anything that might give her an opportunity.

The fire had burned down during the night until it was just a heap of ashes this morning. Benjy's gun lay on the ground beside her, a few feet away. Dave saw her eyeing it and said sharply, "Don't you do it, sister. Reach for that Colt and I'll shoot you. I swear, I'm fed up enough to do it."

Denny believed him. She saw the anger and weariness in his eyes and knew he would do what he said.

But the gun wasn't the only weapon she had. Something hard pressed into the back of her bare right thigh where she was sitting on the ground. A few moments earlier, she had figured out that it was the hilt of the knife she was feeling. She must have moved around some in her sleep, and then when she sat up so quickly, her leg had come down on the knife, hiding it from the two men. Probably they believed she had lost it during the night, if they gave it any thought at all.

She had to make sure they didn't think about it now, and she knew one sure way to distract them.

"All right," she said. "I know when I'm licked. You haven't hurt me except when I was trying to fight you, so I'll cooperate from here on out."

Benjy nodded emphatically and said, "Now you're gettin' smart."

"I'd really like to dry these clothes some more

before we head back to your camp, though," she went on. "They're still damp enough that they're uncomfortable."

She reached down, grasped the bottom of her shirt and undershirt, and peeled both garments up and over her head. She clutched the clothes in the hand she put on the ground to brace herself as she got to her feet, and as she rose, she had the knife hidden under them. When she was standing, she took a deep breath and raised her other hand to push her tangled hair out of her face.

"Let me hang these up on a branch for a little while," she said as she stepped toward Dave.

Benjy's eyes were about to bulge right out of their sockets, just as Denny expected. Even Dave, hard-nosed professional owlhoot though he tried to be, was staring at her. His mouth hung open a little. He lowered the gun slightly.

Denny had the clothes in both hands now. As Benjy let out a whistle of admiration and started to say "Holeee—" Denny used her left hand to fling the damp garments into Dave's face, blinding him and causing him to take a startled step backward.

Denny dived after the clothes. She slammed her left forearm against Dave's gun hand, driving it farther toward the ground, and at the same time she shoved the knife into his chest with her other hand. She aimed for the heart and put all the power she had behind the thrust.

The gun boomed as Dave spasmed and jerked the trigger involuntarily, but the bullet must have gone into the ground. Denny knew she wasn't hit. The knife had penetrated Dave's chest all the way to the hilt. She tried to pull it free, but it stuck and she knew she didn't have time to struggle with it. Dave's eyes were huge with pain and shock now, rather than lust. His breath rattled grotesquely in his throat as he started to collapse.

Denny made a grab for Dave's gun but missed it. Instead, she inadvertently snagged the shirt she had thrown in his face. Unarmed now, she bulled past the dying man and ran.

Over the wild pounding of her heart, she heard Benjy's feet slapping on the ground behind her. Now that he had recovered from his surprise, he was giving chase, and his longer legs should have given him an advantage. But she was younger and had always been a fast runner. As a child, she had run races against some of the boys in England—never Louis, because his heart wouldn't have stood up to the strain—and Denny won those races often enough to annoy the boys.

She knew she might be running for her life now, which gave her even more of an incentive. With Dave dead and no longer able to keep his big, rawboned partner under control, there was no telling what Benjy might do if he caught her.

Well, she amended, she knew *one* thing he would try to do—and she wasn't going to allow that to happen.

She flashed into the trees, weaved around the trunks, and ducked under low-hanging branches, barely slowing down as she did so. Benjy would have a harder time of it, since he was bigger and clumsier. Denny had to take advantage of this chance to gain ground on him.

After several minutes of desperate flight, she came to a gully that was dry at the moment, although water probably ran through it whenever there were heavy rains. She slid down into it. Brush scraped and clawed at her bare flesh. She forced her way through the growth and stumbled along the bottom of the gully.

Up ahead, a couple of trees had fallen and lay at angles to each other across the gully, forming a little niche underneath them. That might be a place she could hide for a while. She picked up a broken branch and poked around in the area underneath the deadfalls to make sure no snakes or other varmints were lurking in there. Leaves, pine needles, and other detritus had blown under the trunks.

Some rats scurried out from a nest. They appeared to be the only inhabitants of the little niche. Denny got down on her knees and crawled under the trees. There was enough room for her to sit up. She pulled the shirt back on and felt a little better once she had.

But she was still barefoot, less than half-dressed, and unarmed, and with a brute like Benjy looking for her, none of that boded well. She hefted the branch she had used to poke around under the trees. It had served that purpose well, but she didn't think it was heavy enough to make much of a club.

She caught her breath as she heard something crunching through the brush not far away, making too much noise to be an animal. That left only one possibility.

Benjy.

Denny held her breath as the searching footsteps came closer. She clutched the branch tightly. It was all she had. If she could ram its jagged end into his already injured face, it might discourage him . . .

The noises stopped.

Still not breathing, Denny listened intently. Where

had he gone? He had to be somewhere close. Had he spotted her under the tree trunks and was sneaking up on her, trying to employ stealth now? Benjy didn't seem like the stealthy type, but she couldn't count on that.

A moment later, she learned just how much she couldn't count on it, as boot leather scraped on one of the trunks right above her head. Benjy jumped off the deadfall, landed in the gully, and reached into Denny's hiding place to close a hand around her left ankle.

"Got you now!" he crowed as he roughly dragged her out into the open.

CHAPTER 38

Big Rock

Brice had breakfast at the boardinghouse where he lived, enjoying the spread of flapjacks, ham, hash browns, and fried eggs that his landlady set out. The company wasn't bad, either. The townspeople who lived here were friendly and liked having a lawman as a fellow boarder, whenever he was in town, that is. Brice's work as a deputy marshal kept him out on the trail quite a bit, but he maintained the rented room in Big Rock for when he wasn't assigned to a case.

After he finished eating, he figured he would go by the telegraph office and see if there had been any more replies to his wires. They were still trickling in, but so far they hadn't achieved any positive results. The gang of bank robbers that had left a trail of looted vaults and dead bodies behind them in Wyoming seemed to have vanished off the face of the earth.

Brice hoped it was just a matter of time until they struck again and he got a lead on them. That feeling sort of bothered him, though, because it was almost like he was wishing for a crime to be committed and that went against the grain for a lawman. But he wasn't sure what else he could do at this point.

Monte Carson's office was on Brice's way. He stopped in to say hello to the sheriff, who was pouring himself a cup of coffee from the battered old pot simmering on the stove.

After they'd said hello and Brice had accepted the sheriff's offer of a cup of the steaming black brew, Monte asked, "Have you had any luck with those wires you sent out?"

"I was just thinking about that," Brice admitted. He shook his head. "So far, not a thing—"

The door of the sheriff's office opened quickly and a young cowboy hurried in, leaving the door ajar behind him. Brice and Monte both turned to look at him in surprise. The youngster came to an abrupt halt and said, "Howdy, Sheriff. You, too, Marshal Rogers. I'm mighty glad the two of you are here together. Smoke told me to find you both."

"Your name's Orrie, isn't it?" Monte said. "You ride for the Sugarloaf?"

"Yes, sir, both of them things is true. I ride fast, too, so Smoke sent me with a message. Miss Denny's missin'."

Brice choked on the sip of coffee he'd been taking. He set the cup down abruptly enough that some of it sloshed out.

"What do you mean, 'Denny's missing'?" he demanded.

"She rode up to one of the line camps yesterday with supplies for the fellas who're stayin' there," Orrie explained. "But she never came back. Yesterday, after that big ol' storm blew through, Smoke got to worryin' that something might've happened to her.

Her horse could have spooked, ran away with her, and threw her, maybe. So he went to look for her and took some of the crew with him, includin' me."

Brice didn't think it was likely Denny would lose control of any horse unless it was that loco black stallion Rocket. She was too good a rider for that, even in bad weather.

"You didn't find her?" Brice couldn't keep the worry out of his voice as he asked the question.

"No, sir. We rode all the way to that line camp and back, takin' the same trail she would have, and we never saw hide nor hair of her." Orrie shrugged. "Of course, by then it had rained hard enough that ol' Pearlie said he was gonna start roundin' up some boards to build an ark, so it ain't likely there would've been any tracks or other sign left."

Monte said, "If I've ever known a young woman who's able to take care of herself, it's Denny Jensen." Despite that statement, he sounded worried, too. "I reckon Smoke has search parties out again this morning?"

"Yes, sir. He's mighty worried, and so's Miss Sally. The crew's spreadin' out all over the Sugarloaf, and I don't figure our boys'll be too careful about stayin' right on our range, neither. But Smoke thought maybe it'd be a good idea to ask for help from the town, too."

"It sure is." Monte was already on his feet. He reached for his hat and went on, "I'll get some reliable men together and head out there right away."

"You can do that," Brice said, "but I'm going *now,* as soon as I get my horse saddled."

Orrie said, "Let me swap mounts down at the livery stable and I'll ride back with you, Marshal."

Brice shook his head as he strode toward the door.

"Sorry, but I'm not waiting for anybody. You can come with Monte and the other men."

Then he was outside, heading at a fast walk toward the livery stable where he had left his horse.

He broke into a run before he got there.

Denny wound up lying on her back. Being hauled out from her hiding place like that had left some fresh scratches and scrapes on her hide. She couldn't reach Benjy's face from where she was, so she slashed at his legs with the broken branch.

He jumped back out of range of the feeble attack and laughed.

"I don't reckon that's gonna do you much good, sweetheart. I got my gun and knife back now, and a branch ain't no good against them." His expression sobered. "I ain't a-gonna give you the chance to do to me what you done to poor ol' Dave. That was a mighty dirty trick, distractin' us with your feminine charms like you did."

Denny was angry enough that she practically snarled at him as she said, "If you've got any sense, you'll turn and walk away. I don't know why you're doing this, but you're going to be sorry."

"I'll be so sorry that I'll never forgive myself if I pass up this chance." He drew his gun. "You and me are gonna go back up that hill to the camp, and when we get there, we're gonna have ourselves some fun. You might as well get that through your head right here and now."

That was never going to happen, Denny resolved.

She would fight him tooth and nail. She would force him to kill her before she'd submit.

But to do that, she had to be back on her feet. She drew her legs up under her, put a hand on the ground to brace herself, and started to rise.

Benjy grinned again and said, "Now you're bein' reasonable. You just go along with what I say, darlin', and things'll be a whole heap more pleasant for both of us."

He didn't understand. She was getting up so she could fight again—

"Hello!"

The man's voice came from the bank of the gully, maybe ten yards away. Denny jerked her head in that direction. She could make out the figure standing there, but with the sun behind him, she couldn't see him well enough to identify him.

She knew that voice, though.

Benjy whirled around at the unexpected hail. He started to raise his gun, then lowered it instead and said in a puzzled voice, "What—"

That was all he got out before the man on the bank shot him. The gun in the newcomer's hand cracked and spat fire, and Benjy's head lurched backward. He took a step to the side. His grip on his gun loosened so that the weapon turned over on his finger as it hung by the trigger guard for a second, then slipped off and thudded to the ground at his feet.

Benjy made a half turn caused by a last-second paroxysm of nerves and muscles. Denny saw the red-rimmed hole in his forehead and knew the small-caliber bullet had bored into his brain and bounced around inside his skull, turning gray matter to mush and completing its deadly mission. Slowly, Benjy toppled over like one of those trees that had fallen across the gully. He lay in a crumpled heap and didn't move again.

Count Giovanni Malatesta slid down the bank, still holding in his hand the gun that had slain Benjy, and as he reached the bottom of the gully, he called, "Denise! *Cara mia!* Are you all right?"

Denny stepped forward quickly and scooped up the gun Benjy had dropped. She almost lifted it, pointed it at Malatesta, and ordered him to stop right where he was, but then she hesitated. He had just saved her life. Was the hostility she felt toward him just the result of old habits? Old hatreds?

She lowered the gun to her side, allowed him to rush forward, throw his arms around her, and hug her tightly against him. She didn't let go of the gun, though, just in case she changed her mind about shooting him.

"*Cara mia,*" he breathed. "Thank God I found you in time. Where is the other one?"

"Dead," Denny said. "I . . . I killed him . . . earlier."

She tried to keep her voice strong, but it broke from exhaustion and the terrible strain she had been under and the sudden, unexpected relief of knowing that both her captors were dead.

A voice in the back of her brain stubbornly told her she still needed to get away, but she couldn't fight anymore. She stood there trembling and allowed Malatesta to hold her. After a moment she pressed her face against his shirtfront and started to cry.

CHAPTER 39

The Sugarloaf's headquarters appeared deserted when Brice rode in, but someone inside the big house must have heard the swift rataplan of his horse's hoofbeats. As he reined in, the front door opened and Sally Jensen hurried out onto the porch, followed by Inez Sandoval, the housekeeper and cook who worked in the main house.

Sally waved a hand and called, "Brice! Hello!" She came to the porch railing and rested her hands on it, closing them tightly in the anxiety that gripped her. "Have you heard any news about Denise?"

"Only that she's missing," Brice replied. "That's why I'm here, ma'am." Brice tautened the reins as his horse moved around skittishly, perhaps picking up on his own emotional state. "I was hoping you'd have word by the time I got here. Actually, I was hoping somebody would have found her and brought her back by now."

Sally shook her head. "No. Smoke's not back yet. None of them are." She seemed to be trying to keep the dismay out of her voice and off her face, but she wasn't succeeding too well in either of those efforts.

"Well, I rode out here to help with the search, and Monte Carson shouldn't be too far behind me with a lot of other men from Big Rock, so I'm sure we'll find her before too much longer—"

"Señora Jensen!" Inez exclaimed, breaking in to what Brice hoped were words of encouragement. "Look!"

She pointed, and when Brice looked in the direction the housekeeper indicated, he saw a rider heading toward the big house, still a couple of hundred yards away. Brice didn't recognize the man in the dark suit and black hat at first, but then a fair-haired head poked around the newcomer's shoulder to see where they were. Brice realized somebody was riding double with the man—and he knew who that somebody was.

"Denny!" he shouted as he wheeled his horse around and kicked the animal into a run again.

The man urged his mount to a slightly faster gait as well, and the gap closed quickly. Brice recognized Count Giovanni Malatesta and was surprised that the Italian nobleman was the one who had found Denny. Nobody had even said anything about Malatesta being out here searching.

Denny seemed to be urging Malatesta to bring his horse to a stop. He did so, and she slid down from the saddle. As soon as her feet hit the ground, she ran toward Brice. He reined in as well and dismounted with smooth, athletic ease while his horse was still moving. He ran only a couple of steps before Denny reached him. She flung herself into his embrace and threw her arms around his neck. She clung to him with a fierce intensity.

"Brice," she whispered as she pressed her cheek to his. "I was afraid I'd never see you again."

"And I was mighty worried about you," he told her. "Are you all right?"

He felt her nod against his chest.

"Yes. I will be . . . now."

That made him feel good and warm inside. Denny was, without a doubt, the strongest and most self-sufficient woman he had ever known, but she was human, too, and all human beings had moments of weakness, times when feelings of fear and strain and hurt threatened to overwhelm them and they had to turn to someone else for strength.

Evidently, this was one such moment for Denny—and she had come running to him. Even though she had ridden in on Malatesta's horse and he must have been the one who found her, it was *Brice* she wanted to hold her. He stroked her blond curls, which were in tangled disarray, and said softly, "It's all right now."

"I know," she breathed. "I know."

She was wearing boots, jeans, and a flannel shirt, the sort of garb she wore whenever she rode the Sugarloaf range. But she didn't have her hat, her horse, or her carbine, as far as Brice could see. Definitely, she had run into some sort of trouble yesterday.

She wasn't trembling anymore and seemed steadier now. He moved back a little, rested his hands on her shoulders, and said, "What happened to you?" He saw now that her face was scratched and bruised. Rage welled up inside him. "Who did this to you? I'll—"

"No need for anybody to do anything," she said. "Both men responsible for it are dead. I killed one of them, and Count Malatesta killed the other when he rescued me."

Brice glanced at the nobleman, who sat his saddle with a smug look on his handsome face.

"When he did what?"

"Rescued the fair lady from her captors," Malatesta drawled.

"How'd you even know she was missing?" Brice frowned. "Word just reached Big Rock this morning."

Malatesta looked a little annoyed that Brice would ask such a question at a moment like this. He made a casually elegant gesture and said, "As I have already explained to Signorina Jensen, I rode out here yesterday to pay her a visit, and I happened to see men preparing to search for something. At the time, I did not know what . . . or who . . . they sought. But I overheard enough of their conversation to realize that Denise was missing, and so I set out on my own to search. I believed her father and the others might not have welcomed my assistance."

He was probably right about that, Brice thought. Smoke likely would have told Malatesta to go back to Big Rock.

"I had no luck yesterday evening," Malatesta continued, "but I returned this morning and good fortune was with me. I heard a shot, followed the sound, and came upon Denise about to struggle with her remaining captor." He shrugged. "The fellow made threatening gestures, as if he intended to shoot me, but I shot him first."

"And did a good job of it, too," Denny said. "Killed him just about instantly."

"Well . . . I'm sure Denny and her folks appreciate your help," Brice said grudgingly.

"I certainly do." Denny turned and walked back toward Malatesta. He swung down from the saddle. She went on, "Thank you. I know we've had our differences in the past, but I'll never forget what you did this morning."

Then she held out her hand and waited for him to shake it.

Malatesta's mouth tightened. A bitter, angry look came over his face, but he quickly wiped it away and clasped her hand.

"The pleasure was all mine, signorina."

Denny gave his hand a hard pump, then let go of it and turned to walk back over to Brice. She didn't wait for him to make a move but went ahead and took his left hand in her right. This was no formal handshake but rather a more intimate connection, and anyone with eyes could see that.

Sally came down the porch steps and moved toward the others.

"Why don't we all go inside?" she suggested. "Inez has coffee on the stove, and I imagine we could all use a cup after so much worrying."

Malatesta shook his head and said, "My thanks for your generous and gracious offer of hospitality, Signora Jensen, but I should be going."

"No!" Sally said. "You were the one who rescued my daughter."

Malatesta smiled and spread his hands.

"Not really," he said. "I have every confidence in the world that if I had not come along when I did,

Denise would have succeeded in defeating that rascal on her own."

"He was a lot worse than a rascal," Denny said, "and I'm not sure I would have been able to handle him."

"Never doubt yourself, *cara mia.*"

"You still haven't said exactly what happened," Brice reminded her. "Did those two varmints kidnap you? Who were they? What did they want?"

"Ransom, I suppose," Denny said. "They knew who my father is."

"And they went after you anyway, knowing that Smoke Jensen's your pa?" Brice shook his head in amazement. "They sure must have been short on common sense."

"Or else they really wanted money," Denny said. "But we don't have to worry about them anymore." She came up on her toes—not far since she was a tall girl—and brushed a kiss across Brice's cheek. "And I'm home, so everything's going to be all right now."

"I can't argue with that," Brice said. With his arm now linked with hers, he turned toward the house.

"Thank you again, Count," Sally said to Malatesta. "I'm sure my husband will want to speak with you and thank you as well."

"Any time, signora," he said. He took off his hat, flourished it as he executed a bow that made Sally laugh and then blush. She told him good-bye and then turned to follow Denny and Brice into the house.

Malatesta stood stiffly beside his horse, watching them all go.

* * *

He was seething inside as he rode toward Big Rock. His plan had gone . . . not perfectly, of course, but things had proceeded in a reasonable-enough fashion that he should have been able to salvage them and achieve the results he wanted.

Those two louts were supposed to hold Denny captive overnight, and then today, as they were moving her to another camp, actually they would have led her straight to the spot where Malatesta was waiting to "rescue" her.

As things had turned out, he actually had been forced to search for her, but since he'd already been in the vicinity to carry out the plan, he had been able to hear the shot that had led him to them.

Benjy Bridwell and Dave Nelson had believed that Malatesta would simply take Denny away from them at gunpoint. Actually, his intention all along had been to kill them from ambush so they would never be able to tell Denny that he had paid them to kidnap her. A wise man never left anyone alive with information that could be used for blackmail.

Then she would have been grateful to him for saving her, and she would begin to wonder if she was wrong about him. Malatesta knew that the slightest crack in Denny's armor was all he needed to work himself back into her good graces—and her affections.

Instead, Denny had escaped from those idiots not once but twice, and the second time she had killed Nelson. That was no great loss, since he was slated to die anyway, but because of Denny's success at handling the men, she might not feel as grateful to Malatesta as she should have. She might believe she could have handled the situation alone if she had to.

He had said as much, back there at her parents' ranch house, just to make her deny it out of politeness but still plant the seed of doubt in her head.

Anyway, he had killed one of the scoundrels for her! Wasn't that enough to make her feel differently toward him?

Evidently not. She had expressed her appreciation to him with a *handshake*. A handshake—after she had gone running to the arms of that infernal deputy marshal, Brice Rogers.

After that, Malatesta hadn't trusted himself to remain at the Sugarloaf. He had said his farewells and gotten out of there as briskly as possible before he lost his temper out of sheer frustration. It was clear from what he had seen today that Brice Rogers was the main obstacle standing in the way of him getting what he wanted.

The glare on his face gradually turned into a smile as he slouched along in the saddle. He had a plan for dealing with Rogers, too, and it didn't involve killing the man. The last thing he wanted was Denny pining away over a lost love.

No, he would destroy Rogers in her eyes, so that she wouldn't want anything more to do with him. And then, naturally, she would turn to her former lover . . .

Malatesta heeled his rented horse to a faster pace. He was eager to get back to Big Rock now. He had things to do. He had already laid the groundwork, and now he had a plan to put in motion.

And it would start with that saloon girl Rosemarie.

CHAPTER 40

Red Cliff

As the county seat of Eagle County, Red Cliff was somewhat larger than Big Rock, the other main town in the area. None of its saloons were quite as nice as Longmont's, but the Pemberton House wasn't bad.

Most of the customers were dressed well enough that Ned Yeager felt a little out of place as he strolled in there. He went to the bar, rested his hands on the gleaming hardwood, and told the slick-haired bartender, "I'll have a beer."

"Coming up," the apron replied. "Don't think I've seen you around before. You new in town, friend?"

Yeager wanted to snap at the man and tell him he wasn't his friend, and he wasn't in the habit of answering nosy questions, either. But such a sharp response wouldn't serve any purpose, the gunman told himself. He didn't want to attract any attention until he found out why he had been summoned here tonight. So he just nodded and said brusquely, "Yeah, that's right."

A crooked lawyer in Denver named Duncan Price

was the one who lined up most of Yeager's jobs and
kept in touch with the people who hired him to perform his special services. Yeager preferred not to
meet his employers, and usually they felt the same
way about him. Whenever Yeager had something to
report, he would find the nearest telegraph office
and send a carefully worded wire to Price, who would
then contact the client and pass along the news, good
or bad. That system had worked flawlessly for quite
a while.

Then he had gotten a telegram from Price telling
him to be here at the Pemberton House tonight. Price
wouldn't be there himself, according to the wire, but
someone would meet Yeager.

Yeager didn't like it. The whole thing felt wrong to
him. He needed to be spending his time recruiting
more men for his crew, not carrying out some mysterious errand.

Three more men dead . . . He could barely believe
it. That blasted Italian had the luck of the devil, as
well as some dangerous acquaintances.

On a personal level, the loss of Gene Rice had hurt
Yeager pretty badly. He and Rice had ridden together
for quite a while. He had depended on the man,
along with his other old partner, Fred Kent. Billings
and Norris hadn't meant anything to Yeager. They
were just guns, anonymous tools to be used to finish
a job.

Now he was left with Kent and the other newcomer, Ben Steeger. He needed to put the word out
on the circuit that he was looking to hire more men.

He hoped he wouldn't get *them* killed, too.

But meanwhile, he was wasting time here, he

thought as he sipped the beer the bartender set in front of him. It was good, he had to admit that. Considering that he didn't want to be here in the first place, it really would have been a shame if the beer was lousy on top of everything else.

"Mr. Yeager?"

Stiffening, fighting down the urge to drop the beer and reach for his gun instead, Yeager turned his head and saw a man in a dark, sober suit standing next to him. The gent was medium-sized and sallow-faced, and there was absolutely nothing that stood out about him. He was the sort of man you'd glance at once, and by the time a minute passed, you would have forgotten that you'd ever seen him.

"Yeah, that's right," Yeager said slowly. He didn't see how an hombre like this could be any sort of a threat. "What can I do for you?"

"My employer is the one who had Mr. Price summon you here. He'd like to speak with you."

"Price? I didn't think he was going to be here."

"No, I'm speaking of the man I work for. And the man *you* work for."

"And who would that be?" Yeager asked.

The man gestured toward a large table at the rear of the room. Two men sat there, one of them a huge bruiser with a too-small derby on a mostly bald head, the other slick and well dressed. The second man was the one in charge. Yeager had no doubt of that.

None of this odd trio looked like he belonged in Red Cliff, Colorado. On the other hand, Yeager had never been picky about who he took money from. All of it spent the same, no matter what the source.

"All right," he said, "but I'm bringing my beer."

"Fine," the dour man agreed.

Yeager followed him through the room to the table, which was set in an alcove in the Pemberton's rear wall, giving it at least an illusion of privacy. The well-dressed man didn't get up as Yeager approached the table, and neither did his hulking companion. He held out a hand toward an empty chair, though, and said in a voice as smooth as his freshly shaven jawline, "Please, sit down and join us, Mr. Yeager. You *are* Ned Yeager?"

"I am," Yeager said as he set his beer on the table in front of the empty chair. He had carried it in his left hand so his gun hand would be free, a detail that he didn't think the smooth hombre had missed.

"I thought so. You match the description that Mr. Price gave us when we visited his office and asked about you."

Normally, Price would have kept his mouth shut about their working arrangement. He certainly wouldn't have provided Yeager's name and description to anyone. That was the way Yeager wanted it.

He could understand how Price would have had a hard time saying no to these men, however. They gave off a real air of menace, even the unassuming one.

"And who are you?" Yeager asked bluntly.

"The man who has engaged your services. Surely you must have grasped that by now."

"I don't know your name," Yeager pointed out. "You know mine."

The smooth hombre smiled, even though the expression never reached his eyes.

"And turnabout is fair play, as the old saying goes. Very well. My name is Nick Scaramello. My associates and I are from New York City."

Yeager hadn't asked where they were from, but he had known they weren't from these parts. He figured it wouldn't hurt to sit down and listen to what Scaramello had to say, even though he liked to keep plenty of distance between himself and the people he worked for.

He settled himself into the empty chair and said, "I'm listening, Mr. Scaramello."

"In the matter of that traitor and deadbeat Johnny Malatesta, you have so far been unsuccessful in carrying out my wishes."

Yeager frowned and said, "I thought he was some sort of Italian count."

Scaramello shook his head and let out a bark of laughter. He said, "Malatesta is Italian, that much is true, but he's no more a count than I am. That's just a pose. He's a criminal. A killer and a swindler . . . and a man who fails to honor his debts."

"And I'm betting that's the reason you want him dead. He owes you money."

The huge man sitting at Scaramello's right hand said, "Watch your mouth, bub."

Scaramello raised a finger to forestall any more comments from his companion.

"My motives are no concern of yours, Mr. Yeager. But *I* am concerned with your lack of success."

"We've made two good tries at him," Yeager snapped. "One of them should have worked. He got lucky, both times."

"Luck is no excuse for failure," Scaramello said, his voice hardening. "That's why I've decided to take an active hand in this. I've never let luck stop me from getting what I want."

Surprised, Yeager leaned back a little in his chair. "You're firing me?"

"Not at all. In fact, I'm increasing your pay." Scaramello took a wallet from under his coat and removed several bills from it. He dropped them on the table in front of Yeager and went on, "Hire as many men as necessary and keep me advised of your plans. I've decided I'm going to be there when Malatesta dies." Scaramello smiled again. "I want to see his face when he realizes who's responsible for his death."

Yeager looked at the money. He wanted to take it, but he hesitated.

"That's not usually the way I operate," he said.

"I know. That's why I'm paying you extra. Under the circumstances, it seems like a reasonable request."

"Very reasonable," the giant in the derby rumbled.

Yeager shrugged, then reached out and raked in the bills.

"All right," he said. "I guess if you've really got a grudge against this Malatesta, I can see why you'd want to be there. But while my men and I are working, I give the orders."

The giant leaned forward, his hamlike hands balling into fists as he said, "Listen, pal—"

"No, it's all right, Pete," Scaramello said. "Mr. Yeager is a professional. He has a right to call the shots."

"But he ain't accomplished a blamed thing—"

Yeager's lips pulled back from his teeth. "If you think you can do better, you big tub of—"

"Gentlemen, gentlemen, such hostility serves no purpose," Scaramello broke in. "We understand each other, Mr. Yeager, and we'll leave it at that. My friends and I are staying at the best hotel here in Red Cliff.

When you're ready to make another move against Malatesta, just let us know."

"It'll be the last time I go after him, I can promise you that," Yeager declared. "Next time, he dies."

Scaramello picked up a shot glass of whiskey that had sat untouched in front of him until now and said, "I'll drink to that."

A man sat alone at one of the tables in the Pemberton House, nursing a glass of scotch. He was facing away from the bigger table in the alcove at the back of the room, where four men sat. As soon as this lone individual had come into the room and seen who was sitting at that rear table, he had taken care to position himself so that his back was to them.

Angus Crabtree didn't believe that any of them would recognize him, even if they got a good look at him. He had never even seen one of the men, the one who was dressed like a westerner, and he shouldn't have been known to any of the others, even though they were known to him. As a private detective, part of his job was keeping up with the crooks operating in his part of the world.

Tracing Count Giovanni Malatesta to Colorado hadn't been difficult. The fugitive swindler was either incredibly self-confident or just downright stupid. Maybe a little bit of both. But he hadn't taken any pains to cover his tracks. Crabtree had followed his trail to Denver, then here to Red Cliff, and earlier today he had spoken to a railroad porter who told him that the count and his servant had gotten off the train at the next stop, a place called Big Rock.

The porter had babbled on about some sort of gun

battle that broke out as soon as Malatesta got off the train, which was the main reason the man still remembered the incident a couple of weeks later.

Malatesta had survived that outburst of violence. That didn't mean he would survive much longer, Crabtree mused as he sipped the scotch. He was being paid good money to see that that didn't happen.

His curiosity was aroused, though. He felt certain it had absolutely nothing to do with the job that had brought *him* to this Colorado backwater, but he couldn't help but wonder . . .

What was a slick mobster from Little Italy like Nick Scaramello doing in a place like Red Cliff?

CHAPTER 41

The Sugarloaf

"Well, I still say we ought to have the man come out here for dinner," Smoke declared. "After he helped you like he did, Denny, we owe him."

"Trust me, Pa, you don't," Denny said. "I would have gotten away without Malatesta's help."

"There's no way of knowing that, is there?"

Smoke looked at his daughter, saw the determined expression on her face, and shook his head.

"No, I reckon there's not," he agreed. "And since you feel so strongly on the matter—"

"I do."

"We'll say no more about inviting him out here."

"Good," Denny said. She was sitting in the big arm-chair in front of the desk in Smoke's study. He had called her in here to discuss the idea of having Count Giovanni Malatesta out to the ranch—and Denny had shot that down with a speed worthy of her gun-fighter father.

Smoke leaned back in his leather chair, looked thoughtful, and said, "Of course, there's nothing stopping me from buying the fella a fine dinner at Longmont's as a way of saying thank you for what he did."

Denny's lips tightened. "You think that's better than having him out here?"

"He wouldn't be on Jensen range that way. It would be a, what do they call it, neutral site."

"Yeah, I suppose it would," Denny said with a frown. "And I'm reminded of who I get my stubborn nature from."

"Your mother, obviously."

Denny blew out an exasperated breath. "Sure. I get it all from her."

"And I thought we might invite Marshal Rogers, too."

Denny leaned forward and frowned. "Brice?"

"Yep. The two of you are friends, aren't you? I mean, your mother told me about how he was here when the count brought you home and you ran to him and hugged him." Smoke smiled. "I'll bet a hat Count Malatesta didn't care much for that."

Denny looked intently at her father for a moment, then said, "You don't miss much, do you?"

"I try not to," Smoke said.

Denny leaned back, thought for several long seconds, and finally nodded.

"All right, Pa. You do what you feel like you need to do. I'll even go along. But I'm warning you, don't trust Malatesta for a second." She took a breath. "That's how folks wind up getting hurt."

Smoke cocked his head a little and said, "Do I want to ask you for any more details about that?"

"No. You don't."

"All right," he said, nodding. "I'll send word to Big

Rock and ask the count to have dinner with us at Longmont's tomorrow evening. And Brice, too. Maybe it'll be an eventful evening."

"I hope not," Denny said. But the way things had been going, she wasn't going to depend on that.

Big Rock

"I'm not sure I've ever seen you looking lovelier," Smoke said to Sally as they sat at Louis Longmont's private table the next night. He turned his head to smile at Denny. "Either of you."

No range clothes for Denny this evening. She wore an elegant pale blue gown with white lace at the sleeves and neckline. Her blond curls were swept up and pinned in place in an elaborate arrangement. She had grown accustomed to dressing more comfortably since she had moved back to Colorado permanently, but she had to admit, it was nice to get all fancied up every now and then.

She hoped she would take Giovanni Malatesta's breath away—and then leave him disappointed in the knowledge that he would never have what he had set his sights on.

She also hoped that Brice would be impressed. They had gone through a great deal together, but none of it had involved getting dressed up for an elegant meal.

Sally wore a dark blue gown, more conservative than her daughter's, but no less lovely. Smoke was in a brown tweed suit with a string tie against the snowy white of his shirtfront. He wasn't wearing a gun belt tonight, but Denny happened to know that he had a small-caliber, short-barreled pistol in a shoulder holster under his coat.

Smoke wasn't the only one who was armed. She had a two-shot, .41 caliber derringer in the beaded bag that lay on the table close to her right hand. It might be a new, supposedly more civilized century, but the Jensens had a long-standing habit of packing iron.

Louis Longmont wouldn't be joining them this evening, although this was his private table, tucked away in a semiprivate corner, covered with a cloth of fine Irish linen, set with the best crystal and china and silver. A bottle of wine rested at a slant in a bucket of ice, ready to be opened as soon as the other two guests arrived.

One of them was here now, Denny noted as she saw Louis Longmont himself escorting Count Giovanni Malatesta across the room toward them. Malatesta was well dressed as always, this time in a charcoal-gray suit. Denny could tell he was trying not to smirk in self-satisfaction—but not succeeding too well at that—as he came up to the table with Longmont.

"Enjoy your evening, Count," the former gambler and gunman murmured.

"Oh, I am certain that I shall," Malatesta said, smiling.

He took the hand that Sally held out to him and bent to kiss the back of it, then shook hands with Smoke. Then he turned to Denny.

"*Cara mia,*" he said. She didn't bother telling him not to call her that. It seemed to be a losing battle, and anyway, he would soon see that she wasn't his "beloved." She even allowed him to kiss her hand and didn't pull it away in revulsion.

Smoke had stood up to greet the count. As they all sat down, Malatesta said to Smoke and Sally, "This is a lovely gesture, my friends, but not necessary. Knowing that my humble efforts were of assistance to your beautiful daughter is more than enough thanks for me."

"We just thought it was the right thing to do," Smoke said. "Clearly, you got our invitation all right."

"Your man delivered it to my man, and he conveyed it to me. I very much appreciate your hospitality."

The young cowboy called Orrie was the one who had brought the invitation to town and given it to Arturo, a task which he'd taken great pride in carrying out.

The waiter came over and asked Smoke, "Should I open the wine now, Mr. Jensen?"

"In a minute," Smoke told him. "We're waiting on one more guest."

Malatesta arched an eyebrow and said, "We are?"

"That's right." Smoke nodded toward the entrance. "And here he comes now."

Denny looked around and saw Brice Rogers coming toward the table, carrying his hat in his left hand. He wore a brown suit and an actual cravat with a pearl stickpin. This was one of the few times Denny had seen him this dressed up, and she had to admit that he was pretty handsome. He didn't have a gun belt on, either, but she wondered if he had a gun somewhere on him.

From the corner of her eye, she saw that Malatesta was watching Brice's approach, too. His eyebrows drew down in a scowl.

"I didn't realize the marshal would be joining us," he said.

"Well," Smoke said blandly, "he and Denny are good friends, so Sally and I figured it would be all right. Celebrating her escape from those kidnappers and all."

Malatesta made a little gesture and said, "Of course." His polite, smiling mask was back in place, but for a second Denny had glimpsed the real Giovanni Malatesta. It hadn't been a pretty sight, even dressed up in fancy, expensive clothes.

Brice came up to the table and smiled as he looked around at everyone, even Malatesta.

"Hello," he greeted his hosts. "Mrs. Jensen, you look lovely, as always. Mr. Jensen, it's good to see you again."

"Likewise, Brice," Smoke said. "You know you can call me Smoke, don't you?"

"Yes, sir, I just like to be respectful."

Sally said, "There's nothing wrong with that. More young people should pay attention to their manners these days."

Brice turned to Denny and went on, "Miss Jensen, you look very nice this evening as well."

"Very nice?" Denny repeated.

"Well, I figure you get told how beautiful you are all the time, so you must get a mite tired of hearing it every now and then."

"I'll let you know if I do," she said with a smile. "Until then, feel free to compliment me as much as you like."

Brice smiled and said, "I might just take you up on that." Finally, he turned to Malatesta and nodded politely. "Good evening, Count."

"Marshal," Malatesta said coolly. "How are you?"

"Doing fine."

Smoke waved a hand at the remaining empty chair and said, "Now that the small talk's done with, have a seat, Brice." He nodded to the waiter, who was hovering nearby. "You can open that bottle of wine now."

The man did so and poured drinks for all of them. Smoke lifted his glass and said, "Here's to Count Malatesta, with appreciation for what he's done for our family."

"Yes, thank you so much, Count," Sally said as she raised her glass as well.

Brice added, "I reckon I owe you a debt of gratitude, too, since Denny means quite a bit to me."

Malatesta's smile didn't budge, but Denny thought he looked like he was struggling not to grind his teeth together in anger and frustration. That made her feel better than it probably should have and was almost enough to make her glad that her father had insisted on having this dinner.

"I suppose I should say thank you as well," she murmured.

"Please," Malatesta said, "as welcome as these sentiments are, none of them are necessary." He lifted his glass. "Instead, I suggest that we drink to beauty . . . of which we have two such stunning examples right here at this table."

"I don't reckon anybody could argue with that," Smoke said. "To my wife and daughter. To the Jensen ladies!"

"To the Jensen ladies," Brice echoed.

"To the ladies," Malatesta said.

They all drank. The wine was excellent, Denny thought, and not just for Big Rock. It would have been just as good in San Francisco, New York, even

London or Paris. Louis Longmont spared no expense for special occasions.

Smoke nodded to the waiter, and soon plates with fine steaks and all the trimmings were in front of them. The man made sure their glasses never stayed empty for too long while they were eating.

Sounding like he was just making polite conversation, Brice asked, "How long do you intend to stay in Big Rock, Count? I thought you were making a tour of the West and I sort of figured you would have moved on by now."

"Is that what you wish would have happened?" Malatesta said.

"Not at all. I reckon you're welcome to stay as long as you like. I just thought you would've gotten bored by now."

"I could never grow bored anywhere such an enticing, intriguing person as Denise is."

"You don't have to flatter me, Count," Denny said.

"As close as the two of us have been, you should call me Giovanni, *cara mia.*"

As he said that, he darted a spiteful glance at Brice, as if the reminder that he and Denny had shared a relationship in Venice scored points for him.

Denny quashed that by reaching over and briefly resting her fingertips on the back of Brice's hand.

"I prefer to keep things on a formal basis," she said to Malatesta.

She could tell it was getting more and more difficult for him to maintain his composure. He'd never liked being denied anything he wanted. Maybe if he got annoyed enough, he would give up and leave town. After all the things he'd done, she didn't like the idea of him getting away scot-free, but that might be worth it to be rid of him.

Even if that happened, Denny would then be left having to deal with the aftermath of all this playing up to Brice. She didn't want him getting *too* carried away in thinking he had won her over.

Those things were going through her mind when she became aware that a woman was approaching the table. She was young and pretty in a vacant way. Denny thought she was vaguely familiar but couldn't come up with her name or a reason she knew her. Probably just someone she had seen around town.

But evidently the young woman was on a mission, because she stepped up to the table and said, "Please pardon me for interrupting, folks, but I really need to have a word with Marshal Rogers."

CHAPTER 42

"Miss Sutton," Brice said as he came to his feet. He tried to conceal his surprise at the sight of her. "What are you doing here?"

"I . . . I have to discuss something with you." With a visible effort, she put aside her diffident attitude and lifted her chin in a brief show of defiance. "It's important."

He gestured at the others around the table. "I'm in the middle of dinner—"

"I wouldn't have bothered you unless it was urgent."

He remembered what she had told him of the man boasting about shooting a federal lawman. Maybe she had spotted him again here in town.

He had picked up his napkin from his lap when he got to his feet. He placed it on the table now and said, "I'm sorry about this, folks—"

"Don't worry," Smoke told him. "Most of the time, law business won't wait. You go ahead and talk to the young lady, Brice."

Brice was grateful to Smoke for assuming this was law business—which, of course, it was. Even so,

Denny looked a mite irritated by the interruption. He would deal with it as efficiently as he could.

"I'll be right back," he said. As he turned away from the table, Rosemarie Sutton held her arm out as if she expected him to take it, and he was too much of a gentleman not to. As they started out of Longmont's, the soft warmth of her breast pressed against his arm. He felt his face getting warm, too.

When they were on the boardwalk outside, he said, "Now, what's this all about, Miss Sutton? If you saw that fella again, the one who bragged about shooting a federal lawman, you could have told me about that in there."

"No, that's not it. I . . . I . . . Could we go down there?" She nodded toward the mouth of the alley next to the restaurant and saloon. "Please? Where it's more private?"

Brice hesitated, but then shrugged and nodded. The sooner he listened to what Rosemarie had on her mind, whether it was actually important or not, the sooner he could get back to having dinner with the Jensens.

"All right. Whatever's bothering you, though, you need to just go ahead and tell me."

"I will, I promise."

She took his arm again. They moved along the boardwalk and down the steps into the darkness of the alley. No one was near them on the street, and the alley was thick with shadows. Brice stopped and said, "All right, what is it that's wrong, Miss Sutton?"

She turned to face him, opened her mouth—and screamed at the top of her lungs.

Brice stepped back, shocked by the unexpected cry. Before he could get his wits back about him, she reached into her bag, yanked out a gun, and fired a shot into the air.

"What in blazes!"

As Brice got the surprised words out at last, Rosemarie flung the pistol away into the alley and then screamed again. She grabbed the neckline of her dress and pulled hard on it. The cloth ripped almost down to her waist, exposing the frilly undergarment she wore.

Curious shouts came from people in the street as some of them hurried toward the alley. Brice heard rapid footsteps on the boardwalk in front of Longmont's and turned to see Smoke and Louis Longmont coming quickly to find out what the gunshot and the commotion were about. Each of them had a gun in his hand.

Worst of all, Denny and Sally weren't far behind them. Although Brice was still completely confused, every instinct in his body told him that Rosemarie's shocking behavior might not bode well for him, especially where Denny was concerned.

"What's going on here?" Smoke demanded gruffly.

Rosemarie put her hands over her face and sobbed miserably. That lasted only a moment before she began to beat her fists against Brice's chest and wailed, "Why didn't you let me go ahead and shoot myself? You got me in this condition! Why don't you let me just end it all?"

"Brice, what's this young lady talking about?" Smoke asked. Brice saw the same curiosity on the faces of the other people who were starting to gather around the alley mouth.

"I don't have any earthly idea," he said honestly.

One of the bystanders called, "Say, I know that gal! She works down at the Brown Dirt Cowboy Saloon!"

He didn't have to elaborate on what Rosemarie's job was. Anybody who had been around Big Rock for very long knew that the girls at the Brown Dirt Cowboy not only mingled with the customers and served drinks, they were expected to take the men upstairs and fulfill their other needs.

Rosemarie was crying again. Through her tears, she said, "Brice, honey, how can you lie like that about us? You . . . you know why I'm upset. I told you about the baby, and you said you wouldn't have anything more to do with it or me! And then . . . and then when I tried to . . . to do away with myself . . . you stopped me and . . . and did this!" She gestured at her torn dress. "You can't leave me alone, even now!"

Brice wasn't able to do anything except stare at her in astonishment as the words spilled out of her mouth. At first, what she was saying made no sense to him, but as she went on, things began to get a mite clearer.

He looked at Smoke, who was still frowning, and said, "I don't know anything about a baby, Mr. Jensen. This is the first I've heard of it, I swear. And if this, ah, young lady really is in the family way, I didn't have anything to do with it!"

He moved his gaze over to Denny as he added that last sentence, and he hoped she could tell that he was speaking the truth. He put as much honesty and sincerity into his tone as he could.

"Oh, Brice!" Rosemarie wailed. "How can you say these terrible things!"

He looked at her again and, in a sudden flash of

insight, said, "Somebody put you up to this. I reckon I have a pretty good idea who it was, too."

Brice glanced at the crowd now standing on the boardwalk in front of Longmont's. He didn't see Malatesta among them, but he was willing to bet that the count was somewhere nearby, watching and listening to see if his sordid plan was working.

He had no doubt that Malatesta was behind this act Rosemarie was putting on. He wouldn't be surprised if Malatesta had hired her to come see him that first time, either, laying the groundwork for this scheme if he needed to use it. The scar-faced badman and his boasts were likely complete fiction.

And actually, not very good fiction, either, Brice realized now that he thought about it. He should have seen through Rosemarie's story from the first. A lawman couldn't be that gullible. Normally, he wasn't, but he supposed that as a soiled dove, the young woman was good at lying to men.

"Tell me who got you to say these things," he continued. "It'll go easier for you if you do."

The sharp words made her take a step back and slowed down the crocodile tears.

"I'm telling the truth," she insisted. "You took advantage of me, got me in the family way, turned your back on me when I pleaded with you to marry me, and just now you attacked me. Anybody can see that!"

Brice shook his head and said firmly, "If you keep lying, you're just going to wind up deeper in trouble. The legal kind, not the, ah, being-with-child kind."

"Oh!" She had stopped crying entirely now as she glared at him. "You're terrible!" She turned to look at Denny, who had moved up alongside Smoke and Louis Longmont. "Miss, you really shouldn't have anything to do with the marshal. He's not a good man."

"I haven't seen or heard anything to make me think he's not," Denny replied coolly. "I've known Brice long enough now that I don't believe a word you're saying."

Rosemarie looked back and forth nervously. She was on the verge of complete failure in the mission Malatesta had given her—assuming Brice's hunch was right, and he still believed it was—and she had to know it.

"You just don't believe me because I work in a saloon and I'm not a fancy rich girl like you," she practically spat at Denny.

"No, I don't believe you because you picked the wrong man to accuse of such things."

Louis Longmont stepped down from the board-walk and took off his coat. He said, "Miss, perhaps I'd better accompany you back down to Claude Brown's place." He put the coat around her shoulders and gently pulled it together in front to partially conceal the damage to her dress. "Come along now."

"No . . . you can't . . . I'm telling the truth . . ."

She started crying again, and Brice felt a little sorry for her now because he believed the tears were genuine.

But only a little sorry, because it had been his life she was trying to ruin.

Longmont led her away. Smoke turned to the as-sembled crowd and said, "Appears that poor girl was all mixed up in her head, folks. Best just move along now. No need to stand around and gawk."

Smoke was the most respected man in the valley. People listened to what he had to say. Quite a bit of muttered gossip went on as the crowd began to break up. This would make a good story to tell friends and neighbors in the morning.

And despite the fact that Denny and her parents clearly hadn't believed what Rosemarie was saying, once the gossip got spread around, Brice's reputation would be tainted. Maybe not much, because most folks would follow the Jensens' example and not believe it—but some would. There wasn't a blasted thing Brice could do about it, either. The talk would have to die away on its own and eventually everyone would forget about it.

Brice stepped up onto the boardwalk and said to Smoke and Sally, "Mr. and Mrs. Jensen, I'm mighty sorry about all that."

Sally smiled at him. "There's no need for you to apologize, Brice. We know that poor girl wasn't telling the truth. I feel sorry for her, anyway. She must be deluded."

"Not deluded," Denny said. "She was paid to say those things."

Brice looked at her and lifted an eyebrow. "You think so, too?"

"It's pretty obvious, isn't it? And there's only one person who would benefit from having her spread a bunch of sordid lies about you."

Smoke nodded slowly and said, "Yeah, the same thought occurred to me." He looked around. "I don't see our other guest. Maybe we'd better go find him."

Once they were back inside Longmont's, they saw right away that Malatesta was no longer at the table they had been sharing. The waiter came up to them and said, "That count fella asked me to tell you that he had to leave unexpectedly. He said for me to thank you for dinner, Mr. Jensen . . . even though he didn't finish it."

"He ran out," Denny said. "He must've seen that his plan didn't work, so he left. Like the coward he is."

"Maybe it's time for Count Malatesta to move on from Big Rock," Smoke said. "I'll have a talk with Monte about that."

Brice said, "I'm not sure he's done anything to justify being run out of town. He hasn't actually broken any laws that I know of."

"No?" Denny said. "What about hiring those two saddle tramps to kidnap me so he could pretend to rescue me?"

The others all looked sharply at her. Smoke asked, "How do you know he did that?"

"He has a habit of trying to make himself look better by underhanded means," Denny said, although she didn't offer any further explanation for that statement. Brice wondered if it had something to do with what had happened between her and Malatesta in Venice.

She went on, "When he showed up and shot that second hombre, he asked me what happened to the other one. I didn't think about that at the time, but on the ride back to the Sugarloaf, I started wondering . . . how did he know there were only two of them?"

"That's a mighty good point," Smoke said. "He'd know if he was the one who hired them."

"Exactly."

Brice said, "So when you got to the Sugarloaf . . . when you jumped down off that horse and hugged me . . . you already suspected that Malatesta was behind the whole thing?"

"I was convinced of it," Denny said.

"So that's why you carried on like you did. To get under his skin."

Denny smiled and said, "Well, that's one reason. After everything that had happened, I have to admit it felt pretty good to have you hold me."

She and Brice looked at each for a long moment, before Smoke finally cleared his throat and said, "Maybe if the food hasn't gotten too cold, we ought to go ahead and finish our dinner."

"I think that's an excellent idea," Sally said.

Before Rosemarie Sutton and Louis Longmont reached the Brown Dirt Cowboy Saloon, the young woman said stiffly, "If you don't mind, Mr. Longmont, I really don't feel like going back to work tonight. Would you mind escorting me to my room instead?"

"You don't stay upstairs at the saloon?" Longmont asked, then added, "Forgive me. I suppose that question is a bit . . . indelicate."

"No, I understand," Rosemarie said. "I keep a small place of my own on Woodrow Lane."

Longmont nodded in understanding. Woodrow Lane was the most disreputable street in Big Rock, lined by several brothels and numerous whores' cribs. Some of the girls didn't work anywhere else; others, such as Rosemarie, plied their trade in saloons but also met men outside of there. Claude Brown wasn't a bad man to work for, but he always got his cut of the money. Sometimes a girl needed to earn a little extra cash of her own.

Rosemarie still had most of what that fancy Italian fella had paid her. All she had bought with it were a few supplies and a bit of opium from one of the other girls at the Brown Dirt Cowboy. Malatesta had promised her more, but now that she had failed in her mission, she was sure he wouldn't pay the extra amount. He might even demand some of the money back.

Well, she wasn't going to give it to him. In fact, she might pack up the few possessions she owned and be at the train station early in the morning to catch the first train out of here, no matter where it was headed. Her friends Benjy Bridwell and Dave Nelson were dead—she had heard all about *that* fiasco—and there was nothing keeping her in Big Rock.

"Are you all right, Miss Sutton?" Longmont asked as they drew up in front of one of the tiny cabins on Woodrow Lane, after Rosemarie had nodded toward it to indicate that it was hers.

"I'm fine, I guess." Rosemarie handed him his coat, then wiped at her eyes with the back of her hand. It was an instinctive gesture, designed to win sympathy from a man. Louis Longmont was getting old, but he was still good-looking in a graying, distinguished way. She thought about trying to get him to come in with her. It wouldn't hurt anything to have a little extra money to help her start a new life somewhere else.

"I'll say good night, then," he told her with finality, almost as if he anticipated the suggestion she was considering. He nodded gravely to her as he started to turn away.

"Thank you, Mr. Longmont," she said. He didn't stop, though. He just smiled at her and went on his way, quickly vanishing in the shadows that clogged Woodrow Lane. This wasn't exactly a well-lit part of town.

Rosemarie sighed and went to the door. It wasn't locked. There was nothing in the place worth stealing. She went inside, closed the door behind her, and fumbled around to light the lamp on a small table. She found the matches, scraped one to life on the tabletop, and held the little flame to the wick.

As it caught and a feeble yellow glow welled up, the light revealed Count Giovanni Malatesta sitting on a rickety ladder-back chair against the wall.

Rosemarie gasped and lifted a hand to her mouth. As her heart raced, she willed herself to relax and said, "Oh my goodness, sir, you startled me."

"I wanted to make sure you were all right, Rosemarie," he said as he got to his feet. He'd been sitting with his hat in his lap. He held it in both hands in front of him. "That was a rather unpleasant scene."

"I did it just the way you told me to," she said with a note of dismay in her voice. "It should have worked. Even if that Jensen witch wasn't completely convinced, she should have been at least a little worried that it might be true."

"I underestimated her feelings for that bumpkin lawman," Malatesta said. "Well, one never knows until one tries . . . does one?"

Rosemarie didn't quite follow that, but she figured it was safe to say, "I guess not." Then she added, "We can try something else, if you want to."

She didn't want that. She had been humiliated, and she just wanted to put Big Rock behind her. But if Malatesta insisted—and was willing to pay more—she supposed they could work something out.

However, he shook his head and said, "No, I think we can mark this effort down as a failure, and after tonight, nothing along the same lines would have a chance of succeeding. A shame, really." He put a hand under his coat. "I suppose you'll want a bit more money in order to keep my name out of it and ensure your silence?"

"Well . . ." Rosemarie smiled weakly. "Now that you mention it, that would be nice . . ."

"Of course." Malatesta stood up and moved closer to her. He had to take only a couple of steps to do that, since the cabin was so small. He brought his hand out.

It didn't hold a wallet, though. He grasped a knife, instead, and the blade flickered in the lamplight as it shot forward in his hand and drove into her chest. It happened so quickly that it felt to Rosemarie as if he had punched her lightly, rather than stabbing her, but then she felt a bright explosion of pain deep inside her.

That was her heart, she had time to think. He had stabbed her in the heart, because he didn't want to buy her silence. Because he was afraid of her.

Nobody had ever been afraid of her before. It had always been the other way around.

That was the last thought to go through her brain before darkness swallowed her.

CHAPTER 43

"Got another reply for you, Marshal," Eddie at the telegraph office said the next morning as Brice checked with him. He extended the yellow piece of paper through the window in the counter as he went on, "I was about to send a boy to look for you."

"Thanks," Brice said. He took the flimsy and read the words printed on it. As he did, his fingers tightened on the paper in excitement.

"That's what you've been waiting for, isn't it?" Eddie asked.

"Maybe," Brice said.

"You need to send a reply?"

"Not just yet," Brice said. He left the telegraph office and headed down the street to see Monte Carson.

"Morning," the sheriff greeted Brice as he came in. "Say, I heard about what happened at Longmont's yesterday evening. That's a shame."

"None of it is true," Brice said. He didn't want to be distracted from what had brought him here, but he also felt like he ought to defend himself.

Monte waved a hand and said, "Oh, I figured right

away that it wasn't true. Never believed it was. I know who that Sutton girl is. She's nice-looking enough, I suppose . . . but she's not Denny Jensen." The sheriff chuckled. "No one is."

"Has Denny been to see you this morning? Or Smoke?"

Monte frowned a little and shook his head. "Nope. Should I have been expecting them?"

"Not really."

While they finished their dinner at Longmont's, they had discussed Denny's suspicions of Count Malatesta. Her theory made sense, and Brice would have bet a brand-new hat that she was right: Malatesta had hired those two drifters. But suspicions weren't evidence, and as far as Brice could see, Denny didn't have a lick of proof to support her belief.

For that reason, he had told the Jensens that they would be putting Monte Carson in an awkward position if they insisted that he run Malatesta out of town. No doubt Monte would do it because of how close he and Smoke were, but it wouldn't exactly be legal.

"Well, coffee's on the stove," Monte said when Brice didn't go on. "Help yourself."

"Maybe in a minute." Brice placed the telegraph flimsy on the desk in front of Monte. "Take a look at that first."

Monte leaned forward to read the message. A frown creased his forehead as he did so.

"Burnley, eh?" he said. "I've heard of the place. Don't recollect ever being there."

"I don't think I have, either. It's big enough to have a bank, and from what the town marshal says in that wire, the bunch of owlhoots that drifted down from Wyoming hit it yesterday. Everything about the robbery fits them."

"Yeah. And they killed a bank teller and the marshal's deputy in the process."

Brice nodded. "That's common procedure for them, too. They don't seem to have any regard for human life. They'll snuff out anybody who gets in their way, without the least bit of hesitation. But now I know where they struck last . . . and which direction they were going when they made their getaway."

"You know which direction they started," Monte pointed out. "There's no guarantee they kept going the same way."

Brice thumbed back his hat, went over to the stove, and helped himself to that cup of coffee Monte had offered. He carried it over to the wall where a large map of Colorado was pinned and studied that map while he sipped the coffee.

After a moment, he pointed to the map and said, "If they did keep going in the same direction, that would take them toward this little range of mountains." Brice leaned closer to the map and squinted at the writing on it. "The Prophets. Do you know anything about that area, Monte?"

"Not much," the sheriff replied with a shake of his head. "It's well out of my bailiwick. From what I recall, though, it's pretty rugged and isolated up there. Not really good cattle country, and you can forget about farming."

"That leaves mining."

"Yep, and I think there were some shafts dug and a little color found, enough to start a boom that petered out almost as fast as it started. But it lasted long enough for a town to be established."

Brice peered closely at the map again and said, "Painted Post?"

"That's it."

"An old ghost town like that would be a good place for a gang of bank robbers to hole up."

"You think so?"

"There would be shelter if all the buildings haven't rotted and collapsed. And it's possible there could even be some usable supplies left in the stores, airtights and such, if they're not too old."

Monte shrugged, then nodded.

"Sounds like it might be worth checking out, anyway," he said. "It's a couple of days' ride north of here. Are you going to take a posse with you?"

Brice didn't have to think about that. He shook his head.

"It might be a wild-goose chase. I'll check it out myself first, and if that gang is there, I can ride on to Burnley and round up some help there."

"Just don't try to capture them by yourself. You'd probably be outnumbered eight or ten to one." Monte blew out a breath. "Anybody who went up against odds like that wouldn't stand a chance."

"Except maybe Smoke Jensen, right?" Brice said with a smile.

"Well . . . yeah. But Smoke's a special case. He's dang near supernatural when it comes to fighting."

That was Brice's opinion, too. He had plenty of confidence in his own abilities, but he knew better than to think that he was anywhere near Smoke Jensen's league.

"I'll start putting together some supplies," he said. "And I'd better rent a packhorse from Patterson."

"Good luck. I'm still not sure about you going by

yourself." Monte paused, then went on, "You know, years ago, when he was still a young man, Smoke was a deputy marshal, too. You should swear him in as a temporary deputy and take him along."

Brice shook his head and said, "No, this is my job. And I aim to do it. If those bank robbers are there, I'll bring them in . . . one way or another."

Monte Carson was still in his office, muttering over the paperwork that had cluttered up what was once a nice, simple job, when the door opened again and Smoke Jensen came in this time.

"Well, speak of the devil," Monte said.

Smoke frowned, looked behind him for a second, and then said, "Are you talking about me?"

"Yeah, your name came up a while ago when Brice Rogers was here. Were your ears burning?"

"Not really. What did Brice have to say about me?"

"Nothing, come to think of it. He just asked if you or Denny had been in to see me this morning." The sheriff's eyes narrowed shrewdly. "Did that have anything to do with the incident at Longmont's last night?"

"Yeah, but it's nothing we can prove."

"Well, get yourself a cup of coffee, then light and set and tell me about it."

Smoke did so, concluding by saying, "Denny and I are both convinced Malatesta put the Sutton girl up to it, but we can't prove it. Brice pointed out that without proof, we can't really ask you to run Malatesta out of town."

"I'd do it, though, if that's what you wanted."

"It's not." Smoke took a sip of coffee. "I've taken the law into my own hands plenty of times, when I thought it needed doing. You know that, Monte."

"Yeah, I helped you a few of those times."

Smoke grinned and said, "I know you did. But I guess I'm getting law-abiding in my old age." He paused. "Mostly law-abiding, anyway."

"Getting old is a pathetic state of affairs, isn't it?"

"Reckon the only thing worse is the alternative," Smoke said. "What was Brice doing here, anyway?"

"Marshal Long in Denver told him to track down a gang of bank robbers that seems to be drifting in this direction. Brice finally got a lead on them. Based on the way they were heading when they made their get-away, there's a chance that after their last job, they holed up in an old mining town called Painted Post. He's going up there to find out."

"Up in the Prophets," Smoke said, nodding. "I've been there. I think it's a ghost town these days."

"So it would make a good hideout, wouldn't it?"

"Yeah. Brice went to check it out by himself, you said?"

"That's right."

"He could be riding right into trouble," Smoke said.

"Yeah. But he's a lawman. That's his job. I suggested he take some help with him. He flat-out refused. Which makes me think he wouldn't take it kindly if somebody tried to horn in, well-intentioned or not."

"It won't be me. I have several business deals brewing that could come to a head at any time." Smoke shrugged. "Brice is a smart young fella. I've never known him to do anything that's *too* reckless. Maybe he won't this time, either."

"You haven't said what brings you by this morning, Smoke."

"Those business deals I mentioned. I need to send some telegrams of my own." Smoke drained the last of the coffee in the cup. "And I'd better get at it." He raised a hand in farewell as he left the office. "See you, Monte."

"See you," the lawman said.

He went back to the paperwork, but he hadn't been at it very long when the door opened again. This was turning into a busy morning, he thought as he looked up and set aside the pencil he had been using to enter figures on a sheet of paper.

Claude Brown hesitated in the doorway.

"Come on in, Claude," Monte told him. He and the saloonkeeper weren't close, by any means, but as two longtime residents of Big Rock, they shared a certain bond. "What can I do for you?"

"I'm, uh, sort of worried about one of my girls, Sheriff," Brown told him.

"One of the girls who works for you?"

"That's right. Rosemarie Sutton."

Monte's eyebrows rose. "That's the one who had the run-in with Brice Rogers yesterday evening. Accused him of all sorts of improper things. You know anything about any of that, Claude?"

Curtly, Brown said, "If she was involved with Rogers, it's news to me. I never saw the two of them together. As far as I recall, it's been weeks since he's even been in my place."

"Why are you worried about her?" Monte didn't

offer the man coffee. The bonds of shared citizenship went only so far.

"I had her scheduled early, since she left early last night, but she didn't show up for work today."

"Is that unusual?"

"Very," Brown replied with a nod. "Little Rose-marie likes money."

Monte leaned back in his chair and folded his hands across his belly. "Yeah, but soiled doves aren't exactly the most reliable folks in the world, Claude."

"I know. It's just that this doesn't feel right to me. And after what happened last night with that deputy marshal . . . He might be holding a grudge against her, Sheriff."

"Brice Rogers?" Monte shook his head. "If you're thinking Brice might have hurt her, you're way off. He'd never do that."

"Sometimes folks will do things you'd never dream they would. Anyway, I'm worried about her, and you're the sheriff, so I'm asking you to go down to her place on Woodrow Lane and see if she's there."

"You haven't done that already?"

"No. Figured it might be law business, and I like to stay on the straight and narrow."

Monte managed not to snort out a derisive laugh at that statement. Brown just wanted to avoid as much trouble as possible. But he supposed the saloon-keeper had a point. If a possibility of foul play existed, it was the sheriff's job to check it out.

"All right," he said as he heaved himself to his feet. "I'll go have a look. On Woodrow Lane, you said?"

"Yeah, I can tell you how to find the place." Brown

looked vaguely uncomfortable. "I've, uh, been there a few times."

"No need to explain yourself, Claude. Just give me the directions."

Brown did. Monte put on his hat, settled his gun belt more comfortably around his hips, and started toward the muddy trail at the edge of town that might as well be called Shabby Street instead of Woodrow Lane.

When he got there, the area looked deserted. That was because at this time of day, everyone who lived here was still asleep after being up and working most of the night. They were inside with the curtains drawn tight against the light of day, except for the ones who had to get up to work early shifts at the saloons, such as Rosemarie Sutton.

Claude Brown had provided decent directions. Monte found the little cabin without any trouble. It had a tar paper roof and a slight lean, as if a hard-enough wind might just blow it over. When Monte knocked on the door, it was loose enough to rattle in its frame.

"Miss Sutton?" he called. "This is Sheriff Carson. Are you in there? Miss Sutton?"

No answer. Monte dropped his left hand to the knob and twisted it. The door was unlocked. No surprise there. Out of habit, he wrapped his right hand around the butt of his gun as he twisted the knob with his left. A lawman who stepped into the unknown without being ready to draw had the odds for surviving very long stacked against him.

In fact, as he opened the door and sunlight spilled into the squalid room, instinct made him pull the iron from its holster. A shape sprawled on the floor next to a small table, but as Monte looked closer, he saw that it didn't represent any threat.

In fact, the life had long since faded from Rosemarie Sutton's eyes as they stared in his direction, and the front of her torn dress, as well as the lacy garment underneath it, were dark with dried blood.

CHAPTER 44

Painted Post

Brice Rogers reined his horse to a stop at the edge of some pines atop a narrow ridge, rested his crossed hands on the saddle horn, and leaned forward to ease weary muscles. After a couple of days of fairly hard riding, he was glad to have reached his destination.

A steep, winding trail led down the slope in front of him, but he stayed in the shadows of the trees where he wouldn't be as easy to see if anybody happened to look up at the ridge from the settlement below. He reached into his saddlebags to take out a pair of field glasses.

He was at the eastern end of a gulch that ran westward into the mountains for a mile before coming to an abrupt halt at the base of a towering rock wall. The steep-sided gulch was about a quarter of a mile wide, which allowed room for a main street with a smaller flanking street on each side, plus half a dozen cross streets. Painted Post had been a decent little community at one time, with close to fifty business buildings fronting the main street and at least a hundred dwellings scattered around the side and cross streets.

Just about the time those buildings had been finished, though, the gold veins in the nearby rock wall had petered out, which meant the boomtown had gone bust almost right away.

The business buildings appeared to have been sturdier to start with, since most of them were still standing, Brice saw as he studied the town through the field glasses. A few buildings had collapsed, and the roofs were rotted and falling in on several of the others.

Nearly all the windows he could see were broken. Evidently, the erstwhile citizens of Painted Post hadn't been in a good mood when they pulled up stakes and left.

Most of the cabins were either completely or partially collapsed. They had been constructed hastily to provide basic shelter for the miners working in the tunnels dug into that rock wall at the far end of the gulch. From where he was, Brice could see the openings of those abandoned tunnels, like dark, empty eye sockets in the rock face.

Slowly, he swept his gaze over the entire settlement, searching for any sign that the bank robbers he was after might be here. He didn't see any movement, but he did spot something that made him look again.

Dark, round piles littered the ground inside a corral next to a barn. Had to be horse droppings, he thought, and although he couldn't be sure from this distance how fresh they were, he felt like they must have been deposited there sometime in the past couple of days.

Just because somebody had been here recently and kept their horses in that corral didn't mean they were still here. But it was possible the horses could be inside the barn now, out of sight. From where he was, he could see that the double doors on the front of the building were open but didn't have the right angle to look inside. The fact that the doors were open didn't mean anything, either.

But Brice was suspicious enough that he had to find out. That meant he needed to get closer. He put the field glasses away and patted his horse on the shoulder.

"Sorry, old fella. We can't take the trail down there. It's too much out in the open. We'll have to find another way where there's plenty of cover, and that means your hide will probably get scratched up some. But mine will, too, for whatever comfort that is."

The horse didn't seem impressed by that sentiment. Brice lifted the reins, clucked to the animal, and rode along the ridge, searching for another way down into the gulch.

Alden Simms, Curly Bannister, and Juliana Montero sat at one of the tables inside the saloon that had looked to be in the best shape when they rode into the ghost town. On the faded and peeling sign above the door, the words ACE-HIGH SALOON were still barely visible.

Painted Post had been deserted for quite a while, so none of them expected to find any liquor left in the town, but Curly, who boasted that he had a nose for booze, had uncovered a cache of whiskey bottles inside a dumbwaiter that ran up to the second floor.

Clearly, at some point in the past somebody had placed those bottles in the little chamber, intending to raise them to the second floor, but for some reason they hadn't done it and had then forgotten the bottles were there. That oversight was a blessing for the outlaws who were now the only inhabitants of Painted Post.

The three ringleaders passed one of the bottles back and forth, filling the shot glasses they had found on a shelf behind the bar. Over in a corner at another table, Childers and Billy Ray were playing blackjack for matches. Hamilton and Britt were upstairs, sleeping off the whiskey they had consumed.

Dumont was upstairs, too, but he wasn't sleeping. With all the bullets flying around as they made their getaway from the job in Burnley, Dumont had caught a slug in the left lung. He had clung to life until they got here but crossed the divide shortly thereafter. Hamilton and Britt had promised to bury him, but they hadn't gotten around to it yet. By now enough time had passed that it would be a mighty unpleasant chore if they did, so they might just leave him there in the room at the end of the second-floor hall when they rode away from this ghost town.

What was one more ghost in a place like this, anyway?

Juliana tossed back the whiskey in her glass and asked, "How much longer are we going to stay here? There's nothing to do in this town except shoot rats."

"Practicin' your shootin' won't hurt none, darlin'," Curly told her. He downed his own drink.

Juliana glared at him and said, "I'll put my shooting up against yours any day, whether it's target shooting . . . or the only real way to settle something like that."

Alden chuckled, but he didn't really sound amused.

"You two have been sniping at each other for going on four days now, ever since we got here," he said. "I figure that any posse from Burnley would have caught up to us by now, so we'll pull out soon. Tomorrow morning, I think."

"I'm glad to hear it," Juliana said.

"Aw, it ain't been that bad," Curly argued. "We got free whiskey and a bed that'll do in a pinch."

"A bed full of vermin, you mean." Juliana shrugged. "But I reckon I should be used to that by now, shouldn't I?"

Alden and Curly both laughed at that comment. Curly shoved the bottle toward her, but Juliana shook her head.

"I need to get out and move around a little. Think I'll go down to the old livery stable and check on the horses."

"It's broad daylight out there," Alden objected with a frown.

"Well, barely," Curly said, "what with all them clouds hangin' around."

"You know what I mean. We've been trying not to move around too much when it's light."

Juliana pushed her chair back from the table and stood up.

"Like you said," she told Alden, "if a posse was going to catch up to us, they would have done it by now. But if it'll ease your mind, Alden, I'll be careful. I'll stick to the back alley and not march right down the middle of Main Street."

"I'd like to see that," Curly said with a grin. "Shoot, you're a parade all by your lonesome, gal."

"That was almost a nice thing to say," Juliana said. "You'd better watch it, or you might accidentally turn into a decent human being."

Curly threw back his head and laughed. "No chance o' that!"

Juliana left the saloon through the back door, which sagged considerably on its hinges. She followed the alley behind several other businesses.

As she moved, she listened intently. Other than animal sounds from the trees and brush along both sides of the gulch, everything was quiet and peaceful. She had to give Alden credit. He had picked a good place for them to hide out. He was smart in that way and a lot of other ways.

Sooner or later, she mused, she would have to pick between him and Curly. Both men had been remarkably tolerant about her involvement with each of them, but Juliana had never believed that that arrangement could go on forever. Alden was a lot smarter, no doubt about that, and he didn't annoy the fire out of her like Curly so often did . . . but Alden didn't make her feel like a woman nearly as much as Curly could. It was a dilemma, sure enough.

But she put those thoughts out of her mind as she reached the barn's small rear doorway. The door itself was gone, leaving just the opening. A few nail heads stuck out of the frame.

And on one of those nail heads was a tiny bit of blue cloth, right where a man's arm might have brushed against it and torn off the scrap.

Nobody in the gang had a shirt that particular shade of blue. Juliana knew that instinctively, without thinking about it. The same instinct made her close her hand around the butt of her gun and lift it part of the way out of the holster.

She stopped in the middle of the draw and let the gun slide back down into leather. Until she knew exactly what was going on here, she wanted to play this carefully.

She took off her hat, pulled her poncho over her head, and shook out her hair. She undid the top two buttons on her shirt. Whoever was in there, she wanted to make sure they realized right away she was a woman.

Then she took a deep breath, burst through the open doorway, and exclaimed, "Help me! Oh, please, help me!"

The frightened cry took Brice by surprise. He had worked his way down into the gulch, bloodying his hands and face from the scratches the thick, clawing brush inflicted on him, until he wasn't far from the back of the barn. He had taken a chance by dashing the rest of the way in the open.

Once inside, he had found exactly what he expected to find: fourteen horses in the stalls. Judging by the number of saddles also in the barn, he figured there were eight men in the gang. The other horses would serve as extra mounts and/or pack animals.

The discovery convinced him he had found the gang of bank robbers. Eight-to-one were mighty heavy odds. He would need help in capturing or killing the outlaws—unless he could manage somehow to whittle down their numbers . . .

That was what he was thinking when the young,

dark-haired woman burst into the barn pleading for help. His first thought was that she must have been staying here in Painted Post for some reason when the gang rode in and took over. His second was to notice that she was quite attractive, although in a hard-edged way, as if she had lived through a lot in her relatively young years.

And the third thing that flashed through his mind was the memory that some of the witnesses to the bank robberies had claimed a young woman was a member of the gang.

By the time he realized that, she had lunged closer to him, arms outstretched as if begging for his help. His hand dropped to the gun on his hip, but before he could draw it, she barreled into him with enough force to knock him back off his feet. He hadn't been braced for such an impact.

She landed on top of him and rammed her knee into his groin. Blinding agony exploded through Brice. He tried to fight it off. He managed to raise a hand and grab her by the neck, but he couldn't seem to summon up much strength.

She lifted her arm above her head. Brice's pain-blurred vision focused enough for him to see she held the revolver that had been holstered on her hip when she ran into the barn. It swept down with savage speed and force, and once again an explosion detonated inside Brice, this time in his head rather than his groin. His hand fell away from the girl's throat. Red waves tinged with black washed in from both sides.

"Who are you?" she asked in an angry rasp that seemed to come from far, far away. "Are you a no-good lawman?"

The tiny part of Brice's consciousness that was still

functioning wanted to laugh at that. He *wasn't* any good as a lawman. No good at all. Otherwise he wouldn't have let this owlhoot take him by surprise, and he wouldn't have hesitated for that vital second when he saw she was a woman. That had allowed her to get close enough to him for her attack to succeed. If not for that little hitch in his reaction, he might have drawn fast enough to stop her . . .

But it was too late to worry about that now. Too late for anything except those red tides washing him away to nothingness.

CHAPTER 45

The Sugarloaf, two days earlier

From the barn, Denny saw Monte Carson ride up to the main house. Her eyes were keen enough that she could make out the grim expression on the lawman's face. Something was wrong, and she immediately thought about Brice. That was enough to make it feel like her heart leaped up into her throat.

Inez came to the door in response to the sheriff's knock and ushered Monte into the house. Denny frowned. Her father had just returned from Big Rock not long before, and she knew he had been in his office only a few minutes earlier. Probably still was, so that was where Inez would take the visitor.

Denny left the barn and hurried toward the house, circling it to move along the wall where the window of Smoke's office was located. She could have just barged in and demanded to know what was going on, but she had a feeling that her father and Monte Carson would speak more frankly if they didn't know she was anywhere around.

Sure, it was eavesdropping, but Denny wasn't going to let a little thing like that stop her.

She took off her hat as she crouched under the window and listened intently. She heard Monte's voice right away and knew she had guessed right about where this conversation would take place.

"—don't really believe he had anything to do with it, of course, but he did have that run-in with her at Longmont's," Monte was saying.

"Nobody believed her story, though," Smoke said. "Nobody whose opinion ought to matter to Brice."

So the sheriff *had* come out here to talk about Brice. Denny's hunch had been right.

"Maybe not, but it's understandable why he'd be mad at her anyway."

"Not mad enough to commit murder," Smoke said. "Brice would never do that."

Denny's heart lurched in her chest, then began to slug heavily. *Murder?* And from the sound of it, they were talking about that saloon girl from the Brown Dirt Cowboy, Rosemarie Sutton. The one who had accused Brice of getting her pregnant.

Denny still didn't believe that for even a split second, but she would have before she could ever accept the idea that Brice would kill the young woman. He wasn't capable of such a heinous crime. Or *any* crime, for that matter. Brice Rogers was about as straight-arrow as they came.

"I've asked plenty of questions," Monte went on, "but you know how folks are in that part of town. They don't like to cooperate with the law that much. Nobody admits to seeing anything, and it's even possible they're telling the truth."

"Louis was going to walk the girl back to her place," Smoke said. "You've talked to him?"

"Sure, first thing. He told me she was alive when he

left her there, and he didn't see anything unusual. Nobody suspicious hanging around or anything like that."

"You believe him?"

"Of course I do!" Monte sounded like it was ridiculous to think otherwise, and truly, it was. "Louis and I have known each other as long as you and I have, and I'd trust him with my life. Matter of fact, I have, on more than one occasion."

"Me, too," Smoke said.

"But from the looks of the girl's body, she'd been dead for quite a while when I found her, so she must have been killed pretty soon after Louis left her there last night. How long was Brice at Longmont's after that little disturbance broke up?"

"I reckon we were all there for another half hour or so," Smoke said.

"And you don't know where he went after that?"

"No, I don't. Sally and Denny and I came back out here to the ranch. I suppose Brice went back to the boardinghouse where he lives."

"He could have made a quick trip to Woodrow Lane along the way."

"No," Smoke said flatly. "He may not have a solid alibi, but I still firmly believe he's innocent."

"So do I," Monte said, "but the way things look, I'm going to have to question him, anyway."

"Well, I suppose that's fair enough. Are you going after him, up to that ghost town in the Prophets?"

"No, I don't reckon that's necessary. The girl's already dead; nothing's going to change that. There'll be time enough to talk to Brice once he gets back from this marshaling job he's on."

"I'm glad you feel that way, Monte. He's a devoted

lawman. He wouldn't want anything interfering with an assignment from Marshal Long."

"I just wanted to see what you thought about the situation, Smoke. I'm glad we've got it figured the same way."

"The question is," Smoke said, "if Brice didn't kill the Sutton girl . . . and neither of us believe he did . . . then who did?"

Outside the window, with her heart still hammering in her chest, Denny came up with an answer to that question. The same man who had put Rosemarie up to trying to smear Brice's name might have decided to get rid of her when the attempt failed, just so she could never implicate him in the scheme.

Count Giovanni Malatesta.

Denny moved away from the window and straightened up. Brice might not be in trouble with the law, but he needed to know what was going on. Besides, if Malatesta really had resorted to murder, he might go after Brice next. She wanted to warn him what to expect—and what to look out for.

And, if she was being really honest with herself, she didn't mind having an excuse to trail him up into the Prophet Mountains. If he found the gang of bank robbers he was looking for, he might need some help rounding them up. A job like that held the promise of adventure, and to Denny, that was an almost irresistible lure. He would be annoyed with her, of course—or at least he would pretend to be—but having her around might come in handy. That had happened in the past.

She was sure her mother and father would try to stop her if she told them what she was going to do, though. That was a problem with a simple solution. She just wouldn't say anything to them about it.

Half an hour later, while Smoke and Monte Carson were still talking, after surreptitiously packing some supplies, extra guns, and plenty of ammunition, Denny rode away from the Sugarloaf, heading north. She had always found maps fascinating and had studied the map of Colorado pinned up on the wall of Smoke's office, so she knew where the Prophet Mountains and the settlement of Painted Post were.

She didn't know what she would find at the end of that trail, but there was only one way to find out.

Giovanni Malatesta was not a man to be plagued by self-doubts, but he found himself wondering if killing the prostitute had been the right thing to do.

Logically, it made sense to shut her up permanently, rather than relying on her somewhat shaky discretion. He had always found it best not to leave any loose ends dangling, if possible.

But the worst she could have accused him of was paying her to lie about Rogers. That was a lot less serious than murder.

And the most frustrating part was that it had all been for nothing. Denise and her parents had disregarded Rosemarie's story completely and put all their trust in Rogers. What was it about that blasted man that made everyone adore and believe him?

It was clear to Giovanni now, as clear as anything had ever been.

He would never win Denise over as long as Brice Rogers was still alive.

Therefore, Rogers had to die.

Earlier, he had sent Arturo out to gather the gossip going around in town. Arturo was very good at that and came back to report that while some people suspected Rogers had something to do with the girl's death, overall not many did. The sheriff had questioned a number of Rosemarie's coworkers and acquaintances, as well as Louis Longmont, who had walked her back to her cabin the previous night.

Then Monte Carson had ridden out of town, heading west, and as soon as Arturo said that, Malatesta knew the lawman was going to the Sugarloaf to talk to Smoke Jensen. Carson might be the sheriff, but Malatesta had sensed right away that Jensen was the real power in this valley. Carson would want to get Jensen's opinion on how to proceed with his investigation.

Arturo had one other bit of news: even earlier this morning, before the dead girl's body was discovered, Rogers had ridden out of town, his saddlebags bulging with enough supplies for a trip of several days' duration. None of the gossipers knew where he was going, but it was clear he wasn't going to be in Big Rock for a while.

As soon as he had heard that, Malatesta knew this might be a perfect opportunity to get rid of his rival. Unfortunately, he was no tracker. Without knowing where Rogers was headed, Malatesta stood no chance of finding him.

But the sheriff might know. Carson might intend to find him and bring him back to face questions about Rosemarie's death. Therefore, following the lawman might be worthwhile.

Really, it was the only shot he had right now, Malatesta told himself.

So he had ordered Arturo to put together a pack of supplies for him, and he had rented the same horse he had used before, telling the liveryman that he might be gone for several days, and then he had ridden toward the Sugarloaf, leaving Arturo behind in Big Rock. If the sheriff *hadn't* gone to the Jensen ranch, then he would be out of luck, but if he had, Malatesta intended to pick up his trail there.

The last thing he'd expected, as he sat watching the ranch headquarters from a hilltop, was to see Denise riding away hurriedly and rather stealthily, obviously bent on some important errand. Was *she* looking for Brice Rogers, too? It certainly seemed possible.

Torn between waiting for the sheriff as he had planned or following Denise, Malatesta hesitated for only a moment.

Then he turned his horse and picked out a north-bound route through the trees and over the rolling hills, keeping Denise in sight in the distance ahead of him. If she had looked back at just the right moment, she might have spotted him. But all her attention was directed at what lay ahead of her.

If he could manage it at all, he vowed, what she would find was Brice Rogers's body.

Yeager's camp

Yeager had sent Ben Steeger to Big Rock to scout out the situation. Scaramello had insisted on sending Big Pete along, too, to further represent his interests, as he put it. Yeager didn't like it—but he hadn't liked anything about this job, to be honest. If Scaramello hadn't paid him extra, he might have walked away from it.

Steeger and Pete were both strangers in Big Rock, so it was unlikely that anybody would notice them nosing around. While they were doing that, Yeager had ridden back to the same road ranch where he had recruited Steeger, Billings, and Norris. He had come up with four more men, including one known only as the Norwegian, a tall, blond man with a reputation as a vicious, highly competent killer. That gave them a force of ten men, total, since Scaramello insisted that he would be going along when they made their move against Malatesta, as well as Pete and the dour Anthony Migliazzi, who looked too frail to be much good in a fight.

That was a lot of men to kill one hombre, but they had outnumbered their quarry before and had failed. Yeager was determined that wasn't going to happen again.

He and the others, except for Steeger and Pete, were camped in a clearing about five miles northeast of Big Rock. Scaramello had outfitted himself and his men in Red Cliff, so they had tents, folding canvas chairs, cooking equipment, and other things to make life easier and more comfortable. Yeager was a little jealous, but he was accustomed to riding hard, lonely trails. In the end, all that mattered was getting the job done—and getting paid.

At the moment, Scaramello was sitting in one of those canvas chairs with his legs stretched out in front of him, crossed at the ankle. The boots he wore might have cost almost as much as what he had paid Yeager to kill Giovanni Malatesta. He was sipping a cup of coffee that Migliazzi had brewed in a separate coffeepot.

Fred Kent was rolling dice on a blanket with two of the new men. The third new man was mending his saddle. The Norwegian was sitting by himself, as usual. He didn't care to associate with people any more than he had to.

Yeager heard hoofbeats and called to the others, "Riders coming in." They all put aside whatever they were doing and stood up. Their hands hovered near their guns.

Steeger and Pete appeared, coming through the trees on horseback. Pete grimaced with every step his mount took. He didn't like riding, claimed it was a torture invented by the Devil, and swore that once this was over, he would never get near a horse again, let alone on one.

The newcomers reined in and swung down from their saddles, Pete with considerable awkwardness. Yeager said, "I hope you boys have good news."

"How's this?" Steeger asked. "Malatesta rode out of Big Rock a while ago, and I swear, it sure looked like he was followin' the sheriff. They both wound up at that big ranch called the Sugarloaf."

"They were together?" Yeager asked sharply.

Steeger shook his head. "Nope, like I said, the count was followin' Carson. He hung back and watched the place while *we* watched *him*."

"Did he know you were there?" Scaramello asked.

"No, sir, I don't think so. He never gave any sign of it if he did." Steeger scratched at his jaw. "To tell you the truth, I think I could've plugged him in the back with my rifle, and he never would've knowed what hit him."

"I wouldn't let that happen, Mr. Scaramello," Pete said. "I know you want to see him die up close and personal-like."

Scaramello appeared to think about that. After a moment, he nodded slowly.

"You did right, Pete," he said. "Having him shot dead from ambush wouldn't be nearly as satisfying. Where is he now?"

"Well, that's the odd thing," Steeger said. "Some other fella rode off from the ranch, heading north, and Malatesta followed *him* this time. I thought about trailin' both of 'em but decided it was better to head back here to camp and let you know it looks like Malatesta's gonna be out on his own for a spell, where we can get him. His saddlebags were full, like he was packin' enough supplies to last for several days."

Scaramello looked at Yeager and asked, "Do you have any idea what all this is about?"

"The riding here and there and following people?" Yeager shook his head. "Not a clue. But like Ben said, it's a chance to catch Malatesta out on his own, with nobody to interfere this time."

"Can you pick up his trail from this ranch and follow it?"

The Norwegian spoke up, saying, "If Yeager can't, I can."

"I can pick up his trail," Yeager snapped.

Scaramello gave a curt nod. "Let's get ready to move, then. I want this over, and I want Giovanni Malatesta dead."

CHAPTER 46

Painted Post

Brice made an effort not to groan, move around, or open his eyes as consciousness seeped back into his brain. At first he had no memory of where he was or what had happened to him, but some instinct told him he was recovering from being knocked out. It made sense to see if he could figure out what was going on before he let any potential enemies know he was awake.

The first thing he did was to take stock of his own situation. His head hurt like blazes; that was a given. He tensed the muscles in his arms, just enough to discover that they wouldn't move because his wrists were tied together behind his back. A check of his legs told him that his ankles were bound, too.

So he was tied hand and foot, but he didn't have a gag in his mouth, just a bad taste. It was the bitter, sour taste of defeat lingering under his tongue.

He turned his attention outward to discover what he could hear. A low mutter of men's voices came to his ears. They were muffled, as if they were in another room. He couldn't make out any of the words.

Gradually, he had become aware of light shining on his eyes. It wasn't bright enough to be the sun. The surface on which he lay wasn't rough enough to be the ground, either. It was a plank floor, he decided. He was inside a building, and not the livery barn where he had encountered the woman, because it had a dirt floor.

His captors had taken him somewhere else. Inside one of the old abandoned buildings, more than likely. And now that his brain was functioning fully again, he had no doubt who those captors were. He had fallen into the hands of the outlaw gang he had come here hoping to find.

Slowly, carefully, he opened his eyes a narrow slit. Even though the light coming through an open door into an adjoining room was fairly dim, it was almost enough to make him wince. He controlled the reaction.

But not well enough, because a voice said, "You're finally awake. I'm glad. I thought for a while I'd hit you hard enough to kill you."

That was the woman. She must have been watching him intently to have noticed his reaction to the light. Since she already knew he had regained consciousness, there was no longer any point in pretending otherwise. He opened his eyes and looked around.

He was lying on the floor of a small room with a single small window. The floor had a thick layer of dust on it, undisturbed except where his captors had dragged him in here. No furniture except the ladder-back chair where the woman sat. She wore a hat and poncho now and had her left hand wrapped around the neck of a whiskey bottle. Her right hand rested on her thigh where it would be handy to the gun in the holster that poked out from under the poncho.

He could see only part of the room on the other side of the doorway, but he could tell it was considerably larger. He saw a man with long hair sitting at a table. He was talking, so there had to be other men at the table, too.

The woman took a long enough swallow from the bottle to make it gurgle. When she lowered it, she called, "Hey, the lawdog's awake in here."

The long-haired man pushed his chair back from the table. Other chair legs scraped on the floor. Two men came into the small room while several others waited just on the other side of the door. One of the pair who joined the woman was the long-haired man. The other was shorter, stockier, older, dressed all in black.

The long-haired man hunkered on his heels in front of Brice, reached out, and slapped him lightly on the cheek.

"Welcome back, badge-toter. Or should I be respectful and call you Deputy Marshal Rogers?"

"Reckon you must've found my badge and bona fides," Brice husked. His mouth and throat were dry enough that talking was uncomfortable.

The woman said, "If you were trying to hide them, you made a mighty poor job of it. They were in your pocket."

The stocky man in black said, "He wasn't working undercover. No reason for him to hide his identity. But you *were* looking for us, weren't you, mister?"

Denying it served no purpose, Brice thought.

"If you're the bunch that's been murdering innocent people and robbing banks and trains all across this part of the country, then yeah, I sure was."

"Well, you sure enough found us," the long-haired man said with a grin. "Reckon we'd best be scared, because you're gonna arrest us now, ain't you, Mr. Lawman?"

"Let me talk to him, Curly," the man in black said.

Curly straightened and stepped back. That meant the man in black was the boss, Brice noted, although he wasn't sure the knowledge would do him much good.

"Did you bring a posse with you?"

"Twenty men," Brice answered without hesitation. "They're waiting not far outside of town, and by now they'll be moving in because they'll have figured out something's happened to me."

"Something's going to happen to you, all right." The man in black drew his gun. "I'm going to put a bullet in your knee if you don't tell me the truth. Then, if I think you're still lying to me, I'll shoot your other knee." He smiled thinly. "You've got two elbows, as well. I reckon we'll get the truth out of you sooner or later."

"I've already told you the truth," Brice said. "Whatever you do to me won't change that."

The man in black studied him for a moment, then nodded.

"All right," he said as he raised the gun. "If that's the way you want it."

He pulled back the hammer. The metallic ratcheting sound was loud in the small room. His finger tightened on the trigger.

* * *

Denny had pushed herself and her horse hard enough that she expected to catch up to Brice before he reached Painted Post. She hadn't, which meant that he was traveling pretty fast, too.

This morning, though, she had reached the settlement. Without knowing that Brice had stopped at the same place less than an hour earlier, she reined in and studied the gulch and the ghost town laid out in it.

Then she had stiffened as she saw a familiar figure dart out of some brush and race over to the back door of a large building that looked like a livery barn. That was Brice, she told herself. No mistake about it. The only reason for him to be sneaking around like that was if he believed the outlaws he sought were here.

She was debating whether she should try to go down there and join him when she spotted someone else slipping along the alley behind the buildings. This was a lean hombre in a poncho who paused near the open doorway as if thinking about something. After a moment, the figure discarded hat and poncho, and Denny realized that wasn't an hombre she was looking at, after all. It was a woman, but one who packed a gun and looked like she might know how to use it.

Alarm bells went off in Denny's brain. She started to reach toward the carbine in its saddle sheath, but before she could pull the weapon out, the woman had yelled something and charged into the barn. Denny's guts knotted as she waited for the crash of gunfire.

No shots sounded, though. She watched tensely,

and after a few minutes, the woman reappeared. She was alone. She trotted back down the alley the way she had come.

Frightened that something had happened to Brice, Denny swung up into the saddle and was about to send her mount charging down that steep, winding trail when she realized that if she did so, she would be in plain sight of anyone in the town. She hesitated, torn between fear for Brice and the natural caution of someone who had survived numerous gunfights.

It was a good thing she did hesitate, because mere moments later the woman returned with several men. They would have seen Denny and she would have lost any advantage she might have.

She stayed where she was, concealed in the thick shadows under the trees, and watched as the men carried Brice's limp figure out of the barn and toted him along the alley. They went in the back door of another building.

Denny's heart was racing. She told herself that Brice was just unconscious, not dead. If he'd been dead, they would have left him in the barn or tossed his body in the brush. The fact that they had taken him into another building meant that he was alive.

She tried to convince herself of that, but the only way to know for sure was to get down there.

And if he *was* dead, those outlaws would pay, Denny swore. She would see to that.

For the next half hour, she worked her way down into the gulch, sticking to cover as much as she could because it was possible the outlaws had sentries posted. The whole time, her heart pounded because she expected to hear gunshots at any moment, signifying that Brice's captors had executed him.

But by the time she crouched in the brush not far from the back of the building where they had taken him, no shots had rung out. If Brice had been alive when they took him in there, there was at least a chance he still was.

She looked up and down the alley, searching for any sign of a guard. She didn't see any, but that didn't mean they weren't there.

Excessive caution didn't mean she was going to find out what was happening to Brice. For that she had to get closer, even though it might be dangerous.

She had left the carbine on her horse, back in the brush about fifty yards, but she had her revolver, and the two-shot, .41 caliber derringer she usually carried in her bag when she dressed up was in her jeans pocket if she needed it. She drew the Colt Lightning, straightened up, and dashed across the alley. Pressing her back against the building, she slid along the wall.

There were no windows back here, only a door. She slipped around the corner and spotted a small window not far away. All the glass was broken out of the pane. Keeping low, she moved closer until she could hear what was going on inside.

Her blood seemed to freeze in her veins as she heard a couple of men talking to someone who was obviously Brice. She couldn't risk raising her head enough for a look, but judging by the way they were talking, he was a prisoner. Probably tied up and helpless. And now one of the men was threatening to blast apart his knees and elbows if he didn't tell them what they wanted to know.

Brice was too stubborn, just on general principles, to cooperate with outlaws. They were going to torture him and eventually kill him. Outnumbered or not, Denny couldn't let that happen.

She straightened and ran back to the corner. She rounded it and headed for the open door. Someone inside must have heard her boots hitting the ground, because a man stepped through the door, looked around with a puzzled frown on his face, then yelled, "Hey!" as he spotted her. He clawed at the holstered pistol on his hip.

Denny shot him. She aimed at his chest, but the bullet went a little high because she was running. It didn't matter, because the slug tore through his throat. He jerked his head back as blood spurted several feet onto the dirt in the alley. His knees buckled before he ever cleared leather.

Denny hurdled the falling body and landed inside the building, which, judging by the bar along one side of the room, had been a saloon. A man stood just outside the door of the room where Brice was being held. He whirled toward Denny and got his gun out before she could fire. They pulled trigger at the same time. The outlaw's bullet whipped past Denny's ear, so close she felt the heat of it. Her bullet struck the man in the body and twisted him halfway around. He stayed on his feet, though, and raised his gun for another shot at her.

She dived forward and fired again as she went down. The man's shot sizzled through the air over her head. The slug from her gun punched into his belly, tore through his guts, and doubled him over. He collapsed with a groan.

Another shot roared from somewhere up and to

Denny's right. The bullet chewed splinters from the floorboards less than a foot from her head. She felt a couple of them sting her cheek. She rolled onto her back and saw a man standing on the balcony in front of several rooms on the second floor. Smoke still curled from the muzzle of his gun as he tried to draw a bead on her again.

She snapped a shot at him. The steep angle meant that when the bullet struck him between his nose and mouth, it bored up through his brain and exploded out the top of his head. He dropped his gun, pitched forward, and crashed through the half-rotted railing along the edge of the balcony. He turned half over in the air as he fell and smashed down, landing on his back on one of the tables. The table broke under the impact and dumped him on the floor.

Denny scrambled for another table, got her shoulder under it, and overturned it to use for cover as the three people who had been in the room with Brice burst out of it and opened fire on her. As she hunkered there behind the scant cover, she heard slugs thudding into the table. In a matter of moments, it would be shot to pieces and she wouldn't have any-place to hide.

The batwings were still hanging in the saloon's entrance, although rather crookedly. A man slapped them aside, stepped into the room, and opened fire with the gun in his hand. At first Denny thought he was shooting at her, then realized he was aiming at the three outlaws who had her pinned down.

His entrance had taken them as much by surprise as it had her. As Denny came up on her knees and thrust the Lightning over the table, she saw one of the outlaws staggering back and forth as he pressed a hand to his bloody midsection.

"Alden!" the woman who had captured Brice in the barn cried out as she flung herself at the wounded man while still blazing away at the newcomer. Denny aimed carefully and drilled a bullet through her body. She gasped and stumbled.

At the same time, the man who had just pushed through the batwings shot the third in the trio of owlhoots. The outlaw grunted and fell backward as the slug drove into his chest. All three of them fell in a tangled heap.

The newcomer rushed toward Denny and cried, *"Cara mia!"*

In the middle of all the carnage, she hadn't really recognized Giovanni Malatesta, but somehow she wasn't surprised to find out that he was her rescuer. Still on her knees, she turned toward him—

Another shot blasted, this one from behind Denny. Malatesta stumbled. Denny jerked around, saw that the man she had gut-shot when she first rushed into the abandoned saloon had pushed himself up and managed to raise his gun long enough to fire. She was about to put a bullet through his brain when he dropped the gun, slumped forward, and didn't move again.

Denny looked toward the entrance again. Malatesta had fallen and lay there facedown. He wasn't moving, either. As she came to her feet, she took a step toward him.

Then turned and rushed into the other room instead, calling, "Brice! Brice, are you in here?"

CHAPTER 47

"Denny!"

She had already seen him. She dropped to her knees beside him. His hands were tied behind his back, and his feet were lashed together as well. She holstered the Lightning—it was empty, anyway—and reached in her pocket for her clasp knife.

She cut through the bonds quickly and helped him sit up.

"Are you all right?" she asked.

"I'm fine, but what about you? It sounded like a war out there!"

"It pretty much was," she said with a smile. "But I came through it all right." She wiped away a small smear of blood from her cheek, left there by one of the flying splinters. "Just a scratch, and I mean that literally."

"You killed all of those outlaws by yourself?" Brice asked as she helped him to his feet.

"No . . . not by herself."

The voice came from the doorway. Denny and Brice both looked in that direction and saw Malatesta standing there, the gun still in his hand. His shirt and coat were stained with blood on the left side where he had been hit, but he seemed steady enough on his feet.

The gun he pointed at Brice was certainly steady enough.

"Please, *cara mia*, step away from the marshal."

Denny stared at him. "You're crazy!" she exclaimed. "I'm not going to let you shoot him!"

Malatesta shook his head and said, "After risking my life to save both of you, why would I shoot Marshal Rogers now? I just thought you might be grateful enough for my timely assistance that you would be willing to tend to this annoying wound . . ."

He swayed a little then. He wasn't in as good a shape as he first appeared to be.

"The count's right," Brice said. "He's hurt. Why don't you give him a hand while I check on those outlaws and make sure they're all dead?"

Denny sighed and nodded. She pushed the chair toward Malatesta with her foot and said, "Sit down and I'll have a look."

"Thank you, *cara mia*."

Brice stepped out of the room, bent over to scoop up two of the guns the fallen outlaws had dropped, and began making sure none of them were a threat anymore.

While he was doing that, Denny pulled back Malatesta's coat and shirt, uncovering the deep, bloody bullet gash in his side.

"It's kind of a mess, but you'll live," she told him. "I think I saw some bottles of whiskey out there. I'll get one of them and a rag and clean that wound, then bandage it." Denny paused. "It'll sting like fire when I do."

Malatesta nodded and said, "I understand. Do what you need to do."

Brice appeared in the doorway, still carrying the two guns. "All those outlaws are dead, like I thought. The ones down here, anyway. I'm going to go upstairs and make sure nobody else is lurking around." He nodded toward Malatesta. "He going to live?"

"I think so," Denny said drily.

"Disappointed?" Malatesta asked with a quirk of his mouth.

Brice shook his head and said, "No. In fact, I'm glad, because I want to thank you for your help. Without it, Denny and I might not have gotten out of here alive."

"I did it for Denise's sake, not yours."

"I can accept that," Brice said with a shrug. "I'm obliged to you anyway."

He left to check out the second floor. Denny heard his footsteps going up the stairs. She said to Malatesta, "You haven't told me how you happened to show up in the nick of time like that. What are you even doing here?"

"Following you, of course. Surely you understand by now that I will follow you to the ends of the earth, *cara mia*."

Denny didn't know what to say to that, so instead she told him, "Stay right there," and stepped into the saloon's main room. She headed for the bar, where several partially full bottles of whiskey sat, but she hadn't gotten there when the batwings swung open again.

"Stay right where you are, lady," the man who stepped into the saloon told her as he pointed a gun in her direction.

He was a middle-aged man with a hard, weather-beaten look about him. At first glance, Denny thought she had never seen him before, but then she realized there was something familiar about him. Her mind went back . . . and recalled that day at the train station in Big Rock when Count Giovanni Malatesta had come into her life again.

This hombre was one of those who had tried to kill Malatesta that day, and then again later on the road from Big Rock to the Sugarloaf.

Other men crowded into the saloon behind him and kept coming until there were ten of them standing there. Seven wore range clothes and were typical hard cases. They all held guns.

The other three didn't look like they were from around there. They were well dressed, although one of them was so big and bulky he looked like an ape in a suit. One of that trio, a smooth-shaven, slick-looking gent, stepped forward and said in a faintly accented voice, "Where is Johnny Malatesta?"

As if answering the question himself, Malatesta called from the other room, "Denise, I hear someone talking. Who is out there?"

The slick man smiled slightly and said with evident satisfaction, "Ah."

When Denny didn't answer, Malatesta stepped into the doorway, then stopped short at the sight of the newcomers.

"Nick," he said.

"That's right," the man said. "You never expected to see me again, did you, Johnny? But I never let anybody get away with thinking they can defy me or steal from me. You know that, don't you? You should."

Denny turned her head to glance at Malatesta and asked, "What's going on here?"

"*Cara mia*, I can explain—"

"What's going on, my dear," the man called Nick interrupted, "is that Johnny here is a thief, a swindler, and a killer. But most importantly, he stole from the wrong man. My name is Nick Scaramello. Johnny used to work for me."

Denny's eyes narrowed. "He's a count—"

Scaramello laughed. "About as much as the rats that have taken over this town are. He's nothing. A poor little *paisan* from Sicily who would lie to anyone and kill anyone who got in his way. Oh, I know all about him. He's no nobleman."

Malatesta's face was flushed dark red with rage now. He said, "This man is a liar, Denise, a notorious criminal from New York. Don't believe a word he says."

Scaramello shrugged. "Whether the young lady believes me or not doesn't really matter. I've come all this way to watch you die, Johnny, and I don't intend to be disappointed. Unfortunately, the reasonable thing to do is make sure that no witnesses are left behind, so the young lady will have to go, too."

"Wait a minute," said the first gunman who had entered the saloon. "I've got a better idea, Scaramello. Leave her with me and my boys. We'll make sure she doesn't talk, in the long run. But just gunning her down right here and now would be a waste, don't you think?"

Scaramello considered the suggestion, then shrugged.

"As you wish, Mr. Yeager," he said. He drew a pistol

from under his coat. "Now, it's time to put an end to this."

"It sure is!" Brice called from the second-floor balcony.

He was off to the side and slightly behind the men, who hadn't noticed when he glided out onto the balcony from one of the second-floor rooms because all their attention was focused on Malatesta. But the ringing challenge got their attention fast enough. Several of them whirled and flung their guns up to open fire on him.

Brice pulled his triggers first, blasting down again and again into the saloon's main room with both guns. Flame spouted from their muzzles as gunthunder seemed to shake the walls. Bullets ripped into Scaramello's hired gunmen. The impacts made them jitter grotesquely, and the shots they got off went wild, smashing into the walls.

At the same time, Scaramello snarled and jabbed his gun toward Malatesta, clearly intending to have his revenge no matter what else happened. He was too slow. The gun in Malatesta's hand cracked first, and Scaramello's head jerked as a red-rimmed hole appeared over his left eye. He crumpled to the dusty floor.

The leader of the hired guns swung his weapon toward Malatesta. Denny came up with the derringer from her pocket and fired at the same time as the hard case. Malatesta grunted beside her as the bullet hammered into him. Denny's .41 caliber slug pulped the gunman's right eye and bored on into his brain, leaving him dead on his feet as he dropped the gun and swayed for a second before toppling over.

The big man Scaramello had brought with him was still standing, but several bloodstains marred his shirtfront. Growling and cursing in rage, he tried to climb the stairs to get at Brice. He made it only a few steps before he collapsed facedown and then slowly rolled back to the bottom of the staircase.

"Denny!" Brice called as he rushed down the stairs. He bounded over the massive corpse. "Denny, are you all right?"

She lowered the derringer and hurried into his arms. He held her tightly. She felt his heart slamming in his chest and knew he felt hers doing the same thing.

"I'm all right," she murmured. "I'm all right."

"So am I. Those men—"

"They all look dead to me." Denny pulled her head back to gaze up into Brice's face. "I never saw shooting like that. I'm not sure my father could have done any better."

"I had a powerful reason not to miss," he told her.

"How . . . touching," Malatesta said in a halting voice. Denny and Brice looked around as they heard the click of a gun hammer being drawn back. As they turned to look, they saw Malatesta standing there, bloodier than ever now, obviously hit bad but still on his feet. He aimed the gun in his hand at Brice and went on, "Step away from her."

"Count, you don't have to—" Brice began.

"Step away from her, I said!"

Denny said, "Giovanni, don't. You're hurt—"

"Hurt too badly this time to make it, I fear," he broke in. "Which means . . . I'll never have you . . . *cara mia* . . . but neither will he."

Brice surprised her by letting go of her and stepping to the side. He said, "All right, I'm clear of her, Malatesta. Just don't hurt her. Give me your word."

"You think . . . my word is . . . worth anything?"

"I hope it is."

"Brice, no!" Denny cried.

With a ghastly smile on his face, Malatesta said, "It seems . . . he is willing to give his life . . . for yours . . . *cara mia*. I believe you really are . . . *his* beloved. Willing to die . . . *cara mia*—"

"And I'm willing to kill," Denny said. The derringer, which still had one shot in it, came up in her hand and went off with a wicked crack. Malatesta's head jerked back, drilled cleanly by Denny's shot. With a long, rattling sigh, he folded up on himself and settled into a lifeless heap on the floor.

"I told you and told you to stop calling me that," she said. The derringer slipped from her fingers and thudded to the floor. She turned and went into Brice's waiting arms and started to cry.

She didn't even hear the swift rataplan of hoofbeats sweeping into Painted Post and coming to a stop outside the old saloon.

CHAPTER 48

The Sugarloaf

"Arturo got worried about the count gallivanting off by himself like that," Smoke said to Denny, "so he talked to Monte about it and Monte talked to me. I was already about to ride out with some of the men and look for you, so when I heard that Malatesta had gone missing, too, it made sense that he might be following you. And it was obvious you'd headed for Painted Post, because that was where Brice was going." He shrugged. "Simple."

"You think you know me that well, do you?"

Smoke smiled. "So far, it appears that I do. I was just a mite late to get in on the action this time. That hasn't happened to me very often."

He was right about both things. Smoke, Cal, Pearlie, and half a dozen of the Sugarloaf hands had ridden into Painted Post while the echoes of gunfire were still rolling away through the gulch and the smell of powder smoke hung in the air. That was an odd situation indeed for Smoke Jensen.

But it had ended well, Denny thought as she sat on the front porch of the ranch house with her father, mother, and Brice Rogers. The bank robbers Brice had gone after were wiped out, and the threat of Giovanni Malatesta—and all the trouble he brought with him—was over. They might not know all the details about Malatesta, but Denny didn't care. He was a closed chapter in her life. No, a whole closed *book*.

She was much more interested in the future now.

"Brice," Sally said, "I assume you'll be staying for supper."

He smiled, nodded, and said, "If you'll have me, ma'am."

Sally smiled, too, as she saw the way her daughter clasped the young lawman's hand. She said, "Oh . . . I think we will."

Big Rock

The eastbound train had rolled into the station a short time earlier and would soon depart. Smoke stood on the station platform with Arturo Vincenzo and held out his hand to the man.

"I reckon you could probably find work around here if you wanted to stay in Big Rock," Smoke told him as they shook. "That fella you came to town with may have caused a heap of trouble, but I don't know of a thing you ever did wrong, Arturo."

"Thank you, sir, but I believe I'm going to pay a visit to my old employer, Mr. Conrad Browning." Arturo paused. "Although I believe he goes by the name Conrad Morgan now, since he's adopted his real father's name."

"Yeah, I know him," Smoke said. "Know his pa a

lot better. We've crossed trails a few times. Frank Morgan's a good man, and his son is, too."

"Mr. Morgan . . . Mr. Conrad Morgan, that is . . . told me he would be happy to line up suitable employment for me, now that Count Malatesta has passed on."

Another passenger was walking past on the platform as Arturo said that. Smoke noticed the way the man cut narrowed eyes toward them, a definite reaction to Arturo's statement. The man lingered on the platform, watching the porters load bags into the baggage car. Smoke watched him from the corner of an eye while he and Arturo finished saying their good-byes. Arturo climbed onto the platform at the rear of the passenger car and smiled down at Smoke.

"I just love trains," he said.

Smoke lifted a hand in farewell, but as he turned away, he paused beside the man he had noticed earlier, a middle-aged, horse-faced gent in an eastern suit and derby hat.

"Leaving Big Rock?" Smoke asked as if he was making casual conversation.

"Yeah. I had some work to do here, but as it turned out, somebody else took care of it for me . . . if that's any of your business."

"None at all, friend," Smoke said with a smile. "And I always mind my own business."

A shrill whistle came from the engine as Smoke turned and walked away.

PRAY FOR DEATH
A WILL TANNER, U.S. DEPUTY MARSHAL WESTERN

*U.S. Deputy Marshal Will Tanner is a man of the law,
not a gun for hire. Except when a friend's in danger
and needs the Tanner brand of help
that comes out the barrel of a gun.*

There's serious trouble brewing in the Choctaw
nation, and it goes by the name of Tiny McCoy.
This small-time cattle rustler is expanding his
brand by brewing batches of whiskey in the
Chocktaw territory of Muddy Boggy Creek.
Tiny and his partner have also turned the illegal
brewery into a robbers' roost for outlaws,
cutthroats, and killers of every bent. Local lawman
Jim Little Eagle is under attack and outgunned.
But when he sends a wire to Fort Smith asking
for backup, and U.S. Deputy Marshal Tanner
shows up, Little Eagle knows they're in for one hell
of a bloodbath. If anyone can drive those
murdering devils to their knees
and saying their prayers, it's Will Tanner.

**Look for PRAY FOR DEATH
on sale now where books are sold.**

CHAPTER I

Jim Little Eagle reined his paint gelding to a halt on the bank of Muddy Boggy Creek about fifty yards upstream of the log building bearing the crudely lettered sign that identified it as MAMA'S KITCHEN. The Choctaw policeman had been watching the comings and goings of the typical clientele of the dining room and gambling hall just recently built three miles outside of town. And from what he had observed, there was no doubt that the owner, a man calling himself Tiny McGee, was selling whiskey and employing a prostitute as well. Jim figured it was time to remind McGee that it was illegal to sell whiskey in the Nations. There was little doubt in Jim's mind that the recent complaints from the merchants in town were caused by patrons of Mama's Kitchen. On more than one occasion in the past week, three white drifters had amused themselves by racing their horses through the center of town, firing their firearms, and scaring the people. He was not confident that his visit to Mama's Kitchen would stop the harassment of the citizens of Atoka, because his authority was limited to the policing of the Indian population. He knew that McGee knew this, as all outlaws did, but he felt it his duty to give him notice, anyway.

Inside the log building, Bob Atkins and Stump Grissom sat talking to Tiny McGee at one of the four small tables. A door that led to several rooms in the back of the building opened and Bob's brother Raymond came out, pretending to stagger as he hitched up his trousers and buckled his belt. His antics caused a round of guffaws from the table and a loud response from Bob. "I swear, Raymond, damned if I don't believe Mama's Baby done wore you out!"

Coming out behind him, Ida Simpson commented, "Don't pay no attention to him. He's as rutty as a bull in matin' season." A working girl with signs of wear, but uncertain age, Ida had adopted the name of Baby because it was so appropriate for Mama's Kitchen. Although Mama's was, in effect, a saloon, there was a kitchen and Tiny did sell meals. His cook was a well-traveled woman named Etta Grise, now too old to do the work Baby did. Tiny hoped the name of his establishment might disguise his actual business interests. His plan was to make Boggy Town, the name already given to it by outlaws, a separate little town where outlaws on the run could hole up. And, so far, he had not been visited by any deputy marshals out of Fort Smith.

"I expect Baby's up to givin' you a ride now, Stump," Raymond japed as he sat down at the table.

"Not me," Stump responded. "I ain't thinkin' 'bout nothin' but supper right now." He was about to say more but stopped when he realized everyone was looking past him toward the door. He turned then to see what had captured their attention.

"Well, well," Tiny said, "if it ain't Jim Little Eagle." He sneered openly at the Choctaw policeman standing in the doorway, his rifle cradled in his arms. "What brings you down to Boggy Town? Course, I expect you know I don't serve no Injuns in here."

"I think you sell whiskey to Indians out your back door," Jim answered him. "I come to give you notice that it is illegal to sell whiskey in the Nations, to white man or Indian. I think you already know this. I don't want to put any more drunken Indians in my jail. I think you better stop selling whiskey."

"Damned if he ain't mighty uppity for an Injun," Bob said. "You gonna let him talk to you like that?"

Tiny laughed. "He's the local Choctaw policeman. He knows damn well he ain't got no say-so about anything a white man does." He sneered at Little Eagle. "Ain't that right, Jim?"

"I think you would be wise to take my warning and stop selling whiskey," Jim insisted. "Maybe it would be best if you move your business someplace else. Atoka is a peaceful town."

"This ain't Atoka, this is Boggy Town, and I got as much right to be here as any of them stores in town," Tiny said. "Maybe it'd be best if you take your Injun ass outta here before somebody's gun goes off accidentally." His warning prompted the other three at the table to push their chairs back, preparing for a possible shooting.

With no change in the solemn expression on his face to reveal his frustration, Jim Little Eagle replied, "That would be an unfortunate thing to happen, because my rifle fires by itself when accidents happen. And you are such a big target, white man, you would be hard to miss." When Stump Grissom started to react, Jim whipped his rifle around, ready to fire.

"Let him go, Stump," Tiny warned. "You shoot one of them Injun policemen and there'll be a whole slew of deputy marshals down here." He looked back at Jim. "All right, you've said your peace, so get on outta here and let us get back to mindin' our own business."

Knowing there was nothing he could legally do to close the saloon, Jim backed out the door. With a keen eye still on the door, he climbed on his horse and rode away. He had at least accomplished one thing by making the visit. He verified the suspicion he had that Tiny McGee was operating a saloon. There had been no attempt to hide the whiskey bottle in the middle of the table. He would now notify the marshal in Fort Smith.

Behind him, the four men filed into the kitchen to eat supper. "Soon as we finish eatin'," Bob Atkins suggested, "why don't we take a little ride into town and make sure all them folks are awake."

"Good morning, Will," U.S. Marshal Dan Stone greeted his young deputy when he walked in the door of his office over the jail in Fort Smith. "Are you ready to get back to work?"

"Yes, sir, I surely am," Will replied, and took a seat across from Stone's desk. It was a truthful answer, for he had spent the last three days in town, most of it sitting around Bennett House drinking coffee and listening to Sophie Bennett and her mother talking about the wedding coming up. Out of desperation, he had excused himself from their discussions from time to time, telling them he had to check on his horses and tack. He found himself longing for the hills and open prairies, and that was something that troubled him. His on-again, then off-again, engagement to Sophie had been due to his job as a deputy marshal and the fact that it caused him to be gone most of the time. When he thought about it, he couldn't really blame her for wanting him to go back to the ranch in Texas, a ranch she had never seen. That was another thing that upset her—he had promised to take her there three weeks ago but had to answer a call from Dan Stone to ride with eight other deputies to capture a gang of train robbers targeting the MKT Railroad.

Noticing a look of distraction on Will's face, Stone commented, "You look like your mind's off someplace else." He flashed a smile and asked, "You thinking about that wedding? Is that where your mind was?"

"Yes, sir, I expect it mighta been, but it's back on business now," Will said. Stone had guessed right, but Will felt no inclination to tell his boss that he wasn't sure about getting married. He knew he would, however, because he had asked Sophie to marry him, and she had said yes.

"Good," Stone said. "I'm sending you and Ed Pine down to Atoka to arrest three men who've been terrorizing the town." When he saw Will's questioning expression, he paused before continuing. "I know, you're thinking that sounds like a job for one deputy with a posseman and a cook, but Ed's been pushing me to send him back in the field. So, I told him I would, but only in partnership with another deputy. He feels like he's ready to ride again, but I think he's still a little weak from that chest wound. He just won't admit it." He shook his head as if exasperated. "So, you're the best man to ride with him. He likes you, and he's still beholden to you for going after him when he was left for dead over near Okmulkee. If those three men were in jail, I'd let Ed go without you, but you're gonna have to arrest 'em." He shrugged. "That is, if they're still there by the time you get there, considering it's gonna take you damn near a week." He waited to hear Will's objections, knowing how he disliked being slowed down by a wagon. When Will didn't protest, Stone continued. "Ed's getting the wagon and said he was gonna take Horace Watson to do the cooking." That was fine with Will. He had worked with Horace before, when he was cooking for Alvin Greeley. Greeley was a useless sod, but Will had no complaints about Horace.

"I expect you want us to get started as soon as we can," Will said. "Is Ed takin' care of all the supplies we'll need?" Stone said he was. Will nodded and commented, "Looks like I'll just be his posseman on this trip."

"Pretty much," Stone replied. "You see any problem with that?"

"Nope," Will answered. "Ed oughta know what he's doin'. He's been ridin' with the Marshals Service longer than I have."

"Good," Stone responded. "I knew I could count on you." Will stood up to leave. "Ed's probably still over at the stable, if you want to check with him."

"I'll do that," Will said, and walked out the door.

Will found Ed talking to Vern Tuttle, the owner, when he walked down the street to the stables.

"Here's Will Tanner now," Vern announced when Will came in the door.

"Howdy, Will," Ed Pine greeted him cheerfully. "Have you talked to Dan Stone about ridin' with me?"

"Just came from there," Will replied. "He told me I was fixin' to go to Atoka, that you were in charge on this job, and that I damn sure better not mess up."

Ed chuckled. "Well, I'm glad he laid it on the line for you, so I won't have to do it." Serious then, he said, "I'd appreciate it if you'd check over that list of supplies I loaded on the jail wagon. See if there's anything else you think we'll need." Will took a quick check of the pile of supplies Ed had acquired and found them adequate. "Horace Watson's gonna meet us here at six in the mornin'," Ed informed him. "We can pack most of that food in his wagon."

"Are you plannin' to drive that jail wagon?" Will asked. "'Cause I ain't. Whaddaya say we let Horace pile his cookin' stuff on the jail wagon and he can drive it, instead of takin' two wagons." That sounded like a good idea to Ed. Like Will, he'd rather sit in the saddle than ride on a wagon seat. "It'll take us just as long to get to Atoka, but we'll be free to scout along the way for fresh game, or smoke out any trouble ahead."

They talked with Vern for a while afterward, then Will had a quick visit with his buckskin gelding before telling Ed he would see him in the morning. Ed walked out of the stables with him to say a final word. "Will, I 'preciate you goin' along on this trip. I know Dan don't think I'm ready to ride again."

"Oh, I don't think Dan thinks that at all," Will quickly assured him. "He's just concerned about these three jaspers raisin' hell in Atoka. I think he figures they're more than three harmless drifters. They might be wanted somewhere else, and they might be a handful for one man to handle."

"I reckon we'll see, won't we?" Ed declared.

"I reckon," Will responded. "I'll see you in the mornin'."

As was their usual custom, Ron Sample and Leonard Dickens were sitting in their rocking chairs on the porch at Bennett House when Will walked up from the street. "Ain't it gettin' a little too cold for you boys to sit outside?" Will asked the two elderly boarders as he came up the steps. Never mind the coming of chilly fall weather, it seemed it might take a blizzard to run the two of them inside to smoke their pipes.

"There is a little nip in the air this afternoon," Leonard conceded. "But thanks to Ron, Ruth ran us outta the parlor."

Ron looked at Will and chuckled. "Yep, it didn't set too well with Ruth when I burned a hole in that carpet by the davenport. She made us go set out here on the porch. It wasn't much more'n a little scorched place in the carpet, was it, Leonard? I told her she could pull that rocker over a couple of inches and you wouldn't even notice it. She went on about tryin' to keep the house lookin' decent for your weddin'."

Will glanced at Leonard, who was looking at him, grinning like a Cheshire cat, and he knew there was a little needling coming his way. "No, sir," Leonard said, "we'd best not mess up that weddin'. Right, Will?"

"Hell," Will shot back, "you two ol' buzzards ain't even invited."

They both laughed at that. "Which one of us are you gonna pick to be your best man?" Ron asked.

"You'd be better off pickin' me," Leonard said. "I can still get into my suit I bought for my wife's funeral. It's just like new. I ain't wore it since."

"Maybe Leonard's right," Ron jumped in again. "There ain't much difference in a weddin' and a funeral, anyway. A feller gets his wings clipped at either one of 'em."

He could still hear them laughing after he went inside and closed the door behind him to find Sophie coming down the stairs. "Oh, Will," she said upon seeing him. "Good, you're home. Supper's about ready, so if you have to wash up, you'd best get about it." She paused on the second step, so she could look him in the eye. "Did you go to see Dan Stone today?"

"Yep," he responded. "I reported in, just like I was called to do."

When there was no more from him beyond that simple statement, she gave him that accusing look that he had come to recognize. "You're riding out again, aren't you?"

"Not till tomorrow mornin'," he answered, hoping she would think that at least they had tonight.

"Does he know you're getting married soon?" she asked. "We have so many things to do before then, and it would be nice if you were here to help."

"Sophie, there ain't anything I know to do to help plan a weddin'. You and your mama are goin' to plan everything, anyway. And in the meantime, I have to earn a livin'. So, I can't just sit around Fort Smith every day. When we get married, we're gonna go to Texas, like I told you, and live on the J-Bar-J. And I'll be home all the time." He gave her a smile. "And you'll most likely wish I was back in the Marshals Service."

She shook her head as if perplexed. "Just go wash up for supper." She gave him a quick peck on the cheek before continuing on her way to the kitchen. After supper, she would find out where he was going in the morning and how long he could expect to be gone. In spite of her efforts not to, she was following right along in her mother's footsteps. In love with a deputy marshal, she feared she was destined to realize the same heartbreak her mother suffered when Deputy Marshal Fletcher Pride was murdered by outlaws. Those thoughts brought her mind back to her mother. A strong woman, Ruth Bennett had operated her boardinghouse ever since the death of Sophie's father with never a sign of dependence on anyone. But lately, her mother didn't seem like the determined woman Sophie was accustomed to. Margaret, who had run the kitchen ever since Ruth took over the management of the boardinghouse, noticed a difference in Ruth's demeanor as well, and had commented to Sophie about it. They decided that Sophie's mother was probably working herself into a case of nerves over the upcoming wedding and would recover her old spunk when the knot was tied. Sophie's thoughts were interrupted then when she walked into the kitchen and almost bumped into Margaret coming out into the hall to ring her little dinner bell.

"Where's your mama?" Margaret asked, since Ruth was usually ready to help her set the food on the table.

"She's upstairs," Sophie said. "She was feeling a

little tired and decided to lie down for a while before supper."

"She's been getting tired a lot lately," Margaret commented. "I wonder if she's feeling all right."

"I still think the wedding is giving her a case of nerves," Sophie said. "She'll be all right when that's finally over."

Will was up and ready to leave at five o'clock the next morning. Margaret was in the kitchen, just getting ready to start breakfast when she saw him coming down the back stairs. "You leaving before breakfast?" she asked, and when he said that he was, she insisted on fixing something quick for him. "I've already got the coffeepot on and I'll throw a couple of eggs on the stove for you. Biscuits will be a while yet, but there's some cold corn bread from last night."

"That would suit me just fine," he said right away, and dumped his saddlebags and rifle by the kitchen door. Glancing toward the dining room door, he half expected to see Sophie. They hadn't visited very long after supper the night before because she complained about a headache, so they said good night at half past eight and retired to their separate rooms.

"How long you gonna be gone?" Margaret asked, breaking into his thoughts as she filled a cup for him.

"Couple of weeks, I expect," he answered. "Gotta take a wagon to Atoka and back."

"Well, you be sure and take care of yourself. You won't have much time left before that wedding when you get back."

"I will," he replied, thinking the whole world seemed to revolve around that wedding. It would have been so much easier to simply go to the preacher and let him tie the knot without all the ceremony that was driving Ruth and Sophie crazy. He was willing to bet that Sophie wouldn't have so many headaches if they did. It was with a definite sense of relief that he ate his quick breakfast and was on his way to meet Ed and Horace. "Tell Sophie I'm sorry I missed her this mornin'," he told Margaret as he walked out the back door.

Horace Watson was already at the stable when Will arrived. A few minutes later, Ed appeared, eager to get started. As Will expected, Horace objected to driving the jail wagon instead of taking his chuck wagon, which he had modified to accommodate his every need. He finally surrendered and agreed to do it, but warned them both that this would be the only time. When the jail wagon was loaded up with supplies and Horace's cooking utensils, they started toward the ferry slips down by the river, with Horace and the wagon setting the pace. His regular chuck wagon was left parked where the jail wagon usually sat. A brisk breeze blew in their faces as they set out on a trail that followed the Poteau River to the southwest. Will and Ed rode side by side a little ahead of Horace in the wagon, Will aboard his buckskin gelding named Buster. Ed was riding a horse he had just bought, a big gray he called Smut. The day was bright and sunny. It was chilly, but it was supposed to be this time of year, so none of the three thought much about it.

Since the Sans Bois Mountains were just about the halfway point in the roughly 120-mile trip, they decided to make a brief stop there. Will knew the location of a hideout well known to outlaws holing up in Indian Territory, and Ed was interested in checking to see if it was currently occupied. The hideout had come to be known locally as Robbers Cave. Will had actually made an arrest there on one occasion, but Ed had never been there, and he thought it might be of future use to him if he knew how to find it.

"I used to know an old fellow who had a cabin not far from that hideout," Will said. "His name was Perley Gates, and he was the one who showed me where that cave is. But Perley was gone the last time I went to his cabin. He left a sign on the door to tell anybody who was interested that he was leavin' it for good, and welcome to it." He paused to think about the elflike little man, and it brought a smile to his face. "I ain't run into Perley since. There's no tellin' where he ended up."

"Maybe he changed his mind and came back," Ed said.

"Knowing Perley, he just might have," Will said. The thought served to spark his interest, so he replied, "I wouldn't mind goin' by his place, just in case he did. It ain't far from Robbers Cave. Matter of fact, it's on the way, so it wouldn't delay us much. We could rest the horses there." So that's what they decided to do.

CHAPTER 2

It took two and a half days at the wagon's pace to reach the Sans Bois Mountains and the trail that snaked its way through the narrow valleys that eventually led to a green meadow. On the other side of the meadow Will pointed to a log cabin built back up against a steep slope, and hard to see at first. They pulled up at the edge of the meadow when they spotted a sorrel horse in the small corral next to an open shed on the other side of the cabin. Will recalled that there was no corral there when he had last visited Perley, and his horse was a dark Morgan. "There's somebody in the cabin," he said to Ed, "but I don't think it's Perley. We'd better make sure." He rode ahead a few yards and called out, "Hello, the cabin!"

"Hello, yourself!" a voice came back. "What's your business here? And just so you know, I've got the front sight of a Henry rifle lookin' right at you."

"No need to shoot anybody," Will said. "We were lookin' for a friend of mine, name of Perley Gates. He built that cabin, but it's plain to see Perley's gone. We're U.S. Deputy Marshals on our way to Atoka. Just thought we'd cut through here to see if Perley mighta come back. We won't trouble you any further." He wheeled Buster around and started back out of the meadow but stopped when he heard the man yell behind him.

"Hold on!" the voice called after him. He turned to see a short-legged little old man come up from behind a large boulder at the corner of the porch and proceed to run after them. They pulled up and waited for him. Still holding his rifle as if ready to shoot, he asked, "How do I know you're deputy marshals? I don't see no badges." Both Will and Ed pulled their coats aside to reveal the badges they wore. He looked from one of them to the other, then back to Will, obviously trying to decide what to do. Finally deciding to take the risk and believe the badges were real, he lowered his weapon. "You come lookin' for them two jaspers up there in Robbers Cave?" When he looked again at Ed and Will to see puzzled expressions on both faces, he said, "I hope to hell that's what you came up here for."

"Like he said," Ed replied, "we're on our way to Atoka. We don't know anything about anybody holed up in that hideout. Are they causing some trouble?"

"Well, I'll say they are," the little man responded, as if it was a stupid question.

"What kinda trouble?" Will asked. He couldn't help thinking the new occupant of the cabin reminded him of the original one, even down to the curly white whiskers.

"They've raided my cabin three different times. They'll wait till I go off huntin' and come in here and turn my cabin upside down, lookin' for anythin' they can steal. Last week they stole a four-point buck I was fixin' to butcher, came right up to the house and took it. When you boys showed up, I thought it was them comin' back, and I had my rifle ready for 'em this time."

"What's your name, friend?" Ed asked.

"Merle Teague," he replied.

"All right, Merle," Will said, "we'll take a look up at that cave and see if they're still there. We had planned to stop by there, anyway."

"Horace needs to rest his horses," Ed said, "so while he's doin' that, me and you can go up to that hideout."

They left Horace to unhitch his horses and let them graze while Merle Teague looked over the jail wagon. "You got any coffee on that wagon?" they heard Merle asking as they rode up the ravine next to his cabin. Horace must have said he did, because they heard Merle say he would build up the fire. Will had to laugh when he heard him, for he remembered that every time he had stopped to visit Perley, he was always out of coffee. It got to the point where he brought extra coffee every time he rode this trail.

Will led Ed up to the base of one of the higher hills where nature had formed a corral made of boulders. The opening that served as an entrance to it had three timbers across it that functioned as a gate. Inside were three horses. The two deputies looked the place over from the cover of a thick stand of pine trees. Will pointed to a solid-rock opening up near the top of the slope. "That's the front entrance. The cave is about forty feet long and has a back door. That stream you see runs right through the cave. It's hard to beat for a hideout. One of us can stand near the front and yell for 'em to come out and surrender, while the other one can cover the back door and arrest 'em when they run out the back. You're the lead deputy on this job. Which do you wanna do?"

"What if they don't come out?" Ed asked.

"Then I reckon we'll go in after 'em," Will answered. "Either that or we could steal their horses and make 'em come after them. So, what you want, front or back?"

Ed thought for a few seconds. "I'll stay in front and call 'em out. I don't know exactly where that back door is, so you might be better at that. Is that all right with you?"

"Fine by me," Will said. "You just give me about fifteen minutes to get in position behind that cave." He turned Buster to leave, then paused to warn Ed. "Be sure you've got some cover before you go hollerin' up at that cave. Be careful you don't get shot."

"You don't have to warn me about that," Ed assured him.

Will circled around the hill to come up from behind the stone tunnel. He left Buster in a clump of small trees and climbed up through the rocks until he came to the opening to the small passage that led back into the cave. *If I had forgotten where it was, I coulda found it anyway,* he thought when he approached it and saw smoke drifting up out of the opening in the rocks.

He hadn't been in position longer than a couple of minutes when he heard Ed yell out his warning. "You, in the cave! This is U.S. Deputy Marshal Ed Pine. Come out of there with your hands up!"

There was no response from the cave, so Ed repeated his orders. Inside, Zeke Bowers whispered, "What the hell . . . ?" He gaped, wide-eyed, at his brother, Ike.

"How'd he find this place?" Ike whispered back. "The law ain't supposed to know about this place."

"That bowlegged little rat got the law up here," Zeke said. "What are we gonna do?"

"We need to see if he's by hisself," Ike said. He dropped the piece of venison he had been chewing on and crawled up near the front of the cave to try to see if he could spot Ed. Zeke crawled up behind him.

"Can you see him?"

"Nah, I can't see him," Ike replied. "I can't see the bottom of the cliff unless I crawl out in the open, and I ain't gonna do that."

"Can you see anythin'?" Zeke insisted.

"I told you, I can't see him, but I can see that there ain't no posse settin' down there waitin' for us to come outta here. He might be all by his lonesome."

"There's no use in stallin'," Ed called out again. "You're surrounded. I'm givin' you a chance to come on outta there and make it easy on yourself."

"You got no business botherin' us," Ike shouted back. "We ain't the ones that robbed that store in McAlester."

"Damn, Ike," Zeke whispered. "You shouldn'ta said that. He might notta even knowed about it."

"Come on out with your hands up and we'll talk about it," Ed yelled.

"He's by hisself," Ike said to Zeke. Then he turned his head toward the opening again and yelled, "We ain't comin' out! Looks like you're gonna have to come in and get us!" Back to his brother again, he said, "Let him come on in. We'll fill him so full of holes you can use him for a strainer."

"Hot damn!" Zeke exclaimed. "We ain't never shot

a lawman before. Tell him to come on up here and get us."

"That ain't a good idea today or any other day," Will said, standing twenty-five feet behind them. Both brothers froze for a moment before they were sure, then they spun around, reaching for their guns. Ike was the quickest, so he caught Will's first shot in the shoulder, the result of which knocked him back flat on the stone floor of the cave. His pistol bounced off the solid rock as it dropped from his hand. With a new round already cranked in the chamber of Will's Winchester 73, Zeke found himself looking at sudden death. He wisely dropped his weapon.

"You all right in there, Will?" Ed Pine shouted from in front of the cave, already running toward the entrance after he heard the shots.

"Everything's all right, Ed," Will answered him. "You can come on in." He pointed his rifle at Zeke and motioned with it toward Ike, who was sitting on the floor of the cave holding his arm, a .44 slug in his right shoulder. "You can give your partner a hand with that wound," Will said to Zeke.

"He needs a doctor," Zeke said after a quick look at his brother's wound. "He's bleedin' awful bad."

"Take his bandanna off and stuff it over that wound," Will said. Ed walked in at that moment. "These are the two outlaws that held up that store in McAlester," he said to Ed, hoping Ed would realize he was bluffing. They had received no notice of a store robbery in McAlester before they left Fort Smith.

"Right," Ed came back right away, picking up on Will's bluff. "We figured they'd be here." He holstered his .44 and picked up the two dropped pistols. "Good thing we brought the jail wagon. These two are gonna have plenty of company, but Horace is gonna have to pick up some more supplies in Atoka," he said, thinking about the three men they had actually come for.

"I expect so," Will said, then directed a question to Zeke. "How much of that money have you got left?"

"Ain't got none of it left," Zeke replied.

Still bluffing, Will said, "What? That fellow said you two took over two hundred dollars outta his store."

Both Ike and Zeke reacted immediately. "He's a lyin' horn toad!" Ike exclaimed. "There warn't but thirty-seven dollars in that drawer and we spent all of it that night."

Ed looked at Will and shook his head. Both men were thinking of the cost of transporting the two petty criminals back to jail in Fort Smith. It would amount to more than the two of them had stolen. The temptation to just run them out of the hideout and tell them to get out of the Nations was great. But they had foolishly confessed to the robbery of a store, so they had to arrest them and give them a day in court. "All right," Will finally ordered, "pick up your belongings and we'll walk on outta here, nice and peaceful. If you've got any sense at all, you won't risk your life tryin' to make a run for it."

They marched them down to their horses and waited while Zeke helped Ike up on his horse. Then with each deputy holding the reins of one of the two brothers' horses, they led them back to Merle's cabin, where they were transferred to the jail wagon. Horace Watson's reaction upon seeing the two petty thieves was the same as Ed and Will's. "It's gonna be nice and cozy on the way back to Fort Smith," he observed.

"I'm gonna have to have some more food if we're gonna eat on the way back."

Standing by while the transfer to the jail wagon was taking place, Merle could finally hold his comments no longer. "You're lucky these two lawmen came to getcha 'cause I was fixin' to shoot your sorry asses next time you came stealin' around my place."

"You ain't got nothin' worth stealin'," Zeke responded.

Ike, confident now that he wasn't going to bleed to death, saw fit to join in. "I don't know, Zeke, that deer was pretty good eatin'. We was waitin' for you to go huntin' again."

"Get them two skunks offa my property," Merle demanded.

"That we will," Ed said, and closed the lock on the jail wagon. Will climbed up into the saddle, led them out of the maze of hills that hid Merle's cabin, and picked up the trail to Atoka again. The extra horses were on a rope tied to the back of the jail wagon. Their owners were already complaining after finding they were going to Atoka before making the trip back to Fort Smith.

As they had anticipated, it took them two and a half days to reach Atoka. At the end of each day, they found a stream to camp by. Horace took care of the cooking and the prisoners were released from the wagon and shackled to a long chain for the night, with one end locked around the axle of the wagon. It was the typical fashion in which prisoners were handled, but not the way Will Tanner preferred. He had always felt hampered by a slow-moving wagon and had a running argument with Dan Stone about using one. On this occasion, however, he didn't complain, especially since it was possible they would end up transporting five prisoners back to Fort Smith.

They rolled into Atoka in the early evening and Horace picked a spot near the creek to park the jail wagon and set up his camp. While Ed stayed with him to guard the prisoners, Will rode up Muddy Boggy Creek to Jim Little Eagle's cabin outside of town. The Choctaw policeman walked out of his barn as Will rode into the yard. "Will Tanner!" Jim greeted him. "I thought maybe they send you." He was always glad to see Will. They had worked together many times in the past. "Mary!" Jim called toward the cabin.

In a minute, Mary Light Walker stepped out on the small front porch. "Will Tanner!" She repeated her husband's greeting and stepped off the porch to join them.

"Mary, Jim," Will greeted them in order and stepped down from the saddle. "Stone sent me and Ed Pine, too." When both Jim and Mary looked past him toward the road, Will explained. "Ed's back in town with Horace Watson and a jail wagon. He's set up camp on the other side of the railroad tracks." He went on to explain the acquisition of two prisoners he had not planned on and the need to do something with them while they investigated the problem Jim had wired Fort Smith about. "Anybody in that jail of yours?"

"No," Jim answered. "The jail's empty, has been for a couple of weeks."

"Good," Will said. "Maybe we can put these two jaspers in there for safekeepin' till we come to some kinda answer to your problems here in Atoka."

"You no stay for supper?" Mary asked.

"I reckon not this time," Will replied, "and I surely am disappointed, too. But I've got Ed and Horace and two fellows in the jail wagon back in town. So, I reckon I'll just have to miss out on enjoyin' one of your fine suppers." He shook his head and smacked his lips. "You know when I'm workin' up this way, I always try to hit town here in time to get invited to eat at your table."

She laughed, delighted. "You know you always welcome, Will Tanner."

"I'll saddle my horse," Jim said, "and go back to town with you. Maybe those three drifters will give you a show tonight like they do on some nights." He looked at Mary and said, "You might have to keep my supper warm in the oven till I get back."

"We'll try not to keep you from your supper," Will said. "Just open up that jail for us, then Ed and I can watch the town tonight. If they don't show up in town tonight, maybe we can find out where they're holed up tomorrow."

"No problem there," Jim said at once. "I know where they stay, where every no-good outlaw troublemaker stays. They stay at Mama's Kitchen in Boggy Town."

"Say what?" Will responded, not sure he had heard correctly.

"Mama's Kitchen," Jim repeated. "Big fellow named Tiny McGee built it about three miles east of town on Muddy Boggy Creek. He named it that, so the law might think it's a place to eat, but it's nothing but a saloon."

"Well, I'll be . . ." Will started. "It wasn't here the last time I rode through, and that ain't been but four or five months. And I ain't ever heard of Boggy Town."

"That McGee fellow started calling it that. I think

he's planning to start his own little town for outlaws on the run. He put some buildings up fast," Jim said. "He's selling whiskey to outlaws coming up from Texas, and he's selling rotgut firewater to my people at the back door. He's hauling whiskey in by the barrel, fills his bottles out of the barrels. That's for his white customers. The Indians have to bring a fruit jar to hold their firewater."

"Sounds like your problem is more than three hell-raisers shootin' up the town," Will said. "And it sounds like some big trouble for me, if this Boggy Town catches on."

"That's why I send for marshals," Jim said. "I wanted you to see for yourself."

"This ain't no damn jail," Zeke complained when Jim Little Eagle unlocked the door to the converted storehouse. "This ain't nothin' but a smokehouse. You can't lock us up in there."

He was not far off in his appraisal, but the storehouse had been fixed up to accommodate prisoners, complete with one small window and two straw pallets. Will had used it before to hold prisoners for a short time. "It'll do for you two hams," Will said.

"What about my brother?" Zeke asked. "He's still bleedin' like a stuck hog. He needs a doctor."

"I'm goin' to the doctor's office right now," Will replied. "Then we'll see about gettin' you some supper. Before long, you'll be so comfortable here you won't wanna leave." Will hoped it was still early enough to catch the doctor in his office, so he hurried up the street to get him while Horace filled a water bucket for the prisoners. Ed stayed behind and put an empty bucket inside the jail for the prisoners' convenience. Jim Little Eagle went with Will.

Dr. Franklyn Lowell's office door was locked when they arrived, so they walked around the building and knocked on the back door. In a few minutes, the door opened and Dr. Lowell stood there, glaring down at the two lawmen. "Jim Little Eagle and Will Tanner," he called back over his shoulder to his Choctaw cook and housekeeper. Turning back to Jim and Will, he complained, "It's always suppertime when you two come looking for me. Don't you ever shoot anybody when I'm not fixing to sit down to eat? Who's shot this time?"

"Howdy, Doc," Will greeted him. "Good to see you again, too. We've got a prisoner down in the jail with a bullet in his shoulder. I'd 'preciate it if you could take a look at him." He had used Dr. Lowell's services on other occasions and he couldn't remember a time when it wasn't inconvenient to the stocky little white-whiskered physician.

Recognizing Will's playful bit of sarcasm, Doc snorted to show it didn't bother him. "It's about time you showed up around here," he said. "It's time somebody did something about those three saddle tramps that take delight in shooting up the town. It's just a matter of time before I'm gonna have to take a bullet out of somebody who catches a stray shot."

"Yes, sir," Will responded. "I've got another deputy with me. We're gonna see what we can do. These two men we've got in the jail didn't have anything to do with shootin' up the town and one of 'em needs a doctor. Of course, I'll pay your fee."

Doc turned to face his housekeeper. "How long till those chops are done, Lila?" She told him she had not put them in the pan yet. "Well, wait on that till I get back. I won't be long. Get me my bag." He put on his coat while she hurried to fetch his bag. Will turned to Jim and suggested he might want to ride back and get his supper. Jim agreed and said he'd return after supper.

"You think your three hoodlums are gonna put on a show tonight?" Will asked Jim when they walked back to the jail with Doc Lowell.

"Maybe, maybe not," Jim Little Eagle answered. "They got to get good and drunk first." From what Jim had told them about the three men before, it appeared there was no motive behind their mischief other than the pure enjoyment of scaring the peaceful citizens of the town. His concern was that in their drunkenness, their shots were often wild, causing damage to windows and doors. As Doc had complained, he feared it was only a matter of time before someone was struck by a stray bullet.

"From what you've just told us, there's grounds enough to arrest 'em," Will said. "So, we'll just wait to see if they're still around. Ain't that what you say, Ed?" he asked as they arrived at the jail. Ed smiled and agreed. He knew Will was trying to remember who was supposed to be in charge. "Like I said, you might as well go on home and eat your supper," Will repeated to Jim. "Course, you're welcome to eat with us. Horace is fixin' to fry up some bacon right now."

"Thanks just the same," Jim replied. "I'll go to the house now. I'll be back after I eat." He jumped on his horse and rode back up the creek.

As Doc had told Lila, he didn't take long to remove

the .44 slug from Ike's shoulder. He didn't concern himself with his patient's comfort. Ed Pine commented to Will afterward, "Hell, I coulda done that with my skinnin' knife." Will agreed with him but pointed out that there would probably have been a higher risk of infection. He then reminded Ed that he was just a posseman on this job. Ed was the deputy marshal and, as such, it was his responsibility to pay the doctor. "So that's the way it's gonna be," Ed joked. "All right, I'll pay Dr. Lowell and I'll make sure Dan Stone remembers to pay you a posseman's pay."

"Hey, Doc, I'm gonna need some medicine for my pain," Ike called after the doctor when he went out the door and Ed locked it.

"They're fixing to give you some supper," Doc answered him through the door. "That'll do you just fine."

"He's eat-up with compassion for his patients, ain't he?" Ed commented aside to Will. "I'm glad he didn't do the job on my wounds."

Doc paused to complain before he started back up the street. "Next time you shoot one of these outlaws, bring him to my office instead of dragging me down here." He started again, but stopped to add, "And don't bring him at suppertime."

"Whatever you say, Doc," Will responded.

By the time Doc had finished and collected his fee, Horace had a fire going back at his camp by the creek with side meat in the pan and coffee working away. When it was ready, he brought it up to the jail and Will went in with him to guard the prisoners while Horace laid dinner out for them on the small table in the center of the cell. After the Bowers brothers were fed, Will and Ed went back with Horace to get their supper. The town seemed quiet enough as darkness began to set in, but there were still lights on in a few of the shops. Tom Brant had not taken in his display of long-handled shovels he had in front of his store, and Lottie Mabry's dining room was still busy. The two deputy marshals and their cook sat by the fire drinking coffee, enjoying the peaceful night. Horace produced another coffee cup for Jim Little Eagle to use when he returned to join them.

Connect with Us

Visit us online at
KensingtonBooks.com
to read more from your favorite authors, see books
by series, view reading group guides, and more.

Join us on social media

for sneak peeks, chances to win books and prize packs,
and to share your thoughts with other readers.

facebook.com/kensingtonpublishing
twitter.com/kensingtonbooks

Tell us what you think!

To share your thoughts, submit a review,
or sign up for our eNewsletters, please visit:
KensingtonBooks.com/TellUs.